# IN THE FOOTSTEPS OF THE DAMNED

"I am Nemed," the chieftain said. "These people have come with me to settle here. We have come in peace. Can you tell us who you are?"

The two beings exchanged a look, then Cruc spoke. "So, you are not spirits of the dead. You are new ones."

"You know our tongue, then," said Nemed.

The other nodded. "We know it. We have met those from your lands before, in my father's time. They lived in this same place."

"You know about the people of this place?" asked Diancecht with interest.

"My father's people did."

"Do you know what happened to them?"

The man's mouth lifted in a smile that revealed sharp, yellow teeth, as of a carnivore. "It is certain we know that. We destroyed them."

D1304911

Be sure to ask your bookseller for the Bantam Spectra Books you have missed:

The Gods of Ireland
Book One

# Most Ancient Song

CASEY FLYNN

BANTAM BOOKS

NEW YORK • TORONTO • LONDON • SYDNEY • AUCKLAND

*This edition contains the complete text*
*of the original hardcover edition.*
NOT ONE WORD HAS BEEN OMITTED.

MOST ANCIENT SONG

*A Bantam Spectra Book / February 1991*

SPECTRA *and the portrayal of a boxed "s" are trademarks of Bantam Books, a
division of Bantam Doubleday Dell Publishing Group, Inc.*

*All rights reserved.*
*Copyright © 1991 by Kenneth C. Flint.*
*Cover art copyright © 1991 by Kevin Johnson.*
*No part of this book may be reproduced or transmitted*
*in any form or by any means, electronic or mechanical,*
*including photocopying, recording, or by any information*
*storage and retrieval system, without permission in writing from*
*the publisher.*
*For information address: Bantam Books.*

ISBN 0-553-28832-6

*Published simultaneously in the United States and Canada*

*Bantam Books are published by Bantam Books, a division of Bantam Doubleday Dell
Publishing Group, Inc. Its trademark, consisting of the words "Bantam Books" and the
portrayal of a rooster, is Registered in U.S. Patent and Trademark Office and in other
countries. Marca Registrada. Bantam Books, 666 Fifth Avenue, New York, New York
10103.*

PRINTED IN THE UNITED STATES OF AMERICA

RAI 0 9 8 7 6 5 4 3 2 1

# TO THE MEMORIES OF:

*Lady Augusta Gregory*
*and*
*William Butler Yeats*

Whose efforts during the Irish Renaissance helped preserve the remnants of the ancient Celtic tales.

# Author's Note

I include below a guide for pronouncing some of the more difficult names. I hope you will find it useful. I know *I* do!

| | |
|---|---|
| Cichol Gricenchos | Kee-kol Gry-ken-os |
| Diancecht | Din-kekt |
| Donnchadh | Don-kad (now "Donogh") |
| Faolchu | Fol-ku |
| Goibniu | Gov-nu |
| Luchtine | Luk-tin-a |
| MacDualtach | Mac-Dul-tak |
| Mathgen | Mat-gen |
| Moire | Mor-a |
| Muirgheal | Muriel |
| Murchadh | Mur-kad (now "Murrogh") |
| Sadhbh | Sav |
| Tethra | Tet-ra |
| Toirdealbhach | Turl-bak (now "Turlough") |
| Uile-bheist | Ile-beast |

# Prologue

# The Plain of Death

A billowing mist lay heavily upon the horrid scene.

Its whispering sheets covered like a death linen and mercifully hid the sprawled bodies of the dying scattered across the barren circle.

Here and there a pitiful fire smoldered, forming weak swells of ruddy light in the mist. Around their puny comfort of warmth huddled the miserable lumps of stricken human beings, moaning, coughing, crying out in pain, keening over the still forms of loved ones already gone.

Most seemed too weak even to feed wood or turf to the campfires. So, one by one, the lights were fading out. Of the many hundreds of people in the camp, only a few score were on their feet. Some of them moved from fire to fire, carrying water, vainly administering to the dying. The rest of them were applying their service to a larger number: the dead. Working in pairs they hoisted limp or already stiffening bodies onto four-wheeled carts and dragged them slowly, wearily, endlessly to the center of the plain.

In the center was a vast pit, both wide and deep. Still, it was filled now, filled and heaped high with hundreds upon hundreds of the dead—a great grotesque, tangled mass of bodies growing ever greater. Here other laborers plied shovels, heaving earth upon the mound, pushing more in around the pit's sides in a hopeless attempt to bury the already decomposing corpses. The shovelers wore scraps of rag tied about their faces against the stench of putrifaction that hung dense in the thick, grey air.

At a fire nearby the pit, a man watched the awful work go on. He lay propped against a stone, white faced, breath rasping from shallowly pumping lungs. He was an elderly man of grey-white hair and lined face. He watched the bodies cast into the pit with eyes glittering from tears of anguish that pooled to run down the seamed cheeks.

A figure came out from the windings of the mist and approached him. It was a young man of dark hair and strong countenance. He moved with a vigor that seemed immense in contrast to the rest. He knelt by the old man.

"Partholan," he said, "you should move away from here. This poisonous odor . . ."

"It will make little difference to me," the other wheezed out. "And I must be here, to see my people to their final rest, terrible though it will be."

The young man lifted a pail. "Then drink some water."

Partholan waved it away. "I can no longer swallow it," he said. "My stomach rejects even this by twisting into knots. That pain is worse than the thirst."

"I am sorry, Uncle," the young man said in a helpless way.

"You've done all that anyone could. Tell me, what are the numbers?"

"Of our five thousand, perhaps five hundred remain. Of those, only some two dozen seem untouched by this monstrous plague."

The old man shook his head in despair. "Soon there'll not even be enough to carry our dead to their grave. And the healers? The priests?"

"There was nothing they could do. No magic, no medicine could help. The last of them is dying with the rest."

"Not a dozen days ago we were strong; we were well!" the old man said. "Tuan, what happened?"

"It spread as a gust of strong wind sweeping through the wheat," the young man said. "Another day, one more, and there will be none left."

"Tomorrow," said Partholan. "Beltaine. The day of death. The same day we first came to this land . . . this 'beautiful land!'" He spoke the words bitterly. "Is that why we are destroyed, Nephew? Is it the curse of Bel?"

"No," the young man said. "It's not the gods, Uncle. It is *them*. I know it. They have found some sorcery to do for them what they could not do themselves. They've made us pay for our defiance."

"Tuam," the old man said urgently, "you must not stay."

"What, Uncle?" Tuam said, aghast. "I can't leave you, leave the rest."

"There is nothing more you can do. I am gone. They are all gone. Escape if you can. Take any others who are still untouched. Flee this cursed place. Go far away."

"Abandon you, our families, our friends? Let you die here, unburied and unmourned?"

"You will only condemn yourselves. Don't be a fool. Go now. As your king, it is my last command to you!" Partholan gripped the young man's arm, pulling himself up by an effort of will, body quivering, voice intense. "You must obey me! Promise you will go! Someone must survive!"

"I promise."

The old man released him and lay back, drained of his last strength. His dimming gaze turned to the mass grave. "My people," he said with failing voice. "My poor people." He went limp, eyes rolling back, final breath rattling out of his deflating lungs.

The young man sat in mourning over his dead uncle for some moments. Then he covered the wasted form with a cloth. He rose and went out across the plain, checking at each fire, gleaning the meager number of his people miraculously untouched. At his order they gathered what possessions they could and reluctantly, regretfully stole away, abandoning the dying, leaving their own families and their own comrades helpless, escaping into the mists.

Another day of agony crawled by for those left behind. The few still mobile weakened swiftly, at last joining the rest languishing about the fires. The dead lay ungathered, the last of the workers gone. Slowly the last fires burned out, the last groans faded, the last stirrings ceased. The plain was silent.

Soon, however, there came new sounds. They came from above, from things stirring far up in the surging clouds of grey. There were fluttering noises, and there were sharp, exultant caws. Dark, angular forms, like ragged shawls of deepest black, swooped down. With a last beating of broad wings, great carrion crows settled in to perch upon the dead . . . and then to feed.

But their feast was interrupted.

Something else became visible in the mist—a vast something that was moving out there, an immense shadow, growing larger, darker as it advanced.

The birds panicked, rising in a single clattering, flapping mass to vanish in the mist. The form grew nearer, then halted just beyond the edge of the encampment of the dead.

Though its details remained shrouded in the thick coils of mist, its silhouette could be seen as manlike but of a size over four times more vast, its shoulders and head towering up into the clouds.

Around its legs other forms came into view, some hundred of them, also human shaped and this time of normal size. They moved out ahead of the giant form onto the edge of the plain. All were men of broad feature and swarthy complexion, each wearing a like uniform of grey and a rounded helmet of black metal, each carrying a long, thick rod with a glowing, blue-white tip.

They moved up to the first of the fires with its circle of dead but stopped there, looking at the corpses uncertainly.

"Go on," a resonant voice boomed from the giant figure. "Be certain all are dead."

They still hesitated. One man looked back to the towering form and said quietly, "But, my Commander, the plague . . ."

"The plague has burned out," the voice rumbled. "It is safe."

"But, can we be sure . . ." the man began.

The vast figure stirred. High up, where the head was a vague mass of darkness in the clouds, there was a metallic click and then a shrill rasping sound. A curving line of crimson light appeared, at first only the slimmest thread.

"Will you obey?" boomed the voice. And the thread widened fractionally to a gleaming wire.

"We obey, my Commander," the man said hastily.

He signaled emphatically to the other men, and they moved quickly, fanning out, searching through the encampment, peering down at the dead faces, here and there poking at dead forms with the shining tips of their rods. As they did this, fine tendrils of light shot from the tips, like tiny lightning bolts, playing across the corpses in a blue-white mesh, then flickering out. The lifeless bodies did not respond.

At last satisfied that no one living remained on the awful plain, the men returned to the giant form.

"All are dead, my Commander," said the one who had spoken before.

"Good, Captain," the deep voice said. "Move all their bodies onto the central pile."

The men did so, using the abandoned carts, piling on the stiffened corpses, hauling them to the now filled pit, heaving them unceremoniously onto a mound, which finally reached high above the surrounding plain.

When they had finished, they swiftly left the camp, gathering behind the towering dark form.

The glowing crack in the head-like mass shifted again. With more of the rasping noise, the gap widened further, opening to a hand's width, like the crescent of sun just peeping beyond the black disk of an eclipse, blazing out.

And from the center of the arch of light, there shot a single beam, a jet of intensely shining red, flashing across the plain to the central pile, playing across the mounds of dead.

With an explosion of flame, the tangled remains all seemed to ignite at once. They flared up, the thousands of corpses fueling a roaring funeral pyre that sent columns of greasy yellow smoke boiling higher to discolor the mist.

"When the fire burns down, cover what remains with earth," the giant's thundering voice ordered. "Let their burial mound become a warning. Just so will perish any who come into this land and seek to defy our power."

The figure turned and strode away to be swallowed in the swirling greyness. Behind it the fire blazed bright, sending a cone of golden glow far up into the clouds.

# Part One

# The New Invasion

# Chapter 1

# New Arrivals

The sun flared through a great rift in the overcast, its rays striking a gleam of emerald from the distant line of shore.

"There! There it is!" the young man said with excitement.

He pointed past the upcurved bow of the ship, across the grey and ragged waters to the western horizon and the glowing strip. It had just come into his sight there and seemed to be lifting from the waves into clearer view.

The long, sleek ship was sweeping rapidly toward it, pushed by the brisk and steady wind that swelled its single vast square of sail. The vessel served as the leading point of a wedge formed with four other ships holding tight, parallel courses. The keen-eyed lookouts posted on each of them were also taking note of the landfall with enthusiastic shouts.

The response was a rush to the sides by the scores of people aboard each ship. Their hundreds crowded in along the bulwarks as they gazed out for a first glimpse of the distant shore.

The ranks of faces that now glowed with the flush of rising excitement were of mixed ages but with far fewer elderly or children than young adults. The travelers were as a whole a handsome people of tall and sturdy frame and bold feature. Complexions were fair and hair was generally light. All were simply clad, the men in trousers and tunics of rough wool, the women in long shifts of the same. Soft leather sandals covered the feet of both sexes, and both men and women wore their hair long, hanging loose or caught back in braids. There was little sign of any ornament.

From a curtained lean-to structure in the stern of the lead ship, another man appeared. He was of middle years in looks, his long face growing craggy, his brown hair streaked with first grey. He strode purposefully through the crowd, and they gave way respectfully, letting him reach the ship's side near to the bow. He stood there, staring out intently at the land.

It had already grown much larger, filling the horizon, looming higher against the sky. Features were visible now: the yellow-grey of cliffs, the green of forests atop them, both glowing with a gem-like clarity under the bright sun.

"Nemed, is that it, then?" a spare, golden-haired, and most intense young man asked him. "Is that the Blessed Land we're seeking?"

"Unless the stars and the wind have played us false, it is," the man said slowly. "But only our treading its sod will prove it so."

He turned to another young man who stood nearby. Though Nemed was a tall man, this other topped him by nearly a head and was of a broader, heavily muscled build. The large youth was also of stern and rough-hewn visage, his jaw so massive and squared, his eyebrows so jutting that his mouth and eyes were made to seem disproportionately small.

"Dagda," Nemed said to him, "will you signal the other ships? We will turn north along the coast and seek a landing place."

The hard look of the big man was dispelled as his mouth stretched into a broad grin of pleasure. "I will do that, my Chief," he said most heartily.

So with enthusiastic waves and with bellows backed by the power of his huge lungs, the one called Dagda passed word to the other ships to follow in a turn.

The five ships sailed north along the coast for half a day, seeing only stony shores or more high cliffs. But at last they passed a rugged headland and found themselves in a great curve of sheltering bay. At its back, the shoreline was a flat beach, running smoothly inland, gently rising to a smooth ridge of green hills. At last they had found their safe place to land.

They ran the ships in, dropping sails as they neared shore,

allowing the craft to slide on in through the surf and ground on the sandy beach.

At once dozens of men leaped into the surf, seizing trailing ropes or pushing on the hulls to force the ships farther up out of the sea. Dagda took a main hawser, and his additional strength brought his ship fully from the water onto the sand.

Nemed climbed out and strode in across the beach, followed by the hundreds of his people who swarmed off of the ships, exclaiming in delight at their safe arrival and at being on solid ground once again. He led them from the sand onto the grassy slope beyond, the whole crowd climbing the low hillside to its crest.

Here they stopped, looking out from the vantage point over the country that stretched before them.

"It is surely a wonderful land," the golden-haired young man said with awe.

Ahead lay a vast, rolling territory, densely forested. The trees formed a nearly solid cover for the earth, like a deep-green and thickly textured rug.

"Not exactly the land of lush plains and meadows your ancient fables told of, Nemed," said another. This one was a sandy haired young man with deepset eyes and small chin. His manner was aloof, as if all this were quite beneath him.

"Mathgen, I suppose you expected to find fields already plowed and herds already gathered," the golden-haired one said with a laugh. "Then you wouldn't have had to work!"

"I leave that to the brainless fools like yourself, Nuada," the other returned indignantly. "I've greater uses for my own time."

"Brainless, am I?" Nuada said, angry now. He stepped toward Mathgen challengingly. "Why you pompous . . ."

Nemed stepped between them. "There is no place for this," he admonished sternly. "We must all work together if we're to survive. What Mathgen has pointed out about the land is true. Without an open place where our first settlement can be made, our task certainly becomes harder. We must try to find something suitable."

"I'll take out a searching party," the golden-haired one volunteered.

"Good, Nuada," said a pleased Nemed. "You will search west." He looked around to the massive youth. "And you, Dagda, will take another party toward the north."

"Thank you!" Dagda replied, giving his big grin. "I welcome a chance for exercise after all those days on that tiny boat!"

Nuada looked to the haughty youth. "And you, Mathgen, will take a party south."

Mathgen was dismayed. "I'm no woodsman. I've no desire to go wandering about out there."

"You will still obey me," Nemed told him firmly. "One of your so-great intelligence should surely be able to discover something."

Mathgen glowered but made no more protest.

"Choose out a dozen men apiece," Nemed ordered the three. "And each of you take a brother of the Falva clan. They are the most knowledgeable in tracking and hunting skills."

"How far should we search, Nemed?" Nuada asked.

"Travel three days. Cover as wide an area as you can. Then return. If there is nothing here, then we must take ship and seek another landing place."

"And if all this . . . this *place* is as overgrown as it is here?" asked Mathgen.

"Then things may be difficult," Nemed replied. "If we must clear land, we will miss much of the growing season. That will make the winter a very hard one for us."

So at Nemed's command, the entire company returned to their ships. While the three expedition leaders chose out men to accompany them, the rest of the settlers began to unload the ships and set up temporary camp.

None of the busy pioneers were aware of something that lifted from the sea not far offshore.

It was a head, a more-or-less human head save for gleaming white skin and long silver hair that spread out across the surface in a fan. The face was smooth, fine featured as in one very young, the sex impossible to judge. Bright azure eyes fixed sharply, quizzically upon the laboring newcomers.

The eyes watched with especial interest as the three parties organized and then divided, heading off in three directions from the landing point. The eyes watched them out of sight, and then the head sank, vanishing back beneath the waves.

But soon it reappeared, this time farther north along the shore, distant from the ships and company. It lifted up and moved along like something skimming across the waves, sweeping toward a secluded stretch of beach. As it drew closer, it began to rise up, revealing a long, slender neck, narrow shoulders, and a slim, lithe torso clad in a softly gleaming silver shift.

And as the being's legs came into view, something else did also.

First a long head breached the water, ears perking up, water snorting from wide nostrils. A silver bridle was about the muzzle, the reins stretching to the silver-haired being's hands. The creature's neck and then its back came into view as it rose up, lifting higher the being who sat astride it. Finally, as it came into the shallows near the shore, the creature's sleek, muscled body and lank, sinewy legs came into view.

The rider reined it up as it came fully out of the waves, and it stopped, the seawater streaming from it. It was a peculiar hybrid, seemingly part horse and part reptile. The head and general body form were purely horse, but a hide of greenish scales; webbed, froglike feet; and a mane and tail like flowing seaweed spoke of something amphibious.

The creature stood patiently while the shining being who rode it looked intently toward the north. The blue eyes traced the path Dagda's party had taken up across the hills. Then long, fine-boned hands shook the reins to urge the strange mount ahead.

The creature stretched at once into a lope, crossing the beach, mounting the slope, sweeping over the hillcrest to plunge into the forest, following the men.


The brawny young man called Dagda moved purposefully through the woods with his companions, unaware of the odd beast and rider who followed them stealthily.

The men carried only hunting weapons—knives belted at their waists and long, slender casting spears with broad heads of yellow-brown metal. One of their number went far in advance of the party. He was a wide and squatly built man, but he moved lightly like a deer, slipping through the heavy undergrowth, searching and examining signs.

They traveled north and west, moving in broad sweeps to cover more territory, climbing the highest hills to overlook as much additional land as possible. But there were no signs of large areas of open ground. The forests continued unbroken, dense, and so shadowy that little could grow on their floor.

For three days they traveled outward from the landing site, finding nothing. They camped their third night in a clearing some dozen paces across, the largest one they had yet found. They were a most dispirited company.

All, that is, but the robust Dagda, who seemed to take the hardships with great patience and joviality.

As the others picked in a cursory manner at the roasted meat of a boar they had slain that day, Dagda chewed away with great gusto at an entire, massive haunch.

"What's wrong with you all?" he asked them between huge bites. "You must eat well. You'll need strength for our journey back tomorrow."

"But we've found nothing, Dagda," the squat man replied dismally. "We've failed. Doesn't that mean anything to you?"

"Nonsense, Donnchadh!" Dagda told him with force. "Why, look at this." He swung the haunch around before them. "We've found there is more game here than we've ever seen, haven't we?"

"And fierce predators, too," another man pointed out. "Bears, wolves, great cats . . ."

"We've not had to face them in our old land," put in a third. "There they were chased away or hunted from existence long ago."

"You all talk like old women," Dagda told them. "You didn't come on the journey here without knowing you'd face some hard things."

"Maybe not," the stocky one named Donnchadh said, "but good hunting alone will not sustain our numbers. Too many of us are farmers and herders. We need fields to plant, grasslands to feed our sheep and cows."

"Ah, I still say you're fearing nothing." Dagda cleaned the last meat from the haunch bone and tossed it aside, wiping his mouth with a sleeve. "One of the others will find a place. Maybe not that whining Mathgen, but surely Nuada. He's clever and tough enough to do anything. Now, quit your worrying. Eat up your food, and let's be getting ourselves some rest."

The heartiness and confidence exuding from him did seem to return some cheer to the men. They finished off the carcass with more vigor, then banked their fire and lay down beside it. All were soon asleep.

But halfway through the night, their sleep was interrupted.

A sharp, cracking sound awoke Donnchadh. He sat up, listening intently. Then he moved to Dagda, shaking him awake.

"What is it?" Dagda asked as he sat up, instantly on the alert.

"Something's out there," said Donnchadh. He pointed into the trees. "Over there."

"A prowling bear?"

"Maybe. It's circling us now. Wait. Listen!"

They heard more crackling sounds of movement, coming closer. Then something became visible through the trees. It was something large and glowing with two hazy lights—a silver one topping a green.

Donnchadh and Dagda roused the others as the shining thing turned and began a circling of the camp. The men rose and took up their weapons, moving together defensively to stand staring around them, weapons clutched tightly in readiness, the expressions of most apprehensive.

"It's a most strange thing," one said, eyes tracking the intermittent flashes of the lights as they moved through the trees. "Some creature of the dark."

"Does it mean to kill us?" another asked.

"It hasn't moved closer," said Donnchadh, "as if it means only to let us know it's there."

"Look, there it goes!" cried one.

The light had suddenly started away.

"Come on!" said Dagda, starting after it.

Donnchadh joined him, but the others held back. Dagda stopped at the edge of the clearing to look around at them.

"What are you waiting for?" he demanded.

"If that is some monstrous spirit of this land, aren't we fools to chase it?" one asked.

"We came out to explore this place and seek new things," Dagda told them firmly. *"That* is a new thing. I mean to see just what it is. So stay or come!"

With that he and the squat man went on into the trees. The rest exchanged glances, nodded agreement, then headed after them.

Together the party pursued the eerie lights through the black forest. Their pursuit was long, wearying, and very awkward in the dark. Often men fell. Often they went astray and lost the fleeing lights. But always the lights returned, as if tempting, luring, leading the men on.

And always the men followed, the determined Dagda at their head, his eyes fixed intently on the object of their chase, his jaw set in stubborn determination not to quit.

Still, as the sun rose to send its first rays striking down into the woods, the stamina of the pursuers was nearing its end.

They continued to stumble forward, but they were growing more unsure of the direction. In the morning light, the glowing silver and green seemed to have vanished.

"Please, let's give it up," a weary youth pleaded.

"No, wait!" cried Dagda. "Look there!"

Their quarry was moving in the trees only a few paces before them. Though fainter, its silver and green radiance could still be seen. It paused, then headed on again, straight ahead of them.

Once more they pursued, but this time they came suddenly out of the forest onto what seemed a broad, open hillcrest. They caught just a flash of the strange green creature and its shining rider before the two vanished down below the crest.

The men rushed forward but stopped on the crest, staring ahead.

Before them stretched a long, wide valley of green meadows, all but treeless. A stream ran through it, forming a blue-green and glistening lake in the lowest point at the valley's center.

"It's perfect!" said an astonished Donnchadh.

"Many times enough to support our clans," said another.

"Look, there," said a third, pointing toward the lake. "What are those? Houses?"

One section of the lake's opposite shore rose steeply to the crest of a low, rounded hill. Part of a curving line and a number of rounded lumps were visible there.

"Yes," confirmed Donnchadh. "I'd say that is a palisade surrounding many huts."

"Is this new land already inhabited then?" another said in despair.

"That we will have to see," said Dagda.

They went down the slope into the valley, skirting the lake. There was no more sign of the beast and rider they had pursued here. The pale head with silver hair that lifted from the waters of the lake to watch them with its azure eyes stayed carefully hidden in the cover of lake reeds.

The party moved on toward the settlement. They moved cautiously, looking about for other signs of habitation. But there were no herds, no tilled fields, no human beings.

At last they came around the front of the hill. They found that while the side of it on the lakeshore was steep, the other sides of the circular mound sloped gently outward. To protect these vulnerable sides, a high wall of thick stakes had been erected around the hill's brow. But it was badly rotted, sagging in places. Wide gates on the northwest side stood fully open.

Even more cautiously they mounted the slope and went in through the gates. Beyond the palisade they found several hundred huts of a round shape with wickerwork walls and conical, high-peaked roofs of thatch. All were weatherbeaten, and many had fallen in. There was still no sign of life.

"Deserted for some while, I'd judge," said Donnchadh. They stopped at the village center, near to a much larger structure of an oval shape.

"This must be a meeting hall," said Dagda. "I'll go in. Wait here."

None argued with his decision. They drew close together and looked uncertainly around at the ghostly place as he approached the big hut.

He pushed aside the tattered remnant of a hide hung across the door opening and stepped inside. The air was heavy with the smell of old fires and musty straw and general decay. The room was dusky with thick shadows. Through the gloom the remains of furniture were visible: a table, stools, some empty shelves.

By a ring of stones that formed a central hearth, a bundle of rags lay. Curious, he approached it, prodding gingerly at the bundle with the butt of his hunting spear.

It rolled over with a clatter, and he found himself looking into the face of a gape-jawed skull.

# Chapter 2

# Settlement

The people of Nemed were gathered around the scores of bonfires built along the shore above their beached ships.

Enough of their supplies had been offloaded to provide a comfortable camp. The small seed herds of cattle and sheep were now penned in areas which, to beasts so long confined, must have seemed expansive.

At one of the larger fires sat Nemed himself. He was in deep conversation with Nuada, Mathgen, and the men of their searching parties. Many others of the people of Nemed stood or sat crowded about them to listen.

"So by our third day, the only open country that we'd found was a bogland," Nuada was saying. "It was a treacherous place. We nearly lost Murchadh there." He indicated a stockily built young man who in feature was nearly a twin to Donnchadh. "He had all but sunk from sight beneath the oozing stuff before we got hold of him and dragged him out."

"Is that another perfect bit of our paradise, Nuada?" Mathgen asked caustically.

"At least Nuada traveled out the full three days, Mathgen," shot back a young woman in the surrounding crowd. "He didn't give up and return in less than two."

"And who are you to be giving insult to me, Moire?" he replied to her in outrage.

She moved forward from the others to be revealed in the firelight. She was a tall and striking young woman of boldly handsome features, dark brown eyes, and a wealth of waving hair so raven black that she stood out sharply amongst so many fair-haired ones.

She stepped across the fire to stand challengingly, legs set wide, hands on hips. The light sparked red fire in her angry eyes and struck deep crimson streaks in her shining hair.

"I am a woman who knows why we came here, Mathgen MacDualtach," she said in hard, clear tones. "All of us suffered much in our homeland, prey to the violence and tyranny of the cruel chieftains who ruled us. We would be slaves now, or worse, if we had not listened to the dream of Nemed. He told us we could seek out a new home, build a new life for ourselves and our families that was free of the oppression. We believed him and we chose to follow him. Now we are here, a thousand strong, each of us knowing what it might take to make our place in this land. And there's not *one* of us who isn't ready to make any sacrifice . . . except maybe for *you!*"

Her verbal assault forced him to the defensive. "I did what I could," he grumbled. "The country was too rough. We'd come against high mountains. Ask Toirdealbhach O'Falva. He led our way."

Another stocky young man—once again a near match for Murchadh and Donnchadh—spoke up then, but slowly, considering his words.

"Well, we did come into some high and rugged lands. That's true enough. But we might have crossed them. We might have seen what was beyond."

"Not in three days!" Mathgen insisted. "We had to come back. It was Nemed's own order!"

"Dagda didn't come back," Moire pointed out fiercely. "He has stayed out on the search."

"That ox is more likely only lost," Mathgen said scornfully. "For all we know, he's wandering in circles barely beyond our sight."

This brought an outburst of anger from the crowd, clearly sympathetic to the huge man. And Moire, eyes flaring brighter in rage, started toward Mathgen, hands out as if to grab.

Nemed got quickly to his feet, coming before her.

"Stop, Moire," he ordered firmly. "I know your feelings,

but a brawl will benefit none. Mathgen had good reason for cutting his search short. It *was* my own order to return. And we all . . ." he shot Mathgen a look, *"all* know Dagda is a brave man. So just be calm."

She wasn't mollified. "You're too easy," she told him scoldingly. "If you were Dagda's true friend, you'd strike that one down for his words."

With that she turned and charged out through the circling crowd, vanishing into the dark.

"A most fiery tempered young woman," said Nemed, looking after her.

"A madwoman, I'd call her," said Mathgen, sniffing in disdain.

"Nemed should have let her get at you," Nuada said with a grin. "I'll wager the wagering would have all been on her!"

"Give over this petty bickering," Nemed said sharply. "Such things can't be our concern now." He looked around him at his gathered people, his expression grim. "We must decide what we are going to do. If something *has* happened to Dagda, we must decide how long to stay. Every day which passes, every moment which is lost in waiting is so much less precious time we'll have to establish ourselves. It makes our survival here that much more precarious."

"I say he knew how much time he had to return," said Mathgen bluntly. "We cannot risk a thousand for a dozen."

"A callous view," said Nuada.

"But a most practical one too, I'm afraid," said Nemed. He considered, then sighed resignedly. "We can give them one day more," he announced. "After that we must reload our ships and sail on."

"But what about Dagda's party?" said Murchadh. "What about our brother?"

"Yes," added Toirdealbhach. "Will Donnchadh and the rest just be abandoned?"

"If those of the searching party are alive," Nemed said gravely, "then it is the fates who will have to help them now."

The dawn light streaked across the sea from the east, lighting the white curve of beach. It revealed the hundreds of Nemed's people already beginning the task of reloading their ships.

The morning rays shone bright and sparkling against the

dew-studded grass of the slope above the beach, throwing its crest into sharp relief against the darker western sky. It also showed a solitary figure sitting there upon the crest's highest point. It was that of the woman named Moire.

Another young woman of tall, lean form and flame-red hair climbed up the slope. She carried a waterskin and a bulging sack.

She came up beside Moire. The raven-haired woman seemed unaware of her, her gaze intently searching across the spreading forest land.

"Moire?" the red-haired woman said.

The other stirred and looked around. "Sadhbh, why have you come up here?"

"For worry about you. It's been a day and two whole nights you've sat this vigil alone. You must be starved and dying with the thirst. Here." She set bag and waterskin down.

"I'll take some drink," said Moire, "but I've no stomach for any food."

She lifted the skin and squirted a stream of water into her mouth. The other sat down beside her.

"They're beginning to get ready for our leaving," Sadhbh told her.

"I know." Moire glanced down to the beach, then back to the still-shadowed forest. "But they must be out there, Sadhbh. I feel it . . ." she touched her breast, "in here."

"It's not just your fear for the party, is it?" the other said knowingly. "It's Dagda."

"I have strong feelings for him," Moire said frankly. "I'll not deny them. We've become very close on the journey. My father's growing older and more frail. Mother and I have no one else. Dagda knew that. He was like a brother at first, protecting us and seeing to our needs." She smiled as she considered him. Her voice became soft in her warm reverie. "He's been always most kindhearted to us. That great, rough man, but still so gentle, so openhanded, so giving of himself . . ."

"So it's love now, is it?" said the other with a grin.

"Oh, but you can say nothing about that at all, Sadhbh!" Moire admonished her friend. "Until we've found a home and made a good place for ourselves, there's no time at all for thinking of such things. After that? Well, one day, maybe, if I'm certain he has any feelings like my own, then I . . ."

But she stopped abruptly there, looking down to the ships

again, then back out over the trackless forest. Her hopeful expression faded in the face of the grim reality.

"How can I even think of this, not knowing if I'll even see him again?" she finished dismally.

"He would be very hard to kill," said Sadhbh. "And he has Donnchadh O'Falva with him too. Surely they'd find a way to survive."

"Oh, I've no thought at all that he's dead. I've told you, that much I can feel. It's as if I was a part of him, in him. No, my fear is that we'll sail away before he can return."

"You can't make him come back any more swiftly sitting here," Sadhbh observed.

"Who can know that?" Moire countered. "Maybe he can feel me here, hoping for a first sight of him. Maybe feeling that will give him a keener direction to follow back or add just that bit more length to his stride. Whether it may be or not, Sadhbh, I'll not budge from this spot until the last ship is being pushed off of the strand. And you can tell Nemed *that*!"

So, through the morning, Moire waited there as the others reloaded. And finally the ships were ready. When there was no more to be done, Nemed himself went up the slope to fetch her. With gentle but firm words he at last urged her to the shore.

Still she waited on as the ships were one by one launched and rowed out into the bay. Nemed's own ship was last. Its passengers embarked. It was pushed down to the edge, then out into the surf. It floated, only its bow holding it upon the sand. Nemed and Moire were the only ones left upon the shore.

"There is nothing more you can do," he said to her. "Come, Moire. Please."

She made no reply. He walked out into the surf, stopping by the ship's side. He put a hand to the bulwark and turned, extending the other to her.

"Moire, come," he said again. "Your parents have need of you."

Moire looked once more up to the high crest. It was empty. Reluctantly she turned and strode out into the surf. Nemed helped her into the ship and climbed in after her.

The ship was rowed out to join the others. Their sails lifted, and they began to head out across the bay, toward the curve of headlands and the open sea beyond.

Most looked ahead, but Moire stood in the ship's stern, black hair billowing about her, dark gaze still fixed upon the crest which shrank swiftly away behind them.

The tip of the curve of headlands was close ahead. The ships swept toward it, beginning the turn that would take them around it and out of sight of the wide bay.

"Look there!" she cried, pointing. "Nemed! Look! The hills!"

He turned and looked, joined quickly by the rest. Tiny figures were popping into view there against the sky—three, seven, ten, a dozen figures. They could barely be discerned as the forms of men, but it was clear that one was much larger than the rest.

"Dagda!" Nemed said most thankfully.

And the shipful of people cheered.


The people of Nemed moved up the lush valley in a long column, carrying some of their possessions, hauling more on four-wheeled carts, herding the flocks and herds along with them.

Ahead of the main column, Nemed and an advance party had already reached the abandoned village and were scrutinizing it.

"The people who lived here must have been many times our number," Nuada remarked to his leader, gazing around him at the hundreds of huts.

A man came up to him. He was short but very wiry of frame, with corded muscles and calloused hands that spoke of long years of work, though he looked very young. His head was an emphatic wedge, broad browed and sharp chinned. Large ears, a beak of nose, and tiny mouth gave his features an amusingly hodge-podge look. He seemed nearly to vibrate with excess vitality.

"Enough of these places can be repaired to give all of us good shelter," he briskly reported to Nemed.

"Good, Goibniu," a much-pleased Nemed replied.

"There are smithy and carpentry sheds too," the man added brightly. "They're in bad repair, but no worries, my Chief. We'll get right to work. A day or two and we'll have the forges roarin'!"

He bustled off, passing a pair of men carrying skeletal remains from a hut. A dozen other teams were also bringing out remains from about the village. Under Dagda's supervision the dead were being laid out temporarily in the open area around the meeting hall. A large grave being dug below the fortress hill would soon receive them all.

In the meantime, a lanky man of long features and most dour demeanor was moving along the rows, crouching here and there to examine one of the pitiful heaps of bones. Nuada and Nemed approached him.

"Well, Diancecht," Nemed addressed him, "what have you discovered about them?"

The man rose, straightening his angular body. He spoke in a slow, precise, grave way:

"The indications so far are that there are perhaps two hundred dead here. Most died separately, but some were apparently whole families who died together, often huddled close as if for warmth."

"Diancecht," Nemed said, "you have the most knowledge and the greatest healer's skills among us. What do you say destroyed them?"

"That is very difficult, my Chief," the man said carefully. "There is so little left. It was something very swift, I would judge. Certainly not violence. A pestilence, perhaps. Possibly a famine."

"How could they starve here?" asked Nuada, looking about him at the lush valley.

"A most intriguing point," Diancecht agreed. "Donnchadh has told me there are signs that they had tilled extensive fields. There are also signs that they had cattle, and some sheep. All gone now."

"Like the rest of the people," Nuada said thoughtfully. "Where did they go? We've found no graves, no other bodies. But there must have been thousands more."

"They may have trekked on," suggested Diancecht, "leaving the weak behind."

The first of the main column of Nemed's people were arriving at the village now, moving through the open gates, gazing around in wonder at the vast place.

Nuada looked to them, then turned a concerned gaze to his chieftain.

"Nemed," asked Nuada, "are we safe here?"

"Whatever killed these poor people has been gone for a great while now," Nemed said. "Sickness or drought or famine we will face anywhere we go. The ones who lived in this valley must have labored for years to clear the land, to plow, to nurture stock, to build this place. I think we would be fools not to stay here and reap the benefits of their toil. It is our own best chance of surviving in this land, and the best tribute we could give these dead as well. I say we stay." He looked from Nuada to Diancecht. "Do you agree?"

"I do," the tall man said somberly.

"Yes," said Nuada with conviction. "We stay."

Dagda now approached them in company with Murchadh of the Falva clan.

"We're finished, my Chief," the big man said. "All the dead are here."

"Then you can see to helping our people occupy the village," Nemed told him. "Murchadh, you and your brothers can begin the foraging for food. Tomorrow we will see to beginning a renewal of the fields."

"And the wall?" asked Dagda. "It needs much repair."

"They did not die of violence here," Nemed pointed out. "There seem to be no enemies."

"But there *are* predators," corrected Murchadh.

"Yes," Nuada put in. "These people built a wall for a reason."

"Your argument is a good one," Nemed agreed. "We will restore the wall. But all of these toils can wait until tomorrow. Tonight, my friends, we are going to celebrate!"

So the dead who had once inhabited the village were laid to rest, and the living who would inhabit it anew took their place.

And that night they rejoiced at the first day in their new home. Bonfires blazed high. Merry tunes were played on gracefully curving harps, large leather-covered drums, and slender reed pipes. Men, women, elders, children, families, and friends danced together about the fires that roared up, sending great streamers of red-orange flame and plumes of golden sparks rising far into the clear, star-filled night sky.

Below the village, on the verge of the lake, a softly glowing green figure, part reptilian and part horse, stood in the marshy shallows. A silver form astride it looked up to the cheerful fires, and its childlike face lit with a wide, pleased smile.

At the same time, on a high hill far away, another figure atop a tower of stone stirred fitfully.

It had stood sleeping, propped against a battlement of smooth, grey, seamless stone. Its head lay pillowed on crossed arms, and it snored in deep and rasping waves. But something —some dream or muscle ache—caused it to open tiny glistening eyes deepset behind shaggy brows.

The eyes peered out, first vaguely, then with intent as they focused. With a startled movement, the head lifted.

It was no human head.

The starlight revealed a face like a great boar, with a large, soft, wet-nostriled snout and a tusked, drooping mouth leaking a trail of drool at one side.

The tiny eyes stared fixedly into the night, peering toward the far horizon where a faint, ruddy light from the bonfires showed.

Then the slack mouth moved.

"Fire at the settlement," the creature growled in a tone of fear. "By Great Balor, they've returned from the dead!"

# Chapter 3

# First Meeting

Busy hands worked to rethatch the hut's roof.

The laborer skilfully wove bundles of new straw into the framework of the conical roof all about its smokehole, creating a new peak section that showed bright golden against the age-greyed thatch below.

The man paused in his efforts, turned over to sit up on the sloped roof, and pulled up the waterskin that hung at his belt. It was a bright, clear day for spring and very warm. He drank long to assuage the thirst built by his toil, then sat resting, looking about him at the scene.

It was both a pastoral and a busy one. Around him a dozen others worked at the rethatching of the village huts. Below him hundreds more bustled about the settlement on a variety of chores that ranged from slapping new daub onto wattled walls to drying meat.

The thatcher lifted his gaze to beyond the village wall. From his high point he could look out across the entire valley.

To the south between village and lake, he could see the fields being prepared. Separate plots had been laid out, and men with hand-pushed plows were turning up the sod in furrows. Some fields had all been plowed, and other men were walking the rows, poking seeds into the rich, dark earth.

To the west on the valley's slopes, he could see their precious cows and sheep grazing the lush grasslands. The sheep grazed the steeper upper slopes in a tight mass of yellow-white. The cows ranged below, the dark spots of them widely scattered across the broad, green space.

From here the man's eye traveled up the valley toward the north. No fields had yet been plowed there, no flocks let to graze. Yet his gaze stopped there, staring.

A number of other dark dots were moving far away, traveling slowly down the valley from its uppermost end, heading toward the settlement.

With an expression of curiosity the man watched them approaching, the dots growing, taking on clearer shape as they came.

As he watched them, his curious expression slowly changed to one of concern.

Below him Nemed was moving through the village, inspecting hut reconstruction as the always highly spirited Goibniu described the work being done.

"We're not only restorin' but improvin' the structures as well," the man said with great enthusiasm. He slapped the wooden supports of a doorway hard. "Aye, they'll withstand the strongest gale and hardest rains come winter. I'll wager anything on that, Chieftain."

"Good, Goibniu," Nemed told him. "I knew I could count on your unflagging industriousness. How many are ready now?"

"Nearly fifty, Chieftain. But I've just had to give over the supervision of the work to Luchtine. He's a grand lad, and a true master of the carpenter's arts. I've needed to turn my whole attention to the smithy. Our tools are wearin' out like they were ice meltin' in the sun, the way our folk are using them. Mad with the work fever they are."

"I know," said Nemed with a smile. "It's astonishing what we've accomplished in only these ten days. Crops half planted, houses half rebuilt. A fine work," he slapped a congratulating hand to the smith's shoulder, "and you've been a great part of it. So, I'd best be letting you go back to your forges then. I know that's where your love is."

And with that he left Goibniu, heading across the yard. But as he passed below the hut where the resting thatcher worked, the man hailed him.

"My Chief?"

Nemed stopped and looked up to him. "Yes, Coman?"

"There is someone coming in, my Chief. I've been watching them moving down the valley from the northern end."

"Likely a hunting party," Nemed said dismissingly.

"No, Chieftain. I've watched them for a while as they've come closer. I don't know quite what it is, but there's somethin' strange about 'em. And . . . they're mounted."

"Mounted?" Nemed said, with interest this time. "And how many are they?"

"A score maybe."

"All right, Coman. Thank you. I'll see to it."

"But Chieftain, are they a danger?" the man asked.

"I'm sure not," Nemed assured him. "Just get on with your work."

Yet as Nemed strode away, the man did not take up his work again. He turned his eyes back to the approaching forms, and his look went from concern to growing alarm.

Meantime, Nemed had headed briskly out through the village gates and started around the great curve of the palisade. Repair work on the timber wall was well underway. Man-pulled carts were bringing in suitable logs cut in the forests beyond the valley and adding them to a pile just outside the gates. Here a crew selected the most ideal logs, stripped them, and pointed them on both ends. Another crew then moved each log around to where it was needed.

A great deal of the palisade had already been replaced. Nemed followed around nearly half of its sweeping semicircle before he reached the repair crew. Here Nuada was overseeing the removal of the old logs and the cleaning out of the post-holes.

Dagda was in charge of setting the new logs. He directed six men who lifted the logs, maneuvered them into the holes, wrestled them upright, and then held them in position while others lashed them into place with heavy ropes.

As Nemed approached them, he fell witness to a minor crisis. A log that had seemed secure broke loose suddenly, toppling outward toward the crew below.

They leaped from the way as Dagda himself jumped in, putting up hands to catch the falling log and stop its descent.

His great arm and shoulder muscles bulged with strain as he alone forced the huge log back upright. The others stood watching the feat in amazement until the log was once again set in place. Only then did Nuada order men in to assist his large friend.

The crew took hold of the log and Dagda stepped away, looking to Nuada.

"Thanks for all the help," Dagda said in a sarcastic tone.

Nuada grinned. "I knew you'd have more fun doing it yourself."

Dagda smiled in return. "It *was* good exercise."

Nemed stepped up to them.

"Dagda, Nuada," he hailed. "Sorry to stop your work, but would you two come with me? I need you to see something."

There was an urgent note in Nemed's voice. The two young men exchanged a glance, then unhesitatingly left the crews to join their chieftain in a walk back around the wall.

"What is it, my Chief?" Nuada asked.

"I didn't want to alarm the others, but a thatcher has seen someone coming toward us. He says they are not of our company. I wanted you to see to it with me."

They circled the settlement to the north to have the clearest view. By now the figures could be seen from their lower vantage point. They were halfway down the long valley, still approaching slowly.

At this distance the three men could see distinctly that the ones coming were indeed mounted, though the exact form of mount and rider were still unclear.

"Horses, I think," Nuada said. "I did not know there were any such in this land."

"Then they certainly cannot be our people," said Nemed.

"My Chief," said Dagda, peering at the distant shapes, "I'm not even certain that they are people at all!"

Nemed looked to them. His voice grew urgent. "We must spread the word quickly. Everyone must gather in the village. We must be prepared to greet these visitors."

"I'll arm our men and put them on the walls," said Nuada.

"No," said Nemed quickly. "No sign of hostility. We want to show them that we wish to be friends."

"We must at least close the gates," said Dagda.

"No!" Nemed said with more force. "Nothing threatening at all! There are only a score of them, not a host of war. They must only be coming to see who we are. If they are coming in peace, we must show that we are friendly. Remember, *we* are the invaders here."

"Even so, I don't like taking such a risk," said Dagda.

Nemed put a hand on the big man's arm. His voice was urgent.

"Dagda, you must do as I ask. It could be vital to our whole future here. Please."

Dagda considered. "I think it is a mistake," he said, reluctantly, "but, all right. You are my chieftain. You have my loyalty. They'll see nothing to make them fear. That I promise."

"Thank you, Dagda," Nemed said with great relief. He looked to the approaching riders, hope lighting his face. "And after today, it may be we'll have an ally to help us fulfill our dream."

The gates of the settlement stood wide in welcome.

Many of Nemed's people lined the high walkway within the palisade, peering over the pointed logs. Others formed a large crowd just within the gates. All stared out curiously, raptly, anxiously toward those who came.

The score of riders had already ridden back and forth before the village once at a safe distance. They were now pulled up in a line below the slope, some two hundred paces from the gate, sitting motionless, staring back at the settlers.

Out some twenty paces before the gates, Nemed himself stood with only a dozen men. Two of them were Nuada and Diancecht, flanking their chieftain. The others were elders of the united clans.

"Where is Dagda?" Nemed asked, looking around to the village. "I thought he would join us here."

"He was afraid that just his presence with us might be enough to worry our friends out there," Nuada explained.

"He may be right," agreed Nemed.

"Look," said an elder, pointing, "they're coming up."

The line of mounts, at this distance identifiable as large and thick-girthed horses, lumbered up the slope toward them. The nature of their riders now also became clearly discernable.

"By my ancestors," someone said in consternation, "what are they?"

Though shaped as men, the riders were more like monstrous parodies of Man's form. Some had features less human than bestial. One was slant-eyed and whiskered like a cat. Another sported the bristles, tusks, and snout of a boar. A third had the low forehead, pointed muzzle, and long fangs of a wolf.

Two more had wide, loose, lipless mouths and bulging, wideset eyes more suited to a frog.

Even more awful than these were the beings simply misfigured, as if human heads of a soft clay had been crudely, savagely, diabolically reworked, their features distorted, misplaced, sometimes missing altogether. And the bodies of most were also strangely formed; large, thick, often twisted, often with missing limbs—a hand or foot usually—replaced by claws or stumps of a dark grey metal.

Many sported some armor, largely breastplates and shin and arm guards of the same grey metal but much battered and marked by red-brown streaks. Some carried thick spears with wickedly barbed points. All wore broadswords sheathed at their sides and carried round metal shields.

This bizarre company stopped again some hundred paces down the slope from the gates, eyes taking in the unarmed welcoming party, the fields and herds, the faces of men, women, and children lining the wall. Then two of them dismounted, left their spears and shields with others, and walked on up toward the gate. One was a man of swarthy complexion with a great leather patch across one eye, but otherwise of relatively normal look. His companion was the being with the boar's head.

"Who are you who have come to us?" Nemed called to them as they approached.

No response came from them. They stopped only a few paces away, staring back.

"I am Nemed," the chieftain tried again. "These people have come with me to settle here. We come from across the sea, from the land to the south and east. A great way we've sailed. We have come in peace. Can you tell us who you are?"

The two beings exchanged a look. Then the leather-patched one spoke. His voice was guttural, slow. The words came haltingly, oddly and thickly accented but still intelligible.

"So, you are not spirits of the dead. You are new ones."

"You know our tongue, then," said Nemed.

The other nodded. "We know it. We have met those from your lands before, in my father's time. They lived in this same place."

"You know about the people of this place?" asked Diancecht with interest.

"My father's people did."

"Do you know what happened to them?"

The man's wide mouth lifted in a smile that revealed sharp, yellow teeth as of a carnivore. "It is certain we know that. We destroyed them."

The company with Nemed made sounds of shock at that.

"You destroyed them?" Nemed said, aghast. "Why?"

"This all is our land," the man said, waving around. "Fomor land." He stabbed at his own chest with a thumb. "We are the Fomor. Many lifetimes past we claimed this. Then they came. They refused us tribute. They defied our will. For that, they died."

"How?" asked Diancecht. "What did you do to them?"

"We have much power," the other said vaguely. "None can stand against us." He looked them over again critically with his one glinting eye. "You—you seem very weak. No weapons. No armor. No warriors. You till the land and you herd the beasts. There is no real strength in you."

"We are strong," Nemed countered. "We have worked hard. We have journeyed long. We have come here only to live in peace."

"Your numbers are too few," the other added. "You cannot fight us."

"We don't mean to fight you," Nemed said with some desperation. "Don't you see? We only want this place to live in."

"Then you must pay tribute."

"What kind of tribute?" asked Nemed. "How much?"

"We ask the same of you as our fathers did of them. For the right to live upon this land, each year at the end of the season of growth you will pay us two thirds of your harvested grains and your milk, and two thirds of your own healthy issue for that year."

"Our children?" Nemed said in horror.

"Nemed, we can't pay such as that!" cried Nuada.

"Of course not," Nemed agreed. He appealed to the one-eyed man. "Surely you must see that what you ask is impossible. To give our children . . ."

"It is the tribute we asked of them," the man brusquely interrupted. "It is the same for you."

"But there must be other ways. We can talk . . ."

"No talk," the other snapped. "You must submit or be destroyed. You are too weak. I will show you." He lifted a hand to the boar-faced one. "Neith, kill one," he ordered. His hand swept around to Nemed. "Him!"

At once the creature drew his sword and leaped toward Nemed.

So swiftly did he move that the stunned men had no chance to act in their chief's defense. But as the sword swept up to strike Nemed, something flew in suddenly from the side.

A hunting spear shot under the boarhead's uplifted arm and slammed home, its head driving deep into the side of the broad chest, splitting the heart. The impact of the spear knocked the being sideways from his feet and he crashed down at the feet of Nemed's group, already dead.

The astonished men looked around to see Dagda emerging from behind the pile of logs near the gates, face set in grim satisfaction at the success of his cast.

The one-eyed man growled in rage and went for his own sword hilt. But this time Nuada's reaction was faster. Before the warrior could draw, the young man hurtled into him, enwrapping him with both arms. The two went down together, struggling on the ground.

Now another Fomor in the mounted group acted. The cat-faced one urged his massive steed ahead. The animal loped up toward them while the rider drew out his long sword to attack the unarmed men.

Now unarmed himself, Dagda grabbed up a thick pole of wood trimmed from one of the logs and rushed forward to intercept the charging horse.

They met halfway between. The rider swung a hard blow down at Dagda. The big man lifted his pole to stop it. The sword cut deep into the wood but was turned aside. As the horse swept on past, Dagda spun with a swiftness amazing in one so large. He swept the pole around with all his power behind it, bringing the length square across the warrior's back. Both wood and backbone snapped with the force of the blow. The rider was jolted completely from his seat, sent flying forward, over the horse's head and down to crumple brokenly to the ground.

Dagda turned challengingly to the other mounted beings, massive body set, the shattered remnant of the wood in one hand, awaiting more attacks. Meanwhile, the lithe Nuada had managed to wrestle the one-eyed man's own sword out of his sheath and bring its point up to his throat.

"Tell your warriors to hold place, or have this sword rammed up into your brain," the young man told the other savagely.

The man stopped struggling.

"Hold there!" he shouted to the rest, a shrill note of panic in his voice. "I order you! Nobody move!"

Others of Nemed's people were by this time pouring from the village with hastily snatched-up weapons. Several scores moved out in a broad fan to defend their leaders. The creatures below stayed where they were.

Dagda turned from them and marched up to join his fellows, casting away the splintered stub. He yanked his spear from the slain boarhead and held it cocked and ready over the one-eyed man as Nuada let him up.

The man climbed to his feet, glared around him with his single, balefilled eye.

"You made a great mistake!" he spat out. "No one shames Cruc. I'll see you all die now!"

"It doesn't seem that you're in a position to be making such a threat," said Dagda, poking at him meaningfully with the blood-stained tip of his spear.

"We did not mean this to happen," Nemed told the Fomor in distress. "Please understand. We want to talk. We mean no harm." He looked to Nuada. "Show him, Nuada. Let him go. Give him his sword."

"What?" said Nuada in disbelief. "He tried to kill you."

"A misunderstanding. We must give a sign of peace. Give him his sword."

With great reluctance the young man handed the weapon back. The one called Cruc gingerly took it. He looked at it, then at the spear point Dagda still held poised to strike. Prudently the Fomor slipped the sword away.

"Go back to your people," Nemed pleaded. "Tell them we still wish to talk. Tell them we wish to be friends."

"I will go to them," Cruc said. He cautiously backed away from Dagda to a safe distance, then turned and trotted down the hill to the security of his friends. He climbed onto his horse. Only then did he shout angrily back to them:

"I will go to my people, but there will be no talk. They will come here as a force, and you will die. You are few. You are weak. You are not fighters. Your puny hunting spears will not stop us." His hand swept out to take in the village. "Those ones here before you—they were five times your number. They all died. *You* will die too!"

With that parting barrage, he signaled to his comrades. They turned their mounts and headed away, back up the valley toward the north. The two riderless horses followed them. The two dead beings were left where they had fallen.

The people of Nemed stood looking after the departing Fomor in silent dismay. It was Dagda who spoke first.

"Well," he said in a matter-of-fact tone, "I suppose I should be getting back to my wall repairs then, shouldn't I?"

# Chapter 4

# The First God

From the shelter of the tall rushes that marged the valley lake, the silver-haired being had watched the confrontation at the village intently, its bright eyes filled with great alarm.

When the Fomor had ridden away and the people of Nemed had all disappeared within the palisade, it stealthily emerged from the far side of the lake, once more astride the peculiar reptilian horse. Once distant enough from the village to escape observation, the being urged its mount ahead at full speed, and they left the valley, entering the woods. The hybrid creature threaded a sinuous way through the labyrinth of trees without slowing, kept to a run by the urgently jabbing heels of its slender rider.

A journey that had taken the people of Nemed three days to complete on foot was finished in the span of the single morning. Soon the coastline was ahead, the sea glittering beyond. The strange beast rushed down the hillside, galloped across the beach and without hesitation plunged into the surf.

The waves crested against its broad chest as it pushed out into the sea, still urged by the pale rider. Legs, body, and finally head vanished beneath the waves, carrying down the slender form of the one astride. The last sign of the pale being was silver hair, fanning out across the waves for an instant before being drawn beneath.

Then there was only the rippling sea.

But below the waves the two beings were continuing to move. Off of solid ground the horselike creature was now making use of its broad, webbed feet. All its four legs churned powerfully to propel it at great speed. Its sleek body was stretched out tautly, its long head thrust out far before it on the lean neck. The silver-haired rider also leaned far forward, body and head close to the animal's neck, reducing resistance from the water. The silver hair streamed behind, flowing and twining with the green tendrils of the long mane.

The swimming creature angled downward as it moved out from shore. The bottom dropped away in a steep slope, plunging down into a deep where the sunlight dimmed to a faint, blue-green glowing high above. The ocean floor shelved here, the level but rock-strewn bottom spreading away to be lost in the shadows of distance.

Mount and rider continued on, across the sunken plain, until a vast, dark form came into view, towering up ahead.

It was a mountain, a ragged spire of stone thrusting up abruptly from the sea floor so far that its tip nearly scraped the bottom of the surface waves.

The horselike creature swam around it slowly while the shining rider's bright gaze searched over its surface. The cliffs of its base rose almost sheer from the rocky bed, their rugged faces creating what seemed a solid wall. But at last the rider spied a dark fissure in the stone and tugged the reins, directing the mount toward it.

They glided through the fissure, coming into a round tunnel of smoothly rippled rock. It formed a long, spiraling passage that led upward and inward toward the mountain's heart. Faint light filtering down from a spot high above gleamed softly against the polished whorls of the stone sides. The pair followed the light upward, the spot growing larger, brighter as they approached.

Suddenly they were breaking surface, the two erupting from water into air and light.

not of the outside. This air was contained within a vast
eath the sea, a dome of lustrous rock that arched
s the height of a man and encompassed a space
des across.

come up within a circular pool in the

center of the vast floor. Around it was a shore of clean white sand that ran back to the rising walls of stone.

A number of people were visible there, some two score of them. Most were of a slender build, pale complexion, and light hair similar to the rider's, though not of such an exaggerated type. All were also clearly adults and clearly both male and female; this fact made most evident by the short, clinging garments of vivid hues that they wore.

The rest of the cavern's inhabitants—some dozen of them—differed quite markedly. Their varied complexions and clothing told of different lands and climates, some seemingly quite distant. All were men and of a sturdy type. Still, though different in look and dress, they mixed easily with the shining folk, engaged mainly in the playing of various games or in just lounging about the shore.

All this was clearly visible because of a strange, glowing mist that hung above, concentrated within the top of the huge dome. It sent down a soft but clear white light that reflected from the stone walls. These were of a rose-white quartz with a glossy surface that the reflecting light made luminescent. They imparted to all the interior of the cavern a warm and pleasant tone.

When the horselike beast and rider rose suddenly from the pool, all attention went to them. Everyone quit their activities at once to flock in around the pair as they climbed onto the shore.

The lithe rider leaped down from its mount and gave over the reins to a dark-skinned man in a brightly colored caftan.

"Where is Lir?" it asked a golden-haired woman, speaking in a high, clear, and sprightly voice.

"He's in his private grotto, playing at his vats again," the woman said.

The childlike one nodded and bounded off across the sand. The others followed.

Around the base of the high, curving walls were a number of openings into other caves, also with walls of the smooth, bright stone. Furnishings within these grottos identifed them as private chambers for the cavern's inhabitants. All of them were modest in size but one, which was over twice as large as the rest. It was to this one that the small being and its entourage made their way.

The curious followers stayed outside while the silver-haired one entered. The secondary chamber was furnished simply with chair and benches formed from stone and a large bed of piled rugs and furs. Most of the sandy floor space was taken up by a half-dozen large stone pedestals spaced in a ring.

Each pedestal held one of what the woman had called "vats." They were, more accurately, large basins formed of a crystal-like material so thin and so clear that what they held could be clearly seen through it.

The bottoms of each basin were filled with sand, stones, and aquatic plants, forming a miniature seabed. Shellfish and mollusks crawled about the bottoms or up the sides. Exotic, beautiful, and different varieties of fish swam about in each.

At the moment, a man of tall, lean form was bent over one of the basins, gently poking into its waters with a long finger. He was amiable looking, with features that might have been handsome if it weren't for a rather-too-large hook of nose and a very broad forehead from which receding light-brown hair was combed back sparsely over a high dome of head.

His lips were pursed in concentration and his brows drawn in a frown as he poked into the vat. The small, silver-haired one leaned in beside him to see just what he was poking at.

It was a large, jet black fish with flowing, diaphanous fins. It more hung than swam in the water, moving a bulging body sluggishly along with occasional strokes. Even his prodding finger was not arousing it.

"I simply cannot understand why this one is so slow," the man muttered irritably.

"Because it's so very fat!" the small one said bluntly. "You overfeed it terribly."

The tall man looked around. "Oh, Muirgheal, it's you." He straightened and turned from the basin. "I'm surprised to see you back. I thought you would be gone for days on end, now the warm weather's come."

"It's important, Lir. Something's happened. I had to tell you."

He brightened at this. "So, something's actually happened has it? I see." His manner turned brisk. "Well, come on then! We must do these things properly. I have so few chances at something official."

He led her off, out of the grotto into the main cavern. Those waiting there had overheard and now followed them, looking even more curious than before, chatting in an excited manner about what this news could possibly be.

"I envy you your traveling all about, you know," Lir told

Muirgheal as they crossed the sand floor and circled the central pool. "It is so astoundingly boring here. Without the occasional storm or odd shipwreck, there'd be nothing to do at all."

"Yes, Lir," the other said in a tone of having heard all this many, many times before.

"Why the only new people I've had to speak with in all our years here are these wretched sailors we've rescued from time to time. Fine lads, all of them, but . . ." he leaned down closer and spoke more confidentially, "they're not really ones for wide-ranging conversation. It's all boats and sails and that kind of thing." He sighed.

"I know, Lir," Muirgheal said. "But you *can* leave here whenever you wish."

"Only with the tedious use of magic, and only for a brief time," he said dismissingly. "And even then, where can I really go? To an island covered with trees and rocks and swamps and inhabited by no one but those dreadful Fomor? Not much of a treat, I can tell you."

"That, at least, is different now."

He stopped and looked to the silver-haired being. "What? You mean, there's someone else?"

"A new group. Mortals. That's why I've come."

"Wonderful!" he said elatedly. "Just let me sit down, and you can give your whole report."

They had reached a niche cut into the white quartz wall. A great throne carved of the same stone sat there. It was a sweepingly elegant piece, its back framed by the stylized forms of two leaping dolphins, its curved arms fashioned in the shapes of seahorses. Lir began to settle himself onto its broad seat, but as his posterior touched it, he swiftly came upright again.

"And here's another thing!" he said irritably. "This throne is always so cold!" He lifted a rug from the floor before it to toss across the seat. "Why does everything here have to be made out of stone?" he grumbled as he dropped down again. "Couldn't we have some wood?"

"Lir," said the shining being with just a touch of impatience, "do you wish to hear my news?"

"Oh, yes. Yes!" Lir said, recalled to the matter at hand. His scowl was replaced by renewed eagerness. "By all means. Tell us what's happening."

He leaned forward in an attitude of readiness for intent listening as the silver-haired one stepped up before him. The others moved in a tight semicircle around them, staring avidly as Muirgheal began to speak.

"Some days ago, in my usual circuit of the island, I chanced upon five sailing ships coming toward it. The prevailing winds were pushing them up from the south and east. I followed and watched them land in a bay on the southeast coast."

"Do you know who they were?" asked Lir.

"I've had no way to find out. There are perhaps a thousand of them. They are tall, strong, and fair. They all wear hair long, and the men are beardless. Their clothing is simple, and I think they are tillers of the land, shepherds and herdsmen, perhaps some hunters. There seem to be no noblemen or warriors among them."

"What are their ships like?" asked an olive-skinned man clad in a short tunic of white linen.

"They are long, narrow, with high, curving prows. They have a single sail."

"I have met people like this," the man said. "I think they are of the tribes living on the great peninsula west of my own lands. The Galatae we call them. We have traded with them for many years. I know their speech."

"Thank you for that, Graikos," Lir told him heartily. "I'm glad that you chose to stay with us after we saved you from the sea." He looked back to Muirgheal. "So, continue. What did this folk do after it landed?"

"They began seeking a place where they might settle," Muirgheal said. "But they couldn't find one."

"I'm not surprised, in *that* wilderness. So I suppose they prudently took ship and sailed on." Lir sighed in disappointment. "End of tale. Although that's for the best."

"It's not quite the end of the story, Lir," Muirgheal said with a certain hesitancy now entering her tone. "They did stay. And they found a place. I . . . well, I helped them find one."

"*You* helped them?" he cried in astonishment. "What do you mean? We were sent here only to keep watch on the Fomor! We aren't meant to do anything more!"

"It was only a very small thing," the shining being said defensively. "I felt sorry for them."

"And so you let them come into that cursed island?" Lir raged, getting to his feet, towering over the diminutive Muirgheal. "If you had to do something, you'd have better served them by having me raise a wind to blast them back out to sea."

Muirgheal did not quail. "They were already ashore before I knew what they intended. They seemed most determined to stay. I only meant to make things less difficult."

"How? Muirgheal, exactly what did you do?"

"I helped them find the valley and the old settlement."

"The place where the Partholans lived?"

"Yes. At least there they have a good land to start in and houses, and a wall."

"They are also in the one place where the Fomor would find them most quickly!"

"That would have happened anyway," Muirgheal reasoned, then added with a frown, "But I didn't realize it would be *quite* so soon."

"What?" Lir said in even greater astonishment. "The Fomor have already found them too?"

"Only a small advance party."

"Still, the rest will surely follow," he said grimly. "Muirgheal, your good intentions may very well cause these people to die."

"They don't have to," the silver-haired one replied. "It's why I came to you. You can help them."

"That is *not* why we are here. We are here only to monitor the Fomor activities. We are to act only to warn our people if our island is threatened."

"It can't be *only* that," the other argued.

"It can, it can!" he fired back angrily.

He jumped up from the throne and began to pace back and forth before it, launching into a fuming, growling, exasperated tirade:

"Curse it all! Just why is all this happening to me? I didn't mean to get involved. It's my wandering nature. That's it. That's what's done it to me. That itch to travel a bit, get out, escape the cloying, smothering beauty and comfort and security of that blasted hidden paradise of ours. So I go out for a little adventure. Nothing great. Just a quick jaunt to see the outside world, to find out what's happened in all those lifetimes since we sealed ourselves away. And what happens?"

He stopped to glare around him at his people who listened with patient, "I've-heard-this-many-times-before" expressions. No one replied. They didn't need to.

"*I'll* tell you what happens!" he roared on, taking up the pacing again. "I come upon the blasted, bloody Fomor! I find out they infest this island and are just as deadly as ever before.

And then! And *then*! To make it worse! I tell the Queen! The Fomor are still out there! I say. They're pirating ships and raiding towns and wiping out settlements."

"You couldn't keep that a secret, once you knew," Muirgheal quietly pointed out.

"Oh couldn't I? And what do I get for my troubles?" He waved around him. "This! I get saddled with watchman duty in a dank cavern under the sea." He cast his gaze upward to the cloud-filled dome, adding sarcastically, "Queen Danu, I thank you so much!"

"What we're doing is important," Muirgheal said. "The Fomor *are* our most ancient enemies. They'd certainly not hesitate to attack us if they could. But is watching them enough? Shouldn't we fight them? Shouldn't we help these people to do the same? What benefit to us if the Fomor destroy someone who could become our ally?"

"We are under strict oath not to interfere with events not directly affecting ourselves," he said in a firm, official tone. "Those people are only more mortals. Of little consequence."

"But they are of consequence!" the shining one countered. "They seem quite brave. If they could be given the means to stand up against the Fomor, it would be a victory for us. Lir, we arrived too late to help those poor people who settled there before. We can't just stand by and let it happen again."

Lir shook his head, frowning. "If Queen Danu knew, there wouldn't be words strong enough to describe her anger. For us to risk ourselves or our mission here . . ."

"A little risk, Lir? And weren't you just complaining about your boredom? Couldn't this be something for you to do?"

His frown cleared at that. He considered Muirgheal with more interest. Clearly this element of the being's proposal appealed to him.

"Go on," he said.

"It would be just a little help," the being said coaxingly. "These people have no real weapons. They've no chance of withstanding even the first Fomor attack. But they do have a great will. I know they will fight back, no matter what. *You* could at least give them a chance to meet the Fomor on even terms."

"But how can I help them? They certainly can't know our people are about. I can't reveal my true nature or powers to them."

"There is a way to do it," Muirgheal said, smiling cunningly. "Graikos could be of a great use to you."

"I would be pleased to give any service that I can," Graikos said eagerly, bowing.

"You see, Lir?" the shining one said to its now much-fascinated master. "Let me explain. I promise you will find the adventure a most entertaining one. And they will never know how their help has *really* come."

# Chapter 5

# Help Arrives

It was nighttime at the settlement of Nemed's people.

Within the large, oval meetinghouse, several hundred of the settlers were crowded close to the curve of the outer wall, leaving the area around the central firepit cleared. The ruddy light of the fire revealed their faces drawn in concentration as they listened intently to the argument being waged fiercely by others of their company.

"But we cannot give in to them," the intense young man called Nuada was saying vehemently as he paced around one side of the fire. "It means returning to the same life of brutality and tyranny that we were forced to live before."

"I say capitulate to them," said the haughty one named Mathgen from the opposite side of the pit. "Why risk ourselves at all? Simply pay their tribute and be done with them."

Nuada stopped to stare across the fire at him in disbelief. "What? You could agree to give up our children to them? What kind of . . ."

"Wait now!" Nemed himself ordered sharply from his position midway between the other two. "Nuada, I am sure Mathgen could not mean that we surrender our young. But he is right to say that we must deal with them."

"Negotiate?" said Nuada. "Try to come to fair terms with those creatures?"

"We must try!" Nemed said firmly. "Don't you see? We came here to live in peace, to have our own lands. If there is any way we can insure those things by paying these Fomor a reasonable price, we must try to do it."

"If they will even talk to us, not simply cut us down," said Nuada. "A show of at least some force from us could prove to them that it might be a more prudent course to negotiate."

"It might just as well only make them more savage," countered Mathgen.

"I agree," said Nemed. "We're not warriors."

"But we can still fight," said the big one called Dagda, moving out from the crowd to join them.

"Yes!" said the raven-haired woman named Moire from behind him. "We are not all softling shirkers like Mathgen."

"Woman, you watch your tongue," that outraged man shot back. "You're as much a fool as this great bull is. You mean to fight them? With what? We've no real weapons."

"Goibniu?" Nemed called to the zealous little smith who stood by in the crowd. "What about the weapons? Can anything be done?"

The man moved forward, shaking his head. His manner was unusually subdued, his face drawn in a frown. "I'm sorry, Chieftain. I've got to say I failed you this time." He lifted his arms, revealing the swords he held in each hand. Both were identical in shape, with long, broad blades, but one was of a dark-grey metal, the other a deep yellowish-brown.

"A night and a day I've labored at the making of this," he said, lifting the bronze one for all to see. "I've been able to copy the size and look of this Fomor blade." He held the grey sword up beside it.

"They *are* exact," said Nemed, impressed.

"That they are," said Goibniu, "but you see, the shape's not really the problem, Chieftain. It's the metal." He shook the Fomor sword. "I've never seen anything like it," he said with great annoyance. "Here, I'll show you."

He signaled Dagda toward him and held out the grey sword. "Take this," he directed the big man.

Dagda obeyed, holding the sword out, eying the smith quizzically.

"Just hold it like that," said Goibniu. "Keep it still. I'm going to swing at it."

Dagda held the sword ready. The smith stepped in, swinging his own blade down on it with all his sinewy strength.

There was a dull clang. The Fomor blade bit into the bronze one, slicing so deeply that it nearly cut the sword in two. Goibniu held the damaged weapon up to show the crowd.

"You see? Against that black metal of the Fomor, our own is much too soft. And I've not the means or the knowledge to create anything the like." He looked to Nemed. "Sorry, Chieftain," he said defeatedly. "I never thought I'd be saying it, but there's nothing I can do."

"So that leaves us with no choice," Nemed said. "Any fight we could give would only see us slaughtered. We *must* try to come to terms."

At this the dour Diancecht spoke up, moving in close to the fire:

"My friends," he said in his careful, precise way, "there is one other logical alternative. We could leave here."

"I'm surprised Mathgen didn't suggest *that* craven's course," Moire fired in scathingly.

"I certainly have no wish to return to our homelands," Mathgen quickly returned. "There's nothing at all back there for me. My only chance is out here."

"I didn't mean to imply that returning must be our only course," said Diancecht.

"There *is* no other," Nuada told him sharply. "We know the lands to the east are inhabited and fought over by many fierce warrior tribes. This island we've come to is the last on the very rim of the great world. To the west of it is only endless sea and death for all of us."

"We don't know that for certain," argued Diancecht.

"Still, we must assume that the risk we'd take sailing into the unknown would be as great or greater than what we face here," said Nemed.

"But why *not* think of returning home?" put in young Donnchadh O'Falva from the crowd.

"Aye!" seconded his brother Murchadh. "Maybe our life there was hard, but was it so hard as this?"

"Even that journey, especially with our supplies so low, would be very perilous," Nemed pointed out. "Many would die."

"No matter which way we look," said Nuada, "our choices seem to lie between destruction or surrender."

"We need not simply surrender to the Fomor," Nemed said

emphatically. "We don't know that we can't get acceptable terms from them."

"We'll get nothing at all if they know that we won't fight," growled Dagda.

"We *cannot* fight, don't you see?" Mathgen said in exasperation. "We've no choice *but* to accept their terms."

"I'd rather we battle to the death than give up one child to them!" Nuada all but shouted back.

And so the wrangling started up again, the sides throwing the same arguments back and forth, the discussion growing ever more heated, ever more frustrating as the night drew on.

But then there arose a hubbub amongst those near the door. It grew quickly in volume and spread swiftly through the gathering. The ones arguing by the fire stopped their talk and looked around.

Two men had entered the hut and were moving through the parting crowd. They were not people of Nemed's clans, but strangers.

One was tall, lean, and clothed in rags. He sported an unkempt grey-brown beard, flaring eyebrows and bushy hair that all mixed together, combining with his dress to give him a most disheveled, shaggy air.

Another man of a dark olive complexion and dark eyes followed, wearing a loose shirt of knitted wool over leather trousers, both showing long wear. He was wide bodied and muscular and carried a great bulging sack with ease.

The two came boldly into the center of the room. Those crowded in around them eyed them with mingled suspicion and alarm.

"Please, don't be afraid of us," the bearded man said in a jovial voice, the flash of teeth from a broad smile breaking through the screen of tangled hair like sun shining through a crack in an overcast. "We come among you as friends, which I believe you can well use right now."

"Who are you?" Nemed demanded. "You're not of us. Are you of those Fomor?"

"No, no. Certainly not!" the other said with a denying wave. "I come from . . . well, I suppose you could say I come from all over, really. You can call me Liam." He indicated the other man. "He is called Graikos. He is my assistant."

"You speak our language," said Nuada. "Are you from our homeland?"

"No, I haven't actually visited there. But Graikos knows your people quite well. He taught me your tongue."

Graikos gave a little bow. "I live to serve."

"What are you doing here?" Nuada asked.

"It's my livelihood, actually. I'm a doer of all kinds of little trades. I travel about, offering my services where they're needed."

"How did you know they were needed here?" Diancecht asked. "This island is a wilderness."

"I was just passing by and happened to see your ships," Liam explained lightly. " 'Ah, new settlers!' I told myself. 'Likely they'll need many kinds of help.' So I followed your trail here. It was quite easy. I arrived in time to see your little . . . 'disagreement?' with the Fomor. Just now I was outside here, listening to your talk."

"How did you get into our fortress?" Dagda demanded. "The gates are locked."

"Oh, such things don't hinder me," the bearded one said in an offhand way. "It's one of my little skills. And I have others that I think can be of great value to you!"

"For instance?" asked Nemed.

"Well," the man said brightly, "your smith here gave you one demonstration. Let me give you another. Graikos! The bag!"

The olive-skinned man held up the bag. Liam reached into its depths. He pulled out a sword of a shining silver-grey with a gracefully tapered blade.

"Here, you . . . the large fellow," he gestured to Dagda who still held the Fomor sword. "This time I want *you* to swing at *me.* Get back a good way. Make a run at it. Swing as hard as you can."

"But I can't do that," protested a dismayed Dagda. "I'll kill you!"

"You can let me worry about that," the man told him carelessly.

"You don't have the strength to stop me," Dagda persisted, "not meaning to give offense."

"None's taken," Liam said. "Look, I'll be fine," he added assuringly. "Just go ahead."

"This man is a raving lunatic," Nemed murmured to Nuada. "We can't let him do this."

"Maybe he's not," Nuada murmured back. "Can we pass up any chance for help?"

Reluctantly Nemed shook his head. "All right, Dagda," he called to the big man, "do as he asks."

Clearly unhappy about this, Dagda backed away from the firepit to one end of the long room, the crowd obligingly clearing the floor for him.

Some ten paces away, the bearded stranger stood at ease close before the stone hearth of the firepit, the glinting sword held in one hand, its blade down beside him. He looked completely at ease, smiling broadly.

"Are you really certain about this?" Dagda asked him unhappily.

"Go on," Liam urged.

With a sigh the big man began his charge, swinging up the sword in both hands high over his head.

The other awaited his rush, still not moving.

At full run Dagda charged in. The sword was ready to swing down on Liam's head. Backed by the power of Dagda's muscular arms, it had the potential to cleave the man from crown to belly.

The blade started its sweep down.

Liam swept his sword up in a startlingly swift move, crossing it over in a block to the other.

There was a sharply ringing clang and a bright flare of light at the point of contact. Dagda was knocked backward as if a tremendous force had slammed into his blade with an impact so powerful that he was lifted bodily from his feet and sent crashing down upon the packed-earth floor, the Fomor sword flying from his hand.

"Dagda!" Moire cried in alarm, rushing up to him.

"I . . . I'm all right," he said, sitting up as she knelt beside him. But he shook his head and looked in a stunned way toward the shaggy man who still stood, quite at ease, grinning down at him.

"The sword!" said Nuada. He bent and lifted it from where it had fallen amidst the rushes strewing the floor. This time it was the Fomor blade which had been cut nearly through.

"Amazing," said Goibniu, stepping up to look closely at it.

"More than that," said Diancecht, looking more piercingly at the strange man, eyes narrowed in speculation.

"You're surely much stronger than you look to be," said Dagda, getting to his feet with some effort and Moire's help.

"Can you give us weapons like this?" the smith asked Liam eagerly.

"Perhaps not of *quite* such amazing properties," the stranger casually replied, "but certainly strong enough to more than match the Fomor weapons."

"Tell us how," said Nuada.

"Well, your smith here has the skills and the correct idea," Liam said, looking at the half-severed bronze sword which Goibniu held. "As he told you, it's really just a matter of the metal. You need one much stronger. I can tell you where to find raw materials and how to refine them into something as strong as the Fomor metal. I can help you build the smelter to do that." He looked to Goibniu. "Can you do the rest?"

"I can hardly wait to begin!" the smith told him with great zeal.

"Wait a minute," put in Nemed. "You have to tell us *why* you should do this. We've no wealth. The Fomor have demanded a great tribute. What do you want from us?"

"Just the satisfaction of seeing the Fomor given some comeuppance," Liam said. "The Fomor are nothing but pirates of a most cruel and monstrous kind. My people have suffered from them, as have many others. Graikos' own ship was destroyed by them."

"Yes," the darker man agreed. "They have raided all the sea about here for many years."

"So, beyond some food and a dry sleeping place for two wandering men, we ask nothing," Liam finished simply. He looked around at them searchingly. "I think the question here is: have you the will to accept my help?"

"Well, Nemed?" Nuada said challengingly to his chief. "Here is our chance for weapons. We can now make the choice to fight."

Nemed shook his head. "It's still not good enough. These Fomor are warriors. They may have many times our numbers. We would be overwhelmed."

"Though they're most secretive, I know a bit about them," Liam said. "I know that there are perhaps four thousand of them living in this land. But only a few of their males are of an age and of a fitness to be warriors. They likely have no greater fighting strength than you. But more than that, they are great cowards unless their force is many times as great as their opponent's. With weapons to match theirs, I'm certain you'd have at least an equal chance."

Nemed still looked doubtful. "But what you want us to do

surely can't be done quickly. Finding and gathering these materials, constructing this smelter, forging enough weapons."

"We have time," Liam said. "It will be days before those Fomor reach their one settlement on the north coast. It will be many more before they can mobilize all their force, equip them, and march them here. I know a trick or two as well to speed things along. You can do it."

"What have we to lose?" Nuada said to Nemed earnestly. "My Chief, we can still approach the Fomor unarmed, as you wish. We can try to deal. But if they refuse, we can at least have the weapons ready to defend ourselves. Wouldn't anything else be foolish?"

Nemed met his eye and held it for a long moment in meditation. Then finally he nodded his head.

"Yes," he said in acceptance. "You are right. I have hoped for freedom and for peace. I've no wish to see my people at war. But as things are, there seems no other choice but to prepare."

He went up to Liam and put out a hand to him. "We accept your offer of help," he said.

Liam tossed down his sword and clasped Nemed's hand, beaming in pleasure. As he did, a cheer of acclamation went up from all the crowd.

From all, that is, but a glowering Mathgen.

# Chapter 6

# Preparation

The cauldron of molten ore was hauled out of the fiery depths of the furnace.

The muscles of sweaty and smoke-darkened arms knotted as brawny men used thick metal rods to wrestle the cauldron into position and tip it. The pure liquid metal that floated on the top, still crimson with heat, flowed from a spout into the row of long molds, spilling from one to another to fill them all. The cauldron was tipped back, lifted, and hastily hauled away to dump the cooling slag onto a swiftly growing mound. Meantime, the metal in the molds cooled to hard grey-black ingots.

Nearby the smelter, the bearded one calling himself Liam, closely oversaw the process. But he turned from the work to raise a hand in greeting as he saw the Chieftain Nemed approaching.

Nemed raised a hand in reply. "How do things progress?"

"Very well," Liam said, running an evaluating eye over the working crew. "They've been at it so long now, they've no need of my help. It's a process of itself, working smoothly."

Nemed examined the operation critically as well. There was no question that Liam was right: it *was* very smooth.

Down a path that heavy use had by this time worn in the west slope of the valley, a line of loaded carts was moving, spaced at close intervals, hauled steadily along by determined and strong-bodied men. A parallel line of empty carts was heading back the other way. The full carts carried loads of two kinds—half of them piled with chunks of a glossy black substance, the others with a finer rubble of silver-white mixed with a rust-brown.

All the loads were being carried to the smelter that had been constructed well outside the village walls. At this point they were added to large mounds of the two substances. But while one crew added to the piles, another subtracted, shifting barrowsful to the smelter's gaping maw. Here the black material was shoveled in to fuel the inferno raging within. The rust-and-silver ore was dumped into emptied cauldrons and thrust into the flames to melt it down, keeping the refining process always moving along.

"You've done a miraculous job in showing us the construction of this and teaching us the process," Nemed said. "But it would have been for nothing without your locating those two most amazing substances."

"It's not so difficult really," Liam said modestly. "That metal ore is actually quite easy to spot. Find a great red patch on a rocky hillside and there you are. That black stuff, 'Kol' I believe some call it, is a bit more tricky to locate."

"But you did it so quickly," Nemed said. "And you found them both so close to us as well!"

"I said I had a few tricks," Liam reminded him with a grin.

"Well, you surely are the Man of Many Skills," Nemed said praisingly. "I'm sorry I doubted you."

"*I'm* glad I've been able to help you," the other said with pleasure. "I haven't had such a fine diversion in years. Muirgheal was certainly right."

"Muirgheal?" Nemed said curiously.

"Oh, just an old friend," Liam said quickly, then changed the subject. "Shall we go and see how Goibniu is doing?"

Nemed agreed and the two started toward the village. Another crew of men was now dumping the cooled ingots from their molds and loading them onto carts, readying the molds for a new flow of molten ore. The loaded carts were in turn hauled to the village and through its gates. Liam and Nemed followed one of them along.

"You know, you must see to getting some horses," Liam commented as they walked.

"We couldn't bring any," Nemed said. "We had barely room for the livestock we brought."

"Perhaps you can win some from the Fomor," Liam suggested. "And I believe there are some running wild, in the vales far west and north. Once our present situation is resolved, I might just see to helping you capture some myself."

"It would be a great help," said Nemed. His eye fell musingly on the ingots in the cart before him. "And you know Liam, I've wondered, couldn't this new metal be shaped to plows and hoes and rakes as well as to weapons?"

"It could indeed!" the other said brightly. "You are a clever man, Nemed. Your work would be made several times easier." He clapped an arm across the man's shoulders as they passed in through the gates. "Yes, with your ingenuity and industry—and my help too, of course—you can create a most prosperous settlement here in just a year or two. It'll be great fun."

"Fun?" Nemed echoed, shaking his head and speaking gravely. "No, my friend, I can think of no enjoyment in this until the Fomor have been dealt with and my people are safe."

Liam turned sober, dropping his arm. "Of course, Nemed. I understand."

The two went to the smithy. Here men worked at several blazing forges amidst near-stifling heat and great showers of sparks as they hammered the metal ingots out into long swords and broad spear points. Other men fastened wood grips to the sword hilts or fitted smooth wood hafts into the sockets of the spear points. Racks of hundreds of finished weapons already glinted all about them, along with racks of circular metal shields.

Goibniu saw the two arrive and came to them.

"Enough?" he asked, sweeping an arm about at the full racks.

"Well more than," said Liam. "But you should go on as long as possible."

"Surely we'll do that," said the little man in his eager way, clearly unfatigued even by the nearly continuous work and the intense heat in the smithy. "We can't have too many, if the need comes."

"Then keep at it, Goibniu," Nemed said. "We will leave you to the heat."

They went out of the smithy and into the yard, breathing deeply of its fresh, cool air.

In the yard Nuada and Dagda were drilling a company of

men in swordplay and spear tossing. The men were doing quite well. The two young leaders were being aided by Graikos, who was demonstrating great skill in the use of both weapons.

"The training seems to be going well too," Nemed observed.

"Yes," agreed Liam. "You know, it's most interesting. I find out more about Graikos' skills constantly. He was a soldier himself for many years, it seems, in his homeland. A mercenary. Fought in several quite large wars before he gave it up and went to sea adventuring. A most intriguing fellow. Anyway, it seems your people are turning into warriors quite readily."

"Yes," said Nemed, but with no pleasure. "And in many ways, I have much regret for that."

Liam looked searchingly to him. "You really hate to see this happening, don't you?"

"I don't like my people being trained in violent ways, learning to kill, preparing to face death and pain," Nemed said bluntly. "I gathered them to me because they despised the cruelty and oppression and violence that was their daily lot in our homeland. I hoped we might find a place where such things did not exist. I still hope we can. I hope we can avoid a battle here."

"Nemed, you've worried too much," Liam said assuringly. "You'll be prepared when the Fomor come. You'll be armed and trained and more than their match. They'll leave you alone. I know it!"

"I wish I could be as sure of that as you," Nemed said.

A horn blared loudly. The two men looked around toward a high lookout tower that had been constructed on the north side of the village. A man there was blowing the horn he held in one hand while gesturing excitedly toward the north with his other arm.

"You'll be able to see it for yourself," Liam said. "Here they come."


A host of the monstrous Fomor was massed across the upper end of the valley.

To the front were irregular ranks of several hundred warriors on foot. Behind them were drawn up a much smaller contingent of mounted beings. The weapons bedecking them in profusion made their mass shimmer like a rippling, sunlit sea.

"You seem to have estimated their numbers rightly," said Nuada to Liam, looking the force over. "They are about the same as ours."

The two men stood atop the lookout tower with Nemed. Below them Goibniu and his crew were passing out weapons to every able-bodied man in the village. Dagda and Graikos were organizing the armed men into companies.

"We will make no show of force at first," said Nemed. "I mean to speak to them again—in peace."

"Nemed, they won't listen," Nuada said.

"I'm afraid he's likely quite right," put in Liam.

"We must still give them the chance," Nemed said firmly. "Their supreme leader must be with them. He may be a man of reason."

"If he is a man at all," said Nuada. "At least let a guard go with you."

"No sign of force, I said!" Nemed replied. "I mean to negotiate in peace. That's why I will go alone."

With that he started down the ladder from the tower. The other two looked after him.

"There goes a very stubborn man," said Nuada in exasperation.

"And a man of deep belief," added Liam in an admiring tone.

They followed Nemed down.

Below they found a disputation was taking place.

Diancecht had been told to remain in the village in case of battle and direct a band of women and older men in caring for any wounded. Mathgen was demanding to be allowed to stay behind as well. He was confronting an outraged Dagda attempting to thrust a spear into his hands.

"I will not take that, you bull-brained fool!" Mathgen shouted, pushing the weapon away.

"You'll take it or you'll find yourself eating it!" growled Dagda, leaning over the smaller man threateningly.

Mathgen was not intimidated, firing back, "I am no warrior, and you will not make me be one!"

"You'll fight like the rest of us, you . . ."

"Wait, wait!" called Nemed, moving in to part the two.

"He refuses to join us," Dagda told him.

"I've done no training," argued Mathgen. "I have no skills and certainly no interest in fighting. My talents are of a mental kind."

"None of us wants to fight," said Nuada. "But if we're to survive, we may have to."

"Diancecht won't," Mathgen pointed out.

"He is the only one with healer's skills," said Nuada. "He must stay here."

"My own skills are as valuable as his," Mathgan said arrogantly. He folded his arms in adamant pose. "I *do* refuse to go."

"He has the right," Nemed said quietly, causing Dagda and Nuada to look at him in shock.

"What are you saying?" Nuada asked.

"That we came here for freedom," the chieftain said reasonably. "Everyone must have a free choice. No man can be forced to risk his life, even to help his fellows. To make him do so leaves us no better than those who have oppressed us."

"But he has to do *something*," growled Dagda, "or he's *not* one of us. He doesn't deserve our protection."

Nemed nodded at that. "I agree. Mathgen, if you won't fight, you have to give your help in another way. If your 'talents' are truly as great as Diancecht's, then you must stay with him and aid him in dealing with our wounded, if things come to that."

"What? Care for wounded?" Mathgen said indignantly.

"That, or leave the protection of our palisade," Nemed said bluntly.

Mathgen glowered but made no more argument, wheeling and starting away.

Dagda growled after him as he pushed past, and Mathgen shot a baleful glance back at the big man as he stalked on.

Attention now returned to the urgent matter at hand. The host of the Fomor was drawing slowly but steadily nearer.

While Nuada and Liam went back up the tower to keep watch, Nemed left the village, striding boldly away and down the slope toward the north. Here he stopped to stand alone, a hundred paces from safety.

Upon his appearance the ragged but formidable army of the Fomor pulled to a halt some three hundred paces from the base of the village hill.

Single man and monstrous force faced one another unmoving for long moments. Then a mounted warrior pushed out through the mass of those afoot and rode toward Nemed.

If the chieftain had any hopes that the Fomor leader would be more human and thus more reasonable, they were quickly

dashed. The one who came toward him was more awful than
the rest in appearance. The squat face much resembled a toad's,
with wide, slack mouth, a nose that was only two slits, and eyes
that were protuberances bulging from the sides of the head.
The forehead was low, the crown and face hairless. All the
being's skin was of a yellowish-grey hue, and shining as if
damp.

His body was broad and heavy, with short, thick limbs.
Unlike much of his awful company, he had both hands; but
both his short legs ended in stumps shod with flat metal slabs.

He pulled up before the waiting Nemed, peering down at
the comparatively small being who stood so fearlessly looking
back at him.

"I am the Captain Cichol Gricenchos," he croaked out in a
guttural, heavily accented voice. "Surrender to me now, feeble
man, and we *may* not destroy you utterly."

"There is no need for you to destroy us," said Nemed. "We
do not mean to defy you. We only ask this one piece of land."

"You may have it, if you pay our tribute."

"It is too high. You can't expect us to give up our own
children?"

"If you do not agree, then *all* your men will die, and *all*
your children and your women too will be our slaves."

"Why?" Nemed demanded. "Why must you ask such a terrible tribute?"

"You wish to survive," the being said tersely. "So do we.
This will help insure it."

"But you are strong," Nemed reasoned. "We are a peaceful
people. Can't you take pity on us? Have you none at all?"

The being shook his great head. "None! That too insures
that we will live."

"Then you give me no other choice," Nemed said sadly. He
lifted a hand.

The captain's hand went instantly to the hilt of his sword.
"What do you mean to do?"

"I mean no harm," Nemed said quickly, lifting his arms. "I
am unarmed. Just wait."

Back atop the village watchtower, Nuada was calling out to
those below:

"He signaled! Move out at once!" And he slid down the
ladder, Liam close behind him.

The gates were thrown open. The men immediately began a
march out, directed by Dagda and Graikos. Nuada belted on

his own sword, took up his spear and shield. He looked to Liam who was standing by, simply watching.

"Will you go?" he asked the bearded man.

"No. I'm afraid this you must do without me or Graikos."

"What?" said the dark-skinned man, turning to him in surprise. "But they need my skills!"

"You have already given them," said Liam. "We can't go. Understand. We've done too much already."

"I understand," said Nuada. "You shouldn't risk yourself for us."

"But, Lir . . . Liam!" Graikos began in protest.

"Quiet," Liam said warningly, "or I must leave these people altogether. It can be only as I say."

"If it has to be," said Graikos, but with great chagrin. He tossed his spear and shield onto the ground.

Nuada left them and went off to join Dagda in directing the rest.

Outside, the Fomor captain watched in surprise as the armed people of Nemed streamed out of the gates and formed up in neatly ordered ranks.

"You are not as I was told," he grumbled.

"You see?" Nemed asked him. "We are not helpless. We are armed with weapons the equal of yours. Our numbers are nearly your match. But this is still not a sign that we wish to fight. We only ask to be left alone here."

The disconcerted Fomor recovered, shaking his head. "No. That can't be. You are a vermin. If we allow it, you will spread. You will grow stronger. You will defy us, as *they* did. We must stop you while we have a chance."

"Let us negotiate!" Nemed pleaded. "We can reach a peace."

"To deal with you would only make us weak," the captain said harshly. "There cannot be a compromise."

"Then you will have to defeat us," Nemed said sorrowfully.

"That we will do," said the Fomor. "I will let you join your company. Be armed when we meet again."

The being jerked his mount around and urged it back toward his own warriors. Nemed turned and walked up toward his people. Nuada and Dagda came to meet him.

"Well?" Nuada asked anxiously. "Will they give us peace?"

But there was no need for Nemed to give him answer.

Behind him the Fomor host began its advance.

# Chapter 7

# Battle

"I really never thought that they would fight," the bearded one calling himself Liam said in disbelief.

He and the one named Graikos stood in the watchtower, looking out on the panorama of battle spread before them. The scene was a grim one for the people of Nemed. For after a slow beginning, the Fomor were sweeping the field.

It had taken the exhortations and threats of the Fomor captain to drive the monstrous warriors into their first assault, but that situation had quickly changed. The people of Nemed, trained to fight but not experienced in combat, had been thrown aback by their first sights of gaping wounds and death and by the realization that they must inflict the same.

Their hesitancy had given the Fomor an offensive edge, and the villagers had been driven back. The Fomor, taking courage from their easy first success, had surged forward, a rising bloodlust making them fierce. Now the embattled Nemedians were nearly encircled, the vicious Fomor closing in like wolves upon stricken prey.

"The Fomor are less cowardly than you guessed," Graikos told his master.

"Apparently," the other agreed. "They seem quite desperate to protect their land. Well, that's one piece of vital information to come out of this, at least. Too bad about the rest." Liam looked to Graikos. "Come on then."

"Come on?" echoed Graikos. "Do you mean into the fight?"

"I mean away from here. We certainly can't be caught here when the village falls."

The other stared in dismay. "You can't mean that you intend to abandon them?"

"What else are we to do?" Liam said simply. "Look, we've done all that we could. It was most interesting. But now it's over."

"It was all a game?" said an appalled Graikos. "Is that what you're saying to me? These people didn't mean anything to you?"

"They were very pleasant," Liam conceded. "I am sorry that they couldn't succeed."

"But you're still going to let them die."

Liam shrugged. "They're mortals. Dying is one of the things all of them do, sooner or later. I can't change it."

"You could!" Graikos countered. "Use some magic to stop this! Bring a storm! Bring darkness! Shake the earth!"

"You know I can't risk exposing my true powers," the other replied. "And Queen Danu would certainly know if I used magic so great. Do you know how angry she'd be with me then?"

"You'd be alive, anyway. Those men out there are all going to die! We can at least go fight with them!"

"Graikos, our two swords will do nothing to help them. It will only endanger us and our real mission here."

"You mean *your* mission, Lir," said Graikos, using the disguised man's real name in his anger. "I'm not of your people. I'm going to help."

He started for the ladder, but the bearded man pulled him around with a hand to his shoulder.

"You will not!" Lir said with force. "You may not be *of* us, but you are certainly mine. I saved your life, and you willingly gave your fealty to me. Do you mean to betray that now?"

Graikos met his master's eye for a long moment. Then he shook his head. "No," he said with anguished resignation. "I can't betray my word or my debt to you."

"Then go and prepare our things," Lir ordered. "We have to leave."

"I'll do as you say, but can't we at least stay until there is no other choice?" Graikos said. "They aren't beaten yet."

Lir shrugged. "Very well, a little longer, if you can stand to watch."

And the two turned their attention back to the battlefield.

Below them many others were also anxiously watching the fight.

Women, elderly, and children of Nemed lined the palisade and gazed down in horror at their loved ones caught in the maelstrom.

The raven-haired Moire stood with her friend Sadhbh, her gaze searching through the meleeing men for the larger figure of the Dagda. But even his impressively hulking form was lost amidst the swarms of massive Fomor.

"They need more help," Moire said in frustration. "*I* should take arms. *I* should go out."

"And what good would that be?" asked her friend.

"I'm as strong as many men," she returned stoutly. "I could fight as well!"

"But you aren't trained," the other argued. "You would only be killed."

"At least I would be at Dagda's side, not here, helpless," she said despairingly.

On the field a look of helplessness also creased the face of Nemed.

He stood behind the now muddled ranks of his warriors, staring about him, seemingly stunned by the ferocity of the battle closing in on three sides.

Nuada fought out of the fray to him. The young man's shield and spear were gone. He held his sword two-handed to hack a way through his opponents into the open, showing no reluctance to shed the Fomor blood. He was in fact sprayed in it, his arms drenched in crimson-black to the shoulders, his sword dripping with the gore.

"Nemed, you must act!" he cried out to his chief over the shouts of men and clattering of swords. "Our people don't know what to do!"

Nemed only stared at him blankly.

"You are their leader!" Nuada tried more urgently. "They will follow you. We can strike back."

Nemed finally spoke, his voice filled with hopelessness: "I can't fight them. We . . . we can retreat within the walls."

"We're almost surrounded," Nuada pointed out. "They'll just cut us down if we turn."

"Then, we'll surrender!" Nemed said desperately.

"They won't leave anyone alive!" Nuada grabbed his leader by an arm and shook him. "Nemed think! What's wrong with you? We must attack! Only you can lead it!"

Nemed's dazed and agonized gaze met his. "No. I . . ."

*"There* you are!" a voice croaked triumphantly.

The two men looked around. Cichol Gricenchos had hacked his way through the fighters and now faced them.

"I told you to take arms, feeble man," he rasped as he clumped forward on the broad, metal feet. "This time I will kill you anyway!"

Nuada came up in front of his chieftain, lifting his sword. The captain raised his own sword and shield and charged in.

The battle was a hard, savage one. Nuada was quick and dexterous, driving in many blows. The Fomor, though ponderous of motion, was larger, stronger, and protected by shield and body armor. His return blows landed seldom, but when they did, their power staggered the slender young man.

All others of Nemed's fighting men were occupied. No one came to help. Dagda, caught in the thickest of it, whaled around him with swords in each hand, holding a dozen at bay.

Cichol's massive blows finally told on Nuada. Quickly worn down by fending them off, he was at last staggered badly by one, dropping his guard, leaving an opening.

The captain struck instantly, swinging in a blow at Nuada's head. The young warrior tried to lift his blade to turn it but only succeeded partially. The sword was knocked from his hands by the impact and spun away. The Fomor blade swept on to bite into his side, tearing a long, deep gash.

He grunted, stumbled back and toppled to the earth.

The Fomor stalked in, lifting his sword to strike again. His mouth stretched wide in a grin of victory. The unarmed Nemed was forgotten behind him.

Nemed, until then paralyzed with horror as he watched, was finally galvanized to action by his awakened anger. He grabbed up the fallen sword in both hands and without hesitance slammed its point into the center of Cichol's back with all his strength.

The keen blade drove right through the Fomor, its tip cracking out through his breastbone in a spray of blood. Cichol jerked and came erect, looking more startled than pained. His

bulging eyes swiveled down to see the sword point protruding
from his chest. Then they rolled back as he went suddenly limp,
crashing forward to the ground.

His weight yanked his body free of the killing blade. Nemed
stood over him, gaze flicking from the bloodied sword to the
Fomor's wound, for the moment stunned at what he had done.

The Fomor battling close around him saw their leader fall.
Cries of consternation ran through their company. They
faltered in the fight.

Nemed's warriors took new heart, striking back with force.
The Fomor uncertainty changed to alarm and then to panic.
They began a withdrawal that their counterattacking opponents turned swiftly to a rout. From a position of near defeat,
the Nemedians suddenly found themselves looking after their
fleeing attackers, taken somewhat by surprise. Then Dagda
took the initiative, shouting, "After them, warriors! Run them
down!"

"No!" cried out Nemed. "Let them go! They're beaten! No
more killing!"

The eyes of his people came around to him, some staring in
disbelief at his words.

Dagda moved toward him. "But Nemed, we can finish
them!"

"We must see to our own wounded," Nemed called back.
"Nuada is down."

Hearing this, Dagda at once gave up his argument, rushing
to join Nemed and kneel at Nuada's side.

Gently the big man lifted his comrade as others of their
warriors moved in around them.

"Is he dead?" asked someone.

Nuada moaned.

"We must get him help at once," said Nemed. His eyes went
across the battlefield and the scores of other fallen men scattered about it, many writhing in pain. "We must help all that
we can!"


Nemed, Diancecht, and the disguised Lir stood about the
unconscious form of Nuada lying on the pallet. Graikos
hovered nearby them while Mathgen moved about to tend the
other scores of wounded laid out in the meeting house.

Diancecht had just completed the application of healing
salves and powders to the young warrior's wound. He was now

tightening the strips of cloth binding, already soaked in newly welling blood.

"How is it?" Nemed asked him anxiously.

"It's deep," said the healer, "but not so deep as to kill him alone. If I had means to close the wound, he would recover," he shook his head in regret, "but I don't. As it is, his strength is simply seeping away."

Dagda came into the house and crossed to them.

"All the wounded have been brought into the village," he reported. "We are leaving the clans to keen over and care for their own dead. We lost thirty two, with twice as many wounded."

"And theirs?" asked Nemed.

"We buried their dead together. We let those who were able carry off the rest who might survive, as you asked. The badly hurt I put out of their pain."

"It's the kindest way," said Diancecht.

"Likely more than they'd do for us," growled Dagda.

"We can't know that," Nemed admonished. "We must hope that our victory and our graciousness will convince them to give us peace. I want no more fighting . . ." he looked at his hands, "no more blood."

Diancecht finished his binding of Nuada's wound, covering the young man with a blanket.

"How is he now?" Dagda asked the healer.

"I've done what I can for him," Diancecht hedged. "We can only let him rest and see."

They all moved away from the wounded man. Nemed and Dagda went out of the house to check on the wounded elsewhere. Graikos and his master fell into a murmured conversation. Diancecht moved through the house, checking on other injuries. Across the room Mathgen finished the binding of an arm wound and dropped down exhaustedly on the hearthstones. The healer noted this and went over to him.

"Hard work, eh?" Diancecht said.

Mathgen looked up to him. His haughty manner had been wiped away by the weariness from his long toil. His tunic's chest and sleeves were spattered with his patients' blood. He grimaced in disgust.

"This is the most awful, the most revolting, the most torturous labor I've ever been forced to endure. My only comfort is that I'm not one of these wretched fools."

Diancecht sat down on the hearth beside him. He contemplated the sagging, sullen man for a moment thoughtfully.

"I must confess to having a certain curiosity about you," he at last said in his careful way. "I've never understood why you're with us. You're not like any of the others."

"I'm certainly *not* like the others," Mathgen said, drawing up and speaking with more of his old arrogance. "I've never grubbed in the earth or followed after brainless sheep as they have. I come from people of finer stuff. People of power."

"Then, why did you join Nemed?" Diancecht asked bluntly.

"Oh," the other said, his tone of pride slipping abruptly into one of hesitancy, "well, the power has been lost now. You see my father was a . . . a priest."

"A priest?" Diancecht echoed with a skeptical tone. "And that gave him power?"

The tone prodded Mathgen to elaborate. "He was more," he answered indignantly. "Much more! He was a man of vast knowledge and marvelous skills. He was a seer, a sorcerer, advisor to a king. But . . . he was betrayed." His voice took on a hard edge of bitterness. "His powers grew too strong. The king became jealous and afraid. Our family was stripped of everything. Exiled. He . . . well, he died."

"I am sorry," said the healer.

"Not so much as I," Mathgen said. "I lost the future that should have been mine. I had no other choice but to seek a new place, a place to start again, a place of new opportunity where I could regain riches and power. And when I do, I will go back."

"Go back?" said the healer, clearly intrigued. "To reclaim your father's place?"

"No," Mathgen said with a sharp gleam of malevolence in his deepset eyes. "To take revenge."

"Revenge?" echoed Diancecht. "But the illogic of taking such a destructive course would be . . ."

His argument was interrupted by the entrance of Moire.

"Diancecht," she called softly to him from the door, "you're needed in the house of Clan Bryan. One of the sons is very bad."

"I'll come," he said, rising at once and going out with her.

Mathgen looked after him, then took advantage of his overseer's absence to settle down more comfortably against the hearth. He gave a sigh of relief and closed his eyes in rest.

He took no interest in Graikos and the disguised Lir, still

standing near to the unconscious Nuada, engaged in a whispered but heated discussion.

"And I tell you that simply going back to your little playing with these people is not enough!" Graikos was saying with intensity.

"Why not?" asked Lir. "They've won the battle. The Fomor likely won't bother them anymore. I can return to the amusing pastime of helping them bring some prosperity to this struggling little outpost of humanity. What's wrong with that?"

"What's wrong is that there are sixty men lying wounded around here," Graikos tersely pointed out. "Some of them could die! If you mean to help them, then why can't you do something about that?"

"You know I can't use magic," Lir said. "To heal those men would certainly compromise me."

"And if it did? What of it? Other than that you would lose your entertaining toys."

"Careful, Graikos," Lir said warningly. "Even one so good-natured as I can tolerate only so much. I will *not* use magic of that extent. I can't! I don't dare!"

"Then at least save just one," argued his servant. He gestured toward the unconscious young warrior. "Look at Nuada. He *surely* will die soon. His mind, strength, and spirit are of great worth to these people. At least save him. Could that be such a risk?"

Lir considered. He looked at the pale, shallowly breathing young man. He looked around the room. There was at the moment no one to take any notice of them.

"All right," he said grudgingly, sticking out a hand. "Give me the sack."

Graikos handed over the bulging sack that he kept always with him. Lir opened it and rummaged inside.

"I don't know why I let myself be softened by this," he grumbled as he searched. "Just to save one mortal."

He pulled out something wrapped in cloth and handed the sack back.

"Go watch at the door then," he ordered Graikos. "And remember, if anyone suspects, we'll be away from this place on the instant. Both of us."

"Just save him," the other said, and went off to the door.

Lir sighed and went to Nuada. He kneeled down by the pallet and looked around him again. At the door Graikos peered outside and then signaled that all was clear. Mathgen, by the hearth, seemed soundly asleep.

Lir fell to work. Swiftly but gently he unbound the wound. He unfolded the cloth he had taken from his bag. Within it was a mass of something shiny green. This he lifted and untangled to reveal a length of seaweed with sharp, spiny leaves running up and down its stem.

Bright blood was oozing from the wide and jagged wound. Gingerly Lir laid the strip of seaweed along the cut, its spines touching the whole flesh on either side.

He put a forefinger to each end of the length of plant. His brows and mouth drew into a frown of concentration. He chanted something unintelligible under his breath.

Blue-white flaring light appeared from his fingertips, flickering out along the seaweed in fine tendrils, winking from each of the spine points. The points seemed to catch into the flesh all along the cut. They began to draw the sides of the wound together.

Nuada moaned but stayed unconscious. Lir continued his chanting and intense concentration. The two sides were pulled slowly closer, the spines like sutures drawing them in, knitting the ragged edges together, holding them while the blue light played up and down them.

Suddenly the light gave a last flare and faded away, the final trickles of it sucked back into the fingertips. Lir ceased his mutterings, opened his eyes, and carefully lifted the seaweed, examining the wound.

He smiled in satisfaction. The cut had been mended to no more than a red-white, puffy scar.

Nuada stirred and moaned again. His eyelids fluttered, then lifted. His gaze focused on the bearded man bent over him.

"Liam!" he breathed softly. "Did . . . did we win?"

Lir put a hand on the young man's shoulder and grinned. "That you did, lad," he said.

He didn't note the glint of light in the opened slit of one of Mathgen's watching eyes.

# Part Two

## The Three Plagues

# Chapter 8

# The Beast

A sleek ship of dull silver-grey metal glided in toward shore.

It was an odd craft in many ways. In look it was narrow, long, and featureless except for a step-pyramid of the same metal that arose from the midsection of the deck. It moved with a seeming miraculousness. Not a single crewman was visible anywhere upon it. There were no masts or billowing sails rising above it. No rowing oars protruded from its smooth, blank hull. Still it sailed on, sweeping through an opening between two hooks of neatly dressed stone that jutted far out to sea and formed an artificial bay.

The ship slowed as it entered the bay, swinging slightly to aim toward a row of quays that lined the shore. The dozen identical landing places were also built of the neat blocks of stone. Behind them rose large, flatroofed structures whose grey walls were as smooth and seamless as if each had been fashioned from a single slab of rock.

The ship slowed further, little more than drifting in toward one of the quays. Near the end of the stone platform a small party of Fomor warriors stood waiting. As the strange craft slid in, bumping lightly into the quay, several Fomor leaped at once onto its deck, carrying snubbing hawsers. These they swiftly looped around deck cleats and hauled the ship in, securing it tightly.

A door—before only a near-invisible crack in the smooth face of the pyramid—slid open. The waiting Fomor drew up as at attention, eyes riveted on it. From the blackness beyond a figure emerged, and the Fomor drew up even more stiffly than before, staring in obvious dread.

But the revealed figure seemed nothing to inspire such apprehensive looks. It was a man of broad, coarse, swarthy but otherwise normal features, marked by a neat beard and short-cropped black hair. His trim and muscular body was clad in close-fitting trousers and belted tunic of a like finely textured grey cloth. High boots and gauntlets were of a glossy black leather. He was unarmed except for a short baton of silver metal with a bulbous glass head.

Behind him two others emerged from the ship. These two were also dark, strongly built men and similarly clad. But both carried long rods of metal with odd, glowing tips, and both wore large helmets of dark metal which flared out at sides and back to reach the shoulder blades.

The waiting group watched as these three stepped from the deck and marched up the quay to them, moving with matching, precise, and wide-stepping strides. They stopped close before the Fomor, the two guards flanking their leader.

He gazed at the members of the greeting party superciliously, head up, chin thrust out. His voice was chilly and imperious.

"And just *where* is Cichol Gricenchos?"

Most of the Fomor quivered in open fear, but one of them pushed forward from the bunch. It was the one of single good eye and leather patch who had first confronted the Nemedians.

"He is dead, Captain Tethra," this one said bluntly, clearly not so intimidated by the arrivals. "I have assumed his place. I am Captain Cruc."

The other examined him with a contemptuous eye. "So, 'Captain' you have assumed the leadership of this rabble?"

"I've taken charge of this force," the other amended with some spirit. "They are not rabble, Sir."

"Then can you explain why this tiny band of farmers and herdsmen we were told about can defeat you in battle and kill your leader and send you scrambling for your lives?"

"They had weapons, Captain Tethra. They were trained as

warriors. These things they had kept hidden from us. And they were stronger than we thought, as well."

"And if they're not beaten they'll grow yet stronger," the other said, "and more swiftly than you, you wretched mistakes for men. *Their* offspring will all be strong and whole."

"We know that," Cruc retorted. "And we know what their blood could do for us. But we won't have it from them now. We'll get no tribute at all. We're beaten. My warriors won't attack again. We must have help."

"You know we can't do that!" Tethra said sharply. "You already drain enough from us."

"What, some scraps of food? Some poor castoffs of clothing? Some simple weapons? We're forced to raid widely and constantly to barely survive, and still we must give half our plunder to you! Yet you expect us to wage war with swords and spears while you have weapons like those?" He gestured at the rods the two guards bore.

"We can't waste precious resources on such aberrant creatures as you," Tethra responded sneeringly. "You must see to your own survival or you must perish as useless refuse."

"Why you . . ." Cruc growled, advancing on the captain.

Unconcerned, Tethra merely stepped out and touched the head of his baton to the other's shoulder.

Flares of bright golden light flashed instantly from it to crackle over Cruc. He grimaced in agony and dropped to one knee, drawn taut and vibrating from the immense power surging over him.

"You are too hostile, 'Captain,' " Tethra cooly chided. "You must learn respect for your betters if you wish to keep command."

He stepped back and lifted his baton, releasing Cruc from its power. The one-eyed man abruptly dropped down, just catching himself from toppling, breathing harshly in recovery as he glared up at his tormentor.

"Get on your feet," Tethra brusquely commanded.

Cruc climbed up with an effort, standing unsteadily, fixing the other with a look of mixed hate and fear.

"Now, understand me clearly," Tethra said. "You will get no help from us. You must find some way of dealing with these invaders yourselves."

"They are too strong, I say," Cruc said stubbornly, his punishment not having extinguished all his defiance. "They've no fear of us."

"Not now," said Tethra, "but that might be changed. I understand that you mind a . . . pet of ours, shall we say? A creature left from our past unfortunate experiments in breeding?"

"The Uile-bheist?" said Cruc. "Yes, we've kept it alive for you, penned in a strong vault. It disposes of our useless captives and our own dead and other such garbage."

"It can dispose of these interlopers too. Release it."

"Release it?" Cruc said, aghast. "But it would only attack us!"

"Not if you drive it into the newcomers' domain."

"That would be hard and dangerous. Many of us could die doing it."

"Many more will die if you must face these people yourselves," Tethra reminded him. "This creature will do much of your work for you. It will bring a terror on them, demoralize them, force them to terms—if it doesn't destroy them first."

"Perhaps," said Cruc.

"You have no other choice," the other said. "It is the only help that you will get. Release the animal. Do it now!"

And with that he turned abruptly on his heel and stalked back to his ship, the two guards following.

Cruc and his fellows stood nonplussed, staring after the three as they reboarded their ship and vanished within the central pyramid. The hawsers were released, the ship drifted free. Then, under its unseen power, the sleek vessel backed away from the stone quay, made a graceful turn, and glided silently away, back out to sea.

"We thank you, O Great Ones," Cruc muttered after it in a sarcastic tone. Then he turned to the others.

"Well," he said, putting on a heartier tone, "it appears this thing must be done."

The others exchanged uncertain looks.

"So," said Cruc, gaze shifting from man to man, "which of you will volunteer to release the beast?"


It was Captain Cruc himself who stood on the wide, flat rooftop, peering warily down through a grating into the space beneath.

There was a vast darkness below, a darkness in which the sounds of faint stirrings and of harshly wheezing breaths could be heard.

"I don't like this," said a hairy and wolf-faced man beside him. "They're going to lose dozens getting that thing herded away from here."

Cruc straightened and looked to him. "Better it's them than us, Faolchu. Give the signal."

The wolf-faced man went to the edge of the roof and looked over. He and his captain stood atop a blank-faced, square-cornered building some fifty paces on each side and over three stories in height. Just below where Faolchu stood, a roadway lead to a pair of broad, high metal doors set in the center of one wall.

From these doors ran two lines of Fomor warriors, a hundred in each. They stood in facing ranks, shoulder to shoulder, shields and spears up before them to create a bristling avenue leading toward open country to the south.

Faolchu lifted a hand to a score of other warriors standing in a tight group near to the huge doors.

"Open them!" he called down.

With very obvious reluctance, the group of Fomor approached the doors. Several of them hastily wrestled a thick rod of iron from its brackets, unbarring the door. Ten of them then put their shoulders to each of the panels, grunting and straining to push them inward. Slowly the doors gave, swinging in with a shriek of rusty hinges.

The doors were swung fully open into darkness. The men instantly rushed back from them, pushing out through the lines of their fellows to safety.

The warriors in the two lines gazed fearfully through the opened doors into the black. They tensed, setting themselves more solidly, lifting spears and swords a little higher in defense. They waited.

There was nothing.

Cruc peered down. He also could see nothing in the void below. The creature wasn't moving.

"It's sleeping, maybe," Faolchu suggested.

"More likely just being wary," Cruc returned. "It hates the light. Get me a torch!"

From a nearby brazier, the wolf-faced one took a lighted brand. Cruc grabbed it from him and dropped it through the grate. He followed the glow of its flame as it dropped down, struck something, bounced away.

There came a deep, echoing growl that caused the entire

structure to shudder. Something stirred. There was a confused
scrabbling and rustling sound, growing swiftly louder.

"That's shifting it," Cruc said triumphantly.

He went to the edge of the roof and shouted to those below.

"Stand ready. It's coming now. We must direct it away. You
must hold the lines. I'll kill the first man who falters or fails to
keep it headed right, myself!"

The Fomor stood ready in their two lines. But more than a
few of the lifted spears could be seen to quiver. And nearly all
the eyes were bulged with fear as they stared into the vault
where something had now become visible.

Regardless of Cruc's threat, some of the warriors broke and
ran in horror as a massive form emerged, crawling slowly forth
to be revealed in the light.


The shepherd threw another clump of dried turf onto his
little fire.

It burned with a soft, warm, ruddy glow, sending up a trail
of grey-white smoke whose gentle fragrance scented the soft
spring evening.

He looked up toward a collection of pale white lumps on
the slope above—the nestled sheep of his sleeping flock just
visible in the moonlight. He looked down on the village of
Nemed in the valley below, sleeping too except for a few lights
and a few plumes of smoke making silvery trails against the
night sky.

He sighed in contentment and lay back to look up at the
canopy of stars stretching overhead. His eyes fluttered as he
began to fall asleep.

Suddenly a noise brought him sitting upright, grasping his
staff, gazing around him into the darkness.

It had been a peculiar noise. Not a normal sound of insect
or bird or wind. A throaty, snorting sound.

He looked up to where the sheep lay. None seemed to have
moved. But the sound had come from their direction or beyond.

He rose and moved slowly up the slope toward them. He
stopped short when he heard the sound again—deep, harsh,
and decidedly nearer this time. And following it came another
sound, a continuous rustling sound as of a whole flock rushing
through tall grass, heading right toward him.

Then his sheep were suddenly all upon their feet, baaing in

alarm. They milled in confusion, then bolted, hopping and stumbling over one another in their panic to get away down the slope.

The startled man sidestepped hurriedly as several rushed past him, nearly running him down. He turned to start after them but took only a few steps before a loud growling sound drew his eyes back.

Something had appeared on the slope above. It loomed up, towering over him, blocking out the stars.

He gave a shriek of terror and began to run. But he was too late. The form descended, smashing down upon him, bearing him to the earth.

A bestial roar of victory echoed along the quiet valley, bringing the sleeping people of Nemed instantly awake.

# Chapter 9

# A Hunt

The grisly remains of the bull lay scattered across the slope.

The once massive and muscular animal had been literally torn apart with what must have been enormous violence. Most of the meat from the carcass was gone, stripped away, leaving little but jumbles of bone and skin. The few remaining identifiable portions had been badly chewed.

Dagda knelt and lifted the intact section of a hind leg, examining the marks in the bright sunlight of a clear dawn. The bone was deeply scored.

He looked up to Nemed and Diancecht who stood over him.

"If these are the marks of teeth, then it was a great beast indeed that attacked here," he said.

Nuada was striding up and down over the slope nearby, where the rent corpses of several other cattle were visible. He was scouring the ground carefully with his eyes.

"A great beast," he said. "And yet from these marks it seems it was a large pack of smaller creatures that came here, trampling the grass, overrunning these poor animals."

"A strange pack to stay so closely together when they hunt," said Diancecht.

"But not so close that they weren't able to get hold of several cattle at once before the rest of the herd scattered," Dagda pointed out, tossing down the leg and standing up. He looked up the slope to where the one they knew as Liam stood with his servant Graikos. "Liam, you know more of things than we do. Do you know anything of this?"

"I can say truthfully that I have no idea what it is," the bearded man said.

"Well, one thing is clear," said Nemed heavily, "we can no longer risk either our men or our livestock outside the palisade."

"But we can't keep them locked up inside," Nuada argued. "We can't become prisoners of our own fortress. How can we survive?"

"How can we expect our people to risk themselves over cattle and sheep?" Nemed returned. "How can we risk losing any more of our livestock? Nearly a third have been lost to us now, along with the three herdsmen."

"Then we will have to stop these things," Dagda said simply. "Let me do it."

"How?" asked Nuada. "We don't know when or where they will strike us, save always at night and when we are most vulnerable. Then they vanish again into the forests. You'd never find them there."

"With the help of one of the Falva clan, I would," Dagda said with assurance. "They can track any creature anywhere."

"And if you do find *these* creatures?" said Diancecht.

"I will destroy them," Dagda tersely replied.

"But from the evidence, these things are incredibly savage," Diancecht pointed out.

Dagda shrugged. "They are still only beasts. They can be caught and they can be killed, like any other."

"Not by you alone," said Nemed.

"I could take a score of good fighting men as well, just to be certain," the self-confident man said.

"I'll go," Nuada volunteered.

"No," said Dagda. "Your skills and your cleverness are too much needed here. This is something for me to do."

"I have to agree with him, Nuada," Nemed said. "There is no need for two of my most valued leaders to risk themselves. I only wish it wasn't necessary for either one of you to go."

"Very well, I'll stay," Nuada agreed with reluctance, "but I will at least help you pick out and equip the men, Dagda. When do you wish to go?"

"Today. As soon as possible. I'd like to find these beasts before the fall of another night."

"Then let's be at it quickly," Nemed said.

He, Nuada and Dagda started at once down the hill toward the village. But Diancecht tarried, looking after them.

"Nuada is remarkably healed, don't you think?" he commented, looking around to Liam.

"Yes. It's amazing how quickly a youthful constitution will knit itself," the other returned in a blithe tone.

"Still, this is something more," the healer said in his studied, calculating way. "Miraculous I'd call it." He eyed the bearded man, one brow arched high in speculation. "Would *you* know more of it?"

"Me?" the other said in feigned astonishment. "And why would I?"

"It's only that when I left him, he was dying," Diancecht said. "When I returned, he was all but healed. No one was about then but a dozing Mathgen. But I recalled that you and your servant had been there before."

"And left when you did. Didn't we Graikos?"

The servant nodded emphatically.

"Yes," the healer said slowly, musingly. "Well, I suppose I shouldn't question such wonderous happenings and just be thankful. Still, it is most curious. Most curious indeed."

And with that he went on down the slope.

"Now, you see there?" the bearded man told Graikos irritably. "I told you doing even that bit of magic would be dangerous. Now we have Diancecht suspicious of us. And he is a most clever, most persistent man. From this point on we must be doubly careful. No more magic. Nothing the least bit extraordinary."

"I suppose that means we won't be volunteering to help Dagda in his hunt," said Graikos.

"Of course we will not. I didn't have any notion of doing such a thing anyway. I was speaking the truth when I said I don't know what they face. Without magic we would be of no help to them. Their own skills and strength will be more useful now."

"Still, it seems a great shame," said Graikos, "for you who have such powers to leave them to take such risks."

"Look here," Lir said testily, "for the last time, Graikos, do you want to stay and give at least our natural help and skills to them?"

"Yes, yes," Graikos said grumpily. "You know I do."

"Then kindly keep in mind that anything bringing greater suspicion upon us will see us packing and leaving here for good. There'll be no more miraculous help from us, Graikos. No help at all!"

But though the disguised Lir spoke inflexibly for himself and for his servant, he did not speak for all of his people.

For later that morning, when Dagda and his hunting party left the village, mounted the valley slopes and plunged into the dense woods beyond, a shining figure mounted on a bizarre hybrid steed slipped from the reeds of the lakeshore and swiftly followed after them.

Unknown to Lir the sprightly Muirgheal had taken up guardianship again.

Dagda and his hunting party of heavily armed men tracked their quarry into the dense forestlands.

Soon after entering the trees, they had picked up a trail. It had indicated that whatever they pursued had headed straight west from the valley. The signs were of something moving without subtlety, leaving a wide, straight, well-trampled trail that they had little trouble following.

Through the rest of the morning they followed the track, the canny hunter Toirdealbhach O'Falva at their head. Just after noon they came out of the trees onto the shore of a small deep-blue lake lying at the base of a steep and rocky hillside.

The track led on, circling the lake, vanishing as it started up the slope. O'Falva ranged back and forth along the face of wind-scoured, jumbled rock. Finally he gave it up, returning to the others.

"It's too rough," he told them. "There're no more signs of tracks."

"Could they have gone on beyond these hills?" asked Dagda.

"I don't think so. They've kept within easy traveling distance of our valley. From the looks of the trail here, they have come and gone this way several times. My feeling is that the creatures are up there, somewhere. Still, finding their lair would be near to impossible."

"Then we'll let them come to us," Dagda declared. "We have the afternoon to work. We can set up our trap here. When these beasts use their path again, we'll be ready for them."

---

Dagda stared out intently into the darkness. In the moonlight the trail was just visible to him as a pale streak running away through the blackness of the surrounding woods, fading quickly from sight.

He was crouched behind a line of man-height stakes. Each of them had one end sharpened and the other set solidly in the ground. They formed a barrier across the trail the quarry had made. To either side of the trail another wall of spiked posts could faintly be seen, running away from the barrier at an angle. Thus the quickly erected palisades created a funnel that would hopefully channel anything using the trail right to where Dagda waited.

A faint crackling sound brought him looking around, hand dropping to his ready spear. But it was only Toirdealbhach O'Falva who appeared from the trees to crouch beside him.

"Ah, you're back," the big man said. "Is everything set then?"

"I've checked the entire wall again," O'Falva reported to him. "Fine work our lads have done on it in so little time. It's strong enough to withstand the charge of a whole herd of maddened bulls. If the creatures come along the path this far, they will be hemmed in solidly on three sides."

"Good. And the men?"

"They are on either side of the trail, near the far ends of the barricades, well hidden, waiting to leap out and close the trap when you shout the signal."

"And they know to wait until the beasts have come all the way in? And to lie silent and stand firm no matter what?"

"They do. It's a bold, strong lot you've picked. They'll not disappoint you."

"I know they won't. What about the fires?"

"All but the rekindling fire are out. And that one is thoroughly banked and covered. There'll be no light at all."

"Then we're ready," Dagda declared. "All we can do is wait."

And so the two men checked their weapons to be sure they were close at hand, then both settled themselves as comfortably as they could while still keeping up a vigil on the trail through cracks in the palisade. The night passed very slowly for a time, the white crescent of the moon creeping upward in the clear sky at a nearly imperceptible pace.

"What odds would you give on their coming tonight?" Dagda at last murmured to his companion.

O'Falva shrugged. "Hard to say," he whispered back. "They've just fed well on our own cows. Like many predators, they could very well just lie up resting, maybe for days. On the other hand . . ."

"Yes?"

"Well, if they've sensed we're here, that may well bring 'em out."

"To walk into our trap?"

The hunter shrugged again. "Maybe not."

"What?" Dagda said in surprise. "Are you saying these things might be too clever for that?"

"I'm saying I have a feeling about this—a feeling of something out there that has some cunning, and certainly no fear. Fearful creatures would never have left such a clear trail. It's as if they didn't care whether we followed. Almost as if they wanted us to."

"Come on now, Toirdealbhach," Dagda said scoffingly. "It's only beasts we're facing. And we're armed men, ready for them, not helpless shepherds. This time, *they're* the prey."

"Maybe," said O'Falva not totally assured.

He sat musingly for a time, staring out at the empty trail. Then he gave a little sigh and shook his head.

"Strange," he said, in a sober tone, "but I never thought to be in such a place and facing such a thing when I joined Nemed in coming to this 'land of promise.' "

"Neither did I," Dagda agreed. "It's more exciting than I ever thought it might be."

"You mean, you came *for* this?" the hunter said in astonishment.

"Of course!" Dagda returned. "Why else? Life back there was dull. Every day the same. Nothing to look forward to in the world. This was a chance at new things, new adventures, new challenges."

"Not for me," said the other, "or for my clan. It's a quiet life that we came seeking here. A place where we could roam free, hunt, fish, and raise our families in safety. That's really what all of it's about for us—the family, the security."

Dagda listened gravely to this, considered, and then nodded.

"Do you know, I think I begin to understand you. I had no family. I never had anything to fight for or to care about except myself. Then I met Moire. Her brothers had been killed, her father was growing old. So, I began taking care of them. Now they've become my family. They've made me know there *is* something else. Something worth fighting for, something worth having beyond my own survival."

"It's important to have family," O'Falva said. "Why, without my two brothers, I . . ."

He stopped suddenly, head cocking to listen.

"What is it?" Dagda asked.

"A sound. Very faint. Very far. But . . . something moving. Yes, definitely moving, on the trail. And coming this way."

Dagda tensed. His big fist closed around the pole of his spear. "Could it be them?"

"It could be anything—deer, boar, even a fox."

O'Falva listened again, intently, then shook his head, relaxing.

"No," he said. "No more. It's gone. Faded away."

"It turned around? Went back?"

"It seems so. It was approaching, but something caused it to retreat."

"You don't think they were cunning enough to spy our trap?"

"If they were," said O'Falva, "then they're gone now, and we'll have no chance to catch them."

A shrill, ululating cry lifted suddenly in the night air. It was joined by two others, twining with it in eerie disharmony that rolled away through the forest. Hard upon it came the sound of crashing from up the trail and to the right, and then the scream of a man in agony.

"They've attacked us!" cried Dagda, leaping up.

"From outside the row of spikes!" added O'Falva, grabbing his own spear and rising too. "They've come in behind us!"

The two charged around the barricade, heading for the sounds. They fought their way at their best speed through the tangled underbrush. Meantime, the men hidden on the left side of the trail also rose from cover and headed for the scene, feeling and stumbling their way out past the wall of stakes and across the trail in the blackness.

But the powerful Dagda outdistanced them all, arriving first at the source of the sounds.

It was a place of confusion. Shapes were shifting about rapidly in the dark. There were constant crashings and thuddings; bestial snorts and shrieks and bellows; human cries of fear, rage, pain.

He saw the dim forms of what seemed men milling about not far before him and headed toward them. One of his hunters staggered backward past him and fell, a swath of blood across his chest.

Dagda looked around to him but then swung back as a massive head swooped suddenly down from the dark above.

He had only a quick glimpse of it—the faint glint from rows of teeth in huge, open jaws, the greenish glow of enormous eyes —and then he was jumping back from the attack.

His heels hit a fallen branch and he toppled backwards, thudding to the ground. It was his good fortune. The jaws shut with a loud snap just above him. The head swept past, lifting again. He rolled, coming up to his knees, preparing to rise when a huge form came over him, knocking him down once more.

He found himself beneath a great, dark, heaving mass of something. Its weight pressed down atop his back, flattening him to the earth and pinning him there. His spear had been knocked from his hand. He couldn't reach his sword. He could only lie helpless, face smashed into the sod, as the form lifted and dropped, lifted and dropped atop him.

Then it lifted far enough for him to move. He rolled quickly onto his side, intending to scramble free. But he found his way blocked by a forest of something that looked to be long, lean, knob-joined limbs. He managed to yank his sword from its sheath and swung out savagely at them. His keen blade sliced through two, shearing them off.

In response there instantly came loud shrieks of pain from what seemed several throats close above him. The dark mass hanging over him lurched suddenly upward and away. The remaining limbs lifted and swung with it, several of them whipping across his body, the sharp talons which tipped each one tearing through his tunic, slicing his arm, ripping his forehead.

He gasped in pain, recovered, and climbed to his feet, looking around. He saw the forms of his companions, some afoot, others on the ground. But whatever had attacked them had already vanished.

From out of the black forest there came back to them a single long, terrified, man's scream, rising and fading away.

# Chapter 10

# The Cave

It wasn't until daylight that the hunting party could fully assess its damages.

Two men sported the deep marks of teeth—one in an arm, the other in shoulder and chest. Three more had been trampled upon—two receiving only bruises, the third a broken leg. And two others had vanished.

"We can't find 'em anywhere," one of the party reported to Dagda. He and his fellows had been sweeping the forest about the battle site for any sign of their comrades.

"Carried off, they were," another man said in distress. "I know for certain that poor Angus was grabbed up by something. Great jaws it had, with fine, sharp teeth, like those of a shark!"

"No, no!" disagreed a third. "It was more like a serpent I say. I saw the great length of the thing whipping about in the air above me. Not just one of them. Five or six there were."

"More even than that!" one of the bruised men put in emphatically. "A dozen there were at least. Didn't I feel the many feet of them myself as they were tramping all across me? Small and quick they were too, like a herd of deer bounding along."

"Those are no deer's legs," said Dagda, lifting one of the limbs he had severed.

The men grouped around him, examining the object curiously. It was certainly a leg but of a distinctly reptilian kind. It was lean but sinewy, with a knobby knee and a two-toed foot from which sprouted long, curved, and very pointed talons. Instead of fur or skin, its thick outer covering was made of green-grey scales.

"Well," one of the men said, scratching his head, "I've surely never seen the like."

The others shook heads in agreement.

"Diancecht would have said it was 'most fascinating,' " one pointed out.

"Diancecht might also have been able to tell something of the nature of the creature which walked on it," added Dagda. "Our own poor knowledge is of little use in doing that."

Toirdealbhach O'Falva came from the woods to join them then, accompanied by two others. The company turned hopeful faces toward him.

"Sorry. No luck at all," he told them glumly. "We followed the trail to the hills. Not a sign of the missing two. But we did find this."

He held out a fist-sized rock, and Dagda took it from him. One surface was splattered with a thick, yellowish substance. Dagda looked from it to the cut end of the leg. A like substance had oozed from its split veins.

"Blood!" he said.

"Aye," said O'Falva. "That wound you made was still seepin' drops of it, and right up the hillside. Should be enough to let us track the things."

"Then, if we can't find our fellows," Dagda said fiercely, looking around at the rest, "we can at least have our revenge for them. Get ready to leave at once!"

The wounded men were patched to the hunters' best abilities. Three of them too badly hurt to travel were left in as much comfort as possible in a small hidden camp. The rest took up their arms and followed the young tracker of the Falva clan along the trail and up the rocky hillside that rose steeply above the lake.

He followed the trail of yellow droplets easily, leading the company high up and across the rugged slope. Finally they reached a narrow ledge jutting from a sheer cliff face. Its outer lip was actually thrust out over the water now some hundred feet below.

From the farther end of the ledge, the mouth of a cavern in

the weathered cliff face yawned at them menacingly. The droplets of yellow formed a clear line, straight into its shadows.

The hunters paused at their end of the narrow platform,
peering at the opening warily.

"Now what?" asked one.

"Yes," said Dagda. He looked to the tracker.
"Toirdealbhach, what do you say?"

"Well," the young man said, considering, "I would say that
whatever's in there is certainly nocturnal. They hunt at night
and hide in darkness during the day. So, they must hate the
light."

"Good lad!" Dagda said, grinning and slapping O'Falva on
the back. "You'll have Diancecht himself on the run soon with
logic like that." He looked to the others. "All right then. If
they hate light, we'll *give* them some light."

"How?" asked one.

Dagda looked around them, his gaze stopping on a tight
knot of fir trees sprouting from a jagged outcrop of rock on the
slopes not far below.

"There!" he said, pointing. "We cut the pines. Get branches
and pitch for torches. And we'll build a fire right here."


A single small glimmer of light detached itself from the
outside brightness and moved into the darkness within the
cavern's mouth.

It was quickly followed by another, and then, after a moment's pause, by several more. The pitch-soaked ends of the
pinewood torches flared with a red-gold light, the combined
glow of them revealing the faces of the young men who held
them. One face—Dagda's—was determined. That of O'Falva
showed a hunter's cautiousness. The others' expressions all
were cast in varied gradations of apprehension.

That half of the party who carried torches held casting
spears in their other hands, their round shields slung upon their
backs. The other half held shields and swords. Holding his own
sword and shield ready, Dagda led the way cautiously forward,
O'Falva close beside him with torch upheld, the rest in a tight
knot behind.

They moved inward some distance, maintaining a strict silence. There was nothing to see but the rough walls of the large
cavern. There was nothing to hear but a soft, low rasping from

somewhere ahead—the separate breathing sounds from their quarry joined to create a single constant noise.

They crept on toward it. The sound grew gradually louder ahead. Daylight from beyond the cave mouth faded away behind, finally leaving them in a darkness alleviated only by their puny and flickering torch flames.

Then one man moving near the cavern wall stumbled, fell, and recoiled with a noise of disgust. The others moved in around him as he arose, looking down at the stone floor. Their lights revealed an almost fleshless and gutted torso, and nearby it a badly gnawed and unrecognizable head.

The rest stared, frozen in shock. But Dagda, after only a quick glance, gestured sharply to them and went on, O'Falva following at once. The others hesitated, exchanging glances of much-heightened anxiety, then went on.

The sounds from ahead had grown quite loud now, echoing up the tunnel like rolling thunder. And a heavy, sweet-foul odor of a carnivore's blood-tinged breath also wafted up upon them.

They reached a bend. Dagda signed the rest to wait and eased around the curve of the cavern wall, O'Falva close at his elbow. The light of the single torch shone into a space beyond, so large that the rays couldn't reach roof or sides. A shadowed mound showed not far ahead in the vast darkness. He signaled the others to follow and took a step toward it.

From just before him, a massive head lifted suddenly, its eyelids snapping open to reveal two glowing, yellow-green orbs.

With sharp snorts of alarm, two other heads lifted up, one on either side of the first, their eyes opening as well. The three heads hovered there, a dozen feet overhead, as Dagda's party rounded the corner, their brighter torchlight finally revealing clearly what they faced.

It was a creature more than a dozen paces long, its broad, reptilian body—upheld by scores of slender legs—tapering down to a lean and switching tail. The gap in the row of legs where Dagda had slashed the two away was also visible. The small beginnings of two new legs were already regenerating from the stumps.

From the wide-shouldered upper end of the creature there grew three long necks, lithe, sinewy, as thick as a man's waist, longer than a man's height. At the end of each was a like head, the size of a bull's but flat and serpentlike, with bulging eyes and enormous, tooth-lined jaws.

For a moment there seemed mutual consternation in both monster and men at this meeting.

The men, plainly stunned by the grotesque nature of the thing, stood together in a motionless knot, staring up. In return the three heads stared back with wide, startled eyes. It seemed that Dagda's plan to cow their enemy with light had worked.

But then each of the three heads voiced a sharp, malevolent hiss, and the long body lunged forward in attack.

Dagda raised weapons and set himself, prepared to do battle. The loyal O'Falva stayed right at his side, torch lifted, spear cocked back. But the rest of their party were gripped by panic and made no move to fight. Instead they wheeled as one body, broke and ran, some casting down spears, swords, shields, and even torches in their headlong flight.

Thus abandoned, Dagda and O'Falva were simply overrun. So swiftly did the thing come upon them that they had little chance to fight. One of the heads swept sideways into Dagda's shield. Backed by the great power in the thing's muscular neck, the blow lifted Dagda and sent him flying across the cavern floor to slam against a wall. The breath exploded from him at the impact. He hung a moment against the rugged stone, then toppled to the floor.

Meantime, the jaws of another head had snapped out at O'Falva. He had cast his spear, but it had skittered along the scaled surface of the neck and dropped harmlessly away. Now he turned to run, but not quickly enough. The jaws closed around his middle.

Desperately he struck out with the torch, slamming it across the head's wide, flat nose. This served only to further anger the beast. The jaws tightened. There was a grotesque crackling from his crushed chest bones and he went limp.

In its eagerness to get to the other fleeing men, the creature simply dropped him, ignored the felled Dagda, and went on, shooting up the tunnel on its scores of wildly scrambling legs.

But Dagda, though down, was not yet out. The big man shook his head, drawing in a great breath. He levered himself up, hearing the fading screams of his fleeing comrades. He went to O'Falva and looked down at the hapless young man's dead form.

With a bellow of rage, he charged after the creature, snatching up one of the fallen torches to light his way.

He moved up the rough-floored tunnel at his best speed. Soon light came into view ahead. The tunnel's mouth.

A large shadow was moving there against the outside brightness. It was the creature, body half blocking the opening, tail switching wildly behind, heads thrust forward, into the daylight.

Its anger with those who had invaded its lair had drawn the monster this far into the medium it loathed in a last attempt to destroy them. Though its eyes blinked constantly, nearly blinded by the sunlight, still it struck out viciously and continually with the three heads, snapping at the men.

Under this attack the erstwhile hunters were struggling to move off the ledge and onto the slope beside it. The narrowness of the space allowed them to make this move only one at a time. Desperate attempts by some to push past others had already resulted in three slipping and tumbling down the rocky slope to end in broken heaps at the bottom. Still others were fighting to be next off the ledge while some of their braver fellows waved spears, swords, and shields in an attempt to ward the striking heads away.

It was a largely futile defense. One man was knocked down by a blow of a head against his shield and nearly rolled from the ledge. Another was caught when jaws closed over his head. The monster lifted him, swung the sinewy neck to thrash him as a dog would a caught rodent, then cast the body away.

Dagda came up unnoticed behind the occupied beast. He leaped across the thrashing tail, moved up alongside the sleek body. In an attempt to distract it from the others, he swung out at it with his sword.

Even the creature's scale plating wasn't enough to withstand a blow with all of Dagda's muscle behind it. The keen blade bit deep into the smooth side just above the tail, slicing a deep canyon that filled instantly with a torrent of the thick yellow blood. It was far from a killing wound, but it was certainly a painful one.

His ploy worked. The three heads screamed in unison. They turned away from the other men. The huge body swung around on the myriad legs with an astounding swiftness. Dagda braced himself to do battle with the three sets of clashing jaws.

But the creature's counterattack came not from the heads but from the massive tail.

The tapering length of it whipped around against the warrior, catching him by surprise. In one swift move, the tail struck him across the back, sweeping him out the entrance and across the narrow ledge, toppling him over the precipice.

He fell at first straight downward, then struck a thrusting boulder in a caroming blow that bounced him outward. It was far enough to make him miss a rocky strip of shore at the cliff's base and instead plunge into the deep waters of the lake just beyond.

He sank down into its deep blue waters, stunned, making no struggle, swallowed up by cold and darkness, vanishing from sight.


Nuada strode the walkway of the village palisade restlessly.

At the end of each turn he paused, staring out toward the west and the valley slope and the deep forest beyond. It was just past noon. Well more than a full day since the hunting party had departed. Still there was no sign of its return.

"So, you're worried too?" said a voice.

He looked around to see the raven-haired Moire approaching him along the walkway.

"About Dagda?" he said casually to hide his true concern from her. "Never. I made him promise to take no dangerous risks."

"But you know how he is," she said, stopping beside him, her own gaze searching the distant line of trees. "When he's set on a course, there's nothing that will shift him. Why, he'd take on a full pack of starving wolves alone."

"And beat them," Nuada added.

"Maybe," she said, a tinge of worry coloring her tone.

She continued to stand there, eyes fixed intently on the distance. Nuada's own eyes examined her musingly.

"You came up here to keep watch for him as well, then," he said.

She nodded. "This is the second time since we came into this land that I've kept vigil, convincing myself over and over again that I would surely see him again . . . and alive."

"I understand that," he said. "I know what he means to you."

She looked around to him, her look turning defensive. "That you do not! It's no one who truly knows what I feel save for myself."

"Come, Moire. Haven't I seen how you look at him? The care you take of him? The concern for him in your voice?" He smiled. "Not that *he'd* be aware of any of those things. Oh, he is a good friend, a fine man, most skilled and as openhanded as the best. Still, you must know that in some ways he *is* a bit like a great ox. Once in a while you have to give him a very firm rap with a fine big stick to make him take note."

She also smiled at that. "I suppose you do," she agreed. Then she sobered again. "So, are you saying that I should tell him what I feel?" she asked gravely.

"Certainly you should! You're a good woman Moire. He should know how you really feel."

"Maybe I'll think of it," she said. "Thank you, Nuada. You're a good man too."

They went back to their search of the western skyline, silent now, both musing on their own hopes and fears. For some time longer, nothing more happened but the slow journey of the sun from its high point down toward the horizon.

It had traveled half its route there when the tiny dots came suddenly into view atop the valley slope.

Nuada saw them first.

"There!" he said elatedly, pointing. "It must be them. Come on!"

The two rushed down from the walkway. Swiftly they gathered a party including Nemed, Diancecht, Liam and his servant, and a large group of excited village folk. Unable to wait this welcoming party left the village and headed for the valley slope to meet the party now descending it.

As the two groups drew closer together and the nature of the hunting party's condition grew more clear, the villagers' expressions of elation changed to looks of dismay.

Only some dozen of the score of men who had gone out with the party were returning on their feet. Some of these were limping or helped along by fellows. Three more men were being pulled along on sledges that had been hastily constructed from tree limbs and woven sticks. The other five men of the party were nowhere to be seen. And neither was their massive leader, Dagda himself.

"What happened to you?" an appalled Nemed demanded when they reached the men.

"We found the thing," one man panted out exhaustedly. "A monster it was. One great, savage creature. But three headed and with a hundred legs! We tracked it to its lair. It . . . attacked us."

Diancecht swept his piercing, evaluating gaze over the men. "We must get these wounded to where I can treat them," he said curtly, looking to the crowd. "All the rest of you, help them."

The people moved in to support the hurt men and take over the pulling of the sledges. They headed toward the village.

"Did you kill this creature?" Nemed asked the hunters as they walked together.

The same man shook his head. "No. We had no chance. It came at us from the dark. So fast . . ."

"Never mind that!" Moire said sharply, moving close to him. "What about Dagda?"

"He tried to fight it," the man said.

"Yes," put in another. "He saved us. Distracted it. We escaped, but he was knocked from the cliff, into a lake."

"The creature gave up on us then," said the first man. "We were out of reach. It wanted no more of the daylight. It went back into its cave, and we got away."

"And Dagda?" asked Moire in anguish. "He was dead?"

The man shook his head. "He had to be. If the fall didn't kill him, then he drowned in the lake. Either way, we saw no more sign of him."

"How well did you look?" asked Nuada.

"As well as we could," the man said defensively. "We had to get out ourselves, remember. We had the wounded. We could only go slowly. We had to leave there as soon as we could."

"What?" cried Moire, grabbing the man's arm and wrenching him around to face her. "You left Dagda there so you could run?"

"We had to be out of there before night, don't you understand?" he told her in anguish. "That thing would have come after us again. It hunts at night. We'd have had no chance!"

"It's all right," Nemed said soothingly, patting the man's shoulder. "You were right to come back here."

"These cowards?" Moire said to him angrily.

"No," Nemed corrected. "These sensible men. To save themselves and the wounded was the logical choice. To not risk all for the sake of one."

"Even when that one is Dagda?" Nuada asked.

"Don't you believe that he would have chosen for things to be done this very way?" Nemed returned.

Nuada considered, then reluctantly nodded his head.

"I suppose we must assume that he is dead," said the disguised Lir, avoiding the accusing eye of Graikos.

"No!" said Moire fiercely. "I'll never believe that!"

"Perhaps it might be better to hope he *is*," said the always-practical Diancecht. "If he is not, then I'm afraid that very soon he will be out there with that thing . . . and quite alone."

He and the others looked up toward the sun, now in its last steep dive toward daily extinguishment.

# Chapter 11

# Duel

Dagda stirred and moaned and his eyes fluttered open.

His vision was at first clouded and unsure. It seemed as if something of a hazy, glowing whiteness hung before him.

He squinted, trying to focus upon it. His vision cleared. He was looking at a face with gleaming silver hair and soft, child-like features that hovered close above his own. The features, before drawn in a worried frown, now lighted with a smile of delight as he awakened.

Bewildered by the strange apparition, Dagda blinked. The figure vanished in the instant of that blink. Startled to full wakefulness, the big man sat up.

He sat on the rocky shoreline of the lake. He was now on the side opposite the cliff from which he had plunged. He cast his gaze all about him quickly. He was alone. No living thing but some wheeling birds moved anywhere around the lake or in the fringes of the surrounding woods.

He looked down at himself. His tunic and boots were still damp from his recent immersion. He looked out at the blue lake into whose depths, at last conscious recollection, he had been sinking, preparing to drown.

"How did I *get* here?" he muttered and shook his head.

And how long had he been unconscious? He looked up to

the sky. Already the sun had dropped behind the ridge of the clifftop, leaving the lake and himself in shadow. Clearly he must have lain unconscious for some time.

His gaze dropped from the sky to the ledge high up on the cliff face. From here it was a barely visible line, the opening of the creature's cavern only a small dark smudge. There was nothing moving there, either of monstrous or of human form.

He started to get to his feet. This caused him to moan and bring a hand to his left shoulder. It was badly bruised from his encounter with the boulder on his plummet to the lake. He worked the stiffened joint of it, grimacing with the pain. Then he stood.

He walked around experimentally, stretching his other muscles, working the shoulder more. Then he looked up toward the cliff again. His first task must be to determine what had happened to his men.

He put a hand to his scabbard. It was empty. His sword, along with his shield, was likely at the bottom of the lake. Whatever he was going to do, he would have to do unarmed.

Shrugging his massive shoulders, he started off.

He rounded the lake to the steep but climbable portion of the hillside they had ascended before. Cautiously he made his way back upward to the end of the little ledge. He peered across to the cavern mouth. No sign of the creature. No sign of any of his men, dead or alive.

An image of the dead O'Falva came into his mind. Likely he had become more feed for that creature. Dagda shook his head regretfully. Nothing could be done for the brave young man now.

He went back down the slope. Near the bottom he made a discovery. A gleam of light brought his eye to a sword half buried in newly fallen rubble. A weapon!

Eagerly he seized it up. But his elation died. The weapon was damaged, its blade cracked nearly in half. One cut and it would simply break apart.

Still, he carried it with him as he made his way back eastward from the cliff and to the spot where they had laid their trap the night before.

The camp they had made there was abandoned. The wounded men they had left were gone, along with the rest. The only sign of the hunting party that remained was a single grave made of heaped earth and piled rock. The last resting spot of a man who had died but had at least escaped the creature's maws. The survivors of the party had departed very hastily indeed, to leave one of their dead behind.

But it did mean that some of them had survived. It also meant that the monster hadn't pursued them back here but had presumably remained within its cave. The O'Falva's guess about it shunning the daylight was very likely correct.

That situation, however, would change with the fall of night.

He looked along the faint trail pointing eastward. With any luck the rest of his party would have time to reach the valley and safety before dark. But what about himself?

He looked upward. The sky above the line of western hills was already turning a darker blue. The day was nearing sundown. And night would come even more swiftly in the spreading shadows below the high cliffs.

He wouldn't be able to get far from that creature's lair before full darkness caught him in the forest, alone and unarmed.

He looked down at the damaged sword. Then he lifted it in both hands and gave it a sharp twist. The long blade snapped in half.

Nodding in satisfaction he fell quickly to work.

He found a long, straight sapling. With the hilted stub of his sword he cut and stripped it, fashioning a shaft as thick as his wrist. Carefully he split one end back far enough to insert half of the pointed remnant of the blade. He bound it tightly in place with the leather thongs from his own boots.

He examined the makeshift spear critically. A crude piece, compared to master smith Goibniu's work, but still a formidable weapon, sturdy, huge, and with a menacing point as long as his forearm. He hefted it in one hand. The balance was good. It would serve.

By now the pool of darkness was spreading quickly outward from the cliff base. He slipped the sword's broken haft into his scabbard and started off.

He moved at good speed through the woods, keeping his direction always toward the east, toward the valley, toward home. He tried to stay ahead of the tide of night, but it soon caught him, the dark waves of it flooding in under the trees, filling up the forest. Once again Dagda found himself drowning, but this time in a sea of black.

His movements were hampered and his way was confused. He was forced to move slowly to find his way through the tangled underbrush. He was forced to pause in any open space, sometimes even climb trees to check the stars and the rising moon for his direction.

Still he kept doggedly on, trying to put distance between himself and the creature's lair.

A quarter of the night passed, and he began to feel he was making good progress. It was then that a roar came to him, joined by another and a third, the trio of them echoing through the woods.

He paused and listened. So, the creature was out. It was out, but was it hunting him?

He pushed on further, grumbling in frustration at the slowness of his progress. Another triple-throated roar rippled through the trees. It was distinctly closer this time. And from right behind. The thing was surely coming after him!

He came into a larger clearing. The trunk of a dead oak rose in its center, the skeletal fingers of the leafless branches reaching toward the sky.

He paused to look. Fallen limbs scattered all about the tree were the fuel for a bonfire. A fire! *That* might keep the creature back.

He shook his head. There was no hope that he could do anything. He had neither the makings nor the time needed to kindle a fire.

The monster's roars came again, already noticeably closer. Without light he had little chance to escape. He couldn't outdistance it. The notion of trying to hide from it never even came into his head.

He gripped his spear tight, his expression hardening; he had to face it now. Challenging, fighting, dying in the fight—that was the only warrior's way!

He looked around again. And why not here? Here where he could make a stand with his back to the wide tree bole, where the stars and moon provided at least enough light for him to see his adversary.

So he moved up to the tree and stood back to it, facing toward the west, spear up and ready, body tensed, waiting for it to come.

Very soon there was a rustling sound from right ahead. From the shadows of the trees the monster appeared, the dozens of its spindly legs scurrying to draw the length of its reptilian body forth. It paused halfway into the open, the pale light glistening from its scales. The three heads lifted on the sinuous necks to waver slowly left, right, and forward, the narrow ribbons of forked tongues flicking far out to scent the air.

Then the three heads all moved close together and all thrust forward. The three pairs of glowing yellow eyes all fixed on him.

The monster crawled on out of cover, the rest of its body and the tapered, restlessly whipping tail sliding into view on its long rows of limbs. By the faint light he could just see that its two severed legs had by this time completely regenerated. Slowly the thing approached him, the heads held low, skimming just about the ground.

As it grew closer, the heads spread apart again, the long necks shifting, one left, another far right as it prepared to strike in at him from three sides at once. The three jaws opened wide. He could see down the pulsing throats. He could see the glint on droplets of saliva trailing from the needle-like teeth. He could feel and smell the warm, rancid breaths playing over him.

He set himself, body tensed, legs planted wide. The spear lifted in his hand. His arm cocked the weapon back, muscles bulging, veins and sinews standing out sharply as he concentrated all his power for the throw. He aimed his spear tip for the center head, at a point exactly between the bulbous eyes. If he could kill at least one of the thing's heads . . .

A strange vision burst suddenly from the trees.

It was of a most peculiar mount and rider—a somewhat horselike steed of glowing greenish hide, astride which sat a lithe, small rider whose childlike face and flowing silver hair were familiar to Dagda.

He stared in astonishment as the pair galloped boldly up between himself and his attacker, then pulled to a stop confronting the monster.

The monster too was startled, jerking to a halt, pulling its three heads sharply up.

The rider lifted slender arms high. In that instant its silver body lit with a brilliant glow, a translucent ball of intense white all but exploding outward to surround the figure and its steed.

The glaring light flooded the clearing, turning nighttime to bright day. Stunned, blinded, the huge creature reared up, its forebody lifting completely from the ground, a front dozen legs on either side windmilling frantically in air, the three heads shooting up straight on the long necks, rigid and quivering with strain.

"Now, Dagda!" the high, clear voice of the silver being

came to him from within the ball of light. "Strike! Strike for its breast!"

Galvanized by the plea, he acted. He ran forward, around the glowing being and straight in toward the monster. The massive thing towered above him, the lifted body like a sheer cliff, the three heads like huge serpents writhing high above.

The bright glow shone against the broad surface of the exposed upper belly, revealing the finer scales of a paler yellow-green that covered it. The creature was clearly much more vulnerable here.

Dagda acted without hesitation. He charged right up to the monster, took hold of his spear in both hands, and rammed it into the center of the broad chest with all his power.

The keen tip of the broken blade punctured through the lighter scales. The point plunged deep into the softer flesh beneath, and half the length of the thick wood shaft followed it.

Hot, viscous yellow blood spurted around the hole, gushing out. The three heads snapped upward in agony, jaws opening to vent three shrill screams. Then they began to thrash wildly on the long necks.

Both Dagda and the strange mount with its rider rushed quickly back from the creature. Dagda leaped into the shelter of the dead tree as a head shot down at him, jaws snapping, narrowly missing him as it swept on by. He peered cautiously back out to watch in wonder as the monster's whole figure was seized by convulsions.

The reptilian body first swung violently back and forth, as if in a desperate attempt to dislodge the weapon. But then the creature fell forward, its own weight ramming the spear on through to burst from its back in a spurting geyser of more pumping life's blood. The dozens of legs scrambled frantically, futilely, unable to lift the form again, leaving it to writhe helplessly on the ground. The tail whipped uncontrollably, crashing through the underbrush behind. The heads arched high, slammed down against the ground, swung madly from side to side, crashed into one another. One smashed into the thick trunk where Dagda hid, shivering the whole dead tree. Dagda crouched low in defense as broken twigs and branches pelted down on him.

Finally the three sinuous necks twined, constricting together in a last twisting, clenching torment of death agony. The heads lifted up as one, the tongues flickering out, vibrating, as long, harsh, shuddering death rattles sounded from the trio of gaping jaws. Then, still locked together, they crashed to the earth for the last time.

The violent convulsing of the body and legs went on for several terrible moments more and then began to weaken. The spasms slowly ended. The tail was last, its slender tip giving a final sharp quiver before dropping heavily to earth.

The creature lay still.

Dagda stepped out from the shelter of the tree, staring in awe at the massive creature his single spear had slain.

Then he realized: the silver glow that had so vividly revealed the scene was swiftly dying away.

He looked around. His silver-haired savior had vanished, taking away the light. The darkness fell about him once again.


Morning sun sent shafts of light down, penetrating the forest's gloom, dotting its floor with spreading pools of gold.

The swelling brightness revealed the rescue party of Nemed's people moving through the trees.

There were some fifty warriors this time, all heavily armed. Nuada led them in the hunt for his friend. In the group behind him moved the one calling himself Liam and his servant Graikos. Also keeping stride with the company of men was the woman Moire, dressed and armed as the rest, her black hair pulled back into a tight braid, her face set in lines of fierce determination.

They had only proceeded a short way along the trail the earlier party had made when they stopped, listening.

Something was moving ahead.

Nuada signaled the party to spread out and take up a defensive stance. All crouched, shields up, spears grounded, creating a barricade that bristled with keen points. They waited, their looks tense.

The underbrush ahead shivered, then was thrust aside as a massive form came through.

A collective sigh of released tension swept the party. It was Dagda who came into their view, carrying a large object on one shoulder.

He stopped on seeing them. After a brief look of surprise, his face lit with delight, his mouth stretched into a wide grin.

"You're alive!" Nuada cried as they all rushed forward to greet him.

"More than that," Dagda said, dropping his vast bundle to the ground before them.

They looked down at one of the creature's severed heads, lying gape jawed, staring with blank, bulging eyes.

"You killed it!" Liam said with amazement.

"Well, I had some help," Dagda told him. "It was a rough night."

"I'm sorry we didn't come sooner," Nuada said contritely. "Nemed refused to let us take out a search party before dawn."

"I understand. I'm only glad to see you all . . ."

He cut off as a raven-haired figure pushed through the others and flung itself upon him, enwrapping him with its arms.

"What?" he said in dismay at the sudden hug from what at first seemed one of the men. Then he pulled back from the figure and realized who it was.

"Moire! What are you doing here?"

"And haven't I as much right to be out here as the rest?" she answered.

"You're a girl."

"I am a woman," she hotly returned, "and I can fight as well as any of these."

"But why would you risk yourself to come out here after me?"

"Why? Because I love you, you great fool!" she blurted out in her exasperation.

The men exchanged looks of amusement and little smiles at her public revelation. She swept an abashed gaze around at them, flushing at the realization of what she had said. Dagda himself, taken fully aback by the outburst, only stared in astonishment.

"Ah . . . Dagda," Nuada put in to alleviate the awkward moment, "just how did you kill the creature?"

"A spear," he said absently, still staring in perplexity at Moire, who had turned away, now refusing to meet his eye.

"You said that you had help," said the one they knew as Liam. "Just what did you mean by that?"

This reminder of the strange method of his salvation at last recalled the big man from his stunned condition to the matter at hand.

"Oh. Well, I mean that someone . . . something . . . I'm not certain what, came from nowhere to blind the thing with light so that I could strike. I would have been killed surely without that."

"Someone?" said Nuada. "Something? Not one of us?"

"No, no," Dagda said emphatically. "This was some unnatural creature. Small, with long, silvery hair, riding a strange green animal."

The disguised Lir and his servant exchanged a knowing glance at that.

"That can't be so," Nuada said in a tone of incredulity.

"Are you asking me to doubt my own eyes?" Dagda challenged. "I'm certain that the being saved me twice. First from drowning, then from the jaws of this." He kicked the head, then added marvelingly: "It must have great magic indeed to make such a blaze as I saw come from nowhere." He considered, then looked up to Nuada, the light of a new realization coming into his eyes. "And you know, Nuada, I wonder now if it wasn't also that same being who first led me to our village."

Caught by the atmosphere of supernatural marvel, all in the party looked around them into the mysterious depths of the deep green forest shot through with the slanting golden shafts of light.

"So," said Nuada musingly, "could it really be that there is some power out there, some spirit or god of this land that wishes to do us good?"

Graikos flashed a grin at his master who glowered in return.

"It seems that there is now!" the servant said.

# Chapter 12

# Poison

Diancecht applied a healing salve to the abrasions on Dagda's broad, bared shoulder.

The big man sat upon a pallet in his own small and spartan hut as the healer treated him. Nuada stood by, watching.

"There," Diancecht said, rising from the bed. "That should help to heal the damage more quickly. But you have to lie quiet for a time for it to work."

"But . . ." Dagda began in protest.

The healer raised a staying hand. "No arguments!" he said firmly. "Even *your* body needs a chance to recover from such punishment. You have done enough for us. This is a rest that you've certainly earned."

He gathered up his medicines and went out of the hut. As Dagda slipped his tunic back on, Nuada stepped forward.

"He's right, you know," he told his friend. "You are of great value to us. We need you fully well. Nemed has told everyone to let you alone for a day or two. They've all agreed."

Dagda looked sharply to him. "Not all!" he said. "Nuada, there is one I *have* to see!"

Nuada grinned. "I had a feeling that would be so. And I have the one you're meaning right outside."

He went to the door and lifted the leather door flap. The raven-haired Moire stepped through into the room.

But she stopped just within the door and stood there looking sober and, for her, rather uncomfortable, her eyes cast down. Dagda eyed her gravely. Neither spoke.

Nuada looked from one to another, clearly feeling uncomfortable himself. "Ah, well, I know I'm not needed here," he said quickly. "I'll leave you alone." And he ducked out.

Moire continued to stand stiffly, not meeting Dagda's eyes. He contemplated her musingly for a long moment, then finally spoke:

"I'm very glad to see you, Moire."

"I shouldn't be disturbing you," was her reply. "You need to rest."

"What I need is to talk to you," he said. "It's our first chance to do that alone since . . . since you came upon me in the forest. And I think we've something to talk about. Don't you?"

She shook her head sharply. "I should never have spoken as I did. I brought shame on you and on myself."

"How shame?" he asked. "Unless what you said to me wasn't true. Are you saying that it wasn't, Moire?"

"I . . ." she began, then hesitated. "I'm not certain *what* to say. I spoke out of my relief at seeing you alive. Maybe too hastily, not thinking how you'd feel."

"Could it be that the love you spoke about was a fondness for me as you'd have for a friend, or maybe a brother?" he probed.

"It's not really . . ." she began.

He interrupted. "Because I can see how you might have a feeling like that. I've tried to give help to you and your parents. I've felt about you as if you were family to me. I could understand your having some concern about me out of gratitude."

"It's *not* from gratitude," she said sharply, some of her spirit coming back into her tones. She stepped toward him. "You really can't see that at all, can you? Even though it seems that every one else in this village can."

She stepped up right before him, striking a bold stance, hands on hips. Her voice came now in a sure, straightforward way: "It is surely not some brotherly affection that I feel for you. It is a true, full, woman-to-man love! There, I've said it, and I don't care who knows it or how much it strikes terror into you!"

"Terror?" he said, perplexed. "But . . . it doesn't! There's nothing else I'd so much want to hear. And nothing I was so certain I never *would* hear. Moire, I feel the same way about you."

Now it was her turn to look stupified. "You do?"

"Of course I do. Haven't I thought it from the first time I met you?"

"You have?" she said, and then the true meaning of his words struck her, and her face lit with her delight. She dropped down beside him to throw arms around him in a great hug. He returned it very readily and with great enthusiasm.

"It was no one else I thought about out there, alone in the darkness, that thing pursuing me," he told her. "It wasn't my own life but that you that I thought most about losing."

"And it was you who I feared losing too," she said, "as if I'd lose a part of my own self."

They pulled back to look close into one another's eyes for the first time. His gaze held some puzzlement.

"But why did you hesitate to admit this to me just now?" he asked.

"Because I saw that stunned look in your face when I first spoke of love," she explained. "The horrible thought came to me that you had no feelings to match mine. I'd made a fool of myself, and I'd be best off not to speak of it again."

"I *was* stunned, true enough," he admitted, "but it was with the idea that a woman like you could feel love for the likes of me. It's why I've never spoken of it before. What right had I—rough, ugly bull that I am—to even think of it? A woman as spirited, bright, and handsome as you are surely deserved much better."

"There are no better than you," she told him earnestly, laying her fingers caressingly against his broad cheek. "You are of more gentle hand and more generous heart than the finest of the rest. How could I not choose you over any other man? How could I want any other as companion, husband, father to my sons!"

He reached up and took her hand, holding it tightly in both his own. "I could never wish to hear any grander words," he told her fervently. "It seems then that we have both been fools."

She nodded. "That we have. But no longer. We'll waste no more precious time."

"What do you mean?"

"Twice now since we came here I've kept a vigil for you," she explained. "Twice I've waited through an endless night fearing that I'd never see you again. I've kept my silence, telling myself that I must wait until things are settled, until the time we are at peace and free to think only of ourselves. But last night I knew that such a time might never come. You'll likely be risking yourself for us always. Well, if that's the truth of it, I mean to wait no longer. I don't care what may happen in the future. For here and now I want you, for however much time that may be. I want as much as we can have together. I would be your wife, if you'll have me."

"You said you couldn't want any other companion," he told her. "Well, neither could I. Before I met you, I thought there was no life but adventure, searching, and risk. Now I see life as a chance to stay, to settle, to make a home and family of my own. I'll be husband to you, and gladly."

They embraced again, holding together tightly.

"My love to you," she said. "Our love together, for however long it lasts."

"It will last," he said. "Have no fear of that. Our peace has come. The Fomor are beaten, that creature is destroyed. The time for us has come now, I promise you."


The sleek grey ship slid through the darkness silently, cutting a glowing white wake in the black sea.

On the second level of the vessel's central step-pyramid stood the Fomor captain named Cruc. He clutched tightly to a metal rail to steady himself against the rolling of the ship and stared nervously ahead into the night with his good eye. The chill sea wind swept across him, and he shivered, pulling his long cloak tighter about him.

A door opened in the smooth metal wall behind him, emitting a rectangle of yellow light and a wave of warm air as the grey-uniformed man called Captain Tethra stepped out. Before the Fomor could glimpse anything beyond the door, it swung shut again, cutting off the light and heat. Tethra stepped up to him.

"Surviving, Cruc?" the man asked, but in a careless tone.

"Don't see why I've got to ride this way out here," the Fomor grumbled. "It's freezing."

"Standing orders are that none of your . . . ah . . . 'people' are ever to be let within our ships," Tethra told him superciliously. "We certainly want neither your filth or your stench entrapped inside with us."

The Fomor turned on him, face dark in rage. "Why you preening, strutting . . ." he began.

"Quiet, Cruc," Tethra warned. "Remember where you are. It's a long swim back."

Cruc looked around him at the black sea. He subsided, glowering silently.

"I didn't come out here to listen to you whine," the other went on. "I only came to say that your discomfort is nearly ended. Our destination is now in view ahead."

Cruc turned to gaze forward. From out of the vast darkness beyond the prow, points of light had become visible. Like faint stars at first, the points grew swiftly sharper, steadier, more plentiful as he watched. In moments it was clear that the lights were in a pattern—spaced in horizontal lines, one rank above another, forming a column that rose up higher, higher as the ship approached.

Soon Cruc stared nearly straight upward at a column soaring hundreds of feet from the sea. This close to it and looking from below, he could see that the lights shone out from the sheer and featureless surface of a substance so smooth that the glow spreading across it from the hundreds of points gave it a luster like a sheet of polished ice.

He had only an instant to form this impression, however, before his attention was drawn to what was just ahead.

They were rapidly approaching the base of the towering thing. This lower portion, some fifty feet in height, was not of polished material but of a dull grey, apparently seamless stone. It rose up abruptly from a narrow margin of rocky shore. Directly before the ship's prow, even this strip of shoreline vanished completely, allowing the sea waves to lap right against the stone foundation. Here a pair of grey metal doors, both high and wide, were set into the wall. At the moment, these doors were swinging back, opening the way.

The ship slowed, aiming precisely for the opening. It slid neatly between the doors and entered a cavernous space beyond.

Cruc looked about him at the vast room. It was a complete harbour artificially enclosed. The featureless, square-cornered walls encompassed many acres of water and rose thirty feet to accomodate the high superstructure of the ship. Opposite the doors—already closing behind them—was a long quay of the same seamless stone. A score of piers ran out from it into the water, and a dozen other ships similar in type to Cruc's transport were tied up at them.

Illumination for all this came from rectangular patches of a brilliant white forming several exactly spaced ranks in the wide, flat expanse of ceiling. They bathed everything with a clear and even and amazingly shadowless light.

The ship drew in to one of the piers, sliding to a stop, barely bumping the stone. A crew of grey-uniformed men moved swiftly and efficiently to tie it off and lift a gangplank to its deck. Without delay Tethra guided Cruc briskly down a staircase from the pyramid to the deck, down the ramp from the ship, and up the pier onto the quay.

Two men wearing the flared black helmets and carrying the staffs with glowing tips met them there. One of them fell in at either side and just behind to escort the pair along.

Tethra led the way to one of a row of smaller silver-grey metal doors set in the wall behind the quay. One of the escorts took hold of a handle in the door, sliding the panel back. They entered a small room with walls, floor, and ceiling of a like metal. The door was slid closed. Tethra yanked upward on a short lever protruding from one wall. There was a jerk and then the room began to vibrate.

Up to this point, Cruc had been simply awestruck by all of these marvels. Now he stepped back to press against a wall, going stiff with fear, his one eye wide and nearly popping from his head.

"What's happening?" he said in a strained, piping voice.

"Be easy, fool," Tethra said curtly. "It's only a device to lift us upward into the tower. It's a very long way to walk. Now be silent!"

They rattled upward for a time. Then Tethra flipped the lever back, there came another jerk, and the vibrations stopped. The guard slid back the door. They all stepped out into a high, narrow room.

The tedium of the otherwise stark grey walls was broken with odd decorations spaced at regular intervals. Angular, jutting masses of silver and black metal alternated with large, flat squares painted in complex patterns of geometric shapes, also of silver, black, and grey.

Cruc gave these decorations little attention, his eye fixed apprehensively on a long corridor that lay ahead, its blank and dimly lit walls running away into an ominous blackness.

Tethra urged him on, and they walked up the corridor, the escort close behind. The narrow way opened abruptly into a large space, too dark for any details to be discerned.

But some way ahead of them, something did show. An almost invisible mass loomed there, merely a slightly darker patch within the engulfing black, formless but still somehow exuding a sense of menace and force.

The four stopped within the wedge of pale light that thrust into this blackness from the corridor. Tethra left Cruc flanked with the two guards and stepped forward. The all but unmanned Fomor stood staring as the other moved ahead into the dark, little more than a shadow himself now, to stop close before the hulking form.

"Commander Balor," said Tethra, "I have brought him, as you asked."

There was a soft clicking, and then a voice sounded from the mass; a low and rumbling voice, and with an odd metallic quality as if it echoed from within a large iron pot.

"So I can see," it said. "Not so grotesque a specimen as some. That, at least, is a relief."

This insult gave Cruc back some of his courage.

"My people are of the finest, the purest blood of all our race," he said with what came close to spirit.

"Then you are likely the best your people will ever do," the voice returned. "Your course will be ever downward unless you can act to save yourselves."

"We are trying, Master," Cruc said.

"And you've failed totally," the voice sharply returned. "You have not been able to defeat this one puny group of invaders in battle. And now I am told that even your attempt to intimidate them into submitting has failed."

"Our lookouts reported seeing a band return to their village carrying one of the Uile-bheist's heads," Cruc reported. "Our own search of the forest discovered its body."

"A pity," said the voice. "It was a frightful aberration, but I've had you keep it alive all these years thinking it might have some such use as this. I was certain it would do better."

"It should have been able to defeat a hundred men," Cruc said. "We lost twenty just releasing it. I don't know what force they could have used to kill it."

"It would seem that these people are strong, courageous, and possibly quite clever, too," the voice rumbled. "That would mean three advantages they have over that refuse you call you people, Cruc."

Stung, the Fomor shot back: "We might have been stron enough to destroy them by now if only you had helped!"

A rasping sound came from the dark-shrouded form. Hig up in its mass a thin line appeared, showing a fiery red. ruddy beam of light from it angled down to play across Cru Instantly the Fomor broke out in a profuse sweat.

"Never use that tone of voice here," the voice growle threateningly. "You know what our policy has always been. N risk to our people. No wasting of our resources. Even exposur of our existence could be dangerous. That is why you must b the ones to deal with this threat."

"But how?" Cruc asked in despair. "What way is left t us?"

The line of light narrowed to a hairbreadth crack, shuttin off most of the beam. Cruc breathed in relief, wiping hi streaming brow. There was a long silence from the dark form and the men waited. At last the metallic voice spoke again.

"Astoundingly, you have made a valid point, Cruc. Yo have clearly exhausted all your own resources. And since you defeat *would* be of some inconvenience to us, we are forced t supply some new means to you."

"To destroy them?"

"Hopefully not. Alive and paying tribute, they would be ( great use to you, and to us as well. No, they need to be given more definite, a more powerful example of what kind of forc you could use against them. An extreme example, as it wer Something more guaranteed to put fear into them and weake them as well. Captain Tethra?"

"Yes, Commander?"

"See that Cruc is given an adequate portion of the Nim contaminant. You know the one. Number 344. Just a singl vial," the voice admonished. "That will be more than enoug! And be most careful."

"I will, Commander," Tethra promised. He turned an marched back to Cruc. "Come on then," he ordered sharply and without ceremony hustled the nonplussed Fomor away, th two guards falling in behind.

As they moved back up the corridor, Cruc glanced a la time behind him. He saw the line of crimson light vanish with sharp click, leaving the massive form once more fully shroude in the blackness.

Then they were reentering the metal walled chamber, and a guard was sliding the door closed. Tethra shoved the lever downward. The vibration began again.

"What's happening? Where are we going?" Cruc demanded, totally bewildered by the swift move of events.

"To a storage room deep below the tower," Tethra said brusquely. "I realize this is too much for your simple mind to grasp, Cruc. But all you need to know is that Commander Balor has chosen to give you help, and how that help must be used."

The chamber's motion stopped again. The guard slid the door back and they all stepped out into yet another enormous room.

This one was crowded with boxes made of wood and cylinders of metal formed in neat stacks that touched the high ceiling. Here and there between the piles sat smaller objects of most peculiar shape shrouded in heavy cloths. All was covered with dust, the air thick with mustiness and age, as if long neglected.

"These are things from our ancient days of power," Tethra briefly explained as he led the way along a valley between the mountains of stored materials. "Someday, when our power is adequately restored, we will use them to reassert our proper place in the great world."

They passed through an archway and entered a smaller chamber. The walls of this one were lined with what seemed round metal plates like immense shields, each a man's height in diameter, each bearing a different device of raised figures in interlocking geometric forms.

"Once in a while, the old tales say, one of the inventions of our great society created a problem," Tethra went on, moving along the row of plates, examining each device. "What was to have made our life perfect, ordered, and pure, instead altered our food or air or water and brought sickness, sometimes death to many. Ah! Here it is."

He stopped before one of the metal circles. From within a pocket of his uniform he pulled a ring hung with scores of small, crooked pieces of metal. Cruc watched with fascination as Tethra looked through this collection of metal bits for a time, finally selected one, and slid it into a slot in the center of the disk. There was a sharp series of clicks, then a louder clank. The disk swung outward, revealing itself to be a door.

The door's metal was more than a handbreadth thick. It

swung outward on massive internal hinges at one side, allowing
access to a shallow chamber filled with metal shelves. Each
shelf was crowded with small square vials that seemed made of
a thick glass. Within each vial a liquid substance was visible, all
of the same or a slightly varied golden hue.

Tethra stepped into the area, running his gaze slowly over
each shelf. The front of each vial was etched with small figures
and he perused these very carefully.

"Here," he announced finally, picking one up. "This is the
one."

"What is it?" asked Cruc, peering curiously at the vial.

"A very, very deadly poison," he said. "An accidental by-
product of our civilization so potent that even a droplet of it
could affect hundreds. So insidious that even its touch can in-
fect the human body. Here." And without warning, he tossed it
to Cruc.

The horrified Fomor caught out at it, fumbled it, finally
gripped it tight. He looked white-faced at Tethra who stood
grinning in cruel delight.

"You really are amusing, fool. That vial can't break, and it
can't open accidentally. You're perfectly safe."

Cruc glared at him. "You'll make me look a fool once too
often, Towerman!"

"And just what will you do then?" Tethra returned. "Don't
try my patience, ineffectual freak. We're helping you, and you
had best appreciate it. You do with that vial as we say, and
those interlopers will be begging you to save them before the
winter comes!"

"All right then," Cruc said, swallowing his anger with an
effort. "What do I have to do?"

"We will show you how the vial is to be opened and where
its contents should be poured. After that, you must simply go
and wait for the chance to use it." He smiled, eyes gleaming
with a cold, malicious light. "When the next horror comes
upon those people, it will be coming from within themselves!"

# Chapter 13

# Contamination

The two Fomor watched the Nemedian village from the shelter of a jagged spine of rocks on the valley rim.

One of them was again Captain Cruc himself, lying propped across a rock, peering down at the village through a long tube of silvery metal. Beside him sat a boar-faced warrior of pointed, bristled ears, long tusks, and soft and wet-tipped snout.

It was just past sunset, the last glow draining from the western horizon, stars showing sharply and profusely in a clear sky. A warm night of late spring, with no breeze stirring a sweet and sultry air. Still, there seemed to be many fires burning in the village, making it ablaze with light.

Cruc continued examining the place for some moments, slowly sweeping the tube back and forth, pausing now and again to stare more intently at certain spots. Finally he lowered the tube and pronounced definitely:

"Well, it seems that tonight is going to be the night."

"Oh, yuh?" the other said in thick and guttural tones. "And just how can you be knowing that, Cap'n?"

"Because something's going on down there. Here Torc," he handed over the tube, "take this thing the towermen gave me."

"You mean I finally get to look through?" the boarhead said with childlike delight.

"Yes, yes," Cruc said impatiently. "Now just point that down there and take a look. And don't be startled. It makes things look very large."

The one called Torc examined the tube curiously, then lifted it and peered into one end.

"Ho!" he exclaimed in dismay, jerking his head back. "This thing is broken, Cap'n! It shrank that village down 'til I can't hardly see it!"

"Idiot," growled Cruc, snatching the tube away, reversing it and thrusting it back into Torc's hands. "Try now!"

Torc peered again. "Ah, that is better, Cap'n. Amazin'! Now it's like I was half as far away. I can see right inside. See each of the huts. Even see people movin' around!"

"Look at the main hall, that big hut there in the middle. Do you see what's going on?"

The boarhead looked. Through the miraculous tube he could see the front side and the door of the hall lit brightly by a large bonfire right before it. Scores of people were milling around outside and a constant stream of them was entering the structure.

"I do see, Cap'n!" Torc said excitedly. "Lots of 'em are going inside there."

"Some kind of meeting or ceremony," Cruc guessed. "From what I can tell, everyone in the whole village is going there. And that is going to give us our chance to move."

"Them havin' a gatherin' there don't mean they won't still be havin' their guards about," the boarhead pointed out.

"Maybe, but at least there might not be so many, and this gathering will be some distraction from what we've got to do."

"But enough for us to get down there safe?" Torc asked doubtfully.

Cruc fixed him with a hard look. "Listen, you," he said testily, "we've watched here for a dozen nights now. Every night it's been the same. Not only have they had lookouts on the wall and tower, but there have been some of them out seeing to the herds, bathing in the lake, just strolling about! Tonight, for the first time, there don't seem to be any extra folk around. I do not plan to sit up here all my life waiting for a better chance that will never come. We go!"

"Certainly, Cap'n. Certainly!" the boarface quickly agreed.

They waited longer, watching the village closely. Finally people stopped entering the main hall. Soon after they began to hear the faint strains of sprightly music drifting up to them

hrough the still air. Cruc swept the village one last time with
he tube. No one could be seen moving anywhere within the
valls. Only a single guard seemed to be strolling the palisade
valkway, his gaze scanning solely toward the north. Only one
ookout occupied the high watchtower, and he seemed to be
lozing propped up by his spear.

"The way is even more open than I had hoped," Cruc said
vith glee. He slapped the other's shoulder. "Come. Let's move
uickly while we've the chance!"

The two Fomor moved south along the valley rim, then
rept painstakingly down the slope, slipping from hiding point
o hiding point to finally reach the lakeshore opposite the vil-
age. They pushed their way through a screen of bushes that
ined the shore there to reach the water's edge. From the cover
hey peered cautiously out.

Across the stretch of water sat the village upon its hill,
rilliantly highlighted by the many fires, sharply reflected in the
nirror of the calm lake surface. The sound of the music came
uite clearly to them here, the boom of drums, twang of harps,
nd whistle of pipes combining in another lively tune.

And still, not a soul showed in the village streets.

"All right," Cruc said with satisfaction, "we're safe for
ow. Give me the vial."

The other pulled the square glass container from within his
eather jerkin and handed it over. "Why didn't you just carry it
ourself?" he asked.

"It . . . uh . . . it's your job," Cruc said quickly and
aguely. He examined the vial closely in the poor light. "Now,
vhat did Tethra say? Something about turning the lid to the
ight place and then . . ."

"Just yank the thing out, Cap'n!" said Torc, snatching the
vial back. "Here, I'll do it!"

Cruc stared as his minion simply grabbed the square stop-
oer of the vial and give it a great yank.

"No . . . wait!" he said aghast. "It might spill!"

But Torc kept on yanking, thick muscles bulging with
strain.

"I . . . can't . . . get . . . the . . . cursed . . .
thing . . . out!" he said through gritted teeth. He gave it up,
panting with his exertion.

"Give it back to me, fool!" Cruc snapped, tearing it from
Torc's grasp. "We can't waste any more time. Someone could
appear at any moment. There's a method for this. Now, let me

see . . ." He examined the bottle closely once again. "Ah right! There's a mark on the vial and another on the stopper's rim. I'm to turn the stopper, match them up, and the top will come right off."

He turned the stopper until the two etched marks touched. He put both thumbs against the stopper's base and pressed upward, gently at first, then with increasing force, finally grunting with the effort. It wouldn't budge.

"Come right off, will it, Cap'n?" Torc said, watching the struggle interestedly.

"Shut up, Torc," Cruc growled. He inserted a broad, thick thumbnail into the crack between lid and vial, prying upward. With a pop the stopper at last came free, flying off to drop into the bushes. But there was also a sharp cracking noise and a sharper oath from Cruc.

"Ah!" he said in pain, looking at the thumb. "Broke my nail half off!" He looked at the opened vial. "Well, at least the cursed thing's out. All right, then!" He held the vial out to Torc. "Take it!"

The boarhead took hold of it. Cruc took a few steps back from him.

"Pour it in," Cruc ordered. "Get right up to the edge. Make certain it all goes into the water."

Torc stepped right to the lake's edge, holding the vial out over the water. Then he looked back to his captain.

"There wouldn't be any danger in doin' this, would there, Cap'n?" he asked.

"Of course there's not. It's safe!" Cruc assured him. But when the other turned away from him again, he quickly took another few paces back.

Torc upended the vial. From within, a thick, deep golden substance poured, like purest honey, oozing down in long strands until droplets broke loose to fall into the lake. As each drop touched the water, it began instantly to spread across the surface. By the time the last of the liquid had dribbled into the water, a large patch of the gold, glistening like fat globules floating upon a stew, had crept out several feet from shore and was expanding rapidly.

Torc righted the empty vial and turned to his captain. "All in," he announced.

"So it's done then," Cruc said. He looked at the spreading slick and the empty vial, then across to the bright village. "I'm not certain I like this," he said in grim tones. "This kind of cowardly treachery. A stand-up fight, blade to blade, that's one thing. But this?" He shook his head. "There's a twisted evil to those towermen, that's certain." Then he shrugged. "Well, nothing for it now. Let's be away from here."

"What about the vial, Cap'n?" asked Torc.

"Bring it."

"But the top," Torc said, looking around him. "It flew off somewhere."

Cruc also looked around. In the tangle of brush and the darkness, it was invisible.

"We can't take the time to search," he said irritably. He looked at the open vial. "Even empty, that thing might be dangerous. Leave it too. Toss it away. It'll never be found."

The boarhead tossed the vial into a thicket. It vanished from sight. Cruc nodded and started away, heading back toward the safety of the slope.

"Wait a moment, Cap'n!" Torc said, following after him. "I thought you said it *wasn't* dangerous!"

"Just keep still and keep walking," Cruc shot back. "Let's get away from here before we're seen."

But as they moved off, neither realized that they had *already* been seen. Their curses and tussles over the vial had attracted a temporary but most interested inhabitant of the lake. The silver-haired head of Muirgheal had poked out from a nearby stand of rushes to watch the Fomors' sinister activity.

Now, as they withdrew, the head moved out from the rushes as the being swam closer to see what manner of thing had been dumped into the pristine lake. The stain upon the surface was growing thinner as it spread, but it was still clearly visible as a brighter sheen upon the dark waters. Tentacles from it were expanding outward with astonishing rapidity, reaching out toward the shining being, writhing snakelike almost as if alive.

Muirgheal waited no longer. With a look of horror the being turned, swam swiftly away toward the still unfouled center of the lake, and dived into its deepest point. Only moments afterward, Muirgheal was reemerging, this time on the side of the lake just outside the village palisade, and this time mounted upon the bizarre green steed.

They rode up from the shore, stopping close beside the log wall. The silver-haired one looked back toward the lake. The insidious stain had grown now to cover more than half its waters, so thinned that it was barely visible but still sending its tendrils stretching forth to pollute the pure surface that was left. Muirgheal slid to the ground and spoke urgently to the beast:

"I must enter this place, Augh-iska," the being told it, patting its broad nose. "I have to find Lir. But you must get away from here to hide. You cannot go back into that lake. It's something of great evil that's brewing there. Go to the woods. I'll come for you when I can."

The creature nodded its great head in understanding. Then it turned and loped away, headed for the eastern valley slope and the forest beyond.

Muirgheal watched it safely out of sight. Then the being turned and thrust a slender, pale arm into the crack between two logs. Though the space seemed no wider than a sword's blade is thin, the arm miraculously slid through. The small body followed, slipping inside as simply as if the body had been reduced to no more than a sheet of finest gauze.

Once past the barrier, the body once again expanded to full size and solidness. Muirgheal paused, looking warily around. No one was visible. The gathering was still on. The sound of its bright music still danced in the quiet air.

The silver-haired one began to follow the sound, moving cautiously from hut to hut. But soon the music stopped. Muirgheal moved on toward where it had last been, passing a final row of huts and coming into the cleared central portion of the village where the main hall sat.

Light from the bonfire outside it showed that no one was around. Muirgheal crept up to the oval building and moved about the curved wall to a window. Its wood shutters stood open in response to the evening's warmth.

Very, very carefully, the bright-haired one peeped in.

The hall was packed with nearly the entire population of the village, now standing in rapt silence. At one end of the long room, Nemed himself stood upon a small platform, one hand hovering over each of the two heads bowed before him. They were the heads of Dagda and Moire.

"And there could be no finer sign of our true success in our new settlement than this," the pioneer leader was saying with delight, face beaming. "In the marriage of these two fine examples of our excellent youth, in this first union amongst us since our coming here, we see the future. We look forward to a time of true peace where our families will prosper and where our yet unborn children will know only a life in their own free land."

He cast his gaze upward. "And if there are powers here who look in beneficence on our endeavors, then may they smile especially upon this momentous joining."

He put a hand down upon the top of Dagda's head. "My Dagda, who I feel for as for my own son, I here pass into the care and keeping of Moire, knowing he is drawn there willingly by his own love."

He put the other hand upon her raven-haired head. "And Moire, who we all know as a good and courageous woman, I pass into the care and keeping of Dagda, with the assurance that she goes freely and with full heart."

He raised both hands. The two looked up to him.

Nemed's gaze passed around the room, over the huge crowd. "And now," he intoned, "with the blessings of all of our people, your marriage will be well and eternally joined."

The couple turned to face the others. They raised clasped hands high. At that move, all voices in the company broke forth in a single, hearty, and joyous sound of acclamation.

With the ceremony concluded, the gathering dissolved into a happy, confused mass of celebration. Some mobbed the newlyweds. More mobbed the long tables laden with food and drink.

The bright gaze of Muirgheal scanned the milling crowd carefully. Finally the shining being glimpsed the disguised Lir moving back from the group around Dagda and Moire. He got a large mug of drink for himself and then found a spot by the wall. Here he fell into a talk with Nuada and others of the men.

Muirgheal crept on around the outside of the hall to a spot just opposite the wall from Lir. One slender arm slid into a mere crack in the clay daub surface and poked through the woven sticks of the wattling behind as easily as if slipping through a gaping hole. The hand thrust out into the room just behind Lir, out of sight of the other men. Two fingers of it formed a pincers as it darted in at him.

"Ow!" he exclaimed, slapping a hand to his backside.

"What is it, Liam?" asked Nuada.

"I don't know," he began, turning his head to glance behind him. "Something just . . ."

His gaze fell on the slender, pale hand thrusting out from the wall. One finger of it crooked to make a clear "come to me" sign at him.

"Just twinged," he finished quickly, looking back to Nuada with a smile. "Just these old bones of mine. In fact, you know, I do think they're cramping up on me from just standing about here so long. It you don't mind, I think I'll take a bit of a walk outside."

"Well, I'll go with you," Nuada offered.

"No, no," Lir said, lifting a staying hand. "No need at all for that. I'll be just a few moments. One brisk turn about the village. Stay here. Enjoy the festivities."

And thus excusing himself, he made his way off through the crowd.

He looked around for Graikos as he went, finally spotting the servant tucking into a great pile of food with gusto. Leaving him to it, the disguised man went out alone into the night.

But he did not go unnoticed. For Mathgen—standing alone and aloof as usual, disdainfully scanning the raucous crowd—took note of the bearded man leaving. Curious, he followed Lir outside.

He emerged in time to see the other just disappearing around the curve of the big hut's wall. He followed, but then stopped and pulled back quickly as he heard the man's voice ahead, speaking sharply in irritation:

"I just want to know what kind of madness brought you here, Muirgheal. Do you have any idea how dangerous it is?"

"Of course I do," replied a voice much like a child's. "But . . ."

"I'm already very much put out with you, you know," the other interrupted. "You deliberately disobeyed me. You let Dagda see you. Worse, you helped him with your powers! As a result they've begun to believe some kind of spirit or god is out there. I should exile you for that alone! And now, this!"

Mathgen eased around the curve of the hut slowly. Finally the two figures came into view—the one he knew as Liam and a small silver-haired being. He stared and listened in fascination.

"But I *had* to come," Muirgheal said with urgency. "Please listen, Lir. I saw the Fomor pouring something into the lake. It's a poison. I know it is!"

"Poison?"

"What else would the Fomor sneak here in the night to pour in? You have to warn them."

"Warn them?" Lir echoed. "It would be a bit difficult to do that without the risk of revealing myself to them."

"Then do something yourself. You must have some magic that could destroy it."

"That's an even *more* certain way to let them discover who I am."

"You have to do it!" Muirgheal insisted. "They use that water for drinking, for bathing, for the herds and crops. You have to help them!"

"Now you sound like Graikos," Lir said exasperatedly. "Always at me about it: Help them. Help them. Help them!"

"And what other choice is there except to watch them die?" the shining one challenged hotly.

"Now calm down," he said firmly. "You don't even know for certain that this *is* a poison. First I have to find that out. *Then* I'll decide. Is that enough for you?"

Muirgheal considered, then nodded. "I suppose it has to be."

"All right, then. For now, you must get out of here. Go around the lake to the far side. I'll meet you there later."

"Later?"

"I'm certainly not going to risk bringing suspicion on myself by stealing away now. At this moment they are plunging heedless and headlong into the first celebration they've had since coming here. They are feasting and they are drinking ale at a rate I have never seen. It won't be long before they grow very, very sated indeed and bring things to an end. As soon as it's quiet, I'll come to you. And only then."

"But in the meantime, what of the danger to them?" Muirgheal asked.

"There'll be no danger," he said dismissingly. "Most of them will be too drunk to remember they even *have* a lake until morning. Maybe not even then. So just go."

"I will," the other reluctantly agreed.

"But one other thing, Muirgheal," he said, his voice taking on a low and warning tone, "do no more to help them. No more at all, do you understand? If you make another contact, if you even let one of them catch a glimpse of you again, I swear to you that you will be exiled permanently from this land."

"I . . . I understand," Muirgheal told him, but through teeth gritted in frustration. The silver-haired being turned sharply on its heel and fled away, vanishing into the night.

Lir looked around him to be certain there was still no one about, then started back. He didn't see Mathgen, who swiftly retreated before him. By the time Lir rounded the curve of the meeting hall to the door, the wily eavesdropper had reached the shelter of a heap of logs beside the bonfire.

He peered out from it as Lir went back inside. His eyes were narrowed, glinting with a scheming light. His mouth drew upward in a cunning smile.

"So, my friend," he murmured, "now maybe we'll discover just what you *really* are, 'Lir'!"

# Chapter 14

# The Cleansing

The one known to the Nemedians as Liam stood at one side of the village central hall, marveling at the sight before him.

"These people have much greater stamina than I'd ever have thought," he murmured to himself.

Dagda and Moire had long since gone off to their marriage bed. But the rest of the gathering had hung doggedly on and on, stringing out their revels as long as possible.

Still, it couldn't be much longer now. A majority of the company had surrendered to fatigue, inebriation, and bloated stomachs and gone off to their own beds. A number more—largely male—had been overcome by the uncommon and excessive amount of drink and were dozing where they'd sat or fallen. The disguised Lir scanned the few score who were left, with a calculating eye.

Nemed himself was still present, and—as role model of dignity and decorum to his flock—had stayed reasonably sober. But he was not a young man, and the late hour had made him clearly quite drowsy. Nuada and a few other of the most hardy men and equally hardy women were exceedingly intoxicated but holding up well, singing riotous songs and jigging to the tunes played by what musicians were still able. It was difficult to judge how long they would hold out. For the rest the end was coming speedily. Even as Lir watched, a pair of men went staggering out into the night, arm in arm to keep one another up. One more drained his cup and then went abruptly limp, slipping down from his bench to the floor, already deep in drunken slumber.

But while Lir watched that one falling into sleep, elsewhere in the village another was awakening.

It was the raven-haired Moire who stirred fitfully, opened her eyes, and looked around her at the dark interior of the hut. She had been dozing, but for only a brief time. The long, vigorous, and passionate first lovemaking with her husband had left her far too exhilarated to really rest. She was also very warm, her body all but burning from the close air within the hut and the heat of love, her long shift soaked by perspiration and clinging to her form.

She turned to look at Dagda. The big man was soundly and blissfully asleep, chest heaving rhythmically, face relaxed into soft lines of content and peace. She caressed his arm, running her hand down it, onto his massive thigh. He stirred and gave a soft sigh but stayed asleep.

Her disappointed gaze went from him to the pale outside light shining in around the doorflap. Outside, where she could feel the cooling, soothing breath of the night air on her fevered body.

She climbed from their bed and padded barefoot to the door, pulling back the flap to look out. The marriage cottage for this new pair had been built especially by the master carpenter Luchtine. For privacy's sake it had been erected a bit separately from the rest, outside the circles of the other huts and atop the bluff that overlooked the lake.

The village was all but quiet by this time. She could see no one moving about. The only sound was the faint plinking of a single harp being very badly played.

She took a deep breath. But it was warm and heavily scented by the hanging pungent wood smoke of the many celebration fires. She stepped outside, finding only the still, sultry air that offered no relief.

Then her gaze fell upon the lake stretched out below, clean, glistening, cool. The gently rippling waters shone more brightly than she had ever seen. So inviting. A place for real relief. To plunge into its soothing depths. To feel refreshing waves play across her heated body. And no one around to disturb her or to see.

She glanced back into the hut. Dagda lay breathing slowly, quietly, still soundly asleep. She started down the steep pathway to the lakeshore.

On the shore opposite, meantime, Muirgheal sat hidden in the shelter of the bordering shrubbery. The being fumed impatiently as moment after moment passed without a sign of Lir.

Then a movement from across the lake caught the silver-haired one's eye.

She saw the figure moving down the pathway from the village to the shore. Was it Lir?

The bright eyes focused on the figure, able even with the darkness and distance to take in its details. No. Not Lir. It was the same dark-haired woman that Muirgheal had seen being linked in ceremony to that huge warrior the shining being had helped three times before. Just what was it that she was planning to do there now, alone?

The answer to that soon became abundantly, horribly clear. Moire reached the lakeshore. She paused a moment to look out over the shining waters. The film of poison had spread to cover the whole surface by now, grown so thin as to be all but invisible. Muirgheal's sharp eyes could still detect its unnatural, slimy gleam. Moire's could not.

In a simple, swift move, she slipped the long gown from her tall, lithe form. She stepped to the very edge of the lake, stretching out a toe to test its waters.

Appalled, Muirgheal began to rise, mouth opening to cry a warning, arms lifting to desperately wave her back.

But the threatening words of master Lir came echoing back: ". . . even let them catch a glimpse of you again . . . you will be exiled permanently from this land."

Cowed by the recollection, Muirgheal sank back. The being sat helplessly, peering out, its child's face aged by lines of anguish as Moire stepped into the shallows, waded out, and dived neatly forward to be swallowed by the lake.

She was out of sight for a moment. Then her body shot to the surface in an explosion of white spray. She stood again, waist deep, splashing the water up and over her with both hands. The watching Muirgheal could see it all with agonizing clarity and detail. The water streamed in her long hair. It ran from the bold lines of her face, down her long neck, across her bosom. Her gleaming arms struck shivering silver paths through the surface, lifted to trail droplets in strings of light. All her form glowed with the liquid that covered her.

"By good Danu," Muirgheal breathed in agony. "What am I letting happen here?"

The brushes rustled suddenly nearby. The being turned to see Lir pushing through them to reach the lake's edge. He carried with him the bulging sack that was normally in the care of Graikos. That servant had been left dozing peacefully elsewhere.

"At last!" Muirgheal said. "Lir, please, quickly, warn her!"

"Warn her?" he repeated, at a loss. "Who?"

"That woman, over there!" The being pointed out across the lake.

They looked out. But it was already too late. Moire was emerging from her bath, body still shining from the clinging water.

She stood poised with unconscious grace for a long moment on the shore, letting the air play cooly, deliciously across her, her head back, the thick flow of her dark hair showing in striking contrast against the whiteness of her skin. Then she slipped her gown back on.

"A most healthy young woman," Lir said admiringly as she turned and started back up the path from shore.

"She swam, Lir," Muirgheal pointed out emphatically. "I watched her swim. I didn't stop her. I could have, but I didn't, because you commanded me not to!"

"You did very well," he said calmly. "Why are you so concerned? She seemed quite fine to me. No damage from her swim. Are you certain there really *is* something poisonous here?"

"I thought that's what *you* came here to judge."

"Very well," he said. He set down the sack and fished within it for a time, at last pulling forth a wide, shallow basin of polished silver. He knelt at the water's edge and carefully, neatly, and very slowly scooped a portion of the lake surface inside.

He peered at the basin's contents closely for several moments. He shook the bowl slightly, swirling the liquid against the sides. A faint, thin line of an oily residue showed there.

"Hummm," he finally said in a noncommittal tone. "Well, there *may* be something unusual floating in this. But it's very hard to tell. And there's no way at all to know if there's anything dangerous about it."

"The Fomor poured it from some kind of little jar," Muirgheal said. "They tossed it away right about here."

"See if you can find it," he said. "Anything might be of help."

The shining one at once began to move about through the undergrowth, the piercing eyes searching, probing into every shadow. Soon there was a little cry of victory and Muirgheal was seizing up an object to carry back to Lir.

"This is it," the being said, handing it to him. "And it had some kind of lid that they had quite a time in getting out."

Lir examined the vial with immense interest. He scrutinized the precise shape of it and the transparent material of which it was formed. He peered inside to see a tiny remnant of the amber liquid adhering in the corners at the bottom. Then his eyes fell upon the markings etched into one side.

"By our Great Queen!" he gasped in dismay, looking up to the silver-haired one. "Muirgheal, it's from *them*! From the Great Ones! The Ancient Powers! These Fomor have the help of those within the Tower of Glass!"

"Lir, no!" the other cried in equal shock. "That can't be true!"

"It is. I know this workmanship. I recognize the writing. It has to come from *them*."

"What does it mean?" asked Muirgheal.

"Maybe that they see Nemed's clans as such a threat to them that they have been forced to act themselves."

"But if they've chosen to help, then the danger to these people is many times greater than we thought," the shining being said.

"A fact you should have considered before helping them to settle here," he pointed out. "I told you that blowing their ships far away from this 'blessed isle' would be a greater service."

"I know, I know," Muirgheal said with chagrin. "But that doesn't matter any more. They're here, and they must be warned."

"Warned?" Lir echoed.

"Yes," the other said with rising certainty and force. "They have to be warned. They have to know the truth. *You* have to tell them, Lir. Make it clear what it is they really face. Give them a chance to leave here, if they wish. And if they choose to stay, then tell them you will help them with your full powers."

"Now I'm convinced you have gone totally mad!" Lir said in disbelief. "You want me to just give the whole truth to them? To reveal myself? To expose what I really am?"

"If necessary to save these people, yes," Muirgheal stubbornly returned.

"Well I'm sorry, but that is just what we can *never* do. The last thing we want is to have any direct entanglement with them. It's been bad enough to risk revealing our presence to those Fomor scum. But if the Ones of the Tower ever even *suspect* that we still exist, we will have not only disobeyed our Queen, but betrayed our entire race."

"You don't think knowing the Ancient Ones are directly involved makes it even more important to act?"

"Yes, act. Act to protect ourselves even more carefully. Remember, our task here was to keep watch on our old enemies and make certain that they never encountered us. It was certainly *not* to instigate such a contact ourselves."

"To make certain we stayed well hidden, you mean," Muirgheal argued. "To be sure we could safely continue to live in fear of them as we always have. Well I say no to that. I say our responsibility is to help these others who have earned the Great Ones' wrath, and who have thus become our allies."

"Our 'responsibility' is to insure that those of our own race survive," he shot back in adamant tone, "not to risk them to save some foolish pack of mortals. There will be no more argument about this, Muirgheal. None!"

"Meaning that you will do nothing," the silver-haired being said sullenly.

"I didn't say that," he corrected. "These mortals are fools, but they are also much braver than any I've met before, and eminently more likable. Although it is against my better judgment, I will do what I can to protect them, so long as no one knows of it. In other words, I can see to restoring this lake."

The being brightened. "You can? Then, you know what's been put in it?"

"Well, not precisely," Lir admitted. "The words on that vial mean nothing to me. But I think we can rest assured that if it comes from the Ones of the Tower, it is extremely toxic indeed."

"But can you do something about it? Destroy it?"

"Of course. Well, not destroy it, but cleanse the water. Our sorcerers developed methods for dealing with such horrific creations of the Great Ones long ago. Here," he handed the vial to his companion, "hold this. I've got to find the one."

He again opened the bulging sack and began to fish within it. "It should be here . . . somewhere." He went deeper, hand

searching about within. "No. Must be deeper yet." He thrust
his arm in up to the shoulder, rummaging through objects in
the depths.

"Ah!" he said in triumph, pulling the arm out, a wooden
box clutched in his hand.

Muirgheal looked at the box in curiosity.

"Good thing Danu insisted I come on this mission well
supplied," he said, brushing the dust of antiquity from the polished dark wood and flipping open a gold latch. "It's likely
been centuries since this was last used."

He lifted the lid, revealing a coarse, white, crystalline powder, much like common salt.

"What does it do?" the shining one asked.

"The simplest explanation is a demonstration," he said.
"Just watch."

He went to the lake's edge, overturned the box, and simply
dumped the powder onto the surface.

It reacted instantly and almost as if alive. The grains spread
out, forming a ring that expanded with astonishing rapidity.

Growing thinner as it expanded, it widened out from where
Lir stood until a fine white line of the floating grains had totally
encompassed the lake, touching the whole lakeshore, surrounding the entire slick.

Then, more slowly but as smoothly and steadily, the ring
began to contract, forcing the slime trapped within to do the
same.

"You see," said Lir to a fascinated Muirgheal, "the crystals
are 'trained' I suppose you can say. They have the ability to
encircle, contain, gather in the offending substance. I've no idea
what kind of magic created them."

"Great magic indeed," said Muirgheal, watching the process in awe.

The slick was already only half its previous size; becoming
denser again under the tightening pressure from the ring; growing more dark, more visible; revealing its greasy, ghastly true
form.

"Yes, our sorcerers are quite brilliant," Lir agreed. "The
Ancient Ones could have had this remedy, I understand. It was
offered to them, as were many others for their self-inflicted ills.
Too bad. Had those blind, arrogant fools listened to us instead
of branding us dreamers and lunatics and driving us
away . . ." He sighed and shook his head with regret at what
might have been.

The shining contaminant had by now been compressed to a tiny slick of thick amber substance floating on the lake's surface right before Lir's feet. The confining circle of fine crystals had also grown denser as it contracted, forming a broad, white line.

"Well, that does it, I think," Lir announced. "A most obedient little powder, eh?"

He leaned down with the silver bowl and carefully scooped both the ring and the trapped substance into its confines.

"Just fits," he said, looking into the bowl. "Too bad the crystals can't be separated again. Ah, well. A small sacrifice. Here then, hold out that vial."

Muirgheal obediently held out the container while Lir very cautiously, very steadily poured the bowl's contents in. The vial just held the combined volume of the two materials. He filled it without spilling a single drop.

"Ah good. That's done!" he said with a tone of definite relief. He took the vial from Muirgheal and examined it. The white crystals had all floated to the outside, still surrounding their captive.

"Now what do we do with it?" Muirgheal asked.

"Well, it can't be destroyed, of course, and unfortunately," he said. "That's the trouble with so many of the gruesome creations of the Old Ones. The crystals will help to keep it trapped inside the vial, but only that. Can you find the stopper?"

"Give me a moment."

Muirgheal searched the bushes again and soon retrieved it. He shoved it back into the vial and twisted it tight.

"A job well done," he said. He looked back out over the quiet lake, now glistening naturally beneath the stars, and nodded. "There you are then, Muirgheal. Your lake returned to its pristine self once again, the villagers safe, no harm done and no one's the wiser. All that's left for us is to dispose of this." He lifted the vial.

"Dispose of it?" said Muirgheal. "How?"

"Simple. We take it to somewhere very remote and very desolate, we dig a very, very deep hole, we bury this . . . abomination, and we hope that it is never, never found again. That's the best we can hope for."

"The Augh-iska and I could take it to the bottom of the sea," the shining being suggested. "It might be safer there."

"That's a quite good idea," Lir said. "Where is that beast of yours?"

"I sent it to wait for me in the woods."

"Then let's go to it right now and I'll see you on your way," he said briskly. "The sooner this is dealt with the better."

"I agree," said Muirgheal.

"You can take it down to one of those dreadful deep places so dark that even the fish have their own lights," he said as they started away. "No mortal will ever be able to find it there."

His voice faded and the night swallowed the two. But as they disappeared from the scene, another figure suddenly appeared in it, rising up from the cover of the shrubs not far away.

It was Mathgen, and the image of Lir's bulging sack of wonders still hung tantalizingly before his glinting, covetous eyes.

Meantime, in the village above, Moire had returned to her marriage bed. She lay down close beside her husband who stirred at feeling her warmth once again against him. He rolled toward her, slipping an arm about her shoulders. The two cuddled tightly together.

Moire sighed softly in contentment. Then a look of sharp pain tightened her face. Her hand went to her belly, the palm pressing hard against it.

The abrupt movement roused Dagda to half wakefulness. "What's wrong?" he muttered in a heavy voice.

"It's nothing," she said assuringly, relaxing the pressure of her hand. "A small twinge of muscle. From too much excitement. Too much activity. It's gone now." She kissed him softly on the cheek. "Goodnight my love."

He settled back into sleep, still holding her close. But for a time she lay with her hand pressed to her stomach, staring up into the dark, her brow furrowed by a faint but nagging concern.

# Chapter 15

# Horror

The fall winds keened in the branches of the trees, worrying the last still-clinging leaves.

Within the village of Nemed's people, final preparations for the coming winter were nearing completion. The last chinks in wattled walls and thatched ceilings were being sealed against the rising cold winds. The last supplies of dried and preserved foods were being stored away. Cattle and sheep were being moved to wintering pens close by the village and provided with stacks of feed grasses harvested from the richly producing fields.

Altogether the growing season had been a successful one for the new settlers. The season of death held no terrors for them now that they had adequate food, fuel, and shelter to defend against it.

But while most faced the coming winter calmly, even cheerfully, and went busily about their tasks, in the home of Dagda, there was worry.

The big man paced fretfully about the central firepit where a warm fire blazed against the cold and darkness of the autumn night just falling outside. He paused constantly to look toward a section of the room blocked off by movable wickerwork partitions to form a private chamber. From within it came low voices, occasional soft moans. At wide-spaced but regular intervals there came a sharper cry.

One of the partitions was moved aside enough to allow passage of a man from within the screened room. It was the healer Diancecht.

As the man came out, Dagda caught a brief glimpse across his shoulder into the space. He saw the form of Moire lying upon the bed, her swollen belly visible even beneath the layers of warm coverings.

"Is she all right?" he asked the healer anxiously.

"She has some discomfort," Diancecht said in his careful way. "Of course, that's to be expected. Her time is coming very soon now."

Dagda shook his head. "But it's wrong!" he said. "Her mother's said it to me. I've heard the others whispering of it. This has come too fast."

"Has it indeed?" said Diancecht. "And how can you know that?"

"We've been wed less than half a year now. You know it yourself."

"And?" the healer asked, eying him with lifted eyebrow.

Dagda saw the look, caught the implication, and colored in indignation. "I know what you're thinking. I swear to you now, we had no relationship of that kind until we'd wed. I did honor to her."

"Of course you did," Diancecht said. "But is it possible that . . . she . . ."

Dagda took a step toward him. His color deepened, but in outright anger this time. His voice was a dangerous growl: "Watch your words, healer. It's deadly ground you're treadin' on. Moire is a woman of greater honor than myself."

The doctor's equanimity was for the first time punctured by this. He stepped back, lifting a hand.

"I believe you," he said with great conviction. "Absolutely." There came another sharp sound of pain from beyond the partitions. He glanced to it, then back to the big man. "That, however, is rather unimportant at this point, don't you agree? Whatever the cause for it, your child is coming now."

Dagda's anger subsided before this logic. "Yes, yes," he agreed. "We have to see to Moire."

"Good. Then I had best be off to fetch those who will help deliver it."

"Fetch?" Dagda echoed. "Won't you be doing this yourself?"

"I am a mender of broken bones, a binder of wounds, a healer of sickness," Diancecht explained. "For the bringing of babies into the world there are others much more proficient than I. I will fetch our best midwife, and Moire's mother as well." He put a comforting hand to the worried man's arm. "Have no fears, my friend. They will see to it."

"Go quickly then," Dagda told him.

Diancecht started for the door, but the big man called after him:

"Wait. What about Moire? Can I go in to her?"

Diancecht paused at the door. "You can. But don't tire her," he admonished. "She will be needing all her strength."

He went out into the stiffening wind of what promised to be a blustery night. Dagda moved toward the partitioned area. Carefully he moved one screen aside. Quietly he entered the space. Moire was lying still upon the bed. Her face seemed especially white and small, surrounded by the billowing black mass of her hair. Her breathing was swift and shallow. But her eyes were open, and they turned toward him as he approached.

"My love," she said in a low and fluttering voice.

He knelt beside the bed. He put a massive hand out to gently stroke her brow. "Moire. How do you feel?"

She gave a little grimace. "To tell the truth, I never have felt worse."

"Diancecht says that's to be expected," he said in soothing tones.

"And just how would he know that, being only a man?" she asked with an edge of irritation. "Oh!" she cried. Her body suddenly went taut. "Take my hand!" she ordered through clenched teeth, trusting one out to him.

He grabbed it in both his own and held it tightly while the spasm drew her body rigid, held it quivering, her head thrown back, belly thrust up even higher. Then she relaxed to lie limp, panting for breath.

"My wife," he said in distress, "I wish that I could suffer this pain for you."

"So . . . do . . . I!" she gasped out. Then she fixed her gaze on him, adding with quick regret: "I'm sorry. I know there's only truth in what you said. I'm just so . . . so afraid!"

"I understand," he told her.

"No. No, you don't. I've never felt afraid, not for myself. I feared for you when you were gone. I've felt worry for my parents. But I've never felt fear or helplessness in myself. Now I lie here, taken and ruled by something I can't control, and I feel very afraid."

"There is no need to control it," he told her. "It is nature who rules in this. Things will happen with you as they are supposed to do."

"Will they?" she challenged. "Dagda, there is something in this I can't explain. I know that I know nothing at all about it, but still, the feeling . . . it's so strange. It's . . ."

She cut off as another contraction seized her and drew her rigid, quaking with the strain. He held on tightly to her hand again. A prolonged cry of agony was drawn from her as the pain held on, fading as the spasm at last subsided.

Her body relaxed again, but the ordeal had clearly taken much more out of her. She looked at him, the fear now showing openly in her drawn face and wide, glistening eyes.

"Dagda, if I die . . ." she began.

"That you will not!" he said with certainty. "You are too strong. Stronger than any."

"But listen, please!" she persisted. "If I do, promise me you will remember our time. It was short. But we had that at least. That happy time."

"There will be more of it," he told her. "Don't think of that. Think of this." He put a hand lightly upon the swell of her belly. "Put your mind only to this, Moire. Use all your courage, all your will, and you . . ."

Another spasm interrupted him, and he once more hung on as she was wracked by the contraction's pain.

"Moire," he anxiously said to the panting woman when it had ended, "are you all right?"

The last paroxysm seemed to have left her almost drained of strength. Still, with an effort, she opened her mouth to speak.

But she got no chance. Two robust women of middle age bustled in and briskly took charge.

"Very well, young man, we'll see to this," a sharp-featured and grey-haired one of the pair said brusquely to him. "You just go outside."

He hesitated. But the other woman—whose jet-black hair and handsome features identified her as Moire's mother—took him by an arm and said more gently, "Yes, my son. It's better this way. Please, wait out there."

He allowed her to usher him out of the space. The partition wall was closed tight behind him.

Outside he found Diancecht waiting.

"I thought you might also need someone with you right now," the healer explained with a rare warm smile.

"Thank you," Dagda said with feeling. "You truly are a friend."

Diancecht sat down by the fire to wait. The fretful Dagda took up his continuous pacing again. From inside the space came sounds of direction and encouragement from the two women, mixed with growing sounds of effort and pain.

"Hold on, Moire," came her mother's voice. "It's very close now."

"That's it, girl," said the other woman. "Bear down. Yes, yes, it's coming. More. More. Harder. I see the head. Oh, yes. I see the . . ."

There was a moment of stunned silence. Then a shrill scream of terror rippled through the room, joined quickly by another.

The two men rushed for the place together. Dagda tore aside a partition, revealing the scene beyond.

Midwife and mother had both recoiled from the bed to stand rigid, quaking, eyes staring in horror.

The men's eyes went also to the thing, the object newly born from a now mercifully unconscious Moire, the monstrosity that lay quivering upon the bed.


The fall wind was now sharp and tinged with winter-like chill. The night was black and moonless as Dagda carried the bundle through the village streets to the door of Diancecht's hut, the healer himself close behind.

Diancecht pulled back the door flap to let the big warrior pass inside. The hut's interior was a crowded place, its walls lined with shelves holding jars, basins, cups, and boxes of his healing stuffs; its rafters hung with drying medicinal herbs and leaves; its floor space crowded with tables heaped with yet more of his materials and equipment.

Diancecht quickly swept one of the tables free of its objects and signed Dagda to put his load down there. The big warrior did this with alacrity, stepping back from the bundle to stare at it with an expression that mingled revulsion and relief.

The bearded one they knew as Liam came into the hut.

"What's wrong?" he asked. "I had word you wanted me to come here with all speed and secrecy. What . . ."

He stopped as his eyes fell on the bundle. Its wrapping cloths—white, soft linens meant to swaddle an infant—were stained with a mixture of oozing yellowish liquid and half-clotted, red-brown blood.

"I saw no need for others to know at this point," said Diancecht. "But you were the one whose opinion I had to have on this."

"What is it?" Liam asked in fascination, stepping toward the thing.

"We'll show you," said the healer. "Dagda, unwrap it."

But the big man continued to stand frozen and staring at the object in utter abhorrence.

Diancecht moved up past him to the table. With swift moves he unwrapped the cloths, then stepped back, giving Liam full view.

Now it was the bearded man's turn to stare in shock.

The object born from Moire carried not even a faint resemblance to anything human. It was a featureless, limbless mass, roughly egg-shaped. Its outer surface looked to be a pliant, leathery skin of yellow-gray, coated with a shining, mucus-like slime, and crisscrossed with what seemed to be bulging blue veins. And these veins were constantly, rhythmically throbbing as if blood pulsed through them.

"Can this be something alive?" Diancecht asked Lir.

"I . . . I don't know," he said, stepping closer to examine it. "Where did it come from?"

"Dagda's wife gave birth to it only moments ago," the healer stated flatly.

A spasm of pain crossed the big man's face at that. His eyes squeezed closed as if to block out the awful sight.

"Dagda's wife?" Liam repeated in astonishment.

"Yes, Moire, of the raven hair. Luckily she fell unconscious from the hard birth labor. We brought this away from her before she saw it."

"I know her," said the disguised Lir. An image of the woman was being recalled in his mind; an all-too-vivid picture of her emerging naked from the lake on her wedding night, the polluted waters glistening on her skin. And his own words also came back to toll like a bell of condemnation in his head: ". . . no harm done . . . no harm done . . ."

"By Danu. The Fomor!" he breathed aloud.

"What?" said Diancecht sharply. And Dagda also stepped forward to look down at him in surprise.

He hesitated, then hedged: "I mean, I think it *must* be the Fomor behind this. They've done something to cause it."

"Why would you think that?" challenged Diancecht, fixing him with a curious eye.

"Well, I know the kinds of things they're capable of," said Liam, struggling to keep things vague. "I have experience of them you don't. It's just the kind of thing that could only be caused by their evil. Yes, I say it was the Fomor who did this."

"The Fomor? Did what?" said a weak and fearful voice behind them.

The three men wheeled to see Moire herself standing at the door, wrapped in a bed covering. She was ghastly pale, wobbling badly, but on her feet.

"You took my baby," she said in great distress, moving forward. "Why? What's wrong . . ." She pushed through them before the surprised men could stop her, her gaze falling upon the thing so nakedly revealed.

She recoiled, eyes widening in something far beyond mere horror. And then she fainted.

Dagda caught her toppling form just as her mother and the midwife rushed in.

"You!" the big man snapped in anger. "Why didn't you keep her from here?"

"We couldn't stop her. No power could have kept her from her child."

"There's nothing to be done about it now," Diancecht said reasoningly. He took Moire and passed her into the hands of the women. "Take her back. This time keep her there. And she'll need much comforting when she awakens."

"You might lie to her," Liam suggested. "Convince her this was only a nightmare."

"What do you mean?" asked Moire's mother, glancing toward the thing the bodies of the three men half screened from her. "What do you mean to do?"

"It's best if neither you or she know anything of that," said Liam. His voice took on a commanding tone. "Now take her away from here. Quickly!"

The women complied, taking Moire back to her own hut. The three men returned their attention to the awful thing pulsing upon the table.

"Just what *do* we mean to do?" Diancecht asked.

"Destroy it," Liam said bluntly.

"What?" cried Dagda.

"You called me here for my opinion," Liam said. "You've heard it. Destroy this utterly. Forget it ever existed. That would be best for everyone."

"Then, you know what this thing is?" asked Diancecht.

"No," Liam admitted, "I don't. I don't know precisely what this is, but I know that if the Fomor are involved, you must face the likelihood that it is something very, very bad."

"But it's alive!" said Dagda, looking at the throbbing veins.

"If it is, it's not human, but only some thing that lived and was nurtured within your wife, like a parasite."

"Oh, my gods," Dagda groaned in agony at the grotesque idea.

"Isn't it possible that you are acting hastily?" the always cautious Diancecht put in. "Can we be certain of any of this: of the Fomor part, of this thing's dangerous nature? Perhaps a careful examination . . ."

"Would take time," Liam interrupted. "You haven't any to waste. Every *moment* that passes may be bringing disaster closer. You can't risk it—risk everyone."

"Everyone?" echoed Dagda. "From this one thing?"

"Yes!" Liam said with force. "My innocent friends, you can't even begin to contemplate the evils of which your enemies are capable. Listen to me. Believe me. I've tried to help you, to save you. I wouldn't lie to you. I know!"

Diancecht had listened thoughtfully to this. Now he nodded. "I believe him, Dagda. But it is a terrible decision. And, I'm afraid that it must be yours."

Clearly stunned by the notion, Dagda stood staring down at the object. Then he shook his head. "I . . . I can't make it. I have to think. I need more council. Nemed perhaps. Nuada surely. Maybe they can help. And you, Diancecht," he looked desperately to the healer, "you could examine this. I have to know the whole truth of what it is. Perhaps . . . inside . . ."

As if responding to his notion, there began a violent shuddering of the thing. In an instant the whole surface was bubbling and heaving as if something boiled violently within it.

There came an odd crackling, gurgling sound. The thing split, a long crack opening down one side.

Something slithered forth from it.

It was soft, shiny, legless, like a slug but longer than a hand. One end was tapered, the other blunt, with eyes on waving stalks and a round, sucking mouth. It oozed forth onto the tabletop trailing slime. Another followed it, then several more.

Liam and Dagda, revolted at the sight, stepped back. But the curious Diancecht leaned down toward the first one, scrutinizing it closely.

"Most interesting!" he proclaimed. "What kind of creature . . ."

It contracted its boneless body suddenly and then shot straight at him. Its sucking mouth connected with his neck and fixed there, leechlike.

Diancecht staggered backward, clawing at the thing. His mouth opened and a liquid, choking sound issued from his throat.

Dagda acted quickly. He snatched a smoldering brand up from the healer's fire. He grabbed Diancecht and pressed the wood's glowing tip square against the thing. It writhed and sizzled. The sucking mouth let go and it dropped to the floor. Dagda squashed it noisily with a massive foot.

"Thank you!" gasped the healer. A round mark on his neck was seeping blood.

"Look!" said Liam, pointing to the table.

The others turned to look. Masses of the slug-like things were pouring from the ruptured leathery egg, spewing forth in a torrent of viscous fluid, flooding across the table, dropping to the floor, slithering out in all directions, eye stalks twitching, mouths pulsing hungrily. And the ones which had been first out were already noticeably larger in size, now longer than a man's foot.

"They're growing!" cried Diancecht.

"Get back!" Dagda called in warning to Liam, but too late. Several of the creatures compressed their bodies and leaped; a powerful, spring-like move that sent them flying against the man with great force, knocking him from his feet.

He went down heavily, the sticky creatures swarming over him.

"Get them off him!" said Dagda, handing the brand to Diancecht. And while the healer ran to Liam's help, the big warrior grabbed up two more sticks, both ablaze this time.

Diancecht swiftly burned the creatures from Liam's body and dragged him from the reach of more. Dagda swept out with both torches at the teeming, shimmering mass that now covered half the floor, and they shrank back before the flames.

"Get behind me!" he shouted when he saw Liam again on his feet.

The two men obeyed him and he backed toward the door, swinging the torches to keep away the seemingly endless, rippling wave of creatures rapidly filling the room.

"Burn them!" shouted Liam. "Set everything afire! Burn them all!"

One creature now grown as long as his own forearm leaped at Dagda. He knocked it away with a well-aimed swing of a torch. With a powerful kick he overturned a table atop the advancing mass to slow it, then he stooped to ignite one of the straw pallets that carpeted the floor.

As it blazed up, he rose and touched a torch to a hanging festoon of drying leaves. The flames crackled up the perfect tinder to catch in the ceiling thatch.

The three men reached the door. The creatures were trying to move around the burning pallet and follow, clearly bent on escaping too. Sparks from the flaming ceiling already rained upon them.

"Get outside!" Dagda ordered, pushing the others out behind him.

He paused to jam one flaming stick into the dry sticks of the wattled wall beside the door and backed out. Just outside he stopped to toss his other torch up high onto the roof peak. It caught in the straw at once.

The added fire was by now unnecessary. The interior of the hut was already well ablaze. The creatures were caught within, bubbling, frying, shriveling away. Hundreds of small, shrill screams of death agony twined into one piercing wail.

The flammable hut was by this time fully involved, the roof sending up long tongues of flame into the black night sky. People were rushing in from all about the village. Graikos was one of the first among them.

"Master, are you all right?" he asked the disguised Lir.

"Yes, yes," the man started to assure him. But then he caught sight of Diancecht's wound revealed in the lurid glow from the blazing hut. His eyes dropped to his own arms where three identical rings were streaming blood.

"No!" he corrected. "Get my bag. Quickly." As Graikos ran off, he looked to the healer. "I've some powder that will help us," he explained. "I'm afraid all your own are gone."

"Little enough to pay if we destroyed those horrors," the healer replied.

"If we did," said the other.

With a whoosh the roof of the hut collapsed inward. A whirlwind of flame went coiling up from the inferno within.

"Nothing could survive that," said Dagda, looking into the heart of the blaze.

But even as he spoke, one of the creatures appeared in the doorway, tail smoldering, but still trying to crawl free.

Dagda drew his sword and rammed it through the thing, lifting it up. The creature writhed on the blade. Liquid from within it gushed out, steaming like something molten hot as it ran down the sword, etching its metal.

With a snarl of disgust the warrior threw both sword and impaled creature into the flames and backed away to join the other two men.

There came a sharp cry from behind. He whirled in dismay to see Moire just paces away from him.

She had been moving forward, dragging the two women who had no power to restrain her in her frenzy to return there.

But the sight of Dagda's skewering the wriggling abomination had stopped her, frozen her, left her staring in shuddering abhorrence.

"Moire!" he said.

She didn't hear him. This last shock was finally too much. Her mind could tolerate no more. He saw the light of utter madness flare in her eyes. Her mouth dropped open and she began to scream—a long, high, terrible wail of unbearable pain.

He stepped forward, but she moved more quickly. She broke away from the two women with such force that her own mother was cast onto the ground. She turned and plunged away, driving through the gathering crowd in a burst of crazed power.

"No! Moire! Stop her!" Dagda cried desperately, starting after her.

As swiftly as possible he struggled through the press after her. He came free of the crowd in time to see her running pell-mell through the open gate, her long hair and her blanket streaming behind her.

He put on all the speed he could. Still, when he reached the gate, he was too late.

Moire had already been swallowed by the cold, black night.

# Chapter 16

# The Last Plague

The door slid open, and once more Captain Cruc stepped from the strange lifting chamber into the entry room.

As before, the haughty one called Tethra accompanied him, while armed, helmeted guards flanked them just behind. As before, they immediately began to march briskly up the long corridor toward the space which opened beyond.

Different this time, however, was the fact that the space they headed for was not a black void but a pool of brilliant light.

They came out of the corridor and plunged into the light. Cruc's eyesight soon adjusted to the glare and took in the scene it revealed.

The large room itself was simple, unfurnished, with unadorned walls and a plain ceiling some three stories overhead. The light so starkly disclosing all of this came from enormous windows lining the room's whole outer wall. Each one was some two yards wide and two stories tall. All were set close together to provide an almost uninterrupted panoramic view of the blue daylit sky and the blue-green, sparkling sea as spectacularly seen from some two hundred feet above the ocean surface.

It should have been a most heady sight indeed, for a being

whose life had been lived no more than a story above ground. But Cruc was not overwhelmed. Indeed, he did not even take note of the breathtaking scene. His attention was all fixed on the thing which sat before the windows only a few paces ahead of him.

He was having his first real look at what they all addressed as Commander Balor.

His initial, general impression was that he faced a giant man-like being all clad in dark metal armor. Even seated upon a massive, square-cornered throne, the monstrous figure loomed up over twenty feet. When standing, it would come close to scraping the high ceiling with its head. It was shaped and proportioned like a brawny human's form, with huge arms and legs, broad torso, squared shoulders and barrel chest. But whatever the giant's true nature might have been was fully shielded by the encompassing layer of armor.

Everything was covered by metal. Legs and arms were sheathed and jointed. The body was shielded by a massive breastplate and girdle. Hands were gauntleted and had fully and intricately articulated fingers. The head was the most bizarre and dread-inspiring feature. It appeared much like a huge metal cask, over five feet high, smooth, cylindrical, and totally featureless, save for what seemed to be a visor, a separate half-moon of metal affixed to the helmet's front. This visor was now closed, making the giant seem sightless, or even lifeless. Indeed, the whole look of the thing was more that of a castiron statue than of something alive.

But it *was* alive, and it was clearly aware of the men as well. For as they approached, it stirred. A hand lifted from the arm of the throne and closed into a fist, its index finger thrusting out toward the Fomor.

"So, Cruc, you have failed us again," the metallic voice clanged out from within the vast form.

"No, Commander Balor!" he said, quailing before this overwhelming being. "It wasn't us! We did just as you asked. We poisoned the lake. We saw their people using it! We waited, through the fall, the winter, into the spring. Nothing happened. I swear it!"

"Nothing?" the giant repeated, surprise in its echoing tones. The massive hand dropped back to the throne's arm.

"We saw no signs of disaster, panic, anything. Nothing but the burning of a single hut last fall. And that was likely an accident. There was no effect on the Nemedians at all."

"Impossible," boomed the armored figure.

"It still happened," said Cruc. Having overcome the initial cowing shock of seeing Balor, his courage and aggressiveness was returning somewhat. "That marvelous 'poison' of yours was useless."

"Take care, Cruc," the voice thundered menacingly. "You come too close to insolence."

"Yes, great Balor," the Fomor said with swift contriteness. "But we really can't be blamed for what happened."

"Then what *can* be? Speak up, Cruc. Don't you have any notion as to what might have interfered?"

"Not for myself, Commander. But there are many of my people who are sure they know the answer. The idea's spreading through them like fire through straw. Putting a great fear into them too, as if I didn't have enough troubles with them."

"Just tell us what it is, fool!" Tethra snapped impatiently.

"All right, then. They say it's spirits or magic powers helping them."

"Magic?" Balor's voice echoed sharply.

"Well, yes," said Cruc defensively. "I mean, it isn't just this last thing going wrong, is it? It's all that's happened. Them getting weapons as good as ours almost overnight . . . well, that's one. And how easy they killed that great monster we sent out . . . that's another. And there's even them finding that abandoned village! How'd they do that? It all smacks of something supernatural helping them out."

The metal-clad giant was silent for a long moment in consideration. Then its voice boomed out again. "What do you think, Tethra?"

"I think that these Fomor are mindless beasts who make evil spirits out of their own shadows," he said superciliously.

"And have you an opinion of your own as to what's been happening there?"

"I do not, Commander. If, indeed, these blundering aberrants correctly did as they were supposed to, then that contaminant should have wreaked havoc amongst the invaders. There is no way it can be neutralized."

"No way known to us," Balor corrected. "None *our* science has been able to create."

An expression of astonishment came over Tethra at these words. "What are you meaning?"

"From the look on your face, I can see that you know as

well as I," the giant replied. "There is one possibility: that the Departed Ones are helping these people."

"But that *can't* be, Commander!" Tethra said with force. "They don't exist anymore. Their presence hasn't been detected anywhere in all the centuries since they vanished. They are no more than a vague legend now. There is surely some other, rational explanation."

"And yet you, with all the immense knowledge of our people behind you, can think of none," Balor countered. "Legends may still exist, Captain. And so might *they*. I have felt them. I have expected something like this to happen one day."

"If it could be true," Tethra allowed, "what does it mean?"

"It means we can no longer afford to take chances with these people," the giant's voice clanged out. "Unfortunate. We might have made some most valuable use of them, if they had been subdued. But if there is any possibility that the Departed Ones are providing help, then the invaders are far too dangerous to us. They must be swiftly and utterly destroyed."

"Destroyed?" said Cruc. "But haven't we already tried that? How many different ways? We failed each time. There's no more way for it . . ." he eyed Balor hopefully, "unless *you've* decided to take a hand and . . ."

"No!" the giant boomed. "None of our forces will become directly involved. It is even more imperative now that we stay out of this. If *they* could be about, we must keep all our powers intact and hidden from them."

"Then, what can we do?" asked Cruc.

*"You* will need to do nothing. Or virtually nothing, anyway. The end will come on these invaders just as it came on the invaders before them—the sons of Partholan, thirty years ago."

"You mean to put the sickness upon them?" said Cruc, eyes going wide, a tremor of alarm entering his voice. "The one without a cure?"

"It is the only certain way."

"But I remember the tales of it from my father. It was a horrible pestilence. Our parents lived in fear that it would spread to them as well."

"It did not do so," Balor pointed out.

"Still, what about this time?" Cruc said insistently. "Would you risk all of us too?"

There was a faint, metallic, whirring sound from the giant's head, and then a click. The visor lifted the merest fraction. It revealed a blazing, bright-red light behind it, shining through the crack in a fine line like the slenderest crescent of a crimson moon. And from a point at the center of the arc of light, a single ray shot out, striking down to once again bathe the Fomor captain in its ruddy glow.

Intense heat instantly engulfed the hapless being. His body was at once bathed in sweat. He winced from the searing pain.

"I sense reluctance in you, Cruc," the bell of the armored giant's voice tolled ominously. "Yes, most certainly I would risk all of you to preserve ourselves, with no hesitation at all. All you must do is obey, unquestioningly. Do you understand?"

"Y . . . yes!" Cruc got out through teeth gritted against the agony.

"Good." The visor snapped closed, cutting off the light. "And there is another lesson for you Cruc. Consider the effect if the *full* power of my eye were ever trained upon you."

"I surely will, my Commander," Cruc said, gasping in the cool air, relieved to be alive.

"You have nothing to fear from the sickness, in any case," Balor's voice assured. "All you must do is stay completely out of the way until it has burned itself out. There will be no one left."

"But how do you mean to put the thing upon them?" Cruc asked.

"I said there was virtually nothing for you to do," said the giant. "There is just one little sacrifice. Something of no real importance. You must find amongst your . . . 'people' one suitable volunteer. It must be one more or less normal in appearance. By that, I mean human, as yourself."

"A volunteer?" said Cruc. "But that would mean . . ."

"Yes," said Balor, cutting him off. "He must be prepared to die."

Dagda moved stealthily through the forest underbrush with the two surviving brothers of the O'Falva clan, Murchadh and Donnchadh.

The signs of a new spring were all around them. Lush new growth thickly furred the soaring trees, bright flowers filled the sun-warmed glades, and exultant birds swooped and caroled high above. Altogether, they created a most festive atmosphere, but one clearly making no impact on the grim-faced men.

"Are you certain that it's around here she was seen?" the big warrior asked his companions.

"We are that, Dagda," Donnchadh assured him. "A hunting party caught sight of her in this area only yesterday."

"And there's no question that it was her?"

"They did catch only a quick sight before she fled away," said Murchadh, "but they seemed sure. Although . . . well . . ."

So hesitant was he that Dagda stopped to confront him. "Well what? What is it?"

"Well, it would seem that she has changed quite a lot. But, you know, that would be expected, what with the hardships of living out here so long . . ."

"Yes, yes. I know," Dagda said dismally. "To think that all this while, since she ran away last fall, driven mad by her grief, she may have been living out here. Just the idea of her going through all the winter alone is a torture to me. After all those days of searching the forest for her, only to find nothing. After finally believing that she must be dead. Now this! I tell you, I can't stand it any more!" He shook a massive fist in determination. "I've *got* to find her this time. If she truly is alive . . ."

He cut off as a sound came through the woods: a shrill squealing noise, rising, then abruptly dying away.

"A wild pig!" said Murchadh.

"Aye," said Donnchadh. "Its death squeal. Come on!"

He led the others toward the sound, swiftly and skillfully taking the easiest route through the tangled undergrowth and densely packed trees. Then he slowed, signing them to caution. They crept on forward, reaching a screen of brush. From its shelter the three peeked out.

Beyond was a small clearing. Near its far edge, a large pig was down, a spear sticking up from its broad side. Its belly was split open, its guts spilled upon the ground amidst a spreading pool of fresh blood.

A human form was crouched beside it, back to them, head bent low over the carcass.

"Could that be her?" Murchadh muttered in disbelief.

"I mean to find out," said Dagda, and boldly stepped from the brush into clear view.

The sound of his movement was enough to alarm the being. It wheeled from the dead pig, half rising to assume a defensive stance. Its lips curled back from its teeth in a snarl.

He caught a quick and startling flash of a lean face, of

strings of raw meat ripped from the carcass still dangling from the jaws, of blood streaming down a long neck and vivid against white skin, of a wild mass of dark hair. Then the being moved. Before the stunned Dagda could act, it jerked the spear free from the pig and fled away like a deer into the woods.

He started after it. The two O'Falvas began to follow, but he waved them back.

"No!" he called. "This is for me alone! Stay here!"

He followed, putting all the great power of his legs into the effort, simply crashing headlong through any hindering underbrush, heedless of scrapes. For a short time this heroic effort allowed him to keep the figure in sight, though it was little more than a blur moving through the trees ahead. Finally, however, he lost even this.

He kept stubbornly on in the same direction for a time, then realized the futility of blind pursuit. As he came into another small clearing, he stopped, frustrated, looking searchingly around him at the ringing trees.

A spear shot by, a handbreadth from his face, and sunk home in a tree, shaft quivering.

He whirled toward the direction from which it had come. A figure leaped into view, brandishing a long knife. He stared in mingled wonder and shock at the being he faced. A tangle of jet-black hair billowed about its shoulders. A wrapping of wolf-skin clad its lank body, revealing arms and legs of a hard, lean, and sinewy look. Its face was thin to gauntness, the bold lines of jaw and cheeks protruding sharply, as if it was some wraith of death that challenged Dagda in the spring wood.

But it was no spirit that he confronted. And the face, for all its ghastly change, was still recognizable to him.

"Moire!" he called, fighting back his dismay.

"Moire?" the other growled in a voice hoarse from disuse. "There is no Moire."

"Then, who are you?"

"I take my name from the creatures I live among, that fly free and feed on death," the other rasped. "I am one with them. You can call me after that nightmare bird. I am the Raven Queen—the Morrigan."

"But do you know who I am?"

The wild being contemplated him closely for a time.

"I . . . I know you are a warrior," she said at last.

"I was also a husband," he returned, "with a fine, brave, and loving wife."

"No longer," she snapped. "She's gone. Killed by the terrible thing that was done to her."

"Is that it, then?" he asked in anguish. "Did you run away because you couldn't accept what happened? But it wasn't your fault. It was nothing to do with you!"

"I know that," she grimly replied. "I know it was the Fomor who destroyed your Moire. And it's the Fomor I'm now sworn to hate. It's for them that I am here, making myself harder, more vicious, more cunning. I can steal unknown upon any prey. I can kill it with spear or knife or teeth. My skills are keener now than any man's, or any wolf's. And all that strength, that skill, that hatred I will put to one end: destroying the Fomor. Whenever, however I can, I will slake my own thirst for vengeance in their hot blood, like the battle crow I am."

"No, Moire," he pleaded. "You can't throw away your life . . . our life together. The horror is over. Come back to me."

"For Moire the horror would never be over," she said. "And you, as a man, can never really understand. Nothing would ever wipe out the memories, the feelings of that . . . that thing living and growing inside. And then of seeing it . . ." She cut off that painful line abruptly, shaking her head. "No, no. Only death could end such memories for her. There is no Moire anymore. Only the Morrigan."

"But at least *you* can come back with me now," he offered. "You can have food, shelter, proper clothes . . ."

"I will not," she said adamantly, drawing herself up. "I am a being of the wilds now, not of the haunts of men. My life here keeps me fit. My constant labors keep honed that killing edge I must always have. I will stay here."

"I won't try to make you come," he assured her, "no matter how hard that is. I only hope that, left alone, you will one day change your mind."

"That's a hope you are better off without," she told him sternly. "Forget about me. Grieve for the one you loved. Remember her."

There came sounds of movement in the forest, distant but moving closer. The one now called Morrigan cocked her head to listen.

"Your friends are seeking after you," she said. "Go now, before they come. For the sake of your Moire, let them keep their old memory of her also."

"I will go," he said reluctantly. "But, isn't there anything I can do for you?"

"Only one," she said. "I'm lacking a good sword."

He nodded. He unbuckled his belt with its sheathed weapon and tossed them down before her.

"There's no blade better," he told her.

She nodded. "I know. I'll use it well. Now go!"

Without more delaying he turned and started back. But as he reached the clearing's edge, he paused to glance around.

The raven-haired woman was already gone, melted away into the trees like a woodland spirit.

"Goodbye . . . my wife," the man said, voice choked with his misery.

Donnchadh and Murchadh came into view then, rushing up to him.

"Dagda! There you are," said Murchadh. "You were gone so long!"

"Did you find her?" the other brother asked.

"No," Dagda said quickly and flatly, covering his grief. He turned abruptly and moved off, heading toward home.

The two exchanged a wondering glance, then followed.

"But there was something!" Donnchadh said.

"Yes!" agreed his brother. "And the hunting parties saw . . ."

Dagda cut them off. "The hunting parties were wrong and so were you. It was something else you all saw."

He stopped and turned to face them. His words were terse and clear:

"Listen to me now, and believe. This time, Moire is truly dead!"

# Chapter 17

# Contagion

The party of Fomor warriors came out of the trees and halted on the open crest of a low hill. More of the thickly forested lands spread away before them.

"Well, this is the place," announced Captain Cruc. "One more full day's walk from here to their village, due south."

"We haven't gotten here too soon for me," came a complaining voice from one of the others. "I really cannot stand much more of this."

The one who spoke threw back the hood of his heavy cloak. He revealed himself to be, not a Fomor warrior, but the arrogant towerman named Tethra.

He squirmed and scratched madly at one armpit like a flea-infested hound as he stepped up beside Cruc.

"It's bad enough that these clothes of yours are filthy," he said irritably, "but they're a home for who knows what kinds of vermin as well."

"It was your own Commander's order that you dress as one of us," Cruc reminded him.

"Yes, yes," he sharply returned. "Well, we couldn't take any chance that one of the Departed Ones might discover my presence here."

"You might have stayed on your safe tower island and left this to me," Cruc said.

"What, and let you make a botch of things again?" Tethra said scathingly. "Certainly not. This time we want to see that things go without any mistake. That means *some* intelligence must be applied."

Cruc growled at that. But with an effort, he held back from making a hot reply.

Tethra abandoned his attempt to ease his itching and looked around at the rest of the party. "Very well, the sooner this is taken care of, the better. Let's have that chap come forward."

Cruc signaled. A warrior stepped out from the rest.

"All right, Grinn," Cruc told him. "Prepare."

The Fomor at once began to shed his wealth of accouterments: shield, helmet, breastplate, shin- and armguards, sword, and belt. Without it all, he appeared as a normal if somewhat squat and swarthy young man, clad in simple shirt and trousers of coarse, grey cloth.

"Good enough," Tethra announced, examining him. "They won't be alarmed by some monstrosity. Hopefully, they won't even be sure he's Fomor, at least at first. That should get him into their midst."

"I understand the plan," Cruc told him testily.

"Do you? Good," said Tethra. He looked to the young Fomor. "And what about you? Do *you* understand clearly what you're to do?"

"Yes, Captain," the one named Grinn said, drawing himself to attention and speaking crisply. "I'm to go to the village and tell them I've left my people. I'm to ask to be accepted and use my time among them to spy out what they are doing."

"Very good!" said the towerman. He looked to Cruc with a pleased smile. "This lad will do fine!"

The Fomor captain did not smile in return.

"It's a great honor," the innocent young warrior said, clearly in awe. "For Those of the Tower to entrust me with such . . ."

"Yes, yes," Tethra said curtly. "Never mind all that. So now, there's only one thing left: to see that you don't acquire anything unpleasant from them."

He undid a pouch from his belt and untied its strings.

"Is it really necessary, my Captain?" asked the young Fomor, watching him. "I am very healthy."

"These people are strangers, from far lands that we know

nothing about," Tethra answered in a lecturing tone. "You might be infected, or poisoned by their food, or who knows what? A sick spy would be of little use to us, don't you agree?"

"Yes. Oh, yes sir!" Grinn readily replied.

"And you want to do the very best for us that you can, don't you?"

"Oh yes!" The young Fomor emphatically nodded his head. "Why, of course!"

"Then let us see to it," Tethra said. "Roll up a sleeve."

Grinn did so as Tethra pulled a small metal box out of the pouch. The towerman undid several clasps, opened the box, and carefully lifted an object from inside. It was a long, slender tube of shining gold metal, tapering to a needle-like point at one end.

He stepped up to the young warrior.

"Now, hold out your arm," he ordered Grinn, "and look away. It will be over in just a moment."

Grinn did as he was told. The keen point moved in toward his forearm.

"Wait," said Cruc.

Tethra paused, the needle poised inches from the arm, and looked irritably to him. "Now what?"

Cruc hesitated, then hedged awkwardly: "It's . . . just that . . . that I want to say I'm proud of you, Grinn. It's for the good of all Fomor that you do this. You'll be remembered."

The youth drew himself a little more erect and smiled with pleasure. "Thank you, Captain!"

Tethra shoved the point on in. The fine tip punctured through the skin of the young warrior's forearm. The towerman pressed down a small plunger at the tube's other end. He jerked the point free and stepped back.

"All done," Tethra said briskly. "You'd best get going now. Want to be sure you reach the village in time."

"In time?" Grinn echoed, not understanding.

"I mean, as soon as possible," the other quickly corrected. "No time to waste!"

"Yes, Captain," the youth said. "I'll start now."

"You're not afraid?" Cruc asked him.

"No, Captain," Grinn assured him. "It's the greatest moment of my life!" He gave a jaunty wave. "Well, see you soon!"

And with that, he strode off.

Cruc watched him go as Tethra very carefully packed the pointed metal tube away in box and then pouch.

"Soon," the Fomor said in a voice grim with the irony. He looked to the towerman. "And just how long *has* the poor lad got?"

"Well, the substance begins to turn virulent as soon as it's within a human," the other said matter of factly. "Assuming that your Grinn *is* relatively human, I'd say a day before he begins to feel serious effects. Perhaps another before he becomes too weak to move. More than enough time for him to reach their village."

"And that's all you care about," the Fomor said accusingly.

Tethra shrugged. "That's really all that *is* important, isn't it? Now, if we could get started back?" He began scratching at himself once again. "If I don't get a chance to bathe soon, I will surely die!"

The two men carried the limp form in through the gates of the Nemedian village.

A crowd began to gather around them at once, peering in curiosity at the unconscious young man. Some helped the bearers ease him down upon the ground. A woman supplied a bundled cloak to pillow his head. Another covered him with a blanket.

"Get Diancecht, someone," one of the two men said, and a youth immediately set off at a run.

Nuada arrived, pushing through the others to see the source of their excitement.

"What is this?" he asked.

"We found him this morning," the second of the two men replied. "It was when we went out to plant in the north fields."

"He was just lying there, Nuada," added the first, "just at the roadside. But he was still conscious then, if barely. He moaned and clutched his stomach, in great agony."

"We decided that the best thing was to bring him here, to see the healer," finished the other.

Nuada crouched down beside the form, examining the young, swarthy face, beaded with sweat, drawn taut with pain even in unconsciousness.

"Who is he?" Nuada asked. He looked up at the faces encircling him. "Does anyone know him?"

There were only shakes of heads and murmurs in the negative.

"He's a very young man," one of the women said in sympathy. "No older than my own son."

"But he's surely not one of us," said a man beside her. "Where do you think he's from?"

"He's a Fomor," said another voice, and Nuada looked up to see that the one known to them as Liam was beside him, the servant Graikos close behind as usual.

The simple statement caused a hubbub of amazement in the people of the crowd. Many of them quickly moved back, as if fearful the unconscious man could suddenly rise and snap at them. Others—the more adventurous and intrigued—moved forward.

"How can you be so certain of what he is?" asked Nuada.

"My friend, I assure you that I know of no others in this empty land but yourselves and your enemies," Liam said. "If that's not enough, then believe me that I know one of them at first sight."

"Do you?" said Nuada. "He seems normal to me. No animal's head, no iron claws, no other deformities."

"He's an especially clean specimen, I grant," said Liam, "but there's still a look to him. No, he's a Fomor. Take my word on that."

Finally Diancecht arrived, accompanied by Nemed and Dagda. Many others of the village had also arrived by this time, drawn by the commotion, and formed a densely packed circle around the recumbent figure. But they quickly opened a passage to let their leader, healer, and champion warrior through.

The three came up to the stricken man on the far side from Nuada and Liam.

"What happened?" Nemed asked.

"These two men found him," Nuada said, indicating the pair. "They say he was on the road by the north fields. They brought him to the healer."

"A logical choice," said Diancecht. "He does appear quite ill." He crouched by the figure, putting his hands out toward it. "I should examine him."

"I wouldn't do that," said Liam in a warning tone.

The healer sat back, looking up to him, eyebrow raised in question. "And why not?"

"It could be dangerous," the other replied.

"Liam says he is a Fomor," Nuada put in.

"Fomor?" Dagda repeated, face darkening with rage at the

name. "Then you will surely not touch him, healer. We'll do nothing for the likes of one of them. Cast him out!"

"Cast him out?" said Diancecht. "And just leave the man to die?"

"He's no man. He's a monster," the big warrior stormed. "And no cruelty we could do to him could match what they have done to us. Yes, let him die! Or, just let me kill him now!"

He grabbed for his sword hilt, but Nemed placed a staying hand upon his, speaking soothingly:

"Be easy, Dagda. We cannot act so hastily or in rage. We don't even know for certain that he *is* Fomor."

"If Liam says so, then I believe it," Dagda said stoutly.

"Yes, so do I," Nuada added.

"And I also have reason to believe that our friend's judgments in such things are sound," added Diancecht in his more cautious way. "Still, Liam, is that alone enough to make this one youth dangerous? He seems quite helpless now."

"Perhaps he does," Liam replied, "but no, I still wouldn't trust him. I don't know why, exactly, but I've a feeling—a very unpleasant one. Just what is he doing here? And what's wrong with him? The Fomor are capable of great duplicity. You should all know that by now. Why take chances?"

"Accepting that he *is* Fomor," said Nemed, "must it still be assumed that he came here to do harm? He is, as you've said, alone. He's unarmed. Maybe he came for other reasons."

"Yes!" spoke up one of the men who had carried him in. "When we found him, he could still speak. He talked to us, and in our own tongue. Very faint it was, but understandable. He muttered that he'd left his people. He pleaded to join us."

"You see?" said Nemed. "He was disaffected from them. Sympathetic to us. We *can't* turn him away." He looked to the big champion, his voice taking on a pleading tone. "Dagda, understand: to do that would only make us as evil as you say they are."

"How can you say that?" Dagda asked him in outrage. "How can you even think to ask for kindess? You know what they did to Moire."

"I *don't* know that myself," Nemed countered, "and neither do you. Again, we have only Liam's word for it."

"And you're questioning that word?" Liam challenged. "After all I've done for you?"

"I mean no offense," Nemed said soothingly. "I only question whether the Fomor are quite so villainous as you may have made them seem. It's clear that you have your own reasons to hate them, perhaps much more strongly than we. It might be that you've made them seem more dangerous to keep us set against them. We *do* have only your word that they still seek to destroy us. So far as *I* know, they have left us quite alone since we defeated them in battle, over a year ago. They may want peace."

His words had a clear impact upon the crowd. Many of them nodded in agreement, or muttered words of support.

"You hear?" Nemed said, waving hands about him at his people. "They agree with me."

"So, you still want to blindly believe that goodness will prevail!" Liam said scathingly.

"I want to believe that we can live with them, and not risk more of our people in future conflicts by perpetuating this rivalry needlessly. If taking in this lad might help insure that end, I want to risk it."

An undertone of affirmation rolled through the crowd. Liam looked around at them with a scowl.

"Right then!" he said curtly, with the tone of a hurt child. "If that's your feeling, then I'll voice no more opinions to you. You've survived here thanks to me. I've saved you more often than you know. But *you've* no need of me anymore. *You* can do everything yourselves. Fine then! Do as you wish!"

He turned and stalked away, Graikos following. Dagda, Nuada, and Diancecht looked after him with regret.

"That was unfair to him, Nemed," Nuada told his leader disapprovingly.

"He'll soon see that it's for the best," Nemed assured him, then looked to the healer. "Diancecht, are you willing to see to our visitor?"

"I've vowed to save lives, Nemed," Diancecht replied. "No matter what my own feelings about this youth, I still can't turn away. Bring him to my hut."

"Very good," said Nemed. "Who'll see to moving him?"

"Don't expect me to help," Dagda said, stepping back.

"I'm afraid I must agree with Dagda," Nuada added, stepping around to his friend's side.

"I honor your decision," Nemed told them, and looked around him at the others. "Are there volunteers?"

A number of men readily offered their services. A litter was brought, the young Fomor was gently lifted and laid in it, and then half a dozen carried it to the healer's new hut.

Much of the crowd followed. Nuada and Dagda remained behind, staring after them, faces dark with their misgivings.

Inside the hut the stricken man was transferred to a pallet. Nemed thanked the bearers and ushered them out, leaving only himself and Diancecht with the youth. The healer knelt, feeling his forehead.

"How is he?" asked Nemed.

"It's too early to be certain," the healer replied. "He's very feverish."

"Diancecht, you must save him," Nemed told him urgently. "This one youth might be the beginning of something great. The key to insuring a truly peaceful future for us. To befriend him, save him, show the Fomor our spirit of forgiveness, of generosity . . ."

"I understand, Nemed," the healer said. "I'll do my best for him. But understand me, there are no miracles that *I* can do."

"I have great faith in you," the leader said, going to the door. "You'll save him, and he'll be our symbol of a finer day to come."

And beaming with pleasure at this new promise, Nemed went out.

Diancecht looked back to the unconscious youth. His own expression was guarded, questioning.

*"Is* it a symbol that you'll be to us?" he asked thoughtfully, "or are you a trap?"

It was late in the night that a weary Diancecht came into the main hall.

It was lit dimly by a few candles and the embers of the central fire. Only Nemed and Nuada still occupied it, waiting for some word from their comrade. Dagda had pointedly stayed absent, refusing to be in any way involved. The other Nemedians had long since gone to bed.

The two watched as Diancecht went to the fire, scooped broth from a cauldron there into a bowl, and sat down at the table with them. He lifted the bowl to sip at the steaming liquid, then dropped it back.

"I'm too worn even to eat this!" he said in a dispirited tone unusual for him.

"Things aren't going well then?" Nemed asked in an anxious tone.

The healer shook his head. "A whole day I've worked to

relieve his agonies. I've used every bit of knowledge and every medicine I have. Nothing's worked. Cold cloths do little to ease his fever. He comes to at times, but his words are rambling or incoherent. He has terrible stomach pains; he can't keep any food or liquid down. He's getting weaker."

"And you have no idea at all what it is?" asked Nuada.

"No. I've never seen anything quite like it, neither in progressing so swiftly or striking so violently. And that's what gives me the greatest worry."

"Then, you don't think he'll survive?" asked Nemed, greatly distressed at this disappointing news.

"At his rate of decline, I don't think he'll last more than one day longer," the healer said. He shook his head regretfully. "I'm sorry, Nemed. I said I could do no miracles."

A woman came into the main hall. There was great anxiety in her look.

"Healer, here you are!" she said with relief. "I know it's late, but could you come with me? My husband's feeling very poorly."

"How so?"

"Well, it may be nothing, but he's been ill since dinner. His stomach's in knots, he says."

"I'll come," said Diancecht at once, rising and casting his great weariness away.

But as he started after the woman, Nuada called out to her: "Wait! You're Orfhlaith, aren't you?"

"Yes," she said.

"And isn't your husband Baothghalach?"

"He is."

Nuada looked to the healer in alarm. "Diancecht, he's one of the two who brought in the Fomor yesterday!"

"So," the healer said grimly, "he *is* a trap!"

# Chapter 18

# Pestilence

Sounds of suffering once more filled the main hall of the Nemedians.

Scores of the villagers—men, women, and children alike this time—now lay upon makeshift pallets of straw, filling all the floor of the large room. A dozen of their comrades moved among them, ministering to their needs in whatever way they could. These attempts at help included little more than the laying on of wet cloths to cool hot brows and the speaking of comforting words in an effort to ease the stomach pains. Neither aid was having any effect.

Included in this nursing group were Nemed and Nuada, plus a much disgruntled and revulsed Mathgen, once more pressed into the healer's service. He grudgingly went about what he considered this odious work muttering darkly to himself.

Diancecht came into the hall. Behind him a man carried in a young girl.

"Put her down there," the healer told the distressed man, indicating a single empty pallet near the door. "I'll look to her."

Nuada finished his mopping of a moaning woman's brow and rose, moving to his friend.

"Diancecht, how does it go?" he asked.

"Another two dozen," the healer said, kneeling to examine the girl. "Yes, and this girl too." He looked to the man who hovered anxiously over her. "Can you stay and see to your daughter?" he asked. "There are too few of us here to care for her properly."

"Of course," the man readily agreed, and took Diancecht's place at the girl's side as the healer arose, moving himself in a slow, exhausted way.

"There's no more room here," he told Nuada. "We'll have to begin ministering to all the rest in their own houses."

"How many?" Nuada asked.

"With this one there are nearly two hundred who've come down with it through the past day."

"And have you found any answer for it? Any kind of remedy?"

"None," Diancecht said darkly. "No cure of mine makes any change."

"Would separating the ill from the rest stop it?" Nuada asked.

The healer shook his head. "It moves too quickly from man to man. Those who brought him in went down first. Their families came next, then anyone *they'd* contacted, and so on. I'd guess that by now any one or all of us could have been touched by it."

"So there's nothing we can do?"

"Except to try to fight through it? No." He looked about him at the crowded room. "Dagda's strength could certainly be of great help to us now."

"Yes," Nuada agreed. "Too bad. He left the village after his dispute with Nemed. It was to hunt, he told me, but I think it was really to vent his anger on the sky and trees."

"I understand," said Diancecht. "Who knows but that it might be a blessing for him to be away from this? Tell me then, where is Nemed?"

"Across there, somewhere," Nuada said, looking to one end of the room.

They saw the aging leader rise wearily from one recumbent form and shuffle to the next, a cup in his hands. His shoulders sagged and his eyes were downcast to the suffering people covering the floor about him. He had not seen his healer's return.

"I must tell him where we stand now," Diancecht said, starting toward the man.

But Nuada stopped him. "Wait. You can't tell the worst to him. Not now. He's been laboring all the night to help the sick. He's very worn and very distressed. News like this might finish him. He needs to rest."

Diancecht nodded his understanding and the two men approached their leader.

Nemed had knelt by another stricken young man and was holding out the cup to him. The man was thrashing in his fever and pain. He rolled violently and swung out wildly with his arm, knocking the cup from Nemed's hands. The water was dashed into the older man's face. Nemed dropped back, slumping in exhaustion, staring at the ill one in a helpless, defeated way.

Nuada and Diancecht crouched at either side of him. The healer put a hand to Nemed's shoulder in a gesture of comfort.

Nemed looked up to him. His face was creased by lines of care. Tears of anguish stood in his red-rimmed eyes.

"Oh Diancecht," he said in a frustrated voice, "I don't know what to do! They're so ill. And it's my own doing! My own foolish act!"

"Your act was to show charity to another living being and to give help to your own people," the healer said. "There was nothing wrong in that."

"But look at them!" the older man said, sweeping his gaze around the room. "What's to happen to us?"

Diancecht looked at Nuada. Nuada gave him a hard "be-careful-what-you-say!" look.

"We will get through it," the healer said to his leader carefully. "There are many ill, but no one has died. Even that Fomor lad is still alive. He is very bad, but he also lay unattended for some time."

"Then, you think that there's a chance they'll all recover?"

"Our people are strong, Nemed," Diancecht hedged. "They have a will to fight. They'll all have rest and proper care."

"But if any die . . . for me . . ."

"Don't think that way," Nuada said. "It's only the weariness on you that makes things seem so dark."

"Yes," the healer added firmly. "Right now you can be the best help to us by getting some rest. Your mind must be fully alert. And you must be a fit, strong model to the others."

"I suppose you're right," Nemed agreed with some reluctance.

"Let Nuada see you back to your own house then. Get some sleep. We can see to this for now."

Gently Nuada helped his leader to rise and led him from the hall. Diancecht watched after them, then moved toward the laboring, scowling Mathgen.

"Ah, the great healer at last come back!" Mathgen said sarcastically as he saw the other approach. "Planning to clean vomit and mop sweating, stinking bodies for yourself?"

"I have been doing the same in scores of huts since last evening," the healer sharply pointed out.

"And likely helping those poor beggars as much as I'm helping these here," Mathgen replied. "I don't know why I'm even risking myself. I should get away. Get as far from this cursed place as possible."

"To die out in the wilds alone?" said Diancecht. "For it's likely you'll get this sickness anyway."

"A singularly uncomfortable thought. But it has occurred to me already."

"The best chance for all of us is to find some cure for it. That's why I wanted to talk to you."

"To me?" Mathgen was surprised. "My father's skills didn't run to such things as that. Neither do mine."

"That isn't what I meant." The healer stepped closer, his voice dropping to a confidential tone. "Mathgen, do you have any feeling about Liam?"

This pointed question rather threw the cunning man. "About Liam?" he said in a flustered way. "Uh . . . why . . . no. Of course not."

"I've wondered," Diancecht went on. "I've noted that you seem as curious about him as I."

"Only curious as to how a charlatan can pull such tricks and get away with it," Mathgen said evenly, his aplomb recovered. "That's all he is."

"Are you so certain?" Diancecht probed. "And what about the healing of Nuada? He was here then. So were you. You weren't aware of him doing anything?"

"Nothing at all," the sly one blithely lied, protecting his own knowledge. "Nuada's survival was a fluke. Nothing to do with Liam."

"So, you'd argue that he has no real skills at all? Even if those skills could possibly save us?"

Mathgen considered. He looked around him at the room filled with those in pain.

"Well, it perhaps *might* be that he has *some* skills in real medicine he's picked up," he cautiously conceded. "Clearly, you haven't any yourself."

Diancecht ignored the insult. "I think I'm going to talk to him," he said.

In the hut of the one known to the villagers as Liam, the bearded man himself sat brooding.

His faithful servant Graikos sat nearby, watching him with an expression of disgust.

"Two whole days you've just sat here," he said at last. "There's something going on out there, I tell you. I can hear the sounds of confusion, of fear, of pain. We ought to see what it is."

"No. Not this time," Lir said adamantly. "Whatever it is, they'll have to just see to it themselves. Let them find out what it's like to deal with their own problems for a while. Then maybe they'll appreciate old Liam."

"Now you truly sound like a spoilt child," the other said boldly.

"Well, thank you very much!" Lir said in an offended tone. "After all I've done!"

"All I've done! All I've done!" Graikos insolently mimicked. "That's all you ever say. But has it been that much?"

"What do you mean?"

"Well, consider: if you'd told them who you really were and why you were certain the Fomor were dangerous, this wouldn't have happened. But no. You had to be so clever, so secret about it all, always keeping us outsiders, always separate from the rest."

"That was not done by my own choice," Lir said defensively. "You know well enough that it is on the command of Queen Danu that I've kept my true nature hidden from them."

"Perhaps," Graikos allowed. "Still, from what he knew about things, old Nemed was *right* to think the way he did."

"Right? To question me?"

"Yes, he was," the other said stoutly, "and you won't make me say otherwise."

Exasperated by his servant's impudence, Lir opened his mouth to argue further. But he was interrupted as the door flap was pulled aside and Diancecht came into the hut.

"I'm sorry," the healer said, noting the tense bodies and

expressions of the two. "I've not interrupted something of importance, have I?"

"No, no," Lir said quickly. "Just idle talk."

"Ah. Well, I've come to talk with you about what's happening," the other said, dropping down on a stool.

"And just what is that?" asked Lir.

Diancecht looked at him in surprise. "Why, the plague! You didn't know?"

"I've been here since losing my little skirmish with Nemed. I thought I should keep strictly out of the way."

"Did you? Well, I'm sorry for that, for there is certainly a plague on us. It's sweeping through the village, and I'm afraid it can't be stopped—at least, not by my own skills."

"I thought that something of the kind might come," Lir said. "I did try to warn you."

"Recriminations won't help now," the healer said tersely. "Something's got to be done, and quickly."

"Is it so bad as that?"

"I'm afraid it is as bad as it could possibly be. I've watched the course of this sickness running upon the Fomor boy. It's following the exact same course with our people. In three days more, by my estimates, they will begin to die. By then, with the speed that the illness spreads, the rest of us will have begun to show signs of it as well. And then *we'll* begin to die."

"How many will die?"

"If the violent effects can't be lessened, I don't see how anyone could survive."

"By the gods!" breathed Graikos in horror.

"And how long do you estimate you have?" asked Lir.

"Eight days will likely see most of us dead," Diancecht said bluntly.

"So quickly," murmured the bearded man. "A ruthless plague indeed!"

"That's why I've come to you," the healer said. "I can see no other way to save us. You must help."

"And what makes you think I could do so?" Lir asked, stone faced.

In his methodical way, Diancecht began to list them: "You have skills that I would call miraculous. You gave us the process to make the new metal. I've reason to believe that you healed Nuada. Your 'guess' about Moire was most accurate. And I suspect you have done other things for us that we don't know about. Now, if you do have healing skills—any kind of healing skills—you have to tell me."

"I'm afraid you are wrong," Lir said stubbornly. "I don't *have* to tell you anything."

"Oh, come on, man!" the healer said with uncharacteristic heat. "I can understand why your feelings might have been hurt. But this is a rather excessive way to get revenge for it, isn't it? This isn't some minor bellyache that will teach us a lesson. This is our finish! I can't believe you would go so far to help us, only to let us die in agony to satisfy some petty grudge!"

Lir looked for a long moment into the healer's probing gaze. At last he shook his head.

"No. Of course I couldn't." He looked toward Graikos with a little smile. "I think someone had begun making me see that already."

"Then, you can help?" Diancecht said with new hope.

"I honestly don't know," the other said. "But I can try. First, I must know all I can about what this plague is and where it came from. There is only one who might possibly tell us that."

"The young Fomor who brought the sickness to us," the healer supplied. "I agree. But he is very low. I'm surprised he's lasted so long."

"Let me see him quickly then," Lir said. "It may be that I can still get something from him."

Lir, Graikos, and Diancecht came into the healer's hut.

The young Fomor still lay there, attended by a woman volunteer. The healer thanked her and told her she could go, admonishing her to get some rest herself. Once the men were alone with the youth, Lir knelt down beside him, examining him critically.

Two days of sickness had changed him drastically. The thickly built Fomor had already wasted to shocking gauntness, his swarthy face gone pasty and shriveled to a hollow-eyed death's-head. He lay limp, too weakened even to react to the spasms of pain. The irregular, panting lift and fall of his chest showed he still lived. The eyes glinting faintly through the slits of barely opened lids showed he still clung to consciousness.

"Not much time left," the bearded man concluded. He looked around to Graikos. "The globe!" he ordered.

Without delay the servant fished in the inevitable sack, pulling forth a perfect globe of polished crystal, the size of a clenched fist.

Lir held it out over the young Fomor's head in one palm, making slow, caressing passes over its top curve with his other hand.

"This . . . this thing you're doing—it will not cause him extra pain?" asked the healer, dropping down beside Lir. "I mean, the man is dying."

"And if it did?" Lir asked brutally, "would we have any other choice?"

Diancecht reluctantly shook his head.

"Well, don't fret for him," the other assured. "This little charm should have the opposite effect on him. Watch now, it's beginning to work."

As if the constant rubbing were bringing some warmth into the globe, it began to glow softly, with a clear white light that radiated from its center, bringing a rainbow array of scintillating colors alive to play across the polished surface.

"You feel the pain is fading now," Lir told the Fomor gently. "You may relax. You may rest with greater ease."

Some of the pain that tightened the cadaverous face did fade away. The labored and erratic breathing eased into a quieter rhythm.

"There," said Lir. "Now you feel better. Now you feel more strength."

The eyes opened further. Their lights gleamed with a bit more energy. They looked up to him in puzzlement, surprise. The lips moved.

"I . . . I do feel better," came a voice faint, thick with a gutteral accent but still identifiable as the Nemedian's tongue.

"We are trying to help you," Lir said. "But to do that, you must give help to us."

"How?"

"You must tell us everything you know. You must tell us the truth. Why did you come here?"

"They . . . said . . . I was to . . . to try to join you. To . . . spy."

"And do you know why you are sick?"

"Yes. *They* did it to me. I know it now. They . . . made me sick."

"Why?"

"They . . . lied to me. They sent me here to . . . to bring the sickness to you. To destroy you."

"How do you know?"

"I know what I have. I've heard it described by my grandfather. It was the same thing put upon them . . ."

"Upon whom? Your people?"

"No. Those . . . those others who came here . . . years ago. They lived here then. The sickness was put on them. The Great Ones did that, too."

"Great Ones?" Lir echoed. He exchanged a quick, knowing glance with Graikos.

"Yes. Those . . . of the Tower."

"One of them put this upon you?"

"A captain of them, named Tethra. It . . . it was to be such a great honor!" he added bitterly.

"How was it done?"

"A pointed thing was stuck in me. A medicine . . . to ward off illness . . . he said. It burned. I felt it in me. I . . . should have known."

"Who are these others he's speaking of?" asked a puzzled and fascinated Diancecht.

"I don't know," Lir flatly lied. "But it doesn't matter." He met the healer's gaze squarely. His voice was grim: "If this plague on you is the same that struck those other settlers, then I'm afraid that even my best skills won't be of help to you."

"Why?" asked Diancecht. "What do you mean?"

"I mean that the plague which fell upon those people wiped them out!"

"No," Diancecht argued. "It couldn't have. There must have been thousands living here. We found the remains of only a few scores. The rest must have escaped."

"Only for a time, I'm afraid," Lir said. "The burial mound that marks the resting place of the others lies some two days to the northeast of here."

"How do you know?"

"Oh, a friend who explored all about this isle told me," the disguised man vaguely supplied. "The mound contained the charred remains of thousands buried there. There was no sign that any had survived. I'm sorry, but it seems the Fomor succeeded in destroying them utterly."

"No! No!" gasped the young Fomor. "Not all!"

The two men looked to him again.

"What do you mean?" Lir demanded.

"The . . . the plague wraiths!" he forced out, but his voice failed him there. His face was again growing taut with his pain.

The light in the globe had faded somewhat. Lir rubbed it vigorously again to restore its glow. The youth revived somewhat with it, but much less this time. The globe's power was clearly losing its effect.

"Hold on, lad!" Lir said urgently. "We'll do all that we can for you. But you must tell us: what are 'plague wraiths'?"

"Shadows have . . . have been seen in the forests . . . about . . . the mound. The remains of . . . of fires were found upon it. My . . . my people think they . . . they are spirits of . . . the dead. But . . . but I know . . . that spirits . . . don't light fires."

A sudden spasm of pain took him, jerked him stiff and wrung him tight. He vibrated with the pain, head thrown back, eyes going wide, tongue rattling. Then he went abruptly limp, sinking down in a loose pile of wasted limbs, the last breath sighing from his lips.

Diancecht stared in open shock at the suddenness of the demise.

"What happened?" he asked. "I thought the globe could help him."

"It only helps to mask the pain, not stop its cause," the other said. "I knew it could only work for a while, so near to his end."

"Then you lied to him?"

"To get his help? Yes, I did," Lir easily admitted, and shrugged. "He was a Fomor."

"He was a man," Diancecht countered, "and as much a victim as we are."

"There was no more that could be done for him," Lir answered bluntly, "but there still might be for you."

A light of new hope came into the healer's face. "Does that mean *you* can do something?"

"If the Fomor's words were true," Lir said in a careful way, "then there might just be the faintest chance!"

# Chapter 19

# Burial Mound

"And so it is vital that a party leave at once to reach this place and discover if any of their people did survive."

Diancecht addressed a gravely listening group of the village leaders now gathered in his hut. Their numbers were already visibly thinned by the plague. Nemed and Nuada were there, as were Goibniu and Luchtine, Donnchadh and Murchadh, Graikos and the one they called Liam. But the giant champion Dagda was still conspicuous in his absence.

"Now, let me be clear on this," said Nuada when the healer had finished. "You're saying we've got to find this place, hunt down anyone alive that may be skulking about there, and bring back *blood* from them?" He shook his head doubtfully. "I don't know Diancecht, it sounds like a very long chance to me."

"It is the only chance we have," the healer replied. "Liam and I have determined that."

"And he is, of course, our supreme authority," said Mathgen in a voice touched with sarcasm.

"Quiet," said Nemed sharply. "After what's happened, we will no longer question the wisdom of our friend."

The disguised Lir nodded in acknowledgment of this vote of confidence.

"Who's going out in this party?" asked Nuada.

"Our fleetest and strongest men," the healer supplied. "This mound is two days away. Just the time that it will take to come and go will see most of our people down with the sickness, and some will likely have begun to die."

"I still don't see how this'll be the savin' of us," Goibniu said, scratching his soot-blackened head. "Just what'll this blood do?"

"It will stop the illness," said the healer. "Drive it from our bodies and keep it out. But let Liam explain it to you. The process is his own."

"Oh, not mine!" he said modestly. "Just something I picked up in my traveling. A process developed by a very wonderous race far, far away. They discovered that those who lived through a killing plague had something different about them— something in the makeup of their bodies that protected them. This . . . 'something' could be distilled from the blood of those the sickness left untouched and used to cure the rest."

"All right, we'll say that it will work," Goibniu allowed. "Just how are you meaning to get the blood from these folks, *if* you do find them?"

"Yes," said Nuada. "We surely can't be slashing their throats and hanging them to drain, no matter what our needs."

"That would not be necessary," the healer said. "There is a method, safe and largely painless, for drawing blood. And Liam says we need very little."

"But it's only *you* that know the method," Luchtine pointed out. "Will you be going on this quest?"

"I?" Diancecht seemed uncharacteristically flustered by the question. "Well . . . I . . . I'm afraid I would greatly slow the party down."

"And he's needed here," Liam quickly put in. "The equipment needed for the distilling is complex to set up, and must be ready by the time the blood is brought. Only Diancecht has the skills to help me."

"But bringing these people back here will be a delay too," Luchtine persisted. "Especially if they're not willing to come."

"That's true," put in the smith. "They'll not likely be so anxious to let us take their blood."

"Yes, yes," said the healer, perplexed. "I see. It is a problem."

"I'll go," said a voice.

They turned toward it to see that the speaker was Mathgen.

"You?" Diancecht said, raising an eyebrow in surprise.

"Bleeding is a simple skill I learned from my father," he said casually. "He was no healer, but his . . . experiments required fresh blood from time to time. I can do it. And I'll not slow the rest."

"You mean you're volunteering to go along on this?" Nuada said, openly incredulous.

"It's not altruism, I assure you," Mathgen answered superciliously. "Anything is preferable to staying in this pesthole and doing this odious work."

"I will go as well," said Nuada, giving Mathgen a searching, suspicious look. "Our brilliant comrade here might well be needing some assistance."

"Don't be afraid that I will run away, Nuada," Mathgen told him. "I've nowhere else to go. And this cure could mean my life as much as yours."

"My brother and I will also go," Donnchadh spoke up, his brother nodding agreement. "You'll need the best trackers to find this mound and anyone hiding about it as swiftly as possible."

"And I will go too," said another voice from the door.

They turned to see the champion's massive form filling the opening.

"Dagda!" Nuada said with glee. "You're back!"

"Yes, and it's sorry I am that I was gone."

"I'm the one who is sorry," Nemed said earnestly. "It was my foolishness that drove you away. You were right, as Liam was."

"That's not important now," Dagda said brusquely, brushing the apology away. "Only this is. I overheard enough to know that we must find some people, take blood from them, and bring it back here to save us. But where are this mound and these people to be found?"

"With good fortune, two days' journey to the northeast of here," Liam supplied.

"Then we start now!" Dagda said with force.

Most of those in the stricken village were either too sick or too preoccupied to see the little party off on its quest.

It was only a few score of them who gathered at the gates to watch as Dagda, Nuada, Mathgen, the two O'Falvas and a half dozen of the stoutest warriors headed off up the valley at a brisk trot.

Nemed looked to the sun dropping in the west, then back toward the departing men, shaking his head.

"They'll not get very far before nightfall," he said.

"Any distance they can make will be a help," said the disguised Lir. He looked to the healer. "Well, Diancecht, we'd better get started at our own work."

"Yes," said Nemed. "That you should. I'll oversee the care of the sick for you, healer, for what little good it will do."

"Just see they are comfortable and have as much rest as possible," Diancecht advised. "Tell them they must hold on. Help is only days away."

"I will pray that is the truth," Nemed said wholeheartedly. "Good luck to you." And he went off toward the main hall.

Lir and Diancecht proceeded at once to the healer's new hut. The bearded man looked around him at the medical materials and equipment which Diancecht had scavenged from his burned hut or managed to replace.

"Fine," he said briskly. "Much of this will be helpful." He picked up a finely thrown ceramic jar. "Yes, we'll need several of these." He looked through objects crowding shelves and several tables. "That goblet, those two pitchers, that small brazier, and that silver bowl will be useful too."

He considered. "Let me see . . . we'll need some tubing, beakers, vials . . . oh, and a retort. I should have all those in my bag. Blast that Graikos! I wonder where he's vanished to? I'll have to go back to my hut for the things myself. Diancecht, you can clear one of the tables while I'm gone. We'll set up there."

"All right," said the healer, "but, Liam, I don't see why you told the others that my help was so crucial to this. I've no idea what you're about."

Lir paused and looked back to him. "Oh well, I did need *someone* I could trust to help. And . . . well, I thought you needed a bit better excuse for staying here. One that would better keep the truth from them."

Diancecht's gaze met the other's squarely. This time both brows were arched in surprise. "You know?"

Lir nodded. "Since I first saw you today. I could tell that it was upon you. For how long now?"

"Since this morning," the other admitted. With the secret out, he relaxed his rigid control a little. A grimace of pain crossed his face. "I can't let the rest know. They must keep faith in me."

"Amazing," Lir said in open awe. "To hide your sickness from them all so well. What strength of will it must be taking for you to do that! You know, I think it's that strength, that courage that I admire in your people most. I suppose it's really why I've stayed here to help you. I've never seen the like before."

He reached into a pocket and pulled out the crystal globe, handing it to the other man. "Here, use this as you will. Sorry that it won't do more than mask the pain. But it might at least keep you on your feet a little while longer."

The healer looked at the gleaming ball. "And can I also use it to ease the others' pain?" he asked.

Lir shook his head. "Sorry. You know my feelings there. You've promised to keep the secret of my powers if I helped you. I'm afraid using that globe would reveal a bit too much."

"If they must endure without it, then so must I," Diancecht said, handing it back toward the other.

Lir did not take it. "Don't be a fool, man," he said. "You have to stay on your feet and functioning. They do not."

"If the time comes when there is no other way for me to do what I must, then I will consider it," the healer insisted. "For now, take it."

Lir sighed. "You are a stubborn man," he said, but he took the crystal, repocketing it. "I know you think my secrecy is cruel, yet I assure you, it is necessary if I'm to do anything for you."

"I wish that you could tell me why," Diancecht said.

"Sorry again," Lir said, "but there's just no other way. Now I'll go for the things and we'll get right to work. It won't be so hard to set up. I promise. There is more magic than machinery in the process." He raised a cautioning finger. "But remember: no matter what you'll witness here, you must keep it to yourself and ask no questions!"

"I have given my word to you," the healer said gravely. "I will keep it."

Lir nodded and went out. At a brisk walk he made his way through the nearly deserted avenues of the village to the hut he shared with Graikos. He stepped in through its door flap, then stopped, staring in surprise.

Two figures occupied the room. One was his servant. The other was a slim, childlike being of flowing silver hair.

"Muirgheal!" he said in irritation. "What are you doing here? I warned you about this!"

"I slipped in here quite safely," the shining one said assuringly. "With this sickness on them, there is almost no one about. Anyway, I don't think that matters much anymore."

"What do you mean? Why did you come?"

"That's because of me," Graikos said boldly. "After your meeting with the others, I slipped off down to the lake and told her all that's been going on."

"You?" Lir said. "You had no permission to do that."

"It was right for him to do it," Muirgheal said defendingly. "He thought I should know, and I agree. I mean to help."

"Have you gone completely mad?" Lir asked in disbelief.

"I have not," the childlike being shot back. "I *can* help them. I can lead them to that mound. I'm the one who first found it."

"They can find it just as easily without help," he told her.

"But not as quickly. They can't travel at night. But with me leading them, they can. They can reach there in half the time."

"It doesn't matter," he said angrily. "I forbid it."

"Not this time, Lir," the other said with equal heat. "Each day more that passes means that more of them may die. I will not stand by again and watch suffering that I could prevent."

"You know what it means if you reveal yourself to them," he said threateningly.

The being shrugged. "I don't care what you do to me. It couldn't be as terrible as knowing forever that I did nothing to help. The image of poor Moire haunts me now."

"What happened to her was not your fault. It was done by my order."

"An order my own humanity should have brought me to defy. I was weak before. This time I am not!"

The silver-haired one turned from him and moved toward the hut's back wall. It slipped an arm through a crack in the wattle.

"Wait!" called Lir. "You might be bringing danger upon our own people in doing this."

Muirgheal paused and looked back. "Sacrificing this noble people to protect our own makes us no better than the Fomor. Perhaps you can live with the idea, but I can't. Good-bye, Lir."

And with that the being slipped away through the crack, vanishing from sight.

Lir turned his stunned, infuriated gaze upon his servant.

"Graikos, do you understand what you've done?" he demanded.

The servant gave him a broad smile. "That I most certainly do!"


The sun was slipping swiftly down beyond the trees, draining off its light, leaving rivulets of shadow to trickle into the woods and join into a sea.

As the flood of darkness rose slowly to engulf the questing party, they pressed doggedly ahead, using every last stream of light to find their way on yet a few more, precious paces toward their goal.

From the beginning they had followed a faint trail that the O'Falva brothers had discovered in the woods. It was a broad way that had been well worn by the passage of many thousands of feet. But the following passage of some decades of years had all but obliterated it.

It was more the objects discovered than the near-invisible trail that kept them certain they were going the right way. They hadn't progressed far into the trees before they'd begun to come across the things.

Clearly in their past flight from the village, the people had tried to carry at least some precious belongings with them. But with the effects of the sickness rapidly weakening them, they had soon begun to abandon their baggage along the way. All manner of objects were scattered amongst the trees—finely thrown pottery, intricately ornamented cups and bowls, a once elegant but now warped and stringless harp, a wooden chest filled with rotting clothes, a child's toy cart—all giving grim testimony to the plague's disastrous effect.

But the party hadn't followed this trail of discards very long when they began to come across much more ghastly evidence of the flight: human remains.

Murchadh was the first to come across a skeleton: little more than a tangle of bones and tattered cloth. Then they found others, the numbers growing as they progressed. These were the stragglers, the ones too weakened to keep up with the pace of the exodus, dropping behind, failing, lying down to die.

Finally, however, even these grotesque trail markers were not enough to let the party of Nemedians go forward. When the night had risen fully about them, its darkness was nearly complete. All, including the skilled O'Falvas, were stymied, left with no recourse but to literally feel their way through the dense forest.

They tried this for a short time but then stopped, staring about them at the concealing shroud of black.

"Now what?" asked Nuada in frustration.

"We might try to just guess our way on," said Donnchadh. "But there's a very good chance we'll lose the exact direction, go far off our course, waste even more time than we would just waiting here for daylight."

"Well I, for one, have no wish to stumble about blindly in the dark," Mathgen said curtly. "I say that we stay here."

"It seems there's no other choice," Nuada conceded. "We may as well make camp."

"Wait!" said Murchadh, pointing ahead of them. "Look! What's that?"

They looked. Lights had suddenly become visible, flickering as they moved through the trees, coming steadily closer. Two softly glowing lights, one above the other, the lower green, the upper silver-white.

"Is it Fomor?" one of the warriors asked in fear.

"Or some evil forest spirit?" asked another.

"No," said Dagda. "I'm certain that it's not. I've seen those lights before."

"And so have I," said Donnchadh. "They led us to the settlement."

But unlike that encounter, this time the lights did not stay distant. They continued in toward the waiting company, coming finally through a last screen of trees and into their full view.

All stared in astonishment at the silver-haired being and its peculiar mount. It was Dagda, having had the most experience in meeting the two, who spoke first.

"So, you are real. Not just a vision that I had."

"We are most real," the shining being said in its sprightly voice, giving a little smile. "You may even touch us if you wish proof."

Taking its word, he moved forward while the others watched in uncertainty. The emerald-hued beast calmly awaited his coming. It showed no shyness as he lifted a big hand to gently touch and then stroke its broad nose.

The silver-haired one leaned forward, putting out one of its own contrastingly tiny hands to lightly stroke the champion's broad cheek.

"You see?" it said. "Quite solid."

"Yes," he agreed. "But you are very cold."

The pale hand was quickly withdrawn. "Our proper home is beneath the sea," the being explained as if a bit embarrassed. "Its chill runs in our veins."

"Just who are you?" Nuada demanded, moving up beside Dagda.

"My name is Muirgheal," it answered. "Beyond that, it is unimportant who I am. You need only know that I have come to help you."

"How?"

"By leading you. I know the place you seek. I can guide you through the night . . . if you are willing."

"Why, we could reach our goal in half the time!" said Murchadh.

"Not so quickly!" Mathgen protested. "You mean to run on through these woods all night? It'll be exhausting!"

"Little to pay to bring our people help sooner," Nuada replied.

"But why trust this . . . this creature?" Mathgen argued on. "It could be some malevolent spirit. It could as easily lead us far astray, or even to our deaths!"

"I trust it," Dagda said firmly. "I know it led us to our settlement. So does Donnchadh."

"Yes," that one agreed. "I'm certain it was the lights of these two who led us then."

"And this Muirgheal saved my life," Dagda added, looking to the being. "Twice, wasn't it?"

Muirgheal nodded.

"I thought so," said Dagda. "First from the lake and them from the beast. And the second time you risked your own life for me."

"Good enough," Nuada said heartily. "If Dagda trusts them, then so do I." He looked about him at the rest. "Are there any who disagree?"

All of the others shook their heads but Mathgen.

"I still say that this is foolish," he snapped. "We should stay here."

"Then stay here . . . alone . . . in the darkness," Dagda said. "Is that what you want?"

Mathgen glared at him a moment defiantly. Then reluctantly he shook his head.

"I'll go," he snarled.

"Good!" declared Nuada, turning toward the shining being. "Muirgheal, lead on!"

# Chapter 20

# The Plague Wraiths

They came out of the forest onto a large plain, and the mound was before them.

It rose up from the center of the flat expanse starkly, ominously. Its rounded surface was barren of growth even after all the years since its earth had been piled atop the still-smoldering bones.

The party stopped, staring across to it. There were fewer of them now. Over the past night and day of travel, the onslaught of the plague had taken its toll on them, healthy as they had all seemed at the start. Of the six warriors who had accompanied the party, only three remained. And Donnchadh O'Falva was gone too. Unable to keep pace, they had one by one turned back, hoping to return home before being overcome.

"There," announced Muirgheal, pointing to the mound. "As I promised."

"Then *you* walk now," said Dagda to Mathgen, pulling the man from his shoulder and dropping him down jarringly on his feet.

"Great stupid bear," Mathgen fumed. "How dare you carry me that way? The bouncing nearly jarred loose all my insides."

"I warned you not to keep slowing us," Dagda said.

"We should have just left him behind," said Nuada, "to go back on his own, like the others."

"They were sick," Dagda replied. "There's nothing wrong with this one. We still have need of his skills."

"If he really has them," Nuada added bitingly.

"I have them," Mathgen snarled. "But why I should use them for the likes of you . . ."

"You'll use them," Nuada cut in, stepping close to the other to stare him down, "or you'll find yourself left out here to get by on your own."

"There isn't time for this!" Murchadh said sharply, pulling the two apart. "Now, my brother may be lying back there in the forest dying of this thing. My whole family may be stricken as well by this time. And so may yours. The only way we're going to save them is to work together to get this blood—right now!"

"I'm sorry," Nuada said contritely. "You are right."

"Yes, yes," Mathgen agreed curtly. "So just what do we do next?"

Dagda looked to Muirgheal. "What do you say?" he asked. "You knew where the mound was. Do you know where any of these survivors are as well?"

The shining one shook its head. "I wish I could help you. But I saw no one about when I explored this place before."

"Then I say we start with the mound," Murchadh suggested.

"I agree," said Muirgheal. "It's the best place to find some sign of them."

They approached the mound. It loomed up more hugely, more horribly as they drew close. Dagda looked up at it and shook his head.

"Even seeing it, I can't believe in a burial mound so huge," he said. "Can it really be, or is this only piled stones and clay?"

"See for yourself," Muirgheal advised him, and pointed to a place where rainfall had begun eroding a jagged gully down one smooth slope of sterile, grey-black earth. "Dig there."

Putting down his spear, he used his round metal shield as a huge shovel, scooping out a hole. He had not gone very deep before the earth crumbled away. He stepped back as a section slid down the sloping gully to land at his feet. Then he and the other men stared in horror.

In the exposed space, bones could be seen—scores upon scores of them, blacked by fire, so tangled into a single grotesque mass that no individual skeleton could be distinguished. The many had truly become one in death.

"By all the gods," said Nuada, looking up at the swell of earth above them. "A mound so vast as this, all filled with these remains. Think of the thousands that must be here!"

"Their entire race," said Dagda grimly.

"That we will hope *not*!" Nuada replied.

During this time Murchadh had been moving up the slope in broad sweeps, searching across the surface of the mound. Now, having reached the very top, he called down to them excitedly:

"There are signs here of fires. Many fires."

"So!" said Dagda with relief. "At least we know that *some-one's* been here."

"Most of the fires are old," Murchadh reported. "But one of them looks fairly fresh. I'd say it was from only days ago."

"Are there any signs of trails from there?" Nuada called back.

Murchadh moved around, scanning the bare surface carefully. Then he shook his head.

"No," he said disappointedly, starting back down the slope to them. "This strange ground is very hard packed. And any signs that might have been made here have likely been washed away by the spring rains."

They turned from the mound and stood looking out toward the forests that surrounded the high plain.

"They could be out there anywhere, then," Nuada said. "Probably only a few, in all that great wilderness."

"And probably still in hiding from the Fomor," added Dagda. "It won't be easy finding them."

"Still, we've no choice but to try," Nuada said more briskly, looking to his companions. "Well then, it seems our only chance is to begin a sweep from here, working our way outward, and looking for some sign of them. We should divide up, to cover the most ground."

Dagda looked to the silver-haired one. "Muirgheal, will you help us in the search?"

"Of course I will," the being answered readily. "It's what I'm here for."

"Good!" he said. "Then I'll go with you."

"You needn't do that," Muirgheal told him. "I can search must faster alone."

"I'm certain you can. But these people could very well be dangerous. They might easily think that we're their enemies."

"I can take care of myself quite well," the being assured him.

"That may be, but I still won't have you risking it," he said stubbornly. "I owe too much to you. All of us do."

Muirgheal saw that the big man was not to be denied. The silver-haired head nodded in agreement. "As you wish then."

"All right," said Nuada, "then Mathgen and I will go together." He gave the man a grin. "We've become so close lately, I can't bear to be parted from him."

Mathgen's only answer was a glare.

Nuada turned to the three warriors. "Daithi, you go with Flann," he said to one pair of them, then looked to the third. "And Cumhea, why don't you go with Murchadh."

"Nuada . . ." the man said in a strained way, "I . . . well, I . . ."

"Cumhea?" Nuada said in concern, for the first time noting the pinched, flushed look of the man's face, "what is it?"

"The plague's on him is what," Dagda supplied. "Isn't it, Cumhea?"

"Yes, it is," the man admitted with great vexation. "Since the morning it has been." He put a hand to his belly, wincing at the touch. "I've tried ignoring it, but each step's become an agony now. My insides seem one hard knot."

Nuada clapped a hand to his shoulder. "Don't fight it any longer," he said. "You're a good man to have come this far. Sit down here. Rest."

"I thank you for that," the man said, and eased himself down right where he was, using his spear for support, groaning softly at the pain of movement. "Sorry, Nuada, and the rest of you."

"It's not your fault," Nuada told him. He looked around to the others. "But the same thing might be happening to any one of us at any moment," he said. "We're fast running out of time and searchers as well."

"Then we'd better not waste an instant more," Dagda said tersely. "Let's begin!"

It was a very odd pair indeed that moved through the trees.

In advance went the diminutive Muirgheal, moving on foot, the bright, quick gaze sweeping around for any smallest sign.

The Augh-iska had been left behind this time for fear it might alarm any quarry they came upon. But being afoot did not seem a hindrance to the being. It glided swiftly, silently ahead, slipping through the densest undergrowth as if it were not there.

Behind came Dagda, a towering, lumbering behemoth in contrast, trying to move with an equal stealth, but with as much success as a particularly large ox might have had.

They came into a small clearing and stopped there, looking around.

"Which way now, do you think?" Muirgheal asked him.

"Do you mind if I just rest a bit first?" he said, dropping down on a fallen tree trunk.

"What?" the bright being said in surprise. *"You* are weary?"

"We have traveled a great distance," he said by way of defense. "And you set quite a pace. And we've had no rest at all for these two days. Even I'm not tireless."

Muirgheal moved to him and peered at him closely. He did look very worn, face drawn and, for him, pale. Moreover, sweat stood upon his broad brow and had all but soaked his tunic.

The being moved yet closer, lightly touching his face, asking in a worried tone, "Are you all right? You don't have fever?"

"No, no" he assured with a touch of irritation. "I'm fine. It's just the heat."

It was indeed a very warm day, humid and quite windless within the shelter of the trees, making the atmosphere extremely close.

"All right then," Muirgheal said, and dropped down on the log beside him. "We'll rest. I forget that mortals, even ones such as you, require it at times."

He looked at the shining one who seemed as lively, spry, and dewy fresh as when they'd started.

"And just how is it that you stay so tireless?" he asked. "Have you got some magic power?"

"Oh, no power, really. I've just always been filled with a great energy. 'Charged up with life' my mother calls it. It's why I hate ever having to be at rest."

He considered. "So, you have a mother. And you said you were a being of the sea. You're a most curious . . . person Muirgheal. Do you mind if I ask you exactly what you are?"

"I can tell you that my people have many skills," the other replied. "With them they can live the way they like. Some love to sail the clouds. Some prefer to live and burrow within the earth. My own family has always been most at home in the sea. I'll say that much, but please, don't ask me more."

"Only one other question," he said, "if I don't give any offense. Can I ask you . . . are you boy or girl?"

"What?" Muirgheal said, clearly offended at that. "Why, I'm a girl, of course." The slender figure was drawn up and the chest thrust out as she struck a pose of pride. "A woman, in fact. And for the past hundred years I will have you know."

"Of course," he said hastily. "Certainly. I knew that. And a most comely woman too."

"Am I?" she said, seemingly somewhat abashed by the compliment. "It's not anything I've ever really thought about."

"There are . . . males of your kind as well?" he ventured, uncertain of his ground.

"Of course there are," she said. "I've just never had time or patience for them. I've always wanted to *do* things. To see things. To *be* things! And when I was given the chance to come here, to experience something of the life outside . . ."

He seized upon the word: "Outside?"

"We live in a place separated from the rest," she explained. "Closed off. The greater world has been unknown to most of us for centuries. Anyway, even when my task out here is finished, I'm not certain I could be content to return home."

"And what is that task?" he asked.

"Ah, ah!" she said, raising a warning finger. "No more questioning. You promised!"

"Sorry," he said. "I only wonder what's brought you to risk yourself in helping us."

"Nothing to do with my mission here, I can say," she told him with a smile. "There're some who'd tell you that's just the opposite. No, my helping you has been only my own idea. From the time I first saw you all bringing your ships upon these shores, my heart went out to you. I realized that you were truly living life, not like my own people. They are sheltered, soft, in many ways quite selfish. It seemed to me that there was nothing so important as helping you. For you were what I've dreamed to be."

He put a hand out, engulfing her tiny one. "I will remember what you've done for me . . . for us," he told her with great warmth. "To help us when you owe us so little. Thank you, Muirgheal."

She looked from his hand up to his open, earnest face. She

recalled an image of his wife diving into the poisoned lake and heard the words of Lir echo in her mind: "Muirgheal, your good intentions may very well cause these people to die."

She pulled her hand from his and turned away abruptly so that he would not see the tears welling in her eyes.

"Don't be so quick to praise," she said. "My 'help' may have brought you as much evil as good."

"What?" he said, nonplussed by her swift change. "I don't understand . . ."

"And I pray Danu you may never need to," she said, jumping quickly to her feet. "Now don't you think we should get on?" she asked briskly. "The time's rushing away."

This served effectively to shift his attention back to the desperate matter at hand.

"Yes," he said, standing up. "Of course you're right." He looked up to the little patch of sky visible from the clearing. "The sunlight is beginning to fade already." He looked to her, anxiety in his tones. "Muirgheal, what do you think? Can we really find any of these . . . these 'plague wraiths'?"

"You've no idea how much I hope so," she said.


They crossed the plain back toward the awful mound.

Most of the swollen mass of it was just a looming shadow barely visible against the night sky. But one small section of its slope was faintly lit by the soft, gold glow of a bonfire at its base.

As Muirgheal and Dagda approached, it first seemed to them that only two men sat about it. At one side was Mathgen, barely within the ring of firelight, knees drawn up in a posture of withdrawal, looking sullen. At the other side was Nuada, kneeling beside one of a row of lumps.

"Nuada?" Dagda called.

His friend looked around to see the big warrior and the glowing-haired being coming in.

"Did you find anything?" he asked hopefully.

"Nothing," said Dagda. It was now clear that the row of lumps were human forms huddled on the ground. "What's happened here?"

"It's come on all of them," Nuada said dismally. "Mathgen and I and the pair of you are all that's left." He gestured toward the form he stood beside. "Murchadh was the last, late this afternoon."

Dagda stepped up beside him, looking down at the man. He lay curled up on one side, face pinched with his pain. The three warriors beside him were in like or worse states of agony.

"We'll just have to keep on without them," Dagda said. "There isn't another choice."

"No. No choice," said Nuada.

He began to rise, but the effort caused him to sway suddenly. He stumbled and nearly fell, but Dagda caught him. The big warrior looked closely at his friend's white face and inflamed eyes.

"Nuada . . ." said Dagda.

"Let go," said Nuada irritably. "I'm all right."

He pushed the big man away. But a sudden spasm gripped him, nearly doubling him up. His hands went to his belly and he sat down hard, grunting with the pain.

"By the gods, he's got it too," Mathgen proclaimed in horror.

Dagda knelt by his friend. "Nuada, how long?"

The spasm passed, leaving Nuada panting but able to talk. "Since . . . yesterday," he gasped out. "Just let me rest a moment. I . . . I'll go on."

"He'll go on?" said Mathgen, a rising note of panic in his voice. "Certainly he will. Just like those others lying there. No. He's finished. We all are."

"Quiet, Mathgen," said Dagda, stepping toward the man.

"Why?" said the other, made defiant by his fear. "It doesn't matter now. We can't do anything now. We can't search again 'til dawn. By then we'll all be down."

"I said be quiet!" Dagda growled, stepping up right before him.

"You can't threaten me, you idiot!" said Mathgen, his voice shrill with near hysteria. "You're a dead man. It's on you. It's on all of us. We're dead right now." He screamed it at Dagda. "We're dead! Dead! Dead! De . . ."

The big man's hand swung around, palm out, to slap Mathgen across the side of the face. It was a light blow for the warrior, but still enough to knock the other back, senseless.

"Sorry," Dagda said with only minor contrition, "but I did ask you nicely twice." He turned and walked back to where Nuada sat with Muirgheal standing beside him.

"That was rather excessive, don't you think?" she asked, a bit taken aback by Dagda's use of force.

"Not for him," the warrior said simply.

"But he . . . he was speaking the truth, Dagda," Nuada gasped out through another spasm of pain. It *is* . . . only a matter of . . . time. And you . . . surely can't . . . depend on him."

"You've forgotten about me," said Muirgheal. "You can't search in the dark, but I can."

She pursed her lips and gave a high, sharp whistle. From the darkness beyond the mound there suddenly appeared a blur of green light, sweeping in toward them, halting by the fire to reveal itself as her glowing, hybrid steed. It stood prancing with energy, tossing its flowing mane as she walked to it.

"You see?" she said, taking the reins and patting the beast's wide nose. "With my Augh-iska I can cover a vast territory at great speed."

"What, hunt on that great beast with it glowing like an emerald afire?" said Dagda. "Anyone hiding out there would see you half a forest away. You'd never get close to them."

"Maybe," she replied, "but there's no time for caution now, only for bold chance. Have you any other choice?"

"You have *one*," said an eerie, piping voice from above them. It brought their startled gazes up to a dark figure that had appeared suddenly atop the mound. "You could simply talk to me," it said.

# Chapter 21

# Race Against Death

It did indeed seem as if a wraith of one of the thousands buried in the mound had materialized there on its crest to speak to them. The three below stared upward at the figure in shock for some moments before Dagda managed to find voice:

"Are you one of these . . . of the ones who died here?"

"I am the last," the voice answered, thin, forlorn, and hollow as a fall wind through dried reeds.

"Then you are the only one in this world that can help us," said Nuada. "Please, come down."

"I would ask that the one who seems a child and the strange beast it rides both withdraw some distance first," the figure replied. "They alarm me."

"They are no danger," Dagda assured. "This is Muirgheal. She is our friend."

"That may be, but I will take no chances," was the reply. "I have stayed alive a great many years that way."

"I understand," said Muirgheal. "We will be most happy to move away if you will come to talk."

She swung herself lightly onto the back of her steed and urged it away. The Augh-iska trotted some hundred paces from the mound into the darkness of the plain and stopped there, the softly glowing forms of beast and rider just within sight of the rest.

Apparently satisfied, the figure moved down the slope, into the circle of firelight. What that light revealed to Nuada and Dagda dispelled little of the impression that this was no living being but some ancient specter which they faced.

He seemed a very old man, but his much worn and weathered state made his exact age difficult to assess. The long straggling remains of his hair and his wisps of beard were a grey-white. His clothes were bits and pieces, some scraps of old cloth spliced and patched with deerskin, all so ragged they fluttered about him like the ruffled feathers of a wind-tattered bird. The limbs poking from various rents and remnants were scrawny, parchment skinned, and knob jointed. His face—what was visible through the hair—was deeply etched by lines, hollow cheeked, and very hollow eyed. But from within those black caverns of the sockets, glittering, blue-grey eyes fixed sharply, keenly, searchingly on them.

"You are certainly not Fomor," he said in that odd, airy voice. "Who are you?"

"We are the people of Nemed," Dagda said. "Nemed is our leader. Our clans followed him from the eastern lands to settle here."

"As our own did," the other replied. "But we followed Partholan. He was my own uncle. My name is Tuam."

"I am called Dagda. And this is my friend Nuada."

"It's very pleased we are to meet you, Tuam," Nuada said. "Our situation is most desperate. We . . ."

A new wave of pain took him, jerked him tight, held him rigid a long moment, and then passed, leaving him panting, shaking, and white faced.

"Most desperate indeed," said Tuam, stepping toward Nuada and examining him closely. "So it *is* the same sickness upon you as came on ourselves. I had thought as much when I saw your men being stricken through the day."

"You've been watching us so long?" said Dagda in surprise. "But how could you? From where?"

Tuam pointed back up the mound. "I've hidden right up there since you began searching in the forest. It is the safest place. I found it so when the Fomor were about. Of course, they ceased sending patrols here years ago. They decided it was a spirit of the ones they'd killed still lurking here. They wanted no more part of this place."

"Was it this same plague that killed all your people?" Nuada asked. "What happened to them?"

"They paid for their defiance," the man said bitterly. He sat down crosslegged by the fire, his bony knees thrusting out rather absurdly from the rags. "Thirty-five years ago we came here. We cleared land, built homes, tilled the soil, raised fat herds. We were strong and prosperous. When the Fomor came and demanded a tribute, Partholan laughed. Our force was greater than theirs. We were ready to fight. *We* threatened to destroy *them,* to march on their own stronghold on the northern coast. *That's* when the sickness came upon us."

"Why did you trek here?" asked Dagda. "Was it to escape?"

"At first. But soon we realized it was to have a place to die. As the plague swept through our people and we grew swiftly weaker, Partholan ordered a great burial pit dug in the center of this plain. It was to make it easier to deal with the great numbers of dead. In the end, that meant almost everyone."

"Only . . . only you survived?" Nuada asked through teeth gritted against another onslaught of pain.

"A dozen of us did, but only for a time. The hard life destroyed them soon. It was left to me alone to stay alive."

"Why remain here?" asked Dagda. "Why not go on, perhaps find other people?"

"I had to stay," he said simply. "I had to light the fires. It was on Beltaine that we came into this land—the festival day of our god Bel. And it was on Beltaine that the plague took us. Each year upon that day I light the ritual fire there, atop the mound."

"Why do you do that?" asked Nuada. "Isn't it a risk?"

"Someone must," he said, as if the question surprised him. "Someone has to keep the memory alive. It is important that people know, that they remember, isn't it? Or else, what is left? All these years I've kept my vow to do it, wondering if the last thoughts of our people would die with me. When you came and I saw that you were men like myself, I at first hoped that here at last was someone else who could hear of our fate, take up the memory and carry it on." He shook his head despairingly. "Now I see that I was wrong to hope. You are only victims too, as doomed as we were."

"Maybe not," said Dagda. "That's why we've come to find you."

"What?" the old man said in disbelief. "How can it be so? If this plague is upon your people, nothing can stop it."

"Yes . . . it can," said Nuada. He was speaking more gaspingly now, the effort to speak exhausting him. "We have a way. There is a cure. But only if you help."

"Me? What can I do?"

"You survived," said Nuada. "There is something in you . . . in your blood . . . that kept the plague away. We can use it to save our people but . . . but we must have your blood."

"My blood?"

"Yes," said Dagda quickly, "but not much of it. We don't mean to hurt you. We have a way to take it safely. We only need to . . ."

Tuam raised a silencing hand. "Be easy, large warrior," he said soothingly. "Your request does not frighten me. Of course I will help you."

"You will?" Dagda said in great relief.

"How could I not? I knew there was a reason why I had been left alive." His frail voice was growing stronger as he spoke, filling with a restored vigor at this new hope. "Now I see! This *must* be what it was: I'm meant to give you a chance, to help you survive, to see the Fomor beaten after all. If my blood can save you, I would give all of it, and gladly."

"That is not necessary," Nuada assured him. "Dagda, get Mathgen, quickly. The fates have blessed us, but there's no more time to lose."

Dagda went to the still-unconscious man and shook him, at first gently, to awaken him. It didn't work. Dagda shook harder.

Mathgen snorted and tossed his head groggily, eyes still closed. "Let me alone!" he mumbled thickly and tried to pull away.

"Sorry!" said Dagda. He unceremoniously dragged the man close to the fire, took up a waterskin, and squeezed a hard jet of water squarely into Mathgen's face.

"Ah! No! Stop!" the man burbled and gasped, coming full awake. Then he saw Dagda looming over him and cowered back. "Don't hit me again!"

"That I will not," Dagda assured him. "You've got your work to do." He indicated the man seated nearby. "We've found the last survivor."

Recovering from his fear and disorientation, Mathgen looked at Tuam in astonishment. "You have?"

"That's right. And if you mean to save us—and yourself—you'd best be doing what has to be done."

The logic was not lost on Mathgen. He swiftly moved to pull a leather packet from his shirt and unroll from it the equipment needed for his task.

The objects were simple: a leather thong, a small and keenly pointed knife, a tiny ceramic flask, and some white linen strips. He knelt beside the old man, laying them out upon the ground.

"I don't know what's going on or why," he said, "but it's of little matter now. You—whoever you are—would you mind bearing an arm for me?"

"My name is Tuam," the man said, without hesitation rolling back a ragged sleeve. "Do what you wish."

"So, it's only you now, is it, old man?" Mathgen said, tying the thong about the scrawny arm just above the elbow and drawing it tight. "Are you certain this won't be too much for you?"

"I've lived though much worse, boy," Tuam replied. "And if I die this time, it will be for something of worth."

"Quite a brave old man, eh?" Mathgen said in a snide way. "Well, we'll see." The tight thong had now raised the blue arteries into sharp definition on the man's forearm. Mathgen selected a large one on the inside of the elbow and lifted the little knife. "Hold on then."

The keen point plunged in, quickly and neatly opening the artery. Mathgen untied the thong, and the blood pulsed from the opening in a thin stream, running down the arm. In a deft move, he took up the little flask to catch the crimson liquid as it began to drip.

After an initial wince from the jab, Tuam watched the operation with total calm.

"There really is little pain at all," he commented.

"I know my skills, old man," Mathgen said haughtily.

"When this is over, Tuam," said Dagda, "you could come to live with us."

"What, leave here?" he said, shaking his head. "Ah, no. It's here I belong now. I wouldn't know how to live with others anymore. And *they* need me," he nodded to the mound, "to be their company and light the fires. You understand?"

"I do," Dagda told him. "It's your family here."

It only took moments before the flask was filled. Mathgen first carefully stoppered it and set it aside. He then pressed a pad of the linen to the tiny puncture and tied it in place with a strip of the same material.

"There," he announced. "All finished. A day or two, old man, and you'll be fully healed."

"Most impressive," Tuam pronounced. "But now, what will you do with my blood?"

"We must get it back to our healer," Nuada said. "And as soon as possible."

"Muirgheal could take it now! Tonight!" Dagda said. "With that beast of hers, she could be there before dawn!" He turned to look for her, calling "Muirgheal!"

The Augh-iska still stood where it had stopped, head down, seemingly grazing. But there was no sign of the woman.

"What's happened to her?" asked Dagda in bewilderment. He started toward the animal at a trot. "Muirgheal, where are you?"

Halfway there he saw the soft glow in the grass. The Augh-iska was nuzzling gently at it.

He rushed to the spot, kneeling beside the sprawled form of the silver-haired being.

"Muirgheal!" he said urgently. .

She stirred and with great effort lifted her head.

"Dagda. I . . . I'm sorry. It came upon me so quickly. I was suddenly . . . dizzy. I . . . fell."

"Can you get up?" he asked anxiously. "Can you move at all?"

She tried, her slender body straining, battling to move. Her limbs stirred slightly, but then she gave up, drained by the struggle.

"I'm . . . so weak!" she said in alarm. "Dagda . . . I'm afraid!"

"I'll take you to the fire," he told her. He carefully lifted her, her form like that of a doll in his huge arms, and carried her to the fire, laying her near to Nuada.

"It's come on her as well?" asked Nuada.

"I never thought it would touch me," she moaned. "I never thought it . . . oh!" She drew her legs in suddenly as a jolt of pain hit her. She shuddered through it, then went limp again, murmuring, "By Danu, that hurts!"

"Rest easy," said Dagda, soothingly. "There's nothing you can do."

"Dagda, her horse-thing," Nuada said. "Perhaps you could ride it."

The animal had followed them back and now stood close by, watching its mistress with clearly fretful eyes.

Dagda rose and moved toward it cautiously.

"Be easy, fellow," he told it. "Just stand easy there. Easy."

He lifted a hand toward its bridle, but it would have none of that. It shied away with a lightning move Dagda could not match. It trotted away out of reach to stand again, watching warily.

"That will . . . will do no good," Muirgheal said in a near breathless voice. "It will never leave me. Oh, Dagda, I'm sorry again! I've failed you!"

"No!" he said earnestly, kneeling by her again. "You can't say that. You've done everything you could."

"But you . . . you don't understand. You don't know what I've done. I want to tell you . . ."

He put a hand on hers. "It doesn't matter. There can't be anything that your risks haven't made up for. Now you have to save your strength. We need to see about getting help for you . . . and all of us."

He stood up, looking toward Mathgen.

"Mathgen, we start now," he announced determinedly.

The other man looked at him in shock.

"We? Now?"

"There's no one else. We've got to risk finding our way back in the dark. Our time is used up. For every heartbeat that passes now, more are going to die!"


The two men worked their way through the night-shrouded woods.

They had left the others after making them comfortable by the fire. The old man had promised to keep watch over them. Dagda had taken the lead, following the faint trail and the signs they had made on their journey out to better mark the way. Still, it was very slow going in the dark, and made even slower by the often-stumbling, always-complaining Mathgen.

"I don't see why you've brought me at all," he grumbled. "I can't keep up your pace. I'll hold you back."

"We both have to go," Dagda told him impatiently. "That way, there's more chance one of us will make it."

"That will be you in any case," Mathgen persisted. "You're the one who has the strength of four."

"If I ever had so much," Dagda said, "it's fast draining from me now."

Mathgen stopped, looking after the big man in stunned realization.

"You've got it too!"

"Yes, yes," Dagda admitted brusquely, looking back to him. "Don't make a great thing of it. Since yesterday afternoon I've felt it. But I couldn't let them know. We're their only hope."

"But . . . but you can go on?" Mathgen asked. "I mean, there's *nothing* that can stop *you.*"

"I may at last have found one," he said, wincing at a twinge of stomach pain. "So if I do fail, then it's up to you."

"And just how will I find my way in this, alone?"

"I'll last 'til morning," Dagda promised. "One way or another I will. In daylight even you should be able to follow the trail. Now, come on!"

They pressed ahead. But the long days of effort and the wasting effects of the plague finally began to have their effect even on the powerful Dagda. He began to stumble as the spasms of pain, grown too powerful to ignore, wrung his stomach tight. He was forced to stop and rest more and more often, white faced, soaked in sweat, panting for breath.

When the dawn light finally pierced through the trees to light the forest floor, it revealed a man nearing the end of his endurance, little more than shuffling along.

And Mathgen followed, watching fretfully, clearly waiting for the giant man to fall.

At last he did. A massive pain doubled him up and sent him staggering into a tree. He clung to it a moment, fighting to keep upright. His grip failed and he crashed down, grunting, thrashing on the ground, clutching at his belly as if to crush the thing tormenting his insides.

When the convulsion passed, he remained where he had fallen, chest heaving with his labored breaths.

"Dagda!" said an anxious Mathgen, kneeling by him.

"Now . . . I've an idea . . . how Moire . . . must have felt," Dagda puffed out.

"Can you go on?"

"I . . . think . . ." He tried to sit up, but it was no good. The tortured muscles refused. He fell back, shaking his head. "No. I'm finished. It's you now, Mathgen. You."

Mathgen shook his head violently. "No! You can't do this to me. I can't go. Not alone."

"Listen now," Dagda growled, "you have no other choice. You are all that's left between ourselves and death."

"All right," Mathgen said resignedly. "I understand. Where do I go then?"

"Keep on toward the southeast. Look for the signs. And go as quickly as you can. The plague might come on you too at any moment."

So Mathgen left Dagda and went on, moving through the forest with what speed he had. For half the day he made good distance, but by noon the effort was clearly telling upon him.

He paused to rest and wipe his streaming face. He lifted his waterskin and drank deeply. He grimaced, clutched his stomach, and then dropped to his knees, retching violently.

"My gods!" he murmured in horror when the spell had passed. "The plague!"

He forced himself to his feet and went on, his only chance now to reach the village and deliver the precious blood. The desperation gave him renewed energy.

But it was only for a time. His own long exertion and the rising plague at last defeated him too. He stumbled, fell, and lay stretched on the ground, unable to rise again.

Semiconscious, he lay for some time in the forest, alone in the warm green-gold afternoon forest where only the songs of birds and his soft moaning broke the silence.

Then there came a rustling, and the soft pad of footsteps. They moved closer, closer, stopping right nearby.

Mathgen was rolled over. The movement roused him slightly and he opened his eyes.

Against the sunlight through the treetops above, the outline of a strange, dark figure loomed. It held a spear whose well-honed point hovered just above his throat.

# Chapter 22

# Salvation

A most astounding maze of objects filled the tabletop in the hut of Diancecht.

Beakers, bowls, cups, flagons, jugs, and kettles were connected by troughs of copper, pipes of silver and gold, tubes of a clear and glass-like substance, crisscrossing and intertwining in bewildering complexity.

Through this system there traveled a constant flow of liquid. It began at a glass retort suspended by chains above a glowing brazier. The clear substance within it boiled furiously, welling up into the tapering neck, along a coiling tube, and on into the maze. Somewhere in its travels near the heart of the seemingly absurd jumble, it passed into a curious pulsing object, like a tiny, translucent heart. At every pulse it glowed with violet light. And at every pulse the clear liquid being drawn in at one side was squirted from the other, turned a brilliant sapphire hue.

After some more traveling, coiling, dripping, cascading, and being heated several times in different receptacles, it finally plopped in thick, fat droplets into a basin, forming a jelly-like mass of luminescent green-blue.

Lir was at the moment pouring more clear liquid into the first retort to keep the process going. He was trying to be careful, but an obvious nervousness made his hands unsteady. Several drops spilled, sizzling as they struck the brazier's coals.

"Careful there," remarked Graikos, who stood at his elbow, watching.

"You do it, then," Lir said irritably, thrusting the pitcher into his servant's hands. "Haven't I got a right to be distracted? I mean, what if they're all dead?"

"You've been saying that since Donnchadh and those others came back two days ago. But we've heard no more since. Anyway, the plague shouldn't have killed any of them by now."

"They could still be lying somewhere, dying. Like poor Diancecht there."

They looked across to where the healer lay upon his pallet. The courageous man had finally succumbed to the plague's effects and lay unconscious, drained of color, body shrunken by dehydration and exhaustion, breathing shallowly.

"I think he's very near the end," Lir said. "A day more and it won't matter for him." He turned back in frustration to his assemblage. "It's maddening!" he said with heat. "The transformation process is running smoothly. The distillation works. I could produce the remedy so quickly. I only have to have the blood. Where is the blood!"

"It will come, Lir," Graikos said assuringly. "They have Muirgheal. They have Nuada and Dagda. Nothing can stop them. They will return."

"I'm glad you have such faith," said Lir. "But will it be in time?" He shook his head irritably. "Ah, I can't just stand here watching this liquid bubble uselessly. I'm going out to try to see just how long we do have. Watch over the healer," he ordered Graikos as he went out the door. "I'll be back."

Outside he found that the sour-sweet atmosphere of death hung upon the village.

A cart went by him laden with the contorted, stiffening bodies of the dead, drawn by men who looked little better than dead themselves. He followed it through avenues otherwise deserted, past huts from which moans of pain and death wails sounded, out the village gates and down the hill.

At the base of the slope, the huge furnace of the smelter blazed, its flue sending a greasy grey-black plume of smoke high up in the still air. With most too weakened now to dig graves or cover up the dead, the living had resorted to mass cremation. Using the furnace for the purpose was a grisly but most efficient means.

As the carts arrived, the few men still able wrestled the forms off and carried them to the furnace opening. Without ceremony they flung the bodies—their own friends, family, workmates—into the flames. The smelter created to provide a means for life now consumed the dead, in seconds reducing them to ashes and fragmented skeletal remains.

Nearby, Nemed lay upon a stretcher, propped up, watching the grim labor with dispair. He too was now deeply in the clutches of the plague, wheezing, coughing, wincing with each new throe. As Lir approached, the older man took note, turning a hollow, anguished gaze to him.

"Liam," he said. "Have you any hopeful word for me?"

"I am ready to make the cure," the other replied. "We can begin saving your people very quickly after the blood arrives."

"*If* it arrives."

"Oh, I've no doubt of that," Lir lied, trying to bolster the older man's spirits. "Any time now."

His attempt met no success. Nemed looked back toward the smelter, into the fiery maw. For an instant an incandescent skull was visible there before it was swallowed by the flames.

"We talked once of making plows and hoes," he said slowly, dismally. "Do you remember? It seems so very, very long ago. That brief, glowing moment when I dreamed our goal was won. The dream's burning now. Burning before our eyes."

"Nemed, you should not be in this place," Lir said. "It can do no good for you."

"How can I be elsewhere?" Nemed replied. "Who else can be here to . . . to say good-bye? These are my children. I know the name, the face, the soul of every one who is being cast in there. Why look," he pointed to a newly arrived cart as the bodies were removed, "look there! Gentle dreamer Sadhbh. Boisterous Cormac—only eight years old. Bold, brilliant Aoengus. And Seanan. My Seanan! Another lifelong friend." He looked to Lir, tears streaming down his face. "There can be no more greater torture than this, and no torture more deserved for myself who've killed them all."

"Easy, Nemed," Lir said, patting the man's shoulder comfortingly. "Please, be easy."

The man subsided, exhausted by the outburst, sitting with gaze fixed on the nightmare scene, sobbing quietly. Lir left him, moving on to where he saw Goibniu supervising the cremations.

Even that energy-filled man was clearly near to exhaustion,

but only from constant labor. He seemed one of the few as yet untouched by plague.

"Can't anyone get Nemed away from here?" Lir asked him.

"No one can shift him," the smith answered. "But it's of little matter. He's rarely conscious anymore."

"How many dead?"

"Almost three hundred," Goibniu said bluntly, the tough little man dealing with the grim business practically. "At last count, as many more near dead. The rest . . . well, there are very few now who haven't shown the signs. A matter of time, as Diancecht said. Two days? Three at the most? After that we'll all be dead."

Lir left him and returned to Diancecht's hut. His look and mood had been made all the more solemn by the smith's frank assessment.

Inside, Graikos sat beside the healer, cooling the man's burning forehead with a damp cloth.

"How goes it out there?" he asked his master.

"Worse than I thought," Lir said grumpily. He stepped to the table and contemplated his painstakingly constructed apparatus. "Well, there's nothing more to do now but to keep this junk collection pumping and hope it'll be needed soon," he announced.

He carefully checked over each piece and each connection for any stoppages or leaks. Finding none, he dropped heavily down on a stool and stared at the mass, his eyes following bright bubbles as they scooted along the tubes.

It had a rather hypnotizing effect. Soon the weary man was dozing off, head dropping onto the table atop his folded arms.

But then a light disturbed him. It was a bright, orange-white, flaring light from just ahead.

He walked toward it. Soon he realized it was the smelter he approached, the yawning furnace door filled with fiery glow, the black smoke plume rising high above.

A figure stood before the door—a gaunt form starkly silhouetted against the glaring light. It was someone he knew.

"Nemed?" he said, stepping up to it.

The figure turned. And it was Nemed, but also something terrible—the face half burned, charred bones thrusting out through heat-crisped skin that was cracked and crumbling away.

"We're all dead now," the thing said in a rasping voice. Its arm lifted to point a blackened and still smoking finger at him. "Only you are left. Our friend. Our savior. Isn't it your turn?"

And suddenly a hundred arms were thrust out from the inferno beyond the furnace door. A hundred scorched, skeletal arms stretched out, their bony fingers grabbing at him, seizing him, dragging him toward the searing heat. And there, within the roiling fire, a hundred skulls with blazing eyes and writhing tongues of flame leered out at him.

"Master!" someone called.

It was the voice of Graikos, bringing him awake.

He shook his head to clear it of the dream and looked toward his servant still seated at Diancecht's side. But Graikos was looking toward the door.

"Li . . . Liam," he said with some uncertainty, "we have a visitor."

Lir looked to the doorway. A figure stood silhouetted there —a strange, wild figure of sinewy form, piercing eyes, and raven-black hair.

"Moire?" he said, peering at it. "Is that you?"

"I am called the Morrigan," she said in a brusque way. She pulled a small flask from within her deerskin shirt, holding it out to him. "I am told that you need this!"

A hand moved to softly caress Muirgheal's cheek.

She stirred, opening her eyes. The face of the one who knelt beside her came into focus.

"Lir!" she said with surprise. "Are you really here?"

"I am," he assured her. "We came as soon as we could."

She still lay beside the fire at the base of the mound. It was night. Nearby Graikos and several other men from the village moved about the area with torches, looking to the other stricken who had been left behind. The old man called Tuam who had stayed with them had warily moved some distance away from the new arrivals. But the faithful Augh-iska remained nearby.

"The blood . . . you got it?" she asked Lir. "You made the cure?"

"Yes. I left others to give it out to those in the village. I came to find you."

"Will they recover?"

"Many, I think. Those not too badly taken."

"Dagda? Nuada?"

"We found Dagda on our way here. I gave him a dose." He looked around. A man was just lifting a little bowl to the unconscious Nuada's lips. "Nuada's getting his. It should be in time. But now for you!"

He lifted a bottle and poured out a few drops of a thick, deep-purple liquid into a small goblet.

"Here, drink this," he said, gently lifting her head and holding the cup for her.

She shook her head. "It's too late."

"No, it can't be," he said in dismay. "What do you mean? It's not too late for them."

"They are mortal creatures. Beings of warmth and air. I am something colder. Something of the sea. The plague runs quicker through my veins. I am near the end."

Indeed, the sickness did seem to have affected the sprightly creature differently. Instead of wracking her with fever and fits of pain, it had simply sapped away the vitality of the lithe body, leaving her strange, luminous quality vastly dimmed.

"You can't be dying," he told her firmly. "I won't contemplate it. Now drink."

"I will, for you," she said. She sipped at the dark liquid obediently, and he laid her head gently back.

"Lir," she said, "I want to tell you that I have no regrets in this."

"Never mind," he said. "Just rest. Let the cure work."

"Tell my family that I feel I was fulfilled. Take care of the Augh-iska. Oh, and remember not to overfeed your fish."

"Stop it!" he said, alarmed at the fatalistic talk and at the waning strength of her voice.

"No. Please listen. I have to say it all. I know I brought you into this. I'm not sorry I did. They need us. They deserve our help."

"How can you say that?" he asked. "Look what helping them has brought on you."

"It was by my choice, and I'd chose it again. Lir, *they're* the ones who are important here, not us. Don't you see yet? If we don't help them, we're not really alive. Just tell me you won't leave them. Not now. They'll need you even more now."

"Muirgheal, don't do this," he pleaded. "*I* need *you*! You *have* to stay with me!"

"That's one more order I'm afraid I can't obey," she told him. She lifted a slender hand to clutch his arm. Her fading voice was urgent. "Just promise me you'll help them," she said. "Promise me."

"I . . ." he began. But he stopped as the hand dropped limply from his arm.

Graikos moved up beside him, lifting his torch high.

"Is she all right?" the man asked.

Lir didn't answer. He sat hunched over the still, small form. The torch struck glinting highlights in the silver hair and touched the pale, childlike face with the false warm hue of life.

## Part Three

# The Final Tribute

# Chapter 23

# Hostages

"Some of them survived?" clanged the metallic voice of Balor.

"Yes, Commander," Tethra replied. "A patrol was sent in as you ordered. We told them they would find nothing but the dead."

"And so they should have by now," said the armored giant. This time it stood beside its massive throne, the flat crown of its cylindrical head nearly touching the high ceiling of the huge reception room.

"They observed the village from the hills," the captain explained. "From their report it would seem that approximately half the villagers did not die."

"How is it possible?" Balor asked. "Could it be proof that they do have outside help? Does it mean that the Departed Ones somehow aided them?"

"If so, it was extremely poor aid," Tethra scornfully declared. "Those people are decimated. The estimate is that little more than two hundred warriors remain, and all of them have been badly weakened by the plague. From their speed of recovery, it will be a great while before they can mount anything but a token defense. They may not have been destroyed, but they are all but helpless."

"So! Perhaps we were wrong to believe that they had help,"

the voice rang out. "Perhaps the plague has lost its potency or simply has a lesser effect on them. In any case, this once more changes things. Yes. We no longer need to destroy them utterly. We can return to our first strategy. Let them be thralls, and our poor creatures who think themselves men can after all reap the benefits."

"You mean to let Cruc's rabble deal with the problem?" Tethra asked.

"It would seem safe to let them now," Balor replied. "Send orders to that Fomor scum to march in force at once. If they act swiftly, there will be nothing to thwart them this time."

The village gates burst open from the impact of a ram wielded by two score of burly Fomor warriors.

The handful of spears that had rained down upon them from the walls had been ineffectual in slowing the heavily shielded beings. Now they charged through, followed by a tidal wave of Fomor brandishing weapons and shouting exultant battle cries.

The fierce onslaught was met by a pitifully small defense. Some two score Nemedians, barely recovered from the plague's effects, moved forward to meet the horde, Dagda at their head, Nuada and the one now called the Morrigan at his either hand.

They fought valiantly, desperately, slashing into the oncoming Fomor, even holding them at bay. But they could not keep that up for very long. Their only partially recuperated strength was quickly overtaxed. Their numbers were rapidly outmatched ten to one by the inflowing enemies. They were driven back, retreating through the village toward the center as the Fomor spread out to rampage along every avenue.

Finally the remaining knot of defenders was forced into the central yard before the main hall. There they were trapped, forming a ring to face attackers who moved in from all sides.

They continued to put up what fight they could as the Fomor pressed in closer and closer. Nuada took on four swordsmen at a time. Goibniu laid about him with his blacksmith's maul, cracking skulls and limbs. Dagda, his sword lost, was using the body of a hapless enemy as a club.

The Morrigan, who had escaped all of the plague's weakening effects, fought most savagely. She winnowed about her with her blade, piling up dead and wounded foes. From her throat issued harsh caws of triumph at each new drawing of blood.

Finally Cruc himself pushed through his warriors to confront her. She drove in at once, locking blades with him.

"Give it up now!" he ordered her. "See your friends? Drop your sword or all of them will die."

She glanced around. The fight was over for the others. Dagda was tightly ringed by a dozen men, their spear and sword points poised to sink home. Nuada was disarmed, down on one knee in exhaustion, bleeding from a dozen wounds. Half the remaining defenders were hurt or killed, the rest simply too worn to fight on.

Still, she hesitated, looking back to Cruc with hatred flaring in her eyes. He saw the hate, and his face grew pale with fear.

"Surrender," he said, a bit more urgently this time, "and we will let you live."

"Do it," Dagda told her. "What can you gain by fighting on now?"

"Just more Fomor dead!" she cried. "I want revenge!"

"Don't waste your life!" Nuada pleaded. "There'll be another time!"

This logic at last pierced through the blood lust that had seized her. She disengaged from Cruc, backed away, and dropped her sword.

The Fomor captain's concern was quickly replaced by an air of cockiness.

"A wise choice, woman," he said. "But I promise there will *not* be another time." He looked around to the wolf-headed lieutenant named Faolchu. "See them all disarmed and under heavy guard," he commanded. "And have all the other villagers brought here!"

The Fomor warriors at once began a thorough scouring of the village, searching every hut, rounding up inhabitants, herding them toward the village center. Those recovered from the sickness enough to walk alone helped some of those who could not. The rest of the disabled were toted along by Fomor who upon arrival dumped them ungently to the ground. The yard filled rapidly with the dispirited folk.

Captain Cruc personally searched the main hall. He found a recovering Nemed resting there. Though the aging man was very weak, the Fomor callously prodded him from bed and sent him stumbling outside to join his erstwhile warriors.

Cruc smiled with malicious pleasure as he saw Nemed stagger and nearly fall, only to be caught and upheld by Dagda.

"So, you are not so arrogant now as when you sent me away from here in shame," he crowed.

The boar-headed warrior named Torc came up to him. "We have 'em all here, Cap'n," he reported.

"Search again," Cruc snapped. "Especially for children. I don't want a single one to escape."

"What do you mean to do?" Nuada demanded.

Cruc turned to him. "Worse than we meant to do the first time we met," he said. "But that is your own fault. Your own foolishness in defying us. Then we wanted only tribute from you. Now you will be our slaves."

"You can't make us obey you," Dagda told him.

"We can," Cruc said tersely, "or your children will die!" He looked to the wolf-headed one. "Faolchu, separate the children from the rest. All of them!"

Helpless, the Nemedian adults watched as the Fomor combed through the assembly, pulling out everyone less than twelve years old and driving them together in a separate group. The children huddled close, looking around fearfully, many whimpering or crying aloud.

"You really mean to take all?" Nemed asked in a broken voice.

"All of this lot," Cruc replied. "They will stay with us from here on. They will stay alive, but only so long as you do as we say. You will stay here, grow your crops and raise your livestock." He grinned sardonically. "That's all you wanted anyway, wasn't it? But you will provide two thirds of all you produce to us, along with two thirds of any new issue, to insure your continued . . . 'loyalty,' shall we call it? That will also insure you never grow enough to be a threat again. Do these things without fail, and you can live a peaceful life in your valley, untroubled by us."

"You really expect us to accept such monstrous terms?" Nuada asked.

"You still don't understand," Cruc replied. "These are not terms. They are commands. Your only alternative is death!"

He turned to Faolchu. "Take the children out!"

Nemed and his people watched in agony as the children were loaded into carts and hauled away—some three score of them, all that the plague had left.

With the children gone, the Fomor began to withdraw, a few companies at a time, taking the collected weapons of the villagers with them.

Cruc went with the last group, pausing at the shattered gates to look gloatingly back to them.

"Regain your strength soon!" he advised. "Summer is nearly upon you, and you have much work to do. Come fall, we will be here to collect our share of a bountiful harvest!"

"We *cannot* leave those children in their hands," Nuada fiercely declared.

He was in the main hall along with the others hurt in fight. Their wounds were being treated by a wan but mobile Diancecht, aided by a much more recovered Mathgen. Nemed and the few able clan elders were present as well.

"And just what do you believe we can do about it?" the healer asked as he bound a cut in Goibniu's sinewy arm.

"We can find them and rescue them somehow," Nuada said.

"Somehow?" Goibniu echoed in a skeptical tone. "You don't know anything about where the Fomor are going, what their stronghold is like, or how they'll keep the children once they're there."

"Liam would likely have known these things," said Dagda.

"Yes, we could surely use him now," Diancecht agreed. "Nuada, you're certain he said nothing to you before he disappeared?"

"When he brought the cure to us at the mound, I wasn't even conscious," Nuada replied.

"I was barely so," said Donnchadh. "But he said nothing to me or anyone. He simply took up the body of that . . . that child . . ."

"She was a woman," Dagda corrected.

"If you say so. He took up her body, mounted that strange green beast, Graikos behind him, and they rode away."

"Poor Muirgheal," Dagda said in grief. "She should not have had to die for us."

"Most fascinating," Diancecht mused. "I wish I had met this being. And I would like to have known more of the relationship between her and Liam."

"Do you think he will come back?" Nemed asked him.

"I can't say. However, he is certainly not here to help us with our dilemma now."

"I say that once we're recovered and rearmed, we attack the Fomor and have this out at last," Dagda stated bluntly.

"And what chance will we have then?" asked one of the

men. "Even with everyone well and able to fight, we'll be out-numbered nearly three to one by them. And to attack their own stronghold? Why, they'd wipe us out."

"At least we'd die facing them in a fight instead of cowering here as helpless slaves," said Dagda.

"You'd sacrifice all that are left in a hopeless fight?" Nemed said, aghast at the idea. "No. I forbid it. No more of us will die. Our only choice is to do what they have said."

"Give up our children?" asked Nuada. "Give our crops and herds to them?"

"I think Nemed is right," put in Mathgen, finishing up the treatment of another wounded man. "I mean, we are alive. We can remain so. So can the children. It is certainly a more agree-able prospect than being massacred."

"What, to live a life more sorry, more degraded than the one we left our homeland to escape?" Nuada returned.

"Your arguments are useless," Nemed wearily pointed out. "You ignore the fact that there is nothing else we can do."

"We don't know that!" said Nuada. He stepped close to his chieftain, speaking earnestly: "Nemed, don't just give up now. It *can't* be hopeless. There has to be some way we can act against them, get back the children, even attack them, as Dagda said. I mean to find out."

Nemed eyed his young champion thoughtfully. "How will you do that?"

"I'll follow their host back to its home," he said simply. "I'll spy out where they live, what strengths and weaknesses they have, where the children are kept, anything I can. Then we'll be able to determine just what is possible."

"It is very risky," Nemed said. "You'd have little chance alone."

"He won't be alone," said Dagda. "I'll go with him."

"I too would go," came a rasping voice.

They all turned toward a far, shadowed corner of the room where an angular, dark-haired figure stood alone. So quiet, so withdrawn had the Morrigan been that they had forgotten her. Now she moved out to join the rest.

"I have a special reason to visit them," she said, "and a special reason to see the children saved. Will you have me?"

"Dagda, what do you say?" Nuada asked the champion.

"I say there's no one who more deserves to go."

"Welcome then," said Nuada. He looked to Goibniu. "Smith, are you up to fashioning new weapons for us?"

"Just let me heat my forge," the man said with reborn energy. "You'll get my finest work yet."


In the undersea cavern of Lir, the inhabitants were gathered nearby the central lagoon for a ceremony.

The body of Muirgheal was laid upon a small bier, hands folded upon the breast, face relaxed in soft and peaceful lines, as if she were having a most pleasant dream.

Lir himself—his Liam disguise of beard and ragged clothes now removed—stood at the head of the bier, looking down at the childlike face. The others listened in reverential silence as he spoke:

"I'm not very good at this kind of thing," he said awkwardly. "Until now, I've never lost anyone close to me. All I can think to say is that I've never known a person of more tender nature or of greater capacity for generosity than Muirgheal. She was a being of the cold sea, and the blood ran chill in her, but no heart ever beat with a greater warmth of passion for life."

He lifted a hand. In it he clutched a short, tapered rod of translucent crystal, like a blue-white icicle.

"Now I'll prepare you, Muirgheal, to send you home. You will find your last rest with your family in our enchanted isle."

He touched the tip of the rod lightly to the crown of the silver-haired head. At once a stream of light poured out from it like a thick liquid, flowing down across the slender form to encase it in the glow.

He lifted the rod again. The glow faded. Now Muirgheal was surrounded by a covering like a thick layer of ice, so clear that the view of the woman within it was only slightly blurred.

"There," Lir said. "Her body will be protected on its last journey." He raised his voice to call out: "Augh-iska, we are ready."

From one of the grottos the green hybrid steed instantly emerged. It was now harnessed to a sleek and elegant chariot whose front and sweeping sides were the upthrust head and outspread wings of a silver swan.

Though the vehicle seemed rather large for the single animal, the Augh-iska pulled it easily, taking it across the cavern at a trot to stop beside the bier.

At Lir's signal, several men lifted the encased form and

gently slipped it into the chariot. When they had finished, Lir stepped up close to the beast's head.

"It is only fitting that you, Muirgheal's most faithful companion, should have the honor of carrying her home," he said to it. "And you shall do so, but you have one other task as well. On your way, you must return me to the land of our mortal friends."

"No!" said a vast and strident voice, echoing about the cavern.

It came from above them. They all looked up to the billowing clouds of brilliant light which filled the dome of the cavern and imparted illumination to the vast space.

A form was becoming visible there, like a huge object moving downward through the luminous mist, taking on solidity and color and defined form as it approached.

Finally it was clearly visible: a human face; a woman's face, not youthful but still cleanly featured and unlined; finely sculptured forehead, chin and nose; mouth strong and brows high arching; eyes the chill blue of a clear winter sky.

"Queen Danu!" said Lir, clearly somewhat disconcerted by her sudden appearance.

"As you have not seen fit to communicate with me, our high-druids have sent my image to you," the face replied.

"I'm honored," he said, bowing low.

"Of course you are not," she snapped back in a voice more chilling than her eyes. "Muirgheal's people had some sense of her distress. They had visions of her in an alien land, surrounded by mortal beings. They became certain she was dying, and then dead. I see with great distress that they were right."

"She died very bravely," he said defensively, "helping to save others."

"She died meddling with the mortals' lives," Danu retorted. "She died because you disobeyed my command to stay out of mortal affairs. Your task—your *only* task—was to keep watch on the Fomor actions and to warn us if ever they should come our way. Instead you have all but revealed both your own existence and ours, betrayed the trust in you, risked your people, and caused the death of one of my most loved subjects."

"I will not apologize," he told her boldly. "Muirgheal herself told me that she had no regrets for what she did."

"How dare you or she make such decisions by yourself?" Danu stormed. "It is the safety of the whole of Tir-na-nog that we speak of. It's our security, our very survival that you've endangered by going to this mortals' land. And now you are planning to return?"

"Yes! To finish what has been started, partly thanks to me! They are badly weakened and very vulnerable now. The Fomor certainly are not going to let them alone."

"You cannot become involved in their battles," she said.

"It's our battle too," he called back. "Don't you see? We've got to help them fight. It's something we should have been doing all along. These people are waging what should have always been our war."

"They are mortals. Of no consequence to us," she replied dismissingly.

"They should be *everything* to us!" he argued back. "What have we—the great immortals, the masters of sorcery—become to this outside world? Nothing! We have no worth, not even to ourselves. In the Isle of Enchantment we don't age or know pain. We've escaped the hardships and we live in comfort. But Muirgheal was right: we aren't really alive. We've counted ourselves superior to mortals. But *they* are the important ones. To them life has a value. They can lose it or chose to give it up. Muirgheal learned that from them. Her death *had* value. And I've finally learned from her. I'm going back."

He looked around for Graikos who stood close by as usual, the bulging sack in his hands. "Are you ready?" he asked.

"That I am," the swarthy man eagerly replied.

Lir tossed him the crystal rod and climbed into the chariot's car. Graikos stowed the rod in the sack and climbed in behind him.

"If you do return," the voice of the vast image boomed out ominously, "you will do it without help from us. Your magic will not work for you. Your sack of marvels will become useless."

He looked up to her face, his own hard with determination.

"Your threat won't stop me. But realize that if you do take away my powers, if you prevent me giving them any aid, then you will be as much a cause for the next Fomor villainy as they are themselves." He pointed to the form that lay beside him in the car. "Muirgheal asked me this once, and I now ask you: can you live with that idea?"

He picked up the reins to urge the Augh-iska away. The voice of Danu came to him again, a note of appeal in it this time.

"Wait, Lir. Please think before you act. Do you really know how much it is that you risk?"

He looked at Graikos, then back to her with a defiant grin. "That I most certainly do!" he said.


Goibniu was as good as his word.

It took him only a day and night of intense work to provide beautifully fashioned new swords, shields, and spears. Then the tiny band was off.

Their trio had been made four by the tracker Donnchadh O'Falva, who easily followed the clear trail made by the Fomor host. His brother Murchadh, though he had argued to come, was left behind, still too weakened by the plague for hard travel.

As Dagda left the valley on yet one more desperate mission, he paused at the edge of the forest to look back. The others paused too, following his gaze. The scene spreading below was indeed a serene and beautiful one, but ironically so for a place that had witnessed so much violence and suffering and sorrow.

"The Blessed Land," Dagda murmured. *"Our* land." He looked to the others, his expression troubled. "You know, for the first time I've a feeling that I'll never see it again."

# Chapter 24

# Rescue Mission

"Goibniu!"

The smith stopped his hammering of the heated, half-formed blade to see who had called his name. Graikos and the shaggy-bearded one they knew as Liam stood in the doorway of his workshed.

"You've come back!" he said with delight.

"I have, my friend," the other replied. "Tell me what's happened here. Your gates are smashed, the village seems all but deserted, and you're here alone beating out swords."

"It's a sorrowing place you've come back to," the smith explained. "The folk are mostly within their huts now, caring for the ones still recovering, keening for those who died or for the children lost."

"Children lost?"

"Aye. It was the Fomor who took them for hostages. They stormed the village in force and broke in."

"The Fomor!" said Lir, exchanging a look with Graikos. "I was afraid of something like this. I wish I had been here."

"Wouldn't have done much good if you had been," the smith said. "We hadn't the strength to stop them. Took every child who survived the plague and all our weapons too. Put terrible hard tribute upon us. Made us slaves, they did, unless Nuada and the others find some way."

"Nuada?"

"He, Dagda, Donnchadh, and she that was once called Moire set out after the Fomor to see if the children could be got back."

"Lir," said Graikos, whose eye had been caught by something outside the door, "Nemed's coming."

The tall man looked around to see the village leader, Diancecht, Mathgen, and a contingent of others approaching. They, like Goibniu, looked at him in wonder and delight.

"I was brought word that you had come," said Nemed. "I was afraid to believe it. We thought that we might never see you again."

"Yes. Tell us where you vanished to!" someone demanded.

"That's not for us to ask!" Diancecht said sharply. "I made a vow to this man to ask no questions in exchange for his help. It's a vow you'll all keep as well. He's come back to us. That's all we need to know."

"Thank you for that," Lir said. "Believe me, all of you, the only thing important now is what's happening to you. Goibniu tells me that Dagda and some others have gone after the Fomor. That's a most dangerous thing to do."

"There seemed no other choice," said Nemed. "We knew nothing of the Fomor or where they would take the children."

"I have some knowledge of the Fomor stronghold," Lir told him. "If they mean to rescue those children, they will need a great deal of help. You didn't send any other force with them?"

"There was really no force to send out so quickly," Diancecht explained. "All but a few were still too weakened by the plague. And there were no weapons."

"And now?"

"We're building strength slowly, day by day. In a few days I would estimate that we will have perhaps two hundred men who could fight."

"Too long to wait," said Lir. "Graikos, the bag."

His servant stepped up with it, opening its mouth. Lir rummaged inside, pulling forth a black metal pot. The men watched this feat in wonder. For though the pot alone seemed big enough to fill the bag, his removing it did nothing to diminish the bulging contents.

"Here," he said, setting it down before them. "Cook stew for your people in this. Feed them all well. You will find that

the meal will restore their full vigor to them in a single day."
He looked to Graikos. "And what about weapons? How long to
supply a host?"

"I'm half done already," said the smith with a broad smile.
He gestured at racks partly filled with spears, swords, and
shields. "Been at the makin' of 'em since the others left. I
hoped we'd be in need of 'em soon. Give me a man or two more
to help, and we'll have enough in another day."

"Good man," said Lir, much impressed.

"You think a rescue might succeed?" asked Diancecht.

"With my help and surprise on our side, there's a very good
chance."

"Enough chance to risk the lives of all the hostages?"

"Listen to me, Nemed: I know what these creatures want,"
Lir said grimly. "It isn't hostages. The certainty your children
face in those monsters' hands is something far, far worse than
death!"

The four heads cautiously poked up over the edge of the
hill's crest.

Dagda, Nuada, Donnchadh, and the Morrigan peered
down the rocky slope toward the peculiar broad peninsula that
stretched out before them.

The flat area of shorelands, thrusting abruptly northward
into the sea from an otherwise straight coastline, was peculiar
in its artificial shape. It was as neatly square of corner and flat
of side as if some immense force had cut it that way.

The peninsula was also peculiar for the nature of the town
which sat upon it. From the height and distance of the observ-
ers, its appearance was like that of a game: a playing board
marked out in precise, crisscrossing streets to form equal
squares; each square evenly filled with scores of neat, square
structures, like game pieces set up for play to begin.

Around the outside of the town ran a high thick grey wall,
unbroken save at one point in the southern side where an opening gave way to a broader avenue. The avenue ran inward to
the exact center of the town where another, vastly larger structure towered above the rest. It was also square sided, but pyramidal in shape, like several boxes of diminishing sizes stacked
one upon the other.

"That's it then," said Donnchadh. "The Fomor trail leads
there."

"Is that a village?" Dagda asked.

"It must be," Nuada said. "And if those squares are their houses, many thousands of Fomor could live in it."

"What's that great thing in the middle?" the big champion wondered.

"We can't find out from here," the Morrigan said. "We have to go closer."

They crept down the hillside, moving from its sheltering rockiness into the cover of an immense, reeking garbage pile some hundred paces outside the single entrance to the town. From here they again peered out cautiously.

"Strange," Dagda whispered, examining the smooth grey surface of the wall. "It looks to be stone, but if so it's a single piece! No seams at all."

"There are no guards upon it," said Nuada, running his gaze across the top. "Another proof of their arrogance."

"But there *are* guards at the entrance," the Morrigan pointed out. Before a small, square structure just outside the single opening, a pair of Fomor warriors lounged on stools.

"We've got to get past them," said Nuada.

"You really mean to go inside there?" asked Donnchadh, clearly not relishing the thought.

"There's no other choice," Nuada told him.

"Then we'll need disguises," the Morrigan said. "We have to look like them."

"Taking care of one problem could well take care of both," said Dagda, hefting his spear meaningfully.

"No one else seems to be about," said Nuada. "I think the direct way is the simplest."

The others nodded. Together they moved out from the cover of the rubbish heap and strode boldly, openly toward the entrance.

The guards, both with furry, long-muzzled, wolflike heads, were deep in conversation, and took no note of them at first. When they did become aware, they still took no immediate action, accepting the four as their own. Only when the Nemedians were close did they recognize that there was something wrong. They stood up, drawing swords.

"Who are you?" one challenged them.

"The last thing *you* will ever see," said Dagda.

His spear shot out, propelled with such force that it plunged right through the man, knocking him backward. The second opened his mouth to scream, but died silently instead, his throat torn out by the barbs of the Morrigan's spear.

Dagda drew his sword. "I'll look inside."

"No," said the Morrigan, drawing hers. "Let me."

He nodded agreement, and she moved at once toward the building's single door.

"Are you certain she can handle it?" Nuada asked his large companion.

"We're going to find out right now," Dagda replied.

The Morrigan stepped inside. Three other wolf-headed Fomor sat drinking around a table. They looked up to the leather-clad and wild-haired female in surprise.

"Do you remember me?" she asked.

They dove for their weapons as she charged upon them.

Those waiting outside heard crashing, grunts, the clang of swords, a groan of agony, then silence.

The Morrigan stepped out, holding up a bloodstained cloak. "All right," she announced. "Clothes for everyone."

Soon four figures masked by Fomor armor, cloaks, and hoods were moving through the entrance and up the central avenue into the town.

They expected to see inhabitants at once, but the outer blocks of square structures that they passed appeared deserted, long neglected, their streets choked with trash.

They crossed three intersecting streets before they began to find life. But the life they first found barely qualified as such.

The outmost inhabited precincts of the town seemed the domains of the most horribly deformed of the Fomor. This vast assortment of nightmare creatures dwelt in immense squalor amidst their own rotting offal and waste, wallowing, crawling, hobbling, slithering about the decaying buildings like unspeakable vermin swarming in a long-dead corpse.

The four looked around in revulsion and moved on quickly, getting through that area and into ones where the beings lived and appeared at least somewhat more as humans, though still surrounded by conditions incredibly foul.

From there on, the successive blocks they passed through seemed to be divided into neighborhoods, each one home for clans or companies of Fomor sharing similar physical characteristics. The four passed by one section where the residents were of a decidedly fishlike appearance, then by another where the beings seemed more reptilian. They in turn saw blocks with populations of feline, bovine, equine, canine, and porcine attributes.

For the first time the people of Nemed saw the women and children of the Fomor as well.

The women, formed as the men of their separate clans, lurked mostly within the squalid dens of their square homes. Only an occasional glimpse could be had of one of the wretched beings staring sullenly from a doorway or window. The children—filthy, misshapen whelps dressed in little more than rags —roamed in unchecked gangs, rooting and playing in the trash, sometimes scuffling with bands from rival clans at the intersections.

The frays were vicious and bloody, with no holds barred. The Fomor savagery and fighting style were clearly learned out in the nasty streets, with only the toughest and strongest surviving. The four intruders made wide detours to avoid these wild brawls.

Finally, in the streets closest around the pyramid, they came into an area where the features surrounding them became most like those of normal men. In this sector the filth and decay common in the other sections were largely gone, as well.

They paused on the corner of a crossing of two streets, looking around them. So far no one seemed to be paying them any special notice.

"Now what?" asked Dagda.

"These small buildings all seem to be living places," said Nuada. He nodded at the pyramid. "I say we look in there."

The structure stairstepped upward a full five stories, its flat walls broken only by widely spaced slit windows and a large opening in the base. The avenue they had followed ran directly to this opening, in and out of which Fomor were constantly moving.

Boldly the invaders walked up to the pyramid, joining the crowd to pass inside.

The interior of the building's first and largest level was a single room. It was a gloomy place, lit only by the few slit windows and some lanterns which filled the space with an oil-scented grey haze.

It was being used as a meeting place and market for the Fomor populace. There were areas with tables where drink was being served to reveling warriors. There were stalls which displayed various goods—clothes, weapons, armor, foodstuffs— but of meager amounts and poor quality.

"They haven't much," said Dagda, wrinkling his nose over a cart of exceedingly ripe fish.

"That's why they want ours," Nuada replied, looking around. "Where do you suppose they have the children?"

"We'd better search quickly," Donnchadh said with some anxiousness. "When they find those guards . . ."

"Buried in that mountain of refuse?" said Nuada. "That shouldn't happen soon."

"Just finding them gone might raise an alarm," said the Morrigan. "Donnchadh's right—we must move fast." She pointed out stone staircases on the far side of the room, one leading upward and the other down. "Look there. Let's try below first."

Trying to look as casual as possible, they went to the stairs and headed down.

Two flights brought them to a lower level. A single lantern at the base of the stairs illuminated the scene. Low and narrow corridors ran left, right, and straight ahead. All plunged into deep gloom only a few paces away. The corridors to left and right were closed by thick metal bars running from floor to ceiling. No Fomor were visible in any direction.

"Looks a proper kind of place to be holding folk prisoner," Donnchadh whispered.

Experimentally Dagda took a cut at one of the bars with his sword. There was a sharp sound of metal on metal, and the sword rebounded, its blade notched deeply, the bar left unmarked.

"No getting through these," he muttered.

"Let's try ahead," said Nuada.

They moved tentatively forward a few steps, peering around. There was nothing but blank walls. They felt their way gamely on into the blackness but soon came against a third solid wall that completely blocked the way.

"Nothing here," said Dagda.

"Then let's go back!" said Donnchadh. "Quickly!"

They turned around just as a metallic rattling sounded behind them.

More of the bars were dropping from holes in the roof of the corridor, clanging home in corresponding holes set in the floor.

Dagda rushed to them, grabbing one, trying to wrench it free. His muscles bulged with strain. But even his full strength couldn't lift the metal bar.

"Save your strength," came a voice. "They're locked in place."

They looked out through the bars, back toward the stairs. At their base stood Captain Cruc himself, beaming in delight, a company of Fomor behind him.

With a shriek of rage, the Morrigan instantly launched her spear at him. He was ready for it, lifting his shield in a quick countermove to knock the weapon down. His grin grew wider.

"A useless try. You can't harm us from there and you certainly cannot get out. My little trap worked just as I planned."

"Trap?" said Nuada.

"Of course!" Cruc said gloatingly. "You perfect beings, whole and pure and so superior. You thought I was as much a brainless animal as that strutting Tethra does. Well, now I've shown you all! I thought that your fool bravery might bring you to try something like this. I've kept a lookout for you. You were seen when you killed those guards. You were watched all the way here. You did exactly what I planned you'd do—walk right in there. Caught just like rabbits in a baited snare."

"Then the children are here?" asked Dagda.

"Just down there," Cruc answered, gesturing to the corridor on his left. "So close. Too bad you'll never see them."

"What will you do with us?" asked the Morrigan.

"Nothing. The safest thing to do with you is leave you there to starve."

"Are you starving the children too?" Nuada asked.

"Certainly not," the captain assured him. "They are being well fed. They must be healthy to breed well for us."

"To breed?" Morrigan echoed in horror. "What are you saying? You told us they would be hostages!"

"They are our future!" said Cruc. "The chance to bring new strength to us. The beginning of a whole new life! And thanks to your people, a constant supply of more children to come after, to be raised as our own, to mate and add yet more to our numbers."

"By all the gods!" Nuada cried in revulsion. "You are monsters indeed!"

"We are not monsters!" Cruc shouted in return. "We are men! We are trying to survive! Once, generations ago, we were like you, until the poisons and experiments of those 'Great Ones' in the Tower corrupted our blood. We were cast off by them, sent here, treated as scum fit only to do their bidding. Breeding amongst ourselves only brought greater deformities on us. A few generations more, and we'd all be like those . . . those 'things' you found in the outer precincts. But the pure blood of your children will save us."

"More likely *your* blood will only poison *theirs*!" Nuada countered. "You cannot do this to those innocents!"

"In a few days it will be done," Cruc said with finality. "Tethra will soon be coming from the Tower. He will bring the means to say which of our people have the least tainted blood. The children will be parceled out to them to be raised and readied for breeding."

"Our people will never allow this!" Dagda said. "They'll all fight you once they know!"

"But they will *not* know," Cruc smugly pointed out. *"You* won't return to tell them. And if any more come, they'll be dealt with as easily as you. So good-bye, my friends, for the last time!"

He turned and went up the stairs, his men following. The captives looked after him helplessly.

"Do you think any more of our people will come?" asked Dagda.

"The odds are against it," said Nuada. "Even if they chose to act, they'll be far too weak to send a large enough force for many days. How long do you think we have?"

"We've only food and water for maybe a day or two," said Donnchadh, feeling the waterbag slung at his waist. "After that, we can live perhaps a few days more."

"Then," said Nuada resignedly, "whether they act or not will make little difference to us!"

# Chapter 25

# Treachery

It was, however, only three days later that the force of Nemedians arrived, and in numbers Nuada would not have believed possible, both factors thanks to Lir.

Though the captives could not inform their people of the horrendous fate the Fomor had planned for the children, Lir could and quite graphically did. The result was as he had hoped. Instead of only a few score of young males mobilizing for a rescue force, the entire population of the village had hosted. This last outrage, this final cruelty inflicted upon a people who had wanted only peace had driven them to war.

So now it was over four hundred armed and determined people—all fully reenergized by the food from Lir's miraculous pot—who took concealed positions on the hill above the Fomor town and readied to attack.

"So vast a place," said Nemed, gazing down at the panorama of streets and countless houses. "Won't we still be heavily outnumbered?"

"Most of the Fomor there are too wretched to fight," Lir said. "There're only a few hundred warriors, remember. And even the best of them are more like cattle than men—easily confused, easily frightened. A trick of my own and a surprise assault from you should send most of them running in panic."

"What do we do?" asked Nemed.

"You'll wait here for my signal. By the way, your own people aren't frightened by darkness or lightning storms?"

"What? Well, they're mostly a fearless lot. There are a few, I suppose, who'd be concerned."

"Well, you just tell them that this storm will be on their side," Lir advised. "If I know these Fomor, it'll have them cowering in terror while you move in under its cover."

"I understand. But you mean to raise such a storm? How?"

"One of my tricks, as I said," Lir replied. "And that's all I'll say. But when you see it breaking above the town, take your people in. Make straight for that tower there, in the center." He pointed to the pyramid. "That's where I'm going now."

"Do you have to do that?" Nemed asked. "You said it's a great risk."

"Not for me," Lir said airily. "More tricks, you see. But I mean to be certain that the children are there and safe before I call you in. Whatever else happens, we've got to set them free, right?"

"Right," Nemed agreed. "And what about Dagda and the others?"

"I'm afraid that if they've not come out of there, they're likely dead," Lir told him regretfully. "Still," he added, "I'll be keeping a lookout for them as well."

"Dead too," Nemed added darkly, shaking his head. "Because I didn't listen to their warnings. It's such a fool I've been to think we could live with these beasts and end all violence. The vision of a golden, Blessed Land blinded me."

"You're not the first who's sought a place of peace," said Lir. "The vision's certainly a noble one. But with the likes of these Fomor, there is no compromise. If you give something to them, you have to give them all. My own people found that out long, long ago."

"Your people?" Nemed said, looking at him curiously.

Lir smiled. "Maybe I'll tell you about it someday. Unfortunately their choice wasn't to fight but to run away."

"There'll be no more running for us," Nemed said fiercely. "I mean to see the Fomor pay full price for their treachery this time."

"Good luck to you all then," Lir told him, clapping a hand to his shoulder. "Keep an eye out. I'll raise the storm as soon as possible."

He signaled to faithful Graikos who stood nearby, and the

two started off, slipping down the rocky hillside toward the town.

As Nemed watched them move away, Diancecht came up to him, a shield on one arm, a sword buckled about his lean waist.

"Liam's off then?" he said, clearly disappointed. "I meant to say good-bye."

"He wanted to waste no time," Nemed said. "How is everyone?"

"Ready to fight," he reported.

"Do you really mean to go in with us?" Nemed asked, eying his armament.

"It will do me little good to remain up here with all of you going down there," the healer replied in his careful, reasoning way. "If I'm going to treat the wounded, I'll have to be with you. And to do that without protection for myself would be illogical indeed."

"What about Mathgen? I can't believe he'll choose to go too."

"That I don't know," said the healer. "I haven't seen him since we arrived. He may be skulking, hoping we'll forget about him. Shall I seek him out?"

"Never mind," said Nemed. "He's freely risked himself once for us. I won't force him to go."

What neither knew was that Mathgen had already gone.

At that moment he was creeping most cautiously down through the rocks of the hillside, staying well hidden and at a safe distance behind Lir and Graikos but keeping them in sight.

The two reached the vast rubbish pile, peering out to the entrance of the town. A new contingent of guards was visible there.

"Can't go that way," Lir whispered. "I want to go in completely unobserved. Come on."

He led his servant from the cover of the pile and far out around a corner of the wall to its western side. There were no openings here. Only the blank surface of the formidible defense wall rising some twenty feet above.

"It's certainly much too high to climb," Graikos observed. "Now what?"

"Simple," said Lir. "It would keep out an army of normal intruders, but the Fomor give no account to magic. That is always their greatest flaw. Just give me the hole paint."

"The whole what?"

"Oh, here," said Lir, snatching away the bag. "I'll get it."

He rummaged inside, drawing forth a large brush and a jar. He opened the jar, revealing what seemed a thick, black substance inside. This he scooped out upon the brush and liberally daubed upon the flat grey wall, quickly forming a large circle. It was a peculiar looking spot, not shiny like something wet but of a dull blackness so profound that it appeared to absorb the light.

Lir put the brush and jar away, drawing out the short crystal wand.

"Now to activate it," he said, "I hope."

He muttered some words in a barely audible, sing-song voice, then touched the wand's tip to the center of the spot. The black began instantly to thin, like successive layers of dark cloth being stripped away, until what lay beyond was finally revealed. Graikos stared in astonishment, realizing he was now looking through an opening in the wall to the square buildings of the town on the far side.

"Good," Lir said with relief. "So far sweet, kind, Great Danu's left me with my powers." He shoved the wand away and drew two bundles of clothing from the sack, tossing one to his companion. "Here. Fomor clothes. Must look the part."

In moments the two were climbing through the hole, now disguised in ragged Fomor dress.

As soon as they had gone from sight, Mathgen crept around the corner of the wall and approached the spot. He examined the miraculous hole in awe.

"That amazing sack of tricks again," he murmured. He then peeked cautiously through the wall to see the pair now hiding behind a building just inside, themselves peeking out at the street beyond.

His covetous eye fell on the bulging sack that Graikos carried.

"I must have it," he whispered to himself. "Such power I'd have. Such revenge I'd wreak."

He had no disguise. Entering the Fomor city was most dangerous. Yet he might never have a better chance. His driving need overcame his fears. When Graikos and Lir started on, he followed, climbing through the hole.

The progress of the other two was a slow and zig-zagging trail. They slipped from building to building of the abandoned outer precincts, crossing avenues only after being certain they were deserted, taking no chances.

They at last reached the first of the streets tenanted by the swarming Fomor horrors.

Lir kicked a coiling, wormlike thing away from his ankles and gazed out across a pile of refuse at the area they must now pass through.

"By good Danu," he said with loathing, "no mind, however diseased, could imagine anything like this."

"I'll look ahead, Master," Graikos volunteered. "See if I can't find the best route. Here," he handed the sack to Lir, "hold this."

He went ahead, boldly picking a way through the garbage and grotesque beings. Lir stayed behind the refuse, watching after him.

"What a brave fellow," he said to himself in an admiring tone. "I really must remember to tell him so."

There was a rustling noise behind him.

He had only begun to turn toward it when something struck him hard just behind the ear. He toppled forward onto the littered ground.

It was only moments afterward that Graikos, having scouted ahead two more avenues, made his way back to where he had left his master. He moved past the trash pile to see Lir stretched out on the ground, a figure bent over him.

He stopped in shock. The crouched figure looked up. He saw that it was Mathgen, the bulging sack clasped in one hand.

"You?" he said, confused by the man's presence. "What are you . . ."

He stepped forward. Mathgen's other hand moved. There was a flash of metal in it as it thrust swiftly out.

When Lir's consciousness returned some while later, he opened his eyes to see a squidlike creature about to affix a sucker-lined tentacle to his face.

He sat up abruptly, sending the frightened thing oozing away. He moaned at the pain caused by his sharp movement, putting a hand to the lump on the back of his head. It was then his gaze fell upon the legs protruding from the rubbish.

He moved to them at once, finding that it was Graikos who had fallen into the pile. His Fomor garb had been removed. His eyes were fixed upward with the blank stare of the dead, his face frozen in the lines of his last surprise.

"My friend!" said Lir with anguish, dropping down beside him. "Not you too?" He put a hand to the man's shoulder. "And you never really had your chance to fight, did you?"

Then he realized something else. He looked around him, searching for the sack.

"Gone," he said ruefully, looking back to Graikos. "So that's what you died for. Well, my friend, have satisfaction in that it will do only ill for them!"

His gaze lifted to the pyramid's top which loomed high above. Rage hardened his face and put a sharp edge to his tones:

"I'll do this anyway, you Fomor animals, with my tricks or without! You should have made certain that you'd killed me too!"

The sword blade struck against the wall, raising little more than some sparks and a small, fine spray of dust.

Dagda looked at the spot—a shallow groove cut into the flat surface of the strange hard stone. He looked at his sword edge, notched and blunted after scores of hard strokes.

"Why are you wasting time with that?" Nuada asked him. "You'd be years cutting through that way."

"It's better than just sitting here, doing nothing, waiting to die!" Dagda returned.

"You'll only hurry up your dying wearing yourself down, raising a greater thirst," Donnchadh pointed out. "There's no mor'n a sip of water apiece left now."

"Will drawing it out make a difference?" Dagda asked. "No one's going to help us in time."

"I only wish I might have gotten one more chance at them," the Morrigan said in frustration. "To just die this way . . ."

"Wait!" said Nuada. "Listen." There was a sound of footsteps on the stairs. "Someone's coming."

"It'll only be them bringing the children another meal," said Donnchadh.

And so it was. Two burly Fomor appeared bearing huge trays loaded with bowls. At the base of the stairs they stopped. One man put his tray down. He pressed upon a section of the wall and it slid back, revealing three large cranks. He took hold of the left one and with some exertion began to slowly turn it. The bars across the left-hand corridor rose upward, disappearing into the ceiling holes.

The Fomor stopped cranking and took up his tray again. He and his companion vanished down the corridor.

"If we could only reach those," Nuada said, gazing longingly at the cranks.

"Might as well wish we were skinny enough to slip through these bars," said Dagda. "Muirgheal could have."

"What's that?" said Donnchadh, pointing.

Another figure, a hooded one, had appeared from the shadows of the stairs. This one crept to the bottom to peer up the corridor after the first two. Then it followed silently, drawing its sword out as it went.

"Who in . . ." Dagda began.

"Quiet!" Nuada warned. From out of the left-hand corridor there echoed a low, sharp cry, quickly cut off.

A few heartbeats passed as they waited, watching expectantly. Then the figure stepped back into view, stopping to look at them.

"So you are alive," it said. "That's cheering news."

"I know that voice!" said Dagda with a grin as the figure shrugged back the hood to reveal the familiar face. "Liam!"

"Sorry I didn't say anything before." He gestured up the left corridor with his bloodstained sword. "I had a bit of nasty work to do. Now, let me see about getting you out."

He sheathed his blade and went to the three cranks, examining them. "The middle one, I think," he declared, and took hold of it, forcing it around.

With a faint, rusty squeal, the rods lifted, drawing back into their holes. The four moved quickly to freedom.

"Liam," Dagda said, giving him a great bear hug of joy. "I had a feeling you'd come back."

Lir extricated himself from the near-smothering show of affection. "No time for that," he said briskly. "We've got to act without delay now." He gestured up the left-hand corridor. "Go there. The children's cells are the first four doors. They're only bolted. Free the children and then stay with them."

"But how can we get them out?" asked Nuada.

"We don't need to. Help's coming to them. All of your own people, in fact."

"All of them?"

"Yes. They're finally convinced that they've nothing to lose by challenging the Fomor. Quite a formidable force. They should succeed easily—if I can accomplish my own task, that is. So I need to go back up there and see to it. Meantime, you have to insure that the children stay alive. If anyone comes down—except me, of course—you'll have to kill them."

"Our pleasure," the Morrigan rasped.

He left them to their task and started up. As he came onto the ground level of the pyramid, he looked searchingly around. The Fomor were at their drinking and bartering around the stalls as usual. His foray downstairs had gone unobserved.

He made his way to one of the slit windows in an isolated corner. He looked out, gaze lifting to the sky.

"Great Danu, hear me," he murmured in a pleading way. "I am now asking you for help. I really don't like doing it. I don't *want* to do it. But I have no choice. I've no other resources left. So the fate of these brave people rests with you now, whether you like it or not. You can ignore them, let them and their completely innocent children be horribly destroyed. You can let our most ancient, most hated enemies win. Or, you can help.

"All I'm asking is that you bring a storm . . . just one small lightning storm to set right upon this tower. I know you can hear me and feel where I am. Bring it right to me. Do it for the memory of Muirgheal who saw value enough to sacrifice herself for them. Do it to save me, because I won't abandon them, no matter what. Do it because your heart tells you it is what should be done. But do it! Please!"

He watched the sky tensely. For some while there was nothing but a bright blueness marked by a few serenely drifting clouds.

"Danu," he murmured fervently, "don't forsake me now!"

# Chapter 26

# Attack

A streamer of dark cloud like an angrily switching serpent slithered into Lir's view from the west. It was joined swiftly by another, then many more, sliding across the sky, drawing after them a solid canopy of black.

"Thank you, my most excellent Queen," he said with a grin.

He left the window, making his way back to the stairs and heading down.

At the stairway's bottom he stopped and looked around. The area seemed to be deserted. He started around the corner into the left-hand corridor but came up short with the keen point of a sword pressed against his throat.

It was held by the Morrigan. She lowered it as she saw who he was.

"I think I said 'except me,'" he pointed out.

"You should have given warning," she answered unapologetically. "I'm keeping watch. The others are back there."

He moved past her, up the corridor to the cells. Their doors were open. Nuada and Donnchadh stood outside.

"Where's Dagda?" Lir asked.

"In here," said the big man, coming out of one of the cells. "I was just comforting some of the children. Most of the smallest ones are frightened."

"Quite natural," said Lir. "But what condition are they in?"

"Well enough," said Nuada. "No signs they've been mistreated physically."

"How did it go with you?" asked Donnchadh.

"Things are underway," Lir said. "All we have to do is wait for it to happen."

"How will we know?" asked Dagda.

"We'll hear it."

As if his words were a trigger, a low grumbling sounded down to them from above.

"There," Lir said triumphantly. "First thunder. It'll come soon now!"


"Was that thunder?" asked Captain Cruc.

He went to one of the windows of the room that made up the top, smallest tier of the pyramid. He looked out at a sky by this time filled with a dense overcast.

A false dusk had fallen upon the town. Lightning flickered through the swollen bellies of the clouds and more thunder rumbled ominously. In the streets below, the Fomor were already scampering fearfully for shelter.

"That's certainly come from nowhere," he commented.

"Spring storms are like that," Captain Tethra replied dismissively. He was at a table across the room, stowing a mass of paraphernalia into a heavy bag. "Can we conclude our business now? I want to be away from here."

"So you've found them all so quickly?" asked Cruc, turning from the window and moving toward him.

"Not so difficult. There are pitifully few. Your 'people's' blood is badly tainted. Your own as well." He gave a little smirk. "You don't qualify."

"*I* don't?" said Cruc, taken aback. "I don't believe it."

"And I don't care whether you do or not," Tethra shot back. "You asked for my opinion and you have it. There are two dozen families of acceptable purity. No more. Mate your captive children with the best from them, and you *may* improve your breed."

"You won't keep me out of it," Cruc growled. "You're just against me. I'm of finer stock than any. I'll have one for myself. Maybe more!"

"Fine," Tethra said indifferently, snapping the bag closed. "Defile as many of them with your mongrel blood as you wish.

It'll make little difference. Any improvement will be temporary."

"You're wrong!" Cruc said with greater heat. "This will succeed. You'll see. Someday we'll be of equal purity with you!"

"At the very most this will delay your slipping into totally degraded forms for two or three generations more. That's all."

"Damn you for your superiority," Cruc said in outright rage this time. "*You* made us what we are!"

"Cap'n?" said a voice.

Both men looked around to see the boar-headed warrior named Torc at the room's door.

"What is it?" Cruc snapped.

"We found a man at the docks sir. A stranger. Tryin' to steal a boat he was."

He signaled behind him. Two more warriors came in escorting a prisoner. It was Mathgen, clad in the Fomor disguise he had taken from Graikos.

"And he had this with him, Cap'n," Torc said, lifting a hand.

He held up Lir's bulging sack of tricks.

"Another of them trying to spy us out," said Cruc, looking Mathgen up and down. "Just take this one out and kill him, Torc."

"No! No wait!" Mathgen said quickly. "I've marvels for you. In the sack! Great marvels!"

"What trickery are you trying?" Cruc asked suspiciously. "That's only a sack of rubbish."

"It's not!" Mathgen assured him in a desperate ploy to save his life. "Just look! There are things inside that have magic. Let me live. I can make them work for you. I can give you power!"

"Power?" echoed Cruc, clearly intrigued.

"Magic?" Tethra said, interested as well. "Let me see it."

Torc started toward him. But a loud crack of thunder brought him to a stop, looking upward in fear.

"Cur!" snapped Tethra. "It's only noise! Now be quick!"

The boar-headed one complied, handing over the sack. The man from the tower opened it and peered cautiously inside. Then he reached in, drawing out the pot.

"Most curious," he said, peering into the bag again at the seemingly undiminished contents.

"As I told you," Mathgen announced. "Even the sack is magical. And that pot! I can cook food in it that will give all who eat great energy, no matter how weakened they are."

"Oh, *you* can do that, can you?" asked Tethra with a little smile. He reached into the depths again, rummaging around, finally drawing out the sphere of crystal. "And what can you do with this?"

"I . . . uh . . ." said Mathgen, perplexed by the object he had never seen before and trying to stall. "Well, it's most complex." He put out a hand. "Just let me have it and I'll . . ."

"I think not," said Tethra, dropping the crystal back. More thunder crashed, so close now that the building was shaken by the force. Lightning flared just beyond the slit windows. The three Fomor warriors and Cruc himself quailed openly. Tethra ignored it all, stepping closer to Mathgen.

"Those things aren't yours," he said with certainty. "You don't know how to use them."

"Yes! I do! Certainly!" Mathgen bluffed. "I'm just . . . confused. Give me a while to sort things out . . . to . . ."

"You're a liar," Tethra interrupted, moving up right before the captive. "You might have thought to fool or awe these stupid beasts with your claims. But you can see *I* am of a vastly superior stripe. So tell me: where did you get those things?"

"I say they are mine!" Mathgen stubbornly replied.

"No!" Tethra shot back. "I recognize the magic of the Departed Ones in this. Only *their* sorcerers could create such things. And you . . . you surely are not one of them." His gaze met Mathgen's searchingly, piercingly. "I would know if you were. I would see it in your eyes!"

An immense burst of thunder bounced the room. Hard upon its heels, the wolf-headed one called Faolchu came rushing into the chamber, panting breathlessly.

"Captain!" he gasped out. "The town is invaded! We're under attack!"

"What?"

"From the south gateway, Captain. They're pouring in!"

Cruc grabbed the long magnifying tube from a table and ran to a south window. He peered out, training the tube up the avenue toward the opening in the outer wall. The darkness from the cloud cover made the scene there very dim—a vague seething mass of many people, but definitely moving toward him and very rapidly.

He ran his gaze in, up the avenue. Nearly halfway along, he reached the vanguard of the attacking force. They were sweeping through a light resistance from the Fomor, charging ahead unchecked.

"What happened to our warriors?" Cruc shouted at Faolchu.

"Most were hiding from the storm when the attack struck," the lieutenant explained. "Now they're running or being cut down."

Tethra stepped to the window, pulling the tube away from Cruc and peering through it himself.

"That host has twice the number that we thought they could field," said Cruc.

"And attacking under the cover of the storm while your rabble cowers," added Tethra. "Too convenient." He looked at the bag and then at Mathgen. "Far too convenient," he concluded. "It is more of *their* work." He tossed the tube back to the Fomor chief. "Time to go."

Cruc looked at him in surprise.

"Go?"

"They'll be here in moments. I intend to be safely away by then." He gestured to Mathgen. "Bring that one. He might be useful. Let's move quickly, before we're trapped up here!"

With Tethra carrying Lir's bag and Mathgen in tow, the party headed downward through the pyramid at once. They moved with the best speed they could, but they were still upon the last flight to the ground floor when the first of the Nemedian host, led by Murchadh O'Falva, burst through the main doorway.

Most of the Fomor were huddling in corners, beneath tables, and behind stalls, hiding from the storm. At first only a handful of the most courageous warriors moved to challenge those pouring in.

"Don't lie there, idiots!" Cruc screamed at the rest of his people. "We're being attacked! Get up! Fight! Fight!"

A few more of them, realizing this greater peril, rose up at that and moved into the fray. A ragged defensive line formed across the center of the large room, momentarily stemming the tide.

With the Fomor who were guarding him distracted, Mathgen took the chance to get away. He vaulted across the stair rail from halfway up the flight, dropping to the floor. He staggered but recovered, diving for the cover of the stalls.

Torc and his two warriors started after him, but Tethra restrained them.

"No. You stay with me," he ordered. He looked to Cruc

and Faolchu. "I'm going on," he curtly announced. "You stay here and hold them."

And with that he marched away with the three guards around him, heading for a smaller doorway in the back wall of the room.

Taken aback at his abrupt departure, Cruc looked after him, then turned to look at the battle. His people would not hold long.

"Faolchu, you take charge!" he commanded, then hustled away in Tethra's wake.

The dismayed Faolchu started to call after him but was interrupted by the sudden appearance of a new force.

From the stairway below him, Lir and his four companions charged into the battle. Drawn by the sound of clashing arms above, they had come up from the prison level to join their comrades. With the energy and ferocity of a dozen, they slashed into the back of the Fomor line, scattering its warriors in panic.

In moments they were meeting with those of the attacking party while the remaining Fomor, Faolchu in the forefront, were scrambling to escape.

"Brother!" said Murchadh, hugging Donnchadh. "You're alive!" He looked to Lir. "And you, too! I thought you might have been killed when I saw your bag!"

"My bag?" Lir said. "Where?"

"It was being carried out by Fomor. One of them was different. Not deformed at all, and in an odd, grey dress."

"A towerman! Where did he go!"

"Out that way!" He pointed to the rear door through which the last Fomor able were fleeing, Nemedians in close pursuit.

"I can't let the Tower get that bag!" Lir said, and headed off at once.

The others looked after him in surprise.

"What's he doing?" asked Murchadh. "He can't stop them alone!"

"Then I'm going too," said Dagda, starting after Lir.

"Donnchadh, stay and tell them about the children," Nuada said. And he set off too.

Without a word the Morrigan followed him.

"Have they gone mad?" Murchadh asked his brother.

"Donnchadh!" called a voice.

Both O'Falvas turned to see Nemed himself leading a new

contingent in through the main doorway, Diancecht and Goibniu close behind him.

"You *are* alive!" Nemed said to Donnchadh with joy. "What about the others?"

"Alive so far," Donnchadh replied. "They've gone after the Fomor. The children are all well too." He gestured to the stairway down. "We've left them in the cells just below for safety."

"Diancecht, could you take a contingent down and see to them?" Nemed requested. "Make certain they're we'll protected. *I* mean to go on after the Fomor as well!"

"But Nemed, is that necessary?" the healer questioned in his reasoning way. "The children have been rescued. Shouldn't we withdraw?"

"No!" Nemed fiercely replied. "I won't make that mistake again. We have them on the run. This time we'll see they're *truly* beaten." He gestured with his sword to those around him. "Come on then!"

With a cheer fired by their battle rage, the fighters followed him on, leaving Diancecht behind.

Outside the pyramid they joined a flood of other Nemedians sweeping on in relentless pursuit of the now routed Fomor. Most of the panicking beings were seeking escape by sea, pouring from the streets onto the quays and piers.

Tethra and his Fomor guards had already arrived there, Cruc close behind. They moved out along one of the stone piers to where the sleek metal ship was berthed. At piers all around them, Fomor refugees were piling into their own craft—low, wide, shallow-draft ships with single sails and rows of oars on either side. They were packing the vessels near to overflowing, then casting off as the first pursuers drew near.

Tethra reached his ship's gangway where two of his own helmeted men stood guard with their long power rods. He looked to Torc and the two Fomor with him.

"Far enough for you," he said curtly. "Stay and cast off for us."

"Wait!" shouted Cruc, rushing up to him. "You won't leave me!"

"Stay with your own!" Tethra said.

"You'll take me off," said Cruc, drawing his sword, "or you won't leave either!"

Tethra eyed the combative captain, then looked to the Nemedians moving rapidly closer. This was no time for delaying confrontations.

"Come on then!" he snapped angrily, turning and heading up the gangway, his men close behind.

"Cast off, Torc!" Cruc ordered, following them up.

"Aye, Cap'n!" the boarhead agreed, blindly obedient to the last. He and the other two moved to pull the hawsers from their snubbing cleats.

Lir rushed onto the pier as the last hawsers were being untied. The ship was already drifting out, its still-attached gangway sliding off the pier.

One of the warriors drew and rushed to challenge Lir. Lir tried to duck around him but was blocked and forced to engage.

Torc and the other Fomor cast off the final lines. Lir parried a hard cut and, in a countermove made swift and sure by desperation, slashed his opponent from the way.

He charged for the gangway only to see it slip away and drop into the sea just as he reached the pier's edge.

A burbling white backwash arose at the vessel's stern and built quickly to a churning, high froth as the propelling mechanism rose to full power. The vessel began to slide forward. In seconds it would be completely out of reach.

His eye fell upon one of the loosed hawsers still dangling down the starboard side of the smooth hull to drag in the water near the stern. It was the sole boarding method left.

But Torc was clomping along the pier toward him to attack. Lir had no more time to waste.

He threw his sword, point forward, at the onrushing warrior. The keen weapon struck home, piercing the boarhead's chest, driving deep. As Torc stumbled and went down, Lir crouched and sprang for the dangling line.

He caught it low. His legs up to the knees went into the sea and he was dragged along, slamming against the metal side. As the vessel picked up speed to glide away, he began a desperate climb upward, fighting to keep from being sucked into the waters now boiling furiously from the stern.

# Chapter 27

# Tower of Glass

Just too late to help Lir, Dagda, Nuada, and the Morrigan finally reached the docks.

Around them a dozen Fomor ships crowded with escapees were pulling away, frantically propelled by wildly flailing oars. Nemedians still in pursuit were swarming onto the docks. Some, totally caught up in the frenzy for revenge, were climbing aboard abandoned Fomor ships.

But the eyes of the three were fixed on the strange metal ship and on the familiar figure being dragged along beside.

"What do we do?" said Nuada.

Dagda pointed at a nearby Fomor ship being manned by their fellows. "There. We follow!"

They climbed on board. Nuada quickly took charge, ordering the mooring ropes cut. Dagda grabbed an oar to set a hard, fast rowing pace, and the ship was soon cutting across the waves in pursuit.

Nemed himself had by this time reached the quays. Seeing one ship speeding out and five others preparing to go, he moved at once to join his people.

"Murchadh, Goibniu, take that ship!" he ordered, pointing to one. "Donnchadh, you come with me!"

They rushed to the craft and soon were also heading out to sea.

The pursuit started evenly. For a while the dozen Fomor craft kept their lead over the six Nemedian ones. The sleek ship from the tower glided along in their midst, moving at the same speed. But it moved along effortlessly, pushed by its hidden power. The Fomor ships were driven by brute muscle power, and that power soon began to fade.

One by one the overloaded Fomor craft began to slow and fall behind. The Nemedian ships, lighter, propelled by more organized and more determined oarsmen, began to close the gap.

The ship of Nuada and his companions was moving most swiftly ahead at Dagda's urging. It came level with a faltering enemy ship but passed by, staying fixed on its course dead in the metal ship's wake.

Lir, meantime, had managed to haul himself upward out of the churning waters. He shinnied up the hawser, finally pulling himself across the rail and onto the ship's stern. He was unseen there, behind the pyramidal superstructure, and he crept stealthily around its starboard side to peek out at the main deck.

Tethra stood amidships at the port-side rail, Cruc beside him, both peering back intently toward the Nemedian pursuit. The two guards seemed occupied with watching too. None of the vessel's other crewmen were visible.

Lir eyed his bag sitting on the deck at Tethra's side. He eyed the two guards so close to the edge.

Weaponless he crept up behind them. In a swift move he shoved one guard forward. With a shriek of surprise, the man toppled over the rail.

He moved to seize the bag, but the others whirled on him too quickly. The second guard came in at him, bringing up his rod. Lir's kick caught the center of his weapon, cracking it in two.

The result was startling. The power within the rod was all released at once, flaring out to crackle across the guard's body in whipping snakes of blue-white flame, shaking him violently and knocking him backward off his feet to land on the deck, a pile of smoldering rags, charred flesh, and blackened bones.

But some of the power caught Lir as well. It snared his foot, flickered up his leg, sending him crashing down, momentarily stunned.

He recovered at once, but sat up to find the point of Cruc's sword at his throat, ready to thrust home.

"No!" Tethra ordered. "Let him up."

Reluctantly Cruc moved back a bit, allowing Lir to rise. Tethra picked up the bag and held it out.

"After this, were you?" he asked.

Lir made no answer.

The captain from the tower stepped up to examine him closely. He looked especially into the eyes.

"Yes. Of course you were," he said with certainty. "I didn't believe you existed before. I was wrong. You are one of *them.*"

"I don't know what you mean," Lir told him flatly.

"Certainly you do. After so long we have one of you. You left us and took all your magic, but now we'll have it back." He hefted the sack. "You'll tell us about these. And about so much else. You'll tell us where *all* your people are."

"I'll tell you nothing!"

"You will." Tethra gave a malicious smile. "We haven't your magic skills, but we're very good at persuasion. You'll see. And you *will* talk—in time."

He gestured past the bow. A glowing spot had appeared on the rim of the ocean dead ahead. "See there," he said. "We will soon be at the Tower."

At that moment, high within the tower, first notice was also being taken of them.

"Commander Balor, ships are approaching!" announced a grey-uniformed officer, striding up before the armored giant's huge throne.

"Where?" boomed the metallic voice.

"Due south," said the officer. He stepped to one of the windows, lifting a magnifying tube much larger and longer than Cruc's. "Look there. They are just topping the horizon."

With a faint screeching noise, the barrel head of Balor pivoted fully around on the massive shoulders. The visored single eye pointed toward the sea.

From the high vantage point, with the aid of the powerful lens, the officer was able to see the ships with some detail. Apparently Balor, unaided, could too.

"I see them," the giant rumbled. "A ragged fleet of those Fomor ships, and Tethra's vessel in their midst."

"I believe that the ships in the rear are pursuing the others, Commander," the officer commented.

"Pursuing?" echoed Balor. "Impossible." There was a

pause as both examined the approaching ships, then: "No. You are right. The first ones do seem to be running before the rest. Tethra's as well. How can that be? Our vessels are invulnerable!"

"I don't know, Commander," the officer replied. "But look now! One of the Fomor craft has caught up to another."

It was the craft bearing Goibniu and Murchadh which had come alongside the first of the lagging enemy ships. Already the Nemedians, in full battle fury, were boarding it, carrying on a savage, no-quarter fight with their foes.

"My people are being slaughtered!" Cruc cried out, looking back to the engaged ships.

He, Lir, and Tethra watched as a second laggard was overtaken by another Nemedian ship. Instantly it was boarded as well.

"They've caught another one!" Cruc said in growing agony. He looked to Tethra. "They'll all be caught. They'll all be destroyed! You've got to help."

"Oh?" Tethra said, an eyebrow raised. "And just how?"

"Turn this ship. Run the pursuers down!"

"And risk being boarded ourselves? I think not. I will not chance losing my prizes to save your animals."

"You'll let them all die then?" Cruc asked aghast. "After what they've done for you?"

Tethra shrugged. "We no longer need them." He hefted the bag. "With what's in here . . ." he nodded at Lir, ". . . and what's in that one's mind, we can regain our power, eradicate all the problems that have plagued us, cease to produce more aberrations like yourself. We can grow strong again, go out into the world again, seize what we want for ourselves, not hide away!"

"You can't do that!" cried the Fomor captain. "I won't let you abandon us."

"You?" Tethra sneered at Cruc. "What can you do? Just be grateful that you are with me instead of on one of those ships full of your poor, doomed monsters!"

"Monsters?" Cruc bellowed.

That last, single, cruel word was a mistake. It was finally one insult too many for the beleagured Fomor warrior. Sparked to fury he wheeled upon Tethra and struck out with his sword.

His blade drove full into the center of Tethra's breast. He delivered the blow with a fierce pleasure, his point cracking through the breastbone to impale his longtime tormenter's heart.

Jolted by the blow, Tethra's gloating expression was replaced by one of stunned surprise. In the last instants of life, he looked down at the wound pumping his crimson lifeblood out around the piercing blade, then back up to Cruc's face so close before his own, split by a grin of savage triumph.

"We . . . are . . . not . . . monsters!" the Fomor snarled at the stricken man. With a quick jerk, he pulled the killing sword free.

Tethra toppled forward to crash face down upon the deck. Cruc rolled him over with a kick. The towerman's eyes stared lifelessly upward. His face was still drawn into a mask of disbelief.

"No more of our sacrifice for you," the Fomor captain told him, snatching the bag from his dead hand. "We will use this to give the power to ourselves!" He turned to Lir. "You will now show *me* how these things work."

"I will not," Lir said stubbornly.

Cruc stepped closer, touching his blood-stained blade point to Lir's breast. "You will. Show me some power that will save my ships!"

"Very well," Lir said with seeming reluctance. "I've no choice. Give me the sack."

"You still think I'm such a fool?" the Fomor shot back.

"All right, then. *You* look inside and fetch out that crystal sphere."

Managing to maintain close watch on Lir, Cruc fished in the bag, finally drawing the object out.

"Fine," said Lir. "Now you just hold it in your hand. Hold it tight. And concentrate. Wish for power . . . all the power you could want. Wish for it to fill you up, make you seethe with energy!"

Cruc grew tense, his fist drawing so tight around the sphere that it vibrated with the strain. And in response the sphere began to glow.

"See there!" said Lir. "It's working. Concentrate harder. Wish for more power! More! All of the power it can give. Ask it to flow through you!"

The hand vibrated more violently with increased intensity. Cruc's whole body tightened with the strain. The sphere glowed brighter, brighter, white light shining out with near-blinding glare.

A sudden horror filled Cruc's face. He stared at the gleaming object, his one eye bulging. Then he screamed out, trying to drop the sphere. But his hand seemed frozen, his whole body caught, drawn stiff, unable to move.

"Sorry, Captain!" Lir told him as he snatched up his precious bag, turned, and leapt for the ship's rail.

The explosion consumed the entire ship and the sea around it, hiding them in a mass of light that blossomed outward as it geysered up. A high wave and a blast of air rippled outward from it. But still it was a soundless blast of energy that seemed to simply vaporize the huge mass of metal, dying away in moments to leave no traces at all.

In the tower Balor and a stunned officer watched their vessel so swiftly annihilated.

"Destroyed!" the voice clanged. "How vast a power to do that? It *must* be *them*! They've found us. They're coming! We cannot let them reach here!"

The barrel head swiveled, bringing the visored eye back to the front. With rasps and creaks and clattering the huge form rose from the throne.

"I'm going to the roof!" Balor announced, and started ponderously away.

Out on the sea, the ship of Dagda and his companions, closest to the metal craft, had been nearly overturned by the wind and wave from the tremendous blast. Blown sideways and backward, they recovered with an effort. The big champion, Nuada, and the Morrigan looked out in dismay at the empty, roiling sea where their friend Lir had last been.

Though they were stopped themselves, the other vessels were still going on. The ship carrying Nemed and Donnchadh plus two other craft were still in single-minded pursuit. Nemed's ship was closest to overtaking another victim. But they were also drawing closer to the glass tower, which thrust up stark and gleaming from the sea, its outline now clearly visible.

"Dagda, what's that?" said the Morrigan, noting the strange object for the first time.

"I . . . I don't know," he answered. "It looks like a column of ice!"

"I don't like it," said Nuada. "The Fomor are making right for it. I wish our other ships would turn back."

But the three vessels were pressing on, closing rapidly with their lagging foes.

Ahead the tower loomed ever higher as they approached. And now something else became visible—a black form, human-like, tiny in the distance, that lifted into view on the structure's top.

Nemed had no eyes for either the tower or the ominous figure. His attention was locked on the Fomor ship as they drew alongside.

With a shout of triumph he brandished his sword, preparing to leap aboard.

"Now, Fomor bastards," he cried to his cringing enemies, "you are going to pay!"

A dot of red light appeared on the head of the distant form. From it a streak of light flared out, sweeping across the sea, sending up a trail of steam as it sliced through the waves, finally striking the two engaged ships.

Both Fomor and Nemedian vessel were enveloped in a ball of roaring red-orange flame. It ignited them, consumed them, blasted them in an instant to a shower of crimson sparks that cascaded to the sea to be extinguished.

"By the gods!" Nuada breathed in horror. "Put about!" he shouted to the others. "For your lives, put about and row!"

They fell to their oars. Their ship began to turn. The two ships ahead of them also tried to turn and run.

They failed.

One of them was caught in midturn by the ray. The craft vanished in another burst of fire. The other made it about but got no further. The beam of light played upon it and it died in flames as well.

Dagda and his companions rowed with the energy of fear. They pulled for the shelter of the horizon. They pulled for the safety of distance. They pulled, and the beam followed, drawing its sizzling, steaming trail across the sea, sweeping closer.

The other Nemedian ships, just finishing the slaughterous work on their own prey, were coming into sight ahead. The tower was sinking down beyond the northern curve of sea. Still the beam swept on, nearer, nearer, but widening now as it came.

It struck, a wide, thin oval of reddish light, playing across the ship. They felt a wave of heat, like the blast from a furnace door suddenly opened. Then the heat and the light both died away.

They had passed out of the deadly beam's range.

Still they rowed on, purposefully, steadily, until the tower of glass vanished totally behind them, and the green hills of what they had called their blessed land came into view ahead.

# Epilogue

The surviving people of Nemed gathered on the quays of the Fomor town.

They were a solemn, weary, and dispirited lot. They were also very few. With those who had perished in the annihilated ships and the casualties from the battle in the town, the numbers of the once proud, once courageous settlers who had come so hopefully into this land had been reduced to only some three hundred.

Their children had been rescued. The Fomor had been at least temporarily banished to sea or into hiding in the trash-choked warrens of their city. Now came the need for the Nemedians to decide on their own future.

"We surely can't stay here," one man was saying with conviction. "The Fomor are still out there and in large numbers. More than enough to be a threat if they regain their spirit and counterattack."

"Then we'll fight them," said Dagda. "We'll defeat them again."

"With what host?" another man countered. "With the few men and the women and children who are left? Why, we wouldn't even have won here without the help of Liam's magic."

The name of their vanished savior caused a wave of sorrow to sweep through the crowd.

"I wonder if we'll ever know who he was," wondered Diancecht. "A man of many unusual skills."

"Now *all* those skills are lost to us as well," the arguing man went on. "And there's that . . . that 'thing' out there on that spire of ice. It helped the Fomor. It's surely only a matter of time before it or some other horror worse than the sickness will come upon us. We'll have no chance at all then."

To this there came many sounds of agreement from the gathering.

"How can you all speak of quitting?" Nuada asked. "Just when we've won at last!"

"What have we won?" another stridently put in. "The right to live in terror? To wait and wonder when we'll be attacked or poisoned or enslaved?"

"We're tired, Nuada," said Murchadh heavily. "So very, very tired of the battles and monsters and plagues that have been constantly upon us since we came here. We were never warriors or adventurers. We're mostly simple herders and farmers and craftsmen. We were searching for peace, freedom, a land of our own. We found near extermination instead. Now my brothers are dead, Nemed is dead, and so is his dream. We want no more of this."

"Where can you go?" asked Dagda.

"Home," said Murchadh. "It may be we had little of our own there. It may be that the life is hard and cruel. But we know what to expect. We can survive. My own few clansmen and I mean to return to the village, fetch what we can, and take ship back for our old lands. I think many of the rest will be joining us."

"Well, I will *not* go back," Nuada said with force. "It may be that we've no choice but to leave this island. Still, I will not go back to what we've known. There *must* be someplace else—someplace where Nemed's dream can be made real."

"When we came here, we came to the last land on the ridge of the world," Murchadh pointed out.

"How do we know?" Nuada returned. He pointed westward, into the sea haze that rimmed the curve of the horizon. "How do we know what might lie that way, just beyond our sight?"

"You're right," Dagda told him. "The world back there has no interest for me. I'll go with you."

"Then I go as well," said the Morrigan. "The old life is dead. The old memories hold only agony. In new dangers and new hopes there may be some solace, or at least some forgetting of pain."

"It sounds most unreasonable to say," put in Diancecht, "but I choose also to go with you, Nuada. Like you, I still believe in Nemed's dream."

"And I," said Goibniu.

"And I," said Luchtine.

And some two dozen others added their voices of agreement.

"I'll go with you too, if you'll have me," piped up yet another voice.

From beyond the crowd, Mathgen pushed through to join Nuada and his friends.

"Mathgen!" said Nuada in surprise. "What happened to you?"

"Yes," said the Morrigan suspiciously. "Where were you in the battle?"

"I was nearly killed!" he said defensively, pointing out his own disheveled clothes and a great bruise on his forehead. "I fought with Liam himself to keep his bag from the hands of the Fomor."

"He died succeeding in doing that," said Nuada.

"Yes, so I have found out," said Mathgen with a show of great sorrow. "Too bad."

"But why do you want to go?" Dagda asked Mathgen. "Our way will likely be hard and dangerous."

"I certainly can't go back," Mathgen said simply. "I can't stay here alone. Where else?" He looked toward the west with a glint of covetousness in his dark eyes. "And, who knows what wonders, what wealth, what powers lie hidden somewhere out there?"

"All right," said Nuada. "You may go with us, but only so long as you do your fair share."

"I would think of doing nothing else," Mathgen assured him, bowing low.


The last of Nemed's people returned to the valley that they had planned to make their home forever.

They gathered their belongings, packed up food, collected their herds, and trekked sadly away, leaving the village upon which they had labored so long and lovingly once more abandoned. Retracing the route that had first brought them to the valley, they soon arrived at the landing site where they had left their ships little more than a year before.

It took little time for the surviving people of Nemed to make the craft ready for sea. Two of the five ships were now sufficient to carry those planning the return voyage to their homeland. Nuada, Dagda, and their small company took a third.

When all was prepared, they held a final gathering on the shore, then climbed into their craft. As Murchadh and Nuada each watched the last of their respective groups boarding, Nuada shook his head regretfully.

"There's a great pain in me at remembering how we were when we first landed at this same spot," he said, looking up at the green hills above the beach. "We were all so filled with the joy of the new land, breathing in its grand scents, looking out at its wide countryside, thinking of the new life that we would make."

"I know," Murchadh agreed. "And I'll tell you truly, Nuada, that for all the hardships we suffered here, it is still a most beautiful, rich place. I'd like to hope that one day, when our numbers are restored and our strength recovered, we might yet return."

"I think that's a dream we all have," said Nuada, "to come back and truly make this the Blessed Land Nemed believed it was."

"Then perhaps we will meet again," Murchadh said, clasping hands with him in a gesture of farewell.

"If not in this land, then in the land beyond life," Nuada answered. "Good-bye, my friend . . . all my friends."

Last of all the two men climbed aboard their separate ships. The three vessels sailed away from the shore together, out past the headlands, into the open sea. Here the two groups finally parted, casting their fortunes in opposite directions.

Those with Murchadh O'Falva turned the prows of their craft toward the east and the shores of their old, familiar land.

Those with Nuada set their ship's course for the west.

Nuada, Dagda, Diancecht and the rest looked sternward until the green and shining land had vanished below the curved rim of the world. Then all turned their gaze forward toward the unknown sea that lay beyond their prow.

# Author's Note

My purpose in these books is to present the wonderful tales of
the pre-Christian Celtic peoples of Ireland to modern readers.

This task is most difficult with these Most Ancient Songs—
the oldest Irish tales. These tales comprise the first of the three
cycles of the literature. Called the "Mythological Cycle" they
deal with the development of a race of beings—once mortal—
who will become gods of great power to later races invading
Ireland.

The various tales, originating in Neolithic times, are vague,
fragmented, often confused and even contradictory. Making co-
herent stories out of the pieces creates special problems, but it
also allows (or requires) freer interpretations.

As an example I found the intriguing descriptions of a giant
with a single eye of killing power, a high-rise tower of glass,
and a race of seemingly mutant beings leading me to an inter-
pretation of the Fomor as the remnant of an ancient, scientifi-
cally advanced civilization devastated by their own pollutions
of the earth.

In other aspects I have tried to include elements as pre-
sented in the myths, and to give some flavor of the land and
way of life for the peoples of those long-past times. Dagda,

Nuada, the Morrigan, and others of their friends are especially important figures. For they will haunt and hinder and help the peoples of Ireland through all the cycles and be a part of the Irish culture and character to the present day.

A Special Preview of

*The Gods of Ireland, Book 2*

# The Enchanted Isles

## BY CASEY FLYNN

In the wake of their battle with the Fomor, the peaceful people of Nemed sail far from their Blessed Isle, through a foggy, magical barrier to an archipelago of mysterious, enchanted islands. They explore each island they pass, hoping to find a new home. Caught in a violent storm, their small ship is tossed against the rocks along one island's craggy shore, stranding them there indefinitely. In the hopes of finding an escape, they begin to explore their new surroundings, dismayed by the blight they find, and determined to challenge the giants who caused it. Confronting these beings is their goal, but the quest before the battle may be more perilous than the battle itself. . . .

Before the overcast sun had risen far enough to illuminate the dying forest, the adventurers were already entering the clearing surrounding the ancient oak tree.

They drew up about the massive trunk in a defensive ring, searching about warily, weapons ready. Nothing could be seen moving in the tangled shadows of the dying forest stretching away on all sides. No sound broke the vast and heavy stillness save their own tense breathing.

"No sign of the cats," said Nuada. "We'll need them to guide us."

"I'll bring them," said the Morrigan.

She dropped back her head and gave voice to a loud, throaty roar, in exact mimicry of the cry the cats had given the day before. It echoed away through the silence.

They waited, listening. In moments a roar came in return, quickly joined by a chorus of others. Soon afterward the sinewy shapes of the big cats could be seen approaching through the trees.

The creatures pulled up at the edge of the clearing, forming a tight bunch, staring keenly, guardedly across to the human band.

"Why did you come again in such a force?" the big cat growled. "What do you mean to do?"

"Only to help," Nuada assured them. "To stop the ones who are destroying your isle."

"What, the few of you?" The cat gave a derisive snort. "They are too strong for you."

"That doesn't sound promising," Mathgen observed.

"We have much greater strength than you might think," Dagda told the being. "We wish at least to see if we can help."

"Yes," said the Morrigan. "Show us where these giants are."

"Why should you do this?" the cat asked, still suspicious. "I told you that you did not need to risk yourselves."

"We understand that," Nuada said. "We still wish to do it. We have all decided."

"Indeed?" said the cat, great surprise evident in its gruff tone. It turned to the others and they conferred together for a few moments in low growls. Then the big cat turned back to them.

"We are most amazed by your willingness to help. We would question this seeming unselfishness from such as yourselves, but you can well see that we lose nothing in letting you make the attempt. We will lead you to where the giants live. But the way is very deadly, and the task you face is great. It's quite likely that none of you will survive."

"That we will see," said Nuada. "We have made our choice. We have vowed to help. You'll find we are a people who do not go back on our vows easily. Please, lead on."

So, with the pride of cat-like beings moving ahead of them, the party of would-be saviors traveled inland.

The woods about them grew ever more grotesque as they went. The numbers of dead trees increased, more and more fallen, or canted over in death throes, or thrusting up starkly, skeletally against the sullen sky.

And that sky, too, became ever more unpleasant in appearance as they progressed. From a general, boiling sea of overcast, it changed to even thicker, rolling masses, like distinct, consecutive, and definitely curving ridges of grey-black waves.

They entered an area where only sparsely scattered trees still struggled for a grim, yellow-gray semblance of life. Here each footfall raised a puff of pale grey dust that hung in the still air. As one of the company brushed by the branches of a dead evergreen, a massive cloud of the same dust billowed up from its dried bristles.

On noting that, Dagda swatted at a nearby bush. More of the dust arose from the surfaces of its dead leaves, wafting into his face and up his nose. He snorted and then gave a tremendous sneeze.

Startled by the noise, the cats looked around.

"Careful," the big cat warned. "Don't stir up more of that than you must. It comes from the giants. It's created by their work. It settles down and covers all in its thick coat. It slowly smothers and finally it kills. Breathe in too much of it, and you'll die, too."

"Then just how *do* we breathe?" asked Mathgen.

"As little as possible," said the cat. "That's what we've

learned to do. And it will get worse. I said the way was dangerous. Do you wish to go on?"

"Dust won't turn us back," said Nuada. He looked to the others. "Tear strips from your clothes," he said. "Tie them across your mouths and noses. That should keep it out."

"A most sound idea," Diancecht endorsed.

The adventurers followed his advice, and soon the masked band was again moving on in the cats' wake.

Once more the nature of the forest changed. They had finally reached a territory where no living thing survived. Ahead of them now were only the remains of trees long dead. Their sorry corpses had been stripped of all leaves and needles and bark, and even of branches. Worse, the tops of most of them had been roughly whittled down as if ravaged by fire or eaten by rot.

On entering this section, the cats stopped, turning to those who followed.

"From this point I cannot let the others of my clan go on," the big cat told the humans. "I will not risk them in the more deadly things ahead. But if you still wish to continue, then I will still lead you."

"We're ready," Nuada told him doggedly.

"*You're* ready, you mean!" Mathgen muttered to himself. "I'm not at all sure how much *I* want to go on with this."

The other cats drew up in a line as the humans moved past, following their leader. They sat watching as the adventurers trudged doggedly ahead.

As the band plunged yet deeper into the forest of death, Nuada and his companions found it growing darker with each step. The clouds above were growing thicker, lower, until the company walked in a twilight gloom. The coating of dust was turning from gray to black, blanketing everything like a death shroud. It even began to coat the skin and clothes of the explorers, leaving only the red-rimmed whites of their eyes to stand out strikingly, eerily, like the eyes of some night wraith.

They came upon the banks of a small stream. Its bed may have carried clear, sparkling water once, but now it was a channel for a thick, gray-green sludge adding its acrid stench to the already befouled air.

The curious Dagda leaned down over it, stretching out a finger toward its viscous, oozing surface.

"Don't touch it," warned the cat. It kicked the decayed remnant of a log over the bank. The piece fell upon the surface and began to smoke instantly. Its remaining wood crumbled away and sank into the stuff.

"Very deadly," the creature explained. "It comes down from the lake where the giants live, carrying away their venom to defile all other streams, ponds, springs. We have only to follow it now and it will lead us to its source . . . and thus to them."

They moved along the bank. The sky ceased to become any darker, but the landscape continued to become more bizarre. The remains of the dead trees surrounding them were growing constantly shorter, more eaten or burned away, until some were down to little more than stubs.

A fat drop of liquid plopped into the dust, sending up a small squirt of black cloud. Far away another fell. And another. Then more.

"Rain?" said someone, noting the last strike.

Several of them looked up.

"Ah!" cried Luchtine, slapping a hand to his forehead. "A drop struck me. By the gods . . . it burns!"

"The poison rain!" growled the cat. "The only chance now is to reach the cliffs. Everyone, run!"

The creature took off, and they instantly, unquestioningly followed.

The volume of rain grew swiftly. The drops—thumb-sized globules of an oily yellow-red—grew tighter in their spread. There were more cries of pain as drops struck exposed arms or legs or heads.

"Hold the shields above you," the lion roared back to the others. "Keep off the rain. For your lives!"

All lifted the broad, flat circles of iron to hold over them as they ran. Drops splashed and exploded against the thick metal, sizzling there like hot fat on a heated pan.

In moments the drizzle had become a shower, growing on rapidly toward a full-fledged rain. The company pelted ahead at their best speed, zigzagging their way through a treacherous nightmare landscape thickly dotted with the nubs of what had been countless trees.

Ahead a high wall of rock came into view, already hazy through the thickening screen of rainfall.

"See the opening!" the cat told them. "The cave! Make for the cave!"

The hole was just visible—a large black spot shaped like an open mouth right at the base of the high wall. The stream they had been paralleling seemed to be issuing from there.

They rushed toward it at their best speed. The rain was turning the dusty ground to caustic muck, steaming on the soles of their leather boots. Diancecht, eldest and least physical of the band, stumbled badly, nearly falling headlong into the awful stuff. Dagda seized him up and, as if carrying a grain sack, tossed him over a shoulder. Sheltering both of them beneath his own huge shield, he went on unslowed.

The cat rushed into the shelter of the large opening's stony lip. The first of the adventurers followed in seconds, passing into the darkness beyond. Nuada, one of the first, pulled up just within the mouth, turning back to see his people past into safety.

The rain had by this time increased to near downpour. Still, it seemed that it would be only moments more before everyone would safely reach shelter.

Then one of those near the back of the company slipped.

He staggered, falling sideways. Two more—a young man and woman—stumbled over him. The man went down at once, toppling face forward. The woman made it past a few staggering steps, but then dropped onto her knees.

All three of their shields had fallen, giving no more shelter. The rain, now in torrents, poured over them, soaking them down.

Smoke rose from their skin.

And they began to scream.


The smoke rose up in trickles from places all over their bodies. These grew swiftly into streams, combining, forming a screen of greasy yellow-gray that enveloped each of them. The liquid burned their eyes, filled up their mouths and nostrils, ate at their flesh. In seconds they were left blinded, helpless, thrashing wildly with the intense pain.

At first unaware of their plight, their comrades had run on, each one intent only on reaching the shelter. It was

Nuada, standing at the cave's mouth and looking back, who had first seen them go down. Instantly he had lifted his shield and started back for them.

But a huge form had come into his way, blocking the opening. It was the cat.

"You can't go," it had growled. "You'd have no chance in that."

The screams from outside had by this time drawn everyone's attention back to the stricken three. There were cries of horror and alarm.

"We can't just leave them," someone shouted, and all—save a reluctant Mathgen—surged forward as if to force a way past the huge beast.

"You can't save them," it said with force. "It's too late already. Look!"

The two men who had fallen at full length had now ceased to move, and lay stretched in the soft muck. The woman, still upon her knees, had thrown her head back in a last, gurgling cry, only to freeze that way in a death spasm, upturned face dissolving away.

The rain boiled in the sockets that had held her eyes. It turned her brow, her nose, her cheeks, her lips to soft clay, sending them streaming down to expose jutting bones and teeth of the skull beneath.

Her body went limp, toppling to join the others. Their flesh, too, was swiftly melting away, fully soaked by the downpour, liquifying, sloughing off to join the acidic mire, stripping the bones bare.

Many of the watchers turned away in revulsion at the sight. One retched violently. Some sobbed. Others stared on in grotesque fascination.

The haze of smoke boiling up from the three fully involved forms obscured a clear view of them for some moments. Then it faded, its last streamers dissipating in the rain to reveal what was left. In a few score seconds, three living beings had been reduced to skeletons thrusting starkly up from the gray-black mud. Three familiar faces had become three grimacing skulls.

"By all the gods," muttered Diancecht.

"Now I'm sure," said Mathgen. "I *don't* want to go on with this!"

As if somehow placated by the three deaths, the storm

immediately began to let up. In moments more, the rain died away, leaving a last few fat droplets to plop onto the sodden ground. The tree stubs and the stark bones continued to give off a faint steam from the caustic rain still clinging to them.

The stunned adventurers stood unspeaking, lost in grief, huddling together to give each other comfort. It was the big cat who spoke first, its rumbling voice brisk and contrastingly unemotional.

"Over quickly, as I thought," it said, gazing toward the leaden sky.

"How can you be so uncaring, so unmoved by what we've seen?" Dagda asked.

The animal looked around to him. It rolled its muscled shoulders in a shrug. "Because I've seen it so much before. All the creatures of this island died that way. But you are lucky. These rains come far apart. Even allowing time for the ground to dry enough for safe walking, we should be able to return before another storm begins."

"Return?" echoed Nuada in a puzzled way.

"Yes. Go back. To your ship. I thought that now you would truly believe how hazardous your quest is. It will not get easier. Surely you'll wish to go back."

Nuada looked to Diancecht. "Healer, what do you say?"

"I'll make no more judgments that might sway the others," he said. "They must decide themselves."

"I say that we've more reason to go on than before," one said.

"Yes," another said fiercely. "It's ourselves now that the poison of these giants has harmed. Our own dead to be avenged."

"Those dead may include more of you before we're through," the cat said ominously. "Even all."

"We understand the risk well enough," said Goibniu. He looked about at his companions. "Do any here vote not to go on?"

Mathgen began to lift one arm, but realized he would be the sole dissenter. He subsided, muttering, "Idiots. Idiots!" to himself.

"Very well," said the cat, clearly surprised once more by the humans' tenacity. "Then we go up." It lifted a paw to point back into the darkness. "This opening is a tunnel. It slants upward, a conduit for the stream."

They looked down at the flow of sludge, dimly seen in the shadows. Here it narrowed and ran along a channel grooving the center of the tunnel floor. Only a stride's length separated the dropoff from the tunnel walls on either side.

"This is all overflow from a lake on the plateau atop the cliffs," the cat went on. "It is there we will find the giants' lair."

"Is it a long way?" asked Nuada.

"No, but it is very dark. My eyes can see through it, but yours cannot. I must lead. One of you must hold my tail and the others hold hands with that one in a line. You must not get out of line or release hands. The space between the stream and the tunnel wall is even narrower above. Any deviation from my path could mean the end. Do you all understand?"

They nodded.

The lion led the way, the Morrigan keeping a grip on his tail's tip, the rest strung out behind.

The tunnel ran straight inward a short way, then began a steep climb. The outside light faded away behind them. Without it, they could see that there was light from another source: the stream itself gave off a faint, hazy, greenish glow. Not enough to see more than some vague shadows, but enough to reveal that the channel was cut much more deeply into the slope. The turgid flow of deadly liquid was now over two yards below the edge.

The party made its way upward in silence, each concentrating on footing and staying close to the tunnel wall. The only sounds were their shuffling feet; their labored breathing in the close, fetid air; and the thick, doomful gurgling sound of the poisoned stream flowing downward in its channel so near beside them.

The liquid's odor in the confined space of the tunnel was much worse, and became stronger as they progressed. The sense of being enclosed, trapped, suffocated grew to a near-maddening, near-overwhelming height.

Somewhere ahead of Nuada in the dark, a voice spoke out in sudden panic.

"The edge . . . is . . ."

The rest was swallowed by a wild cry and a crackling sound as a portion of the rocky edge gave way, sliding into the stream, a human form following, toppling from the edge, plunging into the viscid flood.

Others swiftly followed it, yanked off balance in a chain of disaster, one, two, a third toppling over the edge, falling, splashing into the stream's deadly embrace, sucked down so fast there were only brief cries as the dark forms of the victims vanished beneath the luminous ooze.

Nuada had only a heartbeat to register all this before the young woman ahead of him was falling, too. She'd released the hand of the hapless man before her, but retained Nuada's, flailing out madly with her freed arm to save herself.

She failed. Her feet, too near the crumbled edge, slid out from beneath her. She dropped down, yanking him down after her.

But the brief second she had delayed her fall had given him a chance to react. He went down full-length on the narrow path as she dropped toward the stream. She came up short at his arm's length, the jerk nearly tearing her hand from his clasp. Her toes were being licked by the caustic stream.

He hung on desperately, muscles tensed, other arm and legs flung wide to get the most purchase on the ledge.

From up the tunnel there came voices, calls of alarm as the others of the party, stopped now, looked back through the dark, trying to discover what had happened to the rest. "What's wrong?" called one.

"Are you all right?" shouted another.

"We're coming back to help!" promised a third.

"No!" Nuada managed to gasp out through gritted teeth, voice rasping from the strain. "Stay there. Risk no more lives!"

He looked back to the girl dangling below. She was a shadow, no more. He couldn't even see her face. Just that deadly glow behind.

"Hang . . . on!" he told her.

"I can't!" she said weakly, horribly. The burning liquid was eating into the leather of her boots.

"You can!" he said fiercely. "I'll pull you up."

He concentrated, willing all his power to the one arm to

draw her up. For long, long seconds nothing happened as he vibrated from the strain. Then he was winning. She was lifting. He was inching back, bringing her ever upward toward the edge where she might get a grip with her other hand.

As if it were a raptor not to be robbed of its prey, the stream below suddenly surged up. A tongue of the fluid lashed around her legs, the thick strand of slime hanging on like a tentacle, dragging her down.

She gave a single short cry of pain and released his hand. He couldn't hold on alone. Her fingers slid free of his desperate grip.

In shock, he watched the figure drop down, feet first, vanishing in an instant beneath the ooze.

He lay for a moment frozen by anger and agony at the loss. Then renewed calls from ahead forced him back to action. With an effort of cramped muscles he got to his feet and edged along, carefully feeling his way past the spot where half the ledge had broken away, finally reaching the new end of the company.

"Who is it?" the last person in the chain asked him.

"Nuada," he barked, still breathless from his effort.

"But, there were five others between us!" the other said in consternation.

"No more. Pass the word to go on."

"We could have come back to help," said another figure behind the first.

"There was nothing you could have done," Nuada rapped out, "except to get yourselves killed, too."

"But . . ."

"No more talk," he said. "Let's get out of here." He lifted his voice to shout up the line: "Move on!"

The line obeyed. Once more they moved along, even more cautiously now as word of their comrades' loss spread up the line. But the worst seemed past. The nearly strangling concentration of acidic fumes lessened. The slope eased. A circle of daylight came into view above. Soon after they were emerging from the tunnel's other mouth into the daylight.

Only in contrast to the blackness of the tunnel could the illumination be called bright. Little more than a faint glimmer of the sun's glow fought through the heavy blanket of overcast. It gave a gray and dust-hazed light, just adequate to illuminate the new landscape which faced them. But it was not necessarily any great blessing that it did so.

For the bleak and barren scene revealed was that of some nightmare country of complete despair.

The party had come up onto one side of a flat area, a huge, roughly circular plateau. It was land totally desolate, devoid of features, its hard, dried, and soot-blackened earth thickly carved by deep fissures.

The earth formed a border, a broad margin surrounding a central lake. The lake, which might once have been clean water, was now a seething wizard's cauldron of yellow-black ooze, fat bubbles popping up to burst with thick, obscene, splattering burps of sound, letting off blasts of near-overpowering stench.

The foul lake, in turn, formed a surrounding for something else: a feature which rose at the exact center of the plateau.

It was a steep-sided and grotesque cone of hill which thrust up starkly from the stinking slime. Its seamed, black slopes rose up to a jagged peak, a spike-edged rim surrounding a gaping hole from which a geyser of oily smoke spewed.

There could be no doubt in the adventurers' minds that the source of the island's poisoning was here, at this looming cone. The smoke from its awful throat rose and welled out in all directions, forming concentric rings that rolled away to cover the whole sky, to carry smothering dust and caustic rains over all the country around.

Everyone in the party had gone immediately on guard as they entered this dismal scene, staring around for any sign of an enemy. There was none. Indeed, there was no sign of any life at all.

"Where are the giants?" Dagda demanded of their feline guide.

The cat nodded toward the cone. "Inside. It is their workhouse, and their home as well. They never come out."

"Then we'll have to go in," Nuada said grimly.

"Hold on, there," Mathgen said quickly. "Shouldn't we consider what happened below?"

"The edge gave way," Nuada simply explained. "We lost five more comrades."

"And do you mean to ignore it?" the other demanded.

"Of course not. There's simply no place or time to mourn them now. That can come after this is ended."

"But we *can't* go on!" Mathgen wailed in open dismay. "I kept my silence before, but no longer. This is madness!"

"It is our vow," Nuada said.

"Oh, no," Mathgen argued. "It's *your* vow, Nuada. *You* made this choice for us. You talked us into this. You with your fool bravado, your mindless sense of honor, your stupid self-sacrifice. You don't care if you risk everyone."

"That's nonsense, Mathgen," Goibniu said angrily. "Nuada did not make the choice for us."

"He did! He's your leader. You all follow him and you blindly obey! And he's leading you to death."

"I give no orders," said Nuada. "We have no leader. I've said before that all should act only of their free will."

"Before, no one really knew what terrors we'd face," Mathgen reasoned. "Now we mean to enter the lair of these monsters to challenge them, and nearly a third of our force is gone!"

"I can't deny it," Nuada conceded. He looked around at the rest. "It's surely truth that Mathgen's saying. Still, I mean to see this out. I'll give no more reasons or arguments. Follow me whoever will. I'll put no blame on anyone who stays behind."

Look for **The Gods of Ireland, Book 2,**
*The Enchanted Isles*
Coming in July, 1991 from Bantam Spectra

*"A grand conclusion to a revered cycle."* -- *Kirkus Reviews*

# *TEHANU*
## *The Last Book of Earthsea*
### *by*
## *Ursula K. Le Guin*

*"The publication of Tehanu will give lovers of Le Guin's enchanted realm of Earthsea cause for celebration."*
-- *Publishers Weekly*

Once she'd been a priestess, quest-companion to a powerful mage, a student of high magic. Then she gave it all up to be a simple farmer's wife...but an abused child and a dying wizard called her back to a life she'd left behind, and now the adventure begins anew....

*"Tehanu is a major novel by a major novelist...a novel rich in the ways of humanity. Ms. Le Guin's dragons are some of the best in literature.... Admirable and evocative."* -- *New York Times Book Review*

On sale now wherever Bantam Books are sold.

And be sure to look for beautiful new editions of Ursula K. Le Guin's classic novels of Earthsea:

**A Wizard of Earthsea**
**The Tombs of Atuan**
**The Farthest Shore**

AN 194 -- 1/91

"Angus Wells writes with a touch of magic . . .
This is high fantasy of the most
exhilarating kind."
—Robert Holdstock, author of **Mythago Wood**

# THE BOOKS OF THE KINGDOMS

### by
### Angus Wells

Born of fire, feeding on death, Taws, the powerful messenger of an evil god, rises out of a world-spanning forest, sucking life from each man he encounters. His mission: to raise and unite the northern tribes in order to destroy the Kingdoms of the south.

Born of a simple noble and a former acolyte of Kyrie, an order of psychic healers, Prince Kedryn faces his first battle—in defense of the three kingdoms—with all the excitement of the kill. Little does he know that not only is he Taws' hunted prey, but Taws' prophesied destroyer as well. . . .

Read the first two volumes in this exciting fantasy trilogy:

### WRATH OF ASHAR
### THE USURPER

**Now on sale wherever Bantam Spectra Books are sold**

And coming in January, 1991
the stunning conclusion:

**The Third Book of the Kingdoms**

### THE WAY BENEATH

DON'T MISS IT!

AN120

Celtic mythology tells that each person lives many lives. Colin McMahon is discovering that the lives he lived, and the battles he fought, are catching up with him....

# CROMM
# by Kenneth C. Flint

*"A rousing tale of myth and magic.... Highly recommended."* -- Booklist

It began with the dreams...visions of strange and disturbing spectres from a time long ago. Easygoing Colin McMahon has never taken life too seriously, but the images that torment his nights have changes that forever. In his dreams he rides across a battle-torn land, reliving the memories of a fearless young warrior who shares his name -- and losing his heart to a woman as brave as she is beautiful. He helplessly witnesses the brutal rituals of a savage cult that makes blood offerings to Cromm Cruach, the Crooked God. And then the visions begin to invade his waking life, as nightmare creatures wreak havoc and send him on a quest halfway across the world to a confrontation that could change not just his life, but the fate of humanity, forever.

On sale in February wherever Bantam Spectra Books are sold.

AN202 -- 2/91